Daughters

Florence Osmund

ISBN: 1478268336
ISBN-13: 9781478268338
LCCN: 2012913048

DISCLAIMER

This book is dedicated to all those who have struggled with their identity at some point in their lives.

"To thine own self be true." —William Shakespeare

ACKNOWLEDGEMENTS

I have the following people to thank for their assistance in creating this book.

Thank you, friends and family (you know who you are), for supporting me in my writing endeavors and giving me encouragement along the way.

A special thanks to Marge Bousson for giving the manuscript a final "once over" before being published.

Thank you, Carrie Cantor, for your invaluable critique of an early draft of "Daughters." I continue to learn from you and hope some day I will be able to publish a book without your help (and I mean that in the most complimentary way).

Thank you, Claudia Estep, for providing Spanish translations for the dialogue between Rachael and Olivia.

And finally, thank you Team 2 at CreateSpace. It was a pleasure working with you.

CHAPTER 1

Pretenses

Marie combed through her closet for just the right clothes to pack—nothing too fancy, nothing too casual, and definitely nothing too different from those worn by the people she was about to meet. She carefully considered the clothing, holding each piece up to her body in front of the mirror, and imagined how she would feel wearing it, how others would perceive her wearing it. Everything had to be well thought out for this trip. Her life was about to change.

Jonathan Brooks, her father, a man she had met for the first time just two months earlier in September, 1949, was going to arrive at her coach house apartment in less than twelve hours to take her to meet his family—her newfound family—in St. Charles, Illinois, for the Thanksgiving holiday. It was a ten-hour car ride from her home in Atchison, Kansas, and Jonathan promised her they could talk about anything and everything on the way.

"Anything and everything," in Marie's mind, meant nothing was off limits, and she intended to take full advantage of the opportunity. Jonathan had been married with three children when he had met Marie's now deceased mother, and Marie knew very little about their affair. She wanted to know how they met, what they did together, how long the affair lasted, and what caused their breakup. Most of all, she wanted to know what had attracted them to each other in the first place. After all, Jonathan was a Negro, and her mother was white, a rather unlikely pairing in 1923 Chicago.

Discovering who her father was also meant discovering her own ethnicity. With olive skin, nut-brown eyes, and hair the color of raven's wings, Marie could easily pass for white, and for the first twenty-four years of her life, she had. If it weren't for her guilt and self-loathing, she could continue to pass for white, because that would be easier on so many levels. But her strong need to know who she really was and where she belonged drove her to find the answers, the truths about herself, and she was hopeful her father would be able to give her valuable insight.

Not having made much progress with packing, Marie took a quick dinner break. She thought about Jonathan's family as she ate—his wife, Claire; their three grown sons; a daughter-in-law; and two grandchildren. What were the chances Marie would be accepted by all of them, and what kind of relationships would emerge from their first meeting? She didn't know.

Marie's best friend, Karen, who had offered to help her pack, arrived just as Marie was finishing her sandwich. Marie and Karen had met a year and a half earlier, the first week Marie had arrived in Atchison, only days after leaving her husband and home in Chicago. Karen had been a godsend, helping her settle into a new home and lifestyle those first few months, and despite their differences, it didn't take long for the two of them to become fast friends.

Karen's matter-of-fact values caused the two women to be worlds apart when it came to Marie's ethnicity dilemma. If roles were reversed, Marie was certain Karen would accept the situation without any effort to change things—accept the ambiguity of being biracial, accept the bigotry in the world, and the lack of self-esteem Marie feared plagued many Negroes. Karen, Marie was sure, would aim low and settle for mediocrity. Not Marie. Marie had more idealistic goals in mind.

Karen, a year younger than Marie and widowed for three years, walked into Marie's coach house apartment holding a bag from the clothing shop she owned. She handed it to Marie.

"What's this?"

"Just a little going-away present. Open it."

Marie pulled out a teal shirtwaist dress and matching short cropped jacket. "Karen...this is gorgeous." She tore off her clothes and slipped on the dress.

"Like it?"

"Like it? I love it!" Marie hugged her friend. "I don't know what to say. Thank you! I think I'll wear it on the first day."

Karen shot Marie a sheepish grin. "Hoped you'd say that. It looks great on you, hon, but then everything does."

The two women spent the evening picking out the right wardrobe for Marie's two-week visit—skirts and blouses, several pairs of Capri trousers, a variety of sweaters, and nightclothes.

"What about the horses?" Karen asked.

"What about them?" Jonathan owned a horse ranch. He and his family were skilled riders.

"You'll need some riding outfits."

"Shoot. I completely forgot about that." She went to her closet and pulled out two more outfits. Once Marie had become aware of her father's interest in horses, she had started taking riding lessons and bought her own horse shortly afterward—a three-year-old champagne gelding she named J.B., after Jonathan.

She put the riding outfits in her suitcase and looked up at Karen. "I think that does it."

Marie and Karen talked well into the night over a few glasses of wine, something they did often.

"Well, I'm packed and ready to go, but honestly…how does one prepare for something like this?"

"What about your cat?" Marie's cat, Sheana, was sitting on top of her suitcase.

"She senses I'm going away and doesn't like it. The Edwardses have offered to take care of her." Julia and Wayne Edwards were Marie's landlords and lived in "the big house" with their three children.

"She'll miss you."

Marie nodded.

"And so will I," Karen added.

When it was time for Karen to leave, the two women hugged, a little longer than usual, before saying good night. No final words were spoken; none were required—just heartfelt smiles going in both directions in honor of Marie, who was about to engage upon what could turn out to be the most important visit of her life.

* * *

Marie prayed the last gulp of Pepto-Bismol left in the bottle would be enough to settle her stomach. Her head hurt, too, and now she wished she hadn't had that last glass of wine the night before.

Jonathan arrived right on time. Tall and well-built, he wore a robin's egg blue Argyle sweater beneath a brown cashmere coat, which was a nice contrast to his café-au-lait skin. After giving her a fatherly hug, he glanced around her second floor apartment and said, "You did pretty well for yourself, kiddo. I'm proud of you."

She responded with a smile. The coach house was situated well behind the main house, a three-story Victorian occupied by the Edwardses. "This place has been my sanctuary for the past year and a half. I was lucky to find it."

The drawn window between the limo driver and the back seat enabled them to talk in private. Jonathan opened the conversation. "Well, Marie, let me start by telling you about my family, and perhaps more important for you, my roots…our roots." Marie suspected his opening statement would be the essence of…everything. "My father was a mulatto. He was born a slave in 1843. His father—that would be my grandfather—was white and owned a cotton plantation in South Carolina. His mother was one of Grandfather's house slaves." His pause allowed Marie the opportunity for that to sink in. "Are you familiar with the one-drop rule?"

Marie nodded.

"So no matter how much or how little Negro blood you have in you, according to the one-drop rule—which is a white man's rule by the way— you're considered a Negro." His words penetrated into her conscious. Hearing someone say it, him in particular, gave it new meaning. "I wanted to get that out in the open right away. It's important you know who you are.

"My father was raised by his slave mother along side his two half sisters. He wasn't allowed to go to school, of course, so he relied on the white children in the household to teach him to read and write. That was against the law, but they did it anyway, and it was something his dark-skinned half sisters were completely denied."

While Marie knew skin color really did matter, she didn't understand it and didn't want to believe it. It bothered her to hear him talk about it so casually.

"So your grandmother had two Negro daughters before your father was born?"

"Yes."

"So was she married?"

"I'm not sure. My father wasn't sure either."

"Okay. Go on."

"In the mid-1860s, shortly after slavery was abolished, my grandfather gave each of his sons, including my father, several horses and a piece of land. My father made the most of it and became a fairly successful horse breeder down there."

"How old was he then?"

"Early twenties. He worked the ranch and stayed a bachelor until well into his forties. That's when he met and married my mother, a Negro in her twenties, and I was born the next year." He paused, then shrugged. "It's never been clear to me which came first—their marriage or my conception.

"Anyway, my mother died of tuberculosis when I was ten. My father died twelve years later when he was sixty-nine, and I inherited the business." He turned to look at Marie. "Are you following this? Should I slow down?"

"No, please go on. What happened to your grandmother?"

"She died somewhere in her thirties, on the plantation, before my father was given the land. Anyway, I tried to maintain the horse business down there for a few years but struggled at it, and I wasn't a very happy person, shall we say. My white half brothers on neighboring ranches tormented me every chance they got, and between that and the general bigotry of the South, I decided to move my ranch to St. Charles. That was in 1915, when I was twenty-five."

"You didn't mention school. What kind of education did you get?"

"I was able to go through the eighth grade."

"That's amazing."

"What is?"

"That you got as far as you did with only an eighth grade education."

Jonathan chuckled. "What it meant was I did most things the hard way."

"How's that?"

"I spent a lot of time in libraries, and the libraries where I was allowed had limited resources, believe me. I learned accounting and everything else about running a business from books. But even then, when I arrived in St. Charles, I still had a lot to learn."

"So who inspired you? I keep thinking you must have defied all odds to get where you are today."

"This may surprise you, but whenever I feel defeated, I think about a man named Jack Johnson, the first Negro heavyweight boxing champion."

"You're inspired by a boxer?"

"He's more than a boxer in my book. He's an odds breaker. Here's a man, the son of two ex-slaves, who dropped out of school at the age of ten or eleven so he could work to help feed his family, who was told his whole life you can't do that when it came to boxing, and he ended up a boxing sensation. Not only that, but the man had a seventy-four-inch reach. Now I know that doesn't mean much to you, but the average reach for a heavyweight is probably closer to seventy-eight."

"How long ago was that?"

"He won that title in 1908."

"You're kidding."

"Talk about doing something against all odds. And it didn't end there. Apparently he preferred white women over colored ones, and he wasn't discreet about it. Unfortunately, he paid dearly for that."

"What happened?"

"As the story goes, he was arrested for taking a woman across state lines for immoral purposes, shall we say. In reality, he was with his girlfriend who the cops alleged was a prostitute. He skipped bail and fled to Europe for a year or so, and then came back to face the music. Did some time for it in your neck of the woods, in Leavenworth prison."

"Would that have happened if he were white do you think?"

"Hell no. I'll tell you something else that wouldn't have happened if he were white. The way he died. This happened somewhere in the South. I forget which state. Some restaurant refused to serve him. He was pretty much a hot-head, and he high-tailed it out of there like a race car driver. Crashed his car and died. That was just a few years ago."

"Sad story."

"Inspirational story."

"Getting back to your story, were you accepted in St. Charles, more so than in the South I mean?"

"I moved to St. Charles because I had heard there was a nice mix of people there, including some Negroes, but mostly Lithuanians, Native Americans, and Germans. But I found out very quickly no one up north wanted to buy horses from a colored man, so I hired a front man for the business, a white man. For years, my customers didn't even know I existed."

So he pretended too.

"His name is Zach. He's still with me, as is his son. Well, Zach is from the South and knows a little bit about Negro culture. His people were poor, and he found himself living on the outskirts of colored neighborhoods his whole life. Zach and I got to know each other pretty well that first year, and he got it in his head I needed a good woman in my life." Jonathan smirked. "I ignored him for the longest time, and then one day this pretty young light-skinned girl shows up on my doorstep. Come to find out that Zach had sent for her to come for a visit from some small little town in Mississippi, and well, the rest is history."

"Does your wife have any…white in her background?"

"She's not sure. She was raised by a colored family, but never knew who her real parents were. She suspects she's mixed."

Marie nodded. "Please, go on."

"Once my business got established, I slowly started exposing myself to the various horse buyers and was eventually accepted, at least in the horse community."

"But not by others?"

"My neighbors were another story. They didn't know what quite to make of me. I managed to buy this property without a realtor, and to be honest, I think the previous owner sold it to me to get back at his neighbors."

"Because you're a Negro?"

Jonathan laughed. "All of a sudden I was there, and it was too late for them to do anything about it. Anyway, I didn't give them any ammunition to lodge any complaints against me. I had the best kept home, barns, and property. I obeyed every stinkin' law, no matter how trivial. Luckily our ranches are spread pretty far apart, so they don't bother me much. There's a couple down a few ranches who are somewhat neighborly. And of course the Feinsteins. But you know about them."

Gregory Feinstein was a vice president with the National Bank of Chicago, and a neighbor and good friend of Jonathan's. Marie had discovered earlier that Jonathan had asked Greg to oversee her college tuition after her mother died. Years later when Marie's husband threatened to expose Jonathan, Marie went through Greg to alert Jonathan of her husband's threats.

Jonathan let out a heavy sigh.

"You sound tired. Do you want to stop for a bit?"

"No, this is important stuff. Let's go on. After dealing with me directly for a couple of years, one of my customers invited me to join the Central Union Club in Chicago. I was its only Negro member. That's where I met your mother."

Anxious to hear this part of his story, Marie took in a deep breath of air and let it out slowly. Now that the time had come, she was nervous to hear the details.

"It was a male-only club, and Sophia was the person who greeted members as they entered." A wistful expression swept across his face. "She was so beautiful. She had a striking figure, emerald eyes, and olive skin as smooth as porcelain. I was completely taken in by her, and after we talked for the first time, well, I couldn't get her out of my mind."

Marie thought back to the items she'd found in her mother's memory box after she died—the matchbook from the Central Union Club and the photograph of her with several other men, one of whom was Jonathan, although she hadn't known that until recently.

"I frequented the club often after that first meeting, and it wasn't long before we started an affair." He glanced at Marie. "It was wrong, and I'm not going to make any excuses for myself. It was dead wrong, and it wasn't fair to Claire and our three sons."

Jonathan stared out the window for a moment. "It didn't take long. I fell in love with your mother. It was mutual, and it was intense."

"And Claire knew nothing of what was going on?"

"No." He let out an audible sigh. "Let me tell you about Claire and the boys. She had the twins right away, Evan and Arthur. They're thirty now. Both went to college. Neither one ever married. Evan teaches cultural studies at the University of Missouri. Arthur is a lawyer on the south side of Chicago. Most of his clients are colored illiterates who can't afford a lawyer. Our youngest son, Melvin, went to college to be an accountant, but when that didn't pan out, he decided to come work for me. Best accountant I've ever had." His face beamed. "You'll meet them all."

"I can't wait," Marie said through a sincere smile, her stomach doing a series of tight somersaults. "So what do they know about me?"

"I told Claire about you right after our meeting with Greg in September. To be completely honest with you, Marie, I don't think she was all that surprised."

"Really?"

"Yes, really. Our relationship is somewhat complicated, and...well, some day I'll share that with you, but not now. There are too many other things...I need to take a break. Can we talk about you for awhile?"

"Sure."

"You went through life having no reason to believe you were anything but white. Am I right?"

Marie nodded.

"What was your first inclination?"

Marie relayed the story of Mrs. Hollingsworth, a Southern-bred uppity customer who had confronted Marie where she was a manager at the Marshall Field's flagship store in downtown Chicago. The arrogant Mrs. Hollingsworth had referred to Marie as "some half-breed nigger girl." Marie's mother had revealed to her very little about her father, and certainly not the fact he was colored. That incident had been what triggered her desperate search for Jonathan.

Jonathan gave her a heartfelt look. "I am *so* sorry you had to go through that." He reached over and took his daughter's hand. "I've thought so much about you over the years. I've had struggles with my race too. But not like you. Everyone can see I'm a Negro, so there's no question about which public bathroom I have to use, so to speak. But you have different issues. I know. Believe me, I know. And I give you my word, now that I'm in your life, I'll help you through them as much as I can."

Marie responded, her heart dancing its beats. "You can't know how much that would mean to me, Jona...I mean, Dad." When she had first met him, he had asked her to call him "Dad" if she was comfortable with it. She wasn't, but thought it the right thing to do. "More than anything, I want to know more about the Negro culture, *my* culture. I want to know how I can be in both worlds and be accepted. I want to stop pretending to be something I'm not. I want to..."

"Hold on, my dear daughter. Slow down." His smile gave her comfort. "It has taken a hundred years for bigotry to become what it is today in this country, and we're not going to change it in the next two weeks." He methodically patted her hand while he stared out the window, apparently lost in thought. "You can't change people, Marie." He turned toward her. "I think you know that. You can educate them, enlighten them, show them new ways." His gaze turned back toward the window. "And then hope they change. But you can't change them."

"I know, but what I'm doing is ignoring who I really am, and that's tearing me apart."

"I'll never forget what our minister said once: 'God created us different to understand the need for each other.' It took me a long while to accept that explanation, and there are days I still have my doubts, but it's something I hope I never lose sight of." He gave her a loving look. "We'll try to sort this out, I promise you. But you have to realize we're dealing with people with limited and usually flawed views of our people. And they're scared of us, so why would they accept us?"

"I know all that, really I do." She almost called him Dad again, but the more she thought about it, the more she knew she wasn't ready.

"Let me ask you something. And try to answer this as honestly as you can. What did you think about Negroes before you had any idea you were one?"

Marie let her mind go back in time. "Where I lived, the only Negroes I saw were from a distance. In fact, I remember the first one I ever saw was in the restaurant where my mother worked. The kitchen door swung open, and I saw this bent-over black-skinned man washing dishes. It was so foreign to me, I didn't know what to think. And then later on…well, they weren't in my schools, not in college either. Not where I worked. My only exposure to them was in this one jazz club Richard and I sometimes went to."

"Tell me how you met Richard."

She relayed the story about how he'd caught her eye and flirted with her while she was dressing a window display at Marshall Field's. He had enticed her into meeting him for a cup of coffee.

Jonathan shifted in his seat. "And what if he had been colored? Would you have met him for coffee then?"

"Of course not." The words flew from her mouth way too fast.

Jonathan raised an eyebrow. "Okay, *now* tell me how you plan to change people's minds."

Father and daughter held each other's gaze for several seconds before he rolled down the window separating the driver from them and said, "Pull over when you can, Walter. Let's stop for lunch."

Walter, a thin, middle-aged white man dressed in a black chauffeur's outfit, pulled over to a rest stop and proceeded to take picnic lunch items out of the trunk. Halfway through lunch, another car pulled into the parking lot. A family of four emerged from their car and walked toward the only other picnic table. Two young boys sat down on the benches and proceeded to roll a ball back and forth across the table. The parents followed after them with a picnic basket in tow, but when they saw Marie, Jonathan, and Walter, they gathered up the boys and scurried back to the car.

"Case in point?" Jonathan asked.

Marie pursed her lips and nodded. Walter gave Marie and Jonathan a discerning look, but said nothing. He didn't have to.

"Aside from not being that surprised, how did Claire react when you told her about me, if you don't mind my asking?" Marie said after they resumed their journey toward St. Charles.

"At first...well, she didn't speak to me for a few days. Then the first question she asked was what year you were born so she would have that perspective, I guess." He paused. "She's a wonderful woman. You'll like her."

"I'm sure I will."

"I told the kids shortly afterward. I have to admit, they were pretty shocked. Melvin took it the worst. His first wife—she was white—ran off with another man, a white man, shortly after they were married, so he wasn't very understanding. In fact, he didn't talk to me for a whole week. I told him he could be mad at me all he wanted, but what happened happened, and it's time to move on. He'll come around. It may take awhile."

"Will they all be there when we arrive?"

"No, just Claire to start. I wanted the two of you to get to know each other first."

"Is she over the initial shock now? I mean, I know she's not okay with it, but is she...?"

"Is she still upset with me?"

"Something like that."

"She's trying very hard, let's say." He paused. "Tomorrow, everyone will be there for Sunday supper." He seemed to be steering away from talking about Claire's reaction to his bombshell news. "Do you think you're up for it?"

"Yes, I think so." She thought for several seconds. "Do I have a choice?"

Father and daughter laughed effortlessly, like they had known each other for a long time. Then tears welled up in Marie's eyes.

"What's wrong?" he asked.

She swiped away the tears. "I don't know, really. I think I'm just so happy to be here, I can hardly contain myself. But I'm nervous too."

"Well, contain yourself real quick, my dear, 'cause we're here."

CHAPTER 2

Who's This White Lady Again?

Jonathan's house was a sprawling ranch, yielding on three sides to expansive pastures separated by white picket fencing. Dense woods provided a lush backdrop. Walter pulled the car into the circular drive and proceeded to remove Marie's luggage from the trunk. Jonathan led Marie to the front door.

"Ready?"

Marie shot him a guarded smile and nodded, but she was thinking, *maybe not.*

Claire met them at the door. Her face was much softer than Marie had pictured, even with her coarse black hair forced into a pageboy. And she was shorter than Marie had imagined, almost petite. The beige cashmere sweater she wore was not much lighter than her skin color. She was an attractive woman.

Marie had given considerable thought to this meeting, playing over the different possible scenarios in her mind a million times. After all,

Marie was the result of Claire's husband's love affair, and this meeting had strong potential to go very wrong.

The two women make awkward eye contact, and then Claire moved in to embrace her. The quick, inconsequential hug left Marie flat. "Welcome to our home, Marie."

Marie hoped Claire didn't notice the tiny muscle in her upper lip twitching. "Thank you, Claire. Thank you for having me." A few seconds after she said it, she couldn't remember what she had said, or if she had said anything at all. She looked at Jonathan for some sign of reassurance. He nodded and gestured toward the living room.

She glanced around at the seating arrangement. *Where should I sit? Should I sit?* No one was saying anything. Jonathan took her elbow and guided her to the sofa. "Why don't you sit here, Marie? Make yourself comfortable while Walter brings in your luggage, and then you can get settled in your room." Marie looked around the room for Claire. "She's starting dinner." He winked at her. "You're doing fine," he mouthed.

Jonathan eased into what Marie thought might be his favorite chair.

I'm doing fine? No, I don't think so. And I wonder how Claire's doing? That was the briefest welcome she possibly could have given.

Marie took in a breath of air and let it out slowly. She was nervous about not saying anything, but didn't know what to say. She was afraid if she did say something, it would be wrong.

"You okay?" he asked.

"I didn't think I would be this nervous."

"Because of Claire?" he whispered.

"Mm-hmm. I just want her to like me." *I can't believe I just said that.*

After Marie got settled in her room, she sat near Jonathan in the living room and whispered, "Should I go in to see if I can help Claire with dinner?"

He raised his eyebrows and nodded. Marie spent the next hour in the kitchen while Claire prepared dinner. The kitchen was large and one where Marie suspected many family functions and discussions had taken place over the years.

"Can I help you with dinner, Claire?" *May I help you with dinner. Now I'm not even using proper grammar!*

Claire handed Marie a bowl of carrots and a vegetable peeler. "You can peel these if you want." She showed no emotion, no telltale sign of what she might be thinking.

Who was going to start? Should she be the one? She didn't know what to say. During the past weeks, she had practiced so many different things she could say to Claire, but now she couldn't think of any of them.

Claire interrupted her thoughts. "You don't look like anyone in our family, Marie. Do you favor your mother?"

Marie's heartbeat wavered. What exactly did that mean? Was she being sarcastic? She suddenly remembered one of the things she wanted to say to Claire, but now she had to concentrate on Claire's question. *Did she just ask me if I take after my mother?*

"Yes, I do." Her voice stuck in her throat, making it difficult to get the words out. "I have a picture of her when she was in her twenties, and if you didn't know better, you'd think it was me in the picture." *How stupid was that? So now every time she looks at me, she'll see her husband's former lover.*

Claire turned around from the counter to face Marie, gave her a weak smile, and said, "She must have been very beautiful, then." She turned her back toward Marie to continue what she was doing.

A soft flush swept up Marie's neck. *Good grief. How can I turn this around?*

"Thank you. And Claire?"

"Yes?"

Marie swallowed. "Thank you for…well, for welcoming me into your home."

"You're welcome," she said with her back still toward Marie, her voice low and soft, without any inflection.

"You have a lovely home." Had she already say that? Marie's stomach felt like someone had just punched it.

Claire didn't respond. Instead she wiped her hands on a dish towel and sat down beside her. Marie bit the inside of her lip, unable to breathe.

"You have to know this is hard for me."

Marie nodded, afraid to speak. Claire looked past Marie, toward the living room. "I keep telling myself what happened between Jonathan and your mother happened a lifetime ago, and that you had nothing to do with it. But that doesn't make this any easier."

"I know."

"I gave this a lot of thought the past couple of days while Jon was away, fetching you." She leaned back in her chair and looked deeply into Marie's eyes. "I don't know if he told you this, but my first reaction was, 'Don't involve me in this. It's your problem. You deal with it by yourself.'" Her voice softened. "But I know what it's like to not know who your parents are. I never knew mine, so how could I stand by and let that happen to someone else?"

Claire got up from her chair and went back to her food preparation. After a few seconds, she said, "I've forgiven him for what he did, Marie. Now it's time to move on."

Marie wasn't sure what to think. She felt she should say something to quell the dreadful silence that now filled the room.

"Mm-hmm." Idiot! She had just agreed that it was time for Claire to move on. Who was she to agree to that? How insensitive could she be?

Convinced it was better to just keep her mouth shut and be thought a heartless fool than to open it again and remove all doubt, Marie kept silent while she finished peeling the carrots. She had never lacked self-confidence before and didn't like herself much for it now.

Claire didn't say anything more until they sat down to eat. "I know you two have had a lot of time to catch up in the car," Claire said, "but if you don't mind, Marie, can you tell me about yourself?" She let out a nervous laugh. "I'm afraid you'll probably be asked the same questions over and over again by the time your visit is over. As you can imagine, there's an abundance of curiosity running in this family."

"I pretty much expected that." Marie recounted her story, starting with what life was like before her mother died. Then she took them through her college years in New York and her return to Chicago afterward. When she got to her job at Marshall Field's, Claire's facial expression changed. She told Marie that the first time she had gone into that store in 1925, she had been asked to leave.

"Nineteen twenty-five? That was the year I was born," Marie professed.

"Yes, I know." A flash of melancholy swept across Claire's face. "Jonathan was in Chicago for some sort of business, and I had come along." She gave Jonathan a disparaging look. "I can't remember what I did with the children, can you, Jon?" Marie hoped it was her imagination that Claire's words dripped with contempt.

Jonathan shook his head, his thoughts obviously far off. The tension in the room was rising.

"Anyway, I was never so embarrassed in my whole life. I could have afforded to buy just about anything in the store, yet I wasn't good enough to shop there." Claire composed herself before saying, "I got angry." She shook her head. "But then I got over it. Ignorant white people."

Oh dear. This is going to be harder than I thought. Marie continued with her story, ignoring Claire's last comment. "I left Field's in 1948, and I have to admit I don't remember ever seeing a Negro customer in there." *Why did I just say that?*

Jonathan nodded. Claire pursed her lips. Marie went on to tell them about Richard, about how their courtship and marriage had come right out of a fairy tale. The year was 1945. World War II had just ended, and then-twenty-year-old Marie was struggling to support herself on a meager salary as a junior designer at Marshall Field's. By his mid-twenties, Richard was the top salesman in his company, selling high-end medical equipment in a five-state area.

During their courtship, Richard not only showered her with expensive gifts and trips, but was attentive to her every need. Marie had tried to be cautious with Richard, but his charisma overshadowed his flaws, and it had been easy to overlook or explain away his indiscretions. After a quick five-month courtship, Marie and Richard married.

Their first year of marriage was blissful. He bought a two-story brownstone in up-and-coming Lakeview, a neighborhood just north of downtown Chicago. They honeymooned in Hawaii, took weekend trips to New York, and spent more than one Christmas in Aspen. But despite the lavish attention Richard gave to his wife, he also paid considerable homage to his other love—money. His biggest flaw was his inability to juggle his two loves.

After dinner, Marie, Jonathan, and Claire continued their conversation. "What was the first sign Richard was mixed up with the wrong people, Marie?" Jonathan asked.

Marie had asked herself the same question many times before but still didn't have a definitive answer. "When I look back, I think I should have seen things very early on, but you know how that is. I was in love and wanted desperately to start a family, so I'm sure I ignored a lot of things." She paused to recollect days so long gone. "One significant clue was when he attended the funeral of Timmy Buccieri, better known as 'The Bomber.' He was a big-name mobster in Chicago at the time, and there would be no reason for Richard to attend his funeral unless there was some connection."

Marie continued with the account, including the day she'd fled from Richard. After two years of marriage, she had become so frightened by Richard's shady activities, she planned to leave him, but before she could implement her plan, she came home one day and interrupted an important parlay he was having in their home with his so-called business associates. Richard had been so angry with her that he pushed her and caused her to fall down the basement stairs, and then he locked her in the basement. After hearing one of his cohorts say, "She knows too much. She needs to be offed," Marie panicked and escaped through a basement window.

The looks on Jonathan and Claire's faces said it all. Marie turned toward Jonathan. "Did you know back then I was married to him?"

"Yes, I knew, and I suspected he had some shady connections, so I had him checked out." His gaze went to Claire, who had a surprised look on her face. "But I couldn't confirm anything. He's pretty crafty."

"That's one word to describe him." Marie continued with her story, ending with how she'd found her safe haven in Atchison.

Claire shook her head. "You were lucky to get out when you did. Otherwise who knows what he would have done to you."

Marie hoped Claire's comment stemmed from concern for her well-being and not wishful thinking. "You know, Claire, in spite of what happened during our marriage, I know Richard truly loved me, and when he told me earlier this year he had never stopped loving me and wanted me to go back to him, I believed him. I really think he just doesn't know how to balance things in his life. His business, his family, his wife. Somehow everything loses perspective with him when it comes to money. And when he threatened that something might happen to Jonathan…well, I think he said that because he didn't know any other way to convey how he felt about me. I know that sounds illogical, but…"

Claire's expression took on a sudden change. "Just what threats were made against Jonathan?"

What had brought Jonathan and Marie together in the first place was when Richard threatened to expose Jonathan. Two months had passed since that threat, and nothing had happened, but Marie and Jonathan knew it was just a matter of time before something did. While Marie took Richard's threats seriously, she also didn't want to alarm Claire, who apparently was hearing this for the first time.

"Oh, nothing specific. I shouldn't have worded it that way."

Jonathan jumped into the conversation. "As I told you before, Claire, we all think he may expose the fact that I fathered an illegitimate child and try to ruin me, my family, and my business. And now that Marie has told us more about what he has done in the past and how he thinks, I'm thinking that even more." He turned toward Marie. "I had house alarms installed on all the windows and doors a couple of weeks ago. Don't let me forget to show you how they work."

Claire let out a decisive sigh. "Well, I'm getting tired. I think I'll go to bed. You two stay up and continue talking if you want." She walked to the other end of the living room, and without turning around said, "I've heard enough for one night."

Marie waited until Claire was out of earshot. She gave Jonathan a helpless look.

"It'll take time. Just be patient and give her time."

"I can't seem to say anything right."

"Just be yourself. You'll be fine."

Marie sighed. "I think I'll go to bed too. It's been a long day." She got up and headed toward the bedrooms. "Good night, Dad."

"Good night, sweetheart."

Lying in bed, Marie mentally relived every moment of her visit, until a tear made its way down her cheek and onto the pillowcase. She feared tomorrow was going to be an even longer day.

* * *

The next day, one by one, Jonathan and Claire's children, daughter-in-law, and grandchildren arrived for supper. Melvin resembled his father the most: tall, light-skinned, and built like an athlete. His wife, Yolanda, had thin facial features and light skin but was unmistakably a Negro. Jonathan's twin sons had softer, broader features, darker skin, and were a good four inches shorter than their younger brother and their father. Marie was grateful for Arthur's mustache; otherwise, even though they were fraternal twins, she would have had a hard time telling them apart.

At dinner, Jonathan sat at one end of the long table and Claire at the other. Marie had been shown a seat between the older of Melvin's daughters and Arthur, the twin who practiced law on the south side of Chicago. Marie was pretty certain her place at the table had been discussed beforehand.

Marie struggled to appreciate all the conversation and interaction at the dining room table. Jonathan must have noticed and shot her a comforting look periodically throughout the meal. Claire appeared to be enjoying herself more now that her "real" family was all around her, or at least that's what went through Marie's mind.

The chatter of supper conversation was casual and alive. Occasionally Marie was brought into the fold, usually by Jonathan. A couple of times Marie made eye contact with Claire, and when she did, Claire gave her a smile that exuded "I'm only smiling because I have to." Marie smiled back but not without difficulty. All Marie hoped for was a cordial relationship with Claire. If she didn't have at least that, she knew her relationship with Jonathan would be tenuous at best.

Marie glanced over at Melvin a few times while they ate, but he appeared to be preoccupied with something on his plate, or on the other side of the room, or anywhere but in Marie's direction. His conspicuous silence during the meal added awkwardness to the already shaky environment.

After supper, Jonathan lit a fire in the massive fireplace in the living room and turned on the phonograph. Count Basie's piano blues should have created an easygoing atmosphere in which to talk, but Melvin's silence and Claire's indifference toward Marie prevented that.

Everyone listened attentively while Jonathan talked about the book he had recently read. "Keep in mind, *Nineteen Eighty-Four* is just science fiction, but still it makes you think about what it would be like if we lived in a society under the watchful eye of a Big Brother government. No freedom. Back to a slavery of sorts. Pretty bleak." He continued to explain to his wide-eyed family members what totalitarianism was all about. Marie and others in the room cringed when Jonathan cited the book's three slogans of the government: War Is Peace, Freedom Is Slavery, and Ignorance Is Strength.

When he finished talking about the book, Melvin's eight-year-old daughter, Denise, who had been fidgeting the whole time her grandfather had been talking, stared at Marie and then asked her mother, "So who's this white lady again?"

The room grew silent. "She's your aunt, Denise," her mother said. "She's family."

Jonathan scanned the room and smiled. "Maybe now would be as good a time as any to get all the questions out of the way."

With the exception of Melvin, each family member took turns asking Marie questions about herself. Melvin, whom the family called Tré since he was the third born, listened but kept to himself throughout the evening. Marie noticed he didn't even make eye contact with his father except for a fleeting sidelong glance once or twice. By the looks on everyone's faces, Marie could tell she wasn't the only one feeling the tension in the room caused by Melvin.

Toward eight o'clock, Melvin and his family talked about leaving. The girls had school the next day, and it was getting close to their bedtime. Melvin left before anyone could say goodbye, mumbling the entire way out the door. After saying a quick good night, his daughters marched out after him. Yolanda hugged Marie and whispered, "Don't mind him. He'll come around."

Marie gave her a questioning smile and hoped she was right.

CHAPTER 3

The Tallest Tree

Before breakfast the next morning, Jonathan suggested he and Marie take a jaunt on horseback around his 380-acre ranch. The day was sunny and uncharacteristically warm for November. They walked through the fresh morning dew to the barn, leaving a trail of soggy footprints behind them. Jonathan saddled his favorite gelding for himself and a gentle mare for Marie. They kept a slow pace and talked as they rode.

Marie couldn't help but notice how relaxed he sat in the saddle, like he was sitting in his favorite easy chair. She smiled to herself when he started talking more about her mother. She liked hearing him talk about her.

"When I saw her at the Central Union Club that day in 1923, I thought my heart was going to leap out of my chest." He paused for an instant. "I have to explain something to you, something I alluded to earlier in the car." Jonathan shifted his weight to one side of the saddle. "Claire and I love each other very much, but if truth be told, our marriage has always been one of convenience. Before we met, we were both outcasts when it came to personal relationships. With our light skin color, no one wanted us, and we both knew that. When Zach threw us together, it didn't take us long to realize we could at least have each other."

That explained a lot. Not only did Jonathan have an affair, but he had had it with someone he loved, and Claire in all likelihood knew that. It wasn't just an affair. It was his love story. She could only imagine what was going through Claire's mind.

"And so Claire and I got married, and we took care of each other." He sighed. "I don't regret one thing about our marriage, but to be honest..." Something blissful flashed through his eyes. "I was so in love with your mother." He looked at Marie in a way that told her more than words ever could have. She played with the coarse mane of her horse, lost in thought.

"What are you thinking, Marie?"

She shook her head and then met his gaze. She blinked several times to fight back the tears. "You say you don't regret one thing about your marriage. But do you have any regrets about my mother?" she asked in a low, tight voice.

"Your mother was and will always be the love of my life," he said quietly. "I'm telling you things now I've never told another living soul."

"I know."

"Look, I've been with only two women my entire life, and I'll turn fifty-nine next month. Had it not been for your mother, Marie, I would never have known what it is to be in love, really in love, and I'll be eternally grateful to her for that. Was it right to have an extramarital affair? No, of course not. But I don't regret it."

"Why did it end?"

Jonathan stared into Marie's eyes several seconds before responding. She could tell this was a difficult conversation for him. "Right or wrong, I couldn't risk being exposed when she got pregnant with you. I...uh...had to think of Claire, my children, my business. I weighed everything very carefully. At least I thought I did. It was probably the hardest decision I've ever made in my life."

They rode a couple of minutes in silence. Jonathan gazed down for several seconds and then said, "I handled it the best way I could. I don't know. Maybe some would say I took the coward's way out. But keep in mind, I had Claire's best interest at heart too. Now that might sound odd coming from someone who had cheated on her, but I worried what would happen to her if we were to separate."

"If my mother hadn't gotten pregnant, would you have continued seeing her?"

"Probably."

Marie gave her horse a gentle nudge with her heels to get her moving faster, ahead of Jonathan, ahead of the echo of his last word, ahead of the pain.

She stopped her horse when she reached the far corner of the property, Jonathan twenty yards behind her. "I know what you're thinking," he said when he caught up with her.

"Are you sure?"

"You're thinking if it hadn't been for you, your mother would be here now—alive and happy."

"Something like that."

"If it hadn't been for your mother, Marie, I wouldn't be here with you now—alive and happy." He waited for a response but got none. "C'mon, let's head back."

The drone of horse hooves meeting the ground was the only sound that broke the silence while they rode back to the barn. They dismounted their horses. Marie turned to her father and asked, "Did you ever regret not having me in your life?"

He shook his head. "Maybe not at first." He stared down at the dirt floor of the barn for several seconds before meeting her gaze. "But when I saw that first picture of you and looked into those big brown eyes of yours, well...I just wanted to hold you and tell you I loved you."

"But you didn't."

Jonathan shook his head. "No, I didn't." Marie waited for more. "Did I regret that? You're damn right I regretted it. Maybe I made poor decisions in the past, Marie, but I promise you, you will be a part of my life from now on." He put his arms out and embraced her. "I *want* you to be a part of my life." He took a step back from her. "Are we okay?"

Marie cleared her throat of emotion. Discovering the strength of a father's hug was incredible. "Yes, we're okay," she said. "But I don't think Claire and I are okay, and that's bothering me."

"Give her time, sweetheart. She needs time right now."

Later, after a hardy breakfast of blueberry pancakes whipped up by Claire, Jonathan suggested to Marie that they go into town so he could show her around. As they drove the short distance to downtown St. Charles, Jonathan told her a little of the town's history. "It used to be called Charleston. Not sure why they changed it. The interesting thing about this town is that it helped slaves to freedom on the Underground Railroad. There is a well-known runaway slave woman named Joanna Garner who settled here. Some of her family still live here."

"Is that another reason why you chose here to live?"

"That may have been a small part of it. The main reason, of course, was to escape the bigotry that was so prevalent in the South. There were other factors too. I liked the diversity here. But the real reason I'm here is there was plenty of open land for my horses. Cheap land."

They drove down Main Street past the Hotel Baker. "I thought we'd eat there. The hotel has an interesting history. I'll tell you about it over lunch."

Jonathan parked the car in a lot across from a park. "I want to show you something before we go to the restaurant." He led her across the street toward a long park bench. She sat down and allowed the breathy wind to brush across her face for a couple of minutes while she took in the scenery. "Here is where I proposed to Claire. Different bench, but same spot."

A woman walked by with a young girl who appeared to be four or five years old. The girl looked like she was about to approach Marie and Jonathan when the woman grabbed her hand and whisked her away.

Jonathan waited until they were out of earshot. "That's pretty common behavior. They see a colored man, and right away they think I'm some kind of threat. The funny thing is that I may very well have sold that woman's husband a horse at one time or another." He shook his head.

"I've been in her shoes."

Jonathan looked at her. "And?"

"I can relate to her."

Jonathan raised his eyebrows.

"I can't explain it. Fear, maybe? I don't know. Of course, now I don't feel that way, but look what it took for me to get to this point!"

Jonathan laughed. "It's funny, but it's not so funny."

They ate lunch and headed back to the car. On the way home, Jonathan asked Marie what she thought about their new president.

"Karen and I followed Truman and Dewey pretty closely during their campaigns. Like everyone else, we were sure Dewey was going to win. But I'm glad he didn't. I think Truman will do more for the people, especially the poor."

"We'll see how he does on his promises. You mentioned Karen. By any chance would she be the person who came to my door looking for a horse?" His smile told Marie he wasn't upset at the shenanigan she and Karen had pulled in their effort to find him.

"Yes, that would be her. She's my best friend."

When they got home, Claire handed Jonathan a phone message. He took it, went into his office, and closed the door. When he came out, he had a peculiar look on his face.

"I've been invited to participate in a roundtable political discussion in Chicago next week with twenty or so other Illinois businessmen."

"What's the topic of discussion, dear?"

"Truman's first year in office."

"Are you prepared to do that?" Claire asked.

"Well, I can be. I'll have to do a little studying."

"What day is it?"

"The Monday following Thanksgiving. That gives me time."

"You should feel honored to be asked, dear," Claire said.

"I do. There will be a lot of important people there." He glanced at Marie. "But it's going to cut into our visit. I'll have to leave on Sunday, but I should be back late Monday."

"Oh, please don't worry about me. I'll be fine."

Claire looked at Marie and shot her a weak smile. "That will give us a chance to get to know each other better."

Oh dear. Is that a good thing?

"C'mon, girls. Let's go for a ride before dinner."

* * *

The next day Jonathan had business in Geneva and left before Marie awoke. After having a relatively reticent breakfast with Claire, she went out to the barn and had Zach saddle up a horse for her.

"Going out by yourself today, are you Miss Marie?"

"Yes. I think I know my way around well enough now. What do you think?"

"Oh, you'll be fine. Everything is fenced. You can't get too lost. But if you get turned around, just look for the tallest tree." He pointed toward behind the main barn. "That's home."

Marie thanked him and rode off, her mind quickly going to how she could make things better with Claire. Jonathan kept telling her to give it time, but she didn't like the wait.

Glad she had put on a few layers of clothing, Marie flinched at the cool breeze grazing her face, cold enough for her to see the horse's breath shoot out of his nostrils in perfect rhythm with his stride. She headed east and watched the fading ribbons of the morning's sunrise dissipate above the horizon. She enjoyed the peacefulness of the terrain, the strength of the horse between her legs, and the utter contentment of being where she was—home. Well, home of sorts.

She followed a trail that led to the far corner of Jonathan's property, up a slight rise overlooking miles of farmland. She stopped to study the expansive landscape. The configuration of each farm within her view was distinct, but they shared the same basic components: a main barn, several small outbuildings, open fields, and the main house. Some of the houses were situated near the road and others more toward the center of the fields.

Except for the occasional sound of a bird chirping, the air was quiet and calming. Riding had a way of suspending time and place for Marie, allowing her to escape reality. Lost in thought in her own private space, she jumped when she heard a voice behind her.

"Morning." She turned around to see Melvin sitting high on a jet black mare.

"Hi. You startled me."

"Sorry. I didn't mean to." She studied his face but didn't know how to read his expression.

Marie turned back around to face the vast open land. "It's beautiful up here."

"That it is." He guided his horse next to Marie's. "This is my favorite spot on Dad's property. That's why the path is so worn. I come up here every chance I get."

Marie turned to meet his gaze. His skin appeared even lighter when illuminated by the sun. "So Melvin, did you hear about your dad's invitation to the political roundtable discussion in Chicago next week?"

He nodded. "You can call me Tré. Everyone else does."

"Okay, Tré."

"Yes, I heard. Dad's pretty smart, you know. He's well read, and he can hold his own with the best of them, so..."

"I believe that."

He fidgeted in the saddle. "Marie, I didn't just happen to ride up here this morning. Zach told me you headed up this way."

She waited for him to say more, expecting the worst, but hoping for something better.

"I have to apologize for the way I acted on Sunday."

Marie opened her mouth to say something, but Tré held up his hand signaling he wasn't finished. "I need for you to understand something." His eyes focused past her face for a few seconds, into the vast open land. "I was married once before, to a woman named Anna, a white woman. Everyone in my family was against it, but I was young and pretty headstrong back then, I guess I still am, and I was going to do what I wanted to do no matter what anyone else thought or said."

"How long were you married?"

"Less than six months." He dug his hands into his jacket pockets. "One day I woke up and she was gone. Didn't even take all her clothes." He shrugged. "Well, I was crushed and humiliated. More humiliated than anything else. The fact that she left me for a white guy made it that much worse."

"I'm sorry to hear that."

He cocked his head. "Yeah...well, the reason I bring this up is because my experience with a white girl was disastrous on so many levels. I found out later she was cheating on me during most of our short marriage. That was one thing. But just as bad were my dealings with white people in general. The only time I'm ever accepted by whites is when they think I am white." He let out a big sigh. "Then you came along, and I said, 'Oh, great. Now we have another one in the family.'"

Marie laughed. "Another what?"

"Another white. Dad told us you grew up white. Anyway, it brought back all sorts of...unpleasant memories, shall we say." He turned to face her. "Look, I know I shouldn't judge you by my bad experiences."

"So what made you have a change of heart?"

He chuckled. "Yolanda gave me hell when we got home on Sunday. She waited 'til the kids went to bed and let me have it but good," he said, his smile laced with embarrassment. "I slept on the couch that night and did a lot of thinking. In the end, I just felt like a real horse's ass and knew I had to apologize. And I have to tell Mom I'm sorry, and when Dad gets home later, I'll tell him too." He reached out for a handshake.

Not completely sure if his apology was coming from his own heart or his wife's, Marie paused before shaking his hand. "Apology accepted."

She turned her horse around. Tré followed suit. When they emerged from the woods, Marie scrutinized the area in all four directions before spotting it.

"The tallest tree?" he asked.

Her lips folded into a half smile. "How'd you know?"

"Because we all grew up with the same advice: 'If you get turned around, look for the tallest tree,' Zach would say. 'That's home.'"

* * *

The next day was the day before Thanksgiving, and Marie helped Claire prepare the feast. They were expecting eleven for the main midday meal, including Zach and his son. Marie and Claire talked cordially throughout the day while they prepared the food.

"Tell me about your business, Marie," Claire said as she chopped vegetables. Marie had just opened her own interior design business earlier that year. "You must think this place is a disaster given all your education and decorating experience." Her even tone didn't reveal any clue as to whether she was being sarcastic, resentful, or complimentary.

Suddenly it occurred to Marie that perhaps Jonathan's paying for her education had taken away from what he was able to give his other children. She prayed that wasn't the case. "I think you've done a fine job with the decorating, Claire. Your house is so cozy, so inviting." Marie proceeded to tell her about her line of work.

"And so you left Marshall Field's when you fled from your husband?"

"Mm-hmm. I had to, really. Do you want me to slice all the yams?"

"Yes. Would you hand me that bowl, please? So how did you get started in Atchison?"

Marie told her story, including how she had worked at the local phone company in Atchison before starting up her own business, and how she had developed the strong friendship with Karen.

"Maybe someday you can bring her here for a visit. We'd love to meet her."

Marie wasn't sure that Claire's interest in meeting Karen was genuine or something else. She gave her a weak smile and said, "Thank you. I'd like that. But you know, you already have met her."

Claire gave her a puzzled look.

Months earlier, when Marie had begun to suspect her father lived in St. Charles, she and Karen had driven there to check him out. Karen pretended to be interested in buying a horse from him. She was also the one who told Marie that Jonathan Brooks was a Negro. Marie had to see him for herself, so Karen drove to his ranch for the second time, this time with Marie in the passenger seat. When Jonathan had emerged from his home, she had instinctively known he was her father.

Marie relayed the story to Claire, who shook her head. "Getting back to your business, I'm curious as to how you ended up where you are. Let's face it, most women are like me—devoted to housekeeping, raising families, and being a dutiful wife. And most women don't leave their husbands, no matter how difficult the situation is."

Marie wasn't sure if Claire was criticizing her for leaving Richard or thinking about her own set of circumstances. "When I was in college, I studied a woman interior designer named Frances Elkins. You probably never heard of her, but you may have heard of her brother, David Adler, the famous architect." Claire nodded. "Well, she's my hero, my inspiration."

"Why is that?"

"She started out being that typical housewife that you described, married to a man from a very prominent family who made a lot of money and kept her in fine clothes and jewelry. While she wasn't in love with him, she did have three children with him. But that's not what she wanted in life, at least that's not all she wanted in life. She wanted a fulfilling career like her husband, but she knew he would never let her do that, so she left him, divorced him actually, and without any college or training pursued what she loved to do, interior decorating."

"She left her children?"

"No, apparently she took her children with her."

"What time period was that, Marie? Is she still alive?"

"She peaked in her career during the twenties and thirties. Made quite a name for herself. And she did other things she thought could be done, should be done, when others called her crazy. Like establishing her own workshop for the craftsmen who worked on her projects. No woman back then, or even now, would do that. As far as I know she's still alive and living in California."

"Sounds like quite the pioneer."

"She was the first interior designer to incorporate matching her designs with the personalities of her customers. That's something we designers take for granted today, but we owe it to her."

"It's nice to have someone in your life who inspires you to do what you really want to do." Claire looked away for a moment, as if in a distant thought. "I don't think you've said just how you ended up in Atchison. Why Kansas of all places?"

"Five days after I left Richard, I went to Union Station in Chicago trying to figure out where to go, thinking it should be as far away as possible. I was leaning toward Denver when I saw this man lurking around the station. I was pretty sure he was one of Richard's cohorts, and I panicked. I looked at the train schedule posted on the wall and asked the agent for a one-way ticket to Kansas City. It was the town at the top of the list, the next train leaving the station."

"So what you're saying is that had Denver been the next train leaving, you would have settled there? Or Philadelphia, or anywhere else?"

"Probably."

"Funny how fate works, isn't it?"

Marie wished more than anything she could read her. "Yes, it is."

* * *

Family members started arriving late morning, each with their contribution to the holiday meal. Claire cooked an eighteen-pound turkey, a ham, apple-walnut stuffing, mashed potatoes, corn, beans, candied crabapples, and cornbread. For dessert, apple pie, chocolate cake, and the cookies Tré's daughters had baked.

Jonathan asked to say the blessing before the meal. "Please join hands," he began. "Our Father in heaven, we give thanks for the pleasure of our gathering together for this occasion. We give thanks for life, the freedom to enjoy it, and all other blessings. As we partake of this food, we pray for health and strength to carry on and try to live as you would have us live. This we ask, heavenly Father, in the name of Christ.

"On this particular Thanksgiving, we thank you for giving Marie the wisdom and courage to find me, as I didn't have the wisdom and courage to bring her home on my own. We thank you for the mixture of our cultures, blending us into one people under God.

"Please guide us to help those who are less fortunate. We lift up in prayer the victims of poverty and racism, and all others who suffer.

"And finally, we pray that you will bless all those who gather here, and keep us safe. In Jesus' name, amen."

Once the effect of Jonathan's heartfelt prayer dissipated, energetic dinner conversation commenced. In between bites, Marie sat back, taking it all in.

After dinner, the men migrated to the living room for what started out as sports talk but quickly turned into naps. The women spent the next two hours washing dishes and wrapping up leftovers.

Too young to fully understand, Tré's daughters apparently hadn't been told the whole story about Marie, and they were curious, especially after Jonathan's prayer. Denise, the older of the two, wasn't shy about asking questions. Her arms were folded across her chest when she asked the first one. "So, Marie, how can you be our aunt?" Yolanda opened her mouth to say something to her daughter, but then let her continue.

"Because your grandfather is my father," Marie explained.

Denise crinkled her brow. "But you're white."

"Denise!" Yolanda scolded.

"It's okay, Yolanda. I don't mind," Marie said. "Negroes come in all shades, Denise. I'm just very light-skinned." She couldn't believe those words had come out of her mouth. Except for Karen and now the Brookses, she hadn't had a conversation with anyone about her ethnicity or her skin color.

Denise's hands were on her hips. "So we're to call you Aunt Marie?"

"If you want."

"How come you've never been here before?"

"Well, I've been separated from your family for a long time...and now we've found each other."

She shifted her weight. "Is your husband white?"

"Denise!"

"It's okay," Marie said to Yolanda. "I'm married, but I'm not with my husband anymore."

"Why not?" With that, Yolanda took her daughter's arm and guided her out of the kitchen.

Marie's gaze met Claire's, and both women laughed. Claire said, "She'll find out someday. I would have let her continue." She threw up her hands in surrender. "But she's not my child, so I stay out of it." Claire appeared to be letting her guard down a bit, allowing what Marie suspected was her true personality to emerge. It felt good.

The last thing planned for the day was to pick names out of a hat for Christmas presents. Claire explained once the boys were grown and out of the house, they had established the one-gift rule. Marie smiled at the sight of Jonathan's name on her slip of paper.

After everyone had gone, Marie, Claire, and Jonathan sat in the living room relaxing over a glass of wine. "Well, what do you think?" he asked Marie.

"About?"

"About today. How does it feel to be part of this family?" He laughed and looked nervously at Claire before asking Marie, "Have we scared you enough yet?"

Marie smiled while she thought about how to respond. "Quite the opposite. I have dreamt my whole life for a holiday get-together like this…with a family. A family I never had until now. You can't know how good it makes me feel."

"Marie, dear," Claire chimed in, her voice slightly stilted. "I'm not sure just how to put this, but I watched you interact with everyone here today, and I saw someone who felt very relaxed…even when little Denise was asking you all those indelicate questions. I'm not sure most people who were raised in a white family would feel that comfortable around colored people."

"Well, I feel totally comfortable around you." She wondered how Claire would interpret what she had just said.

"And why do you think that is?"

Marie shook her head. "I don't know. Skin color just doesn't matter to me, and as far as I can see, that's the only difference between us." *There I go again. Wrong thing to say.*

Jonathan looked at Marie, then his wife. "On that note, let's go to bed," he said.

CHAPTER 4

To Thine Own Self Be True

Marie jumped at the chance when Jonathan asked her if she wanted to accompany him to the public library the next day to research back issues of newspapers for Truman's political platforms,

Seeing the outside of the library brought back memories of when she and Karen had combed through phonebooks looking for Marie's father. Jonathan touched her arm. "Before we go in, Marie, can you tell me just how you found me?"

They sat in Jonathan's car while she told the story. "After Mrs. Hollingsworth called me...that name, I went to the public library to look at pictures of Negroes. I know that sounds dumb, but I didn't know very much back then. Anyway, I found this book, *What Really Went on in the Big House.* Are you familiar with it?"

Jonathan shook his head.

"Well, in there I saw pictures of mulatto children who looked just like me. And that's when it occurred to me that Mrs. Hollingsworth may have been right. Because remember, I knew nothing about you, and the more I thought about it, the more I wondered just why Mom was so secretive. So after that, every chance I got, I looked for clues. I went to the hospital where I was born, to my schools. I contacted people who knew my mother. But I got nowhere. Then, years later, when Karen and I became friends, I confided in her what I suspected.

"Well, Karen has a keen sense of curiosity, and she went to my college in New York and somehow found out that Gregory Feinstein had something to do with whoever was paying my college tuition. We wanted to know where he lived, so we pored over Chicago and suburban phonebooks."

"Okay. Back up. Why did you do that?"

"Why did we want to know where he lived?"

"Yes."

"Because there was this notation on one of the bank records Karen found at my school referring to a barbecue at Jon's and a date and time, and we thought there might be a connection between Jon and, well, you."

His eyebrows rose. "The note about the barbeque was written on a bank record?"

"Well, not exactly. Karen rubbed a pencil over an imprint that was on the bank document and was able to decipher it."

Jonathan smiled. "I think I want to meet this Karen."

"You already did, remember?"

"That's right. Okay, continue."

"Anyway, we called all the Gregory Feinsteins we found in the phone books until we found the one associated with the bank. So we drove here, to St. Charles, and found his house. Then we looked at all the mailboxes on his street and came here, to the library, and matched up the addresses with names. The only one that made any sense was Brooks Horses." Marie gazed at her father apologetically. "I think you know the rest."

Jonathan shook his head. "All I can say is that you and Karen may have missed your true calling—detectives. By the way, we've invited the

Feinsteins over for dinner tomorrow." He gave her a warm smile. "C'mon, let's go see what Mr. Harry S. Truman is all about."

Marie and her father spent the next several hours reading everything they could get their hands on regarding the new president—newspaper and magazine articles, transcripts of his campaign speeches, and political flyers. Jonathan took copious notes, and when they returned home, he and Marie discussed the various issues: the Soviet Union, economic and social development, the formation of NATO, nuclear weapons, the Cold War, and civil rights—all the topics Truman had spoken about on his "whistle-stop tour" prior to his election.

Impressed with her father's knowledge of political issues, Marie knew there was even more to this man than she had already seen.

* * *

On Saturday, Marie and Jonathan went for a leisurely ride after breakfast. It was gray and overcast, and the temperature had dropped twenty degrees overnight. Claire lent Marie her sheepskin vest for the ride.

"Dad?" It was hard to avoid calling him that sometimes, like now, when she wanted to get his attention.

"Yes, daughter?" Jonathan shot her a sincere smile.

"There's something I brought up in the car ride earlier that I'd like to talk about."

"Sure. What is it?"

"Well, it's about…it's about race." They slowed the horses to a steady gait. "You know when men look at me, they see a white woman."

"No," he corrected her. "When men look at you, they see a beautiful white woman."

Despite the cold, Marie felt the blood rush up her neck. "Thank you. What I'm getting at is that when a man shows an interest in me, it's because he's interested in a white woman. So let's say then he asks me out. I'm at a loss what to do now."

"What's the problem?"

"If I say no, that ends it right then and there, and I may have missed out on a good relationship. But then, of course, I'm not sure anymore if that's the relationship I want to be in anyway."

"Mm-hmm."

"But if I say yes, at some point I have to reveal my true identity. And if I do that on the first date, it will probably be the last date. White men don't want to be seen with a colored woman."

"Sounds like you have this figured out."

"But a Negro man isn't going to want to be with me, either."

He paused for a few seconds. "Look at Tré."

"That didn't work out so well, did it?"

"No, but I'd be hard pressed to say it was because she was white. There were other issues in that marriage."

"Yes, I know."

"I think it's accurate to say most Negro men wouldn't want to be seen with a white woman, but there are plenty of them who wouldn't mind *being* with a white woman, believe me."

"So what am I supposed to do?" Marie asked. "Go through life alone?"

"Claire would tell you there is someone out there for everyone. You just have to find him."

Marie was afraid her own fears would keep her from ever being in a serious relationship—her fear of Richard for one, and not knowing how to deal with her ethnicity for another. Understanding how to manage fear with desire, two diametrically opposed emotions, was something she had yet to figure out.

"So keep saying yes and face the consequences, face the rejections when they find out who I am," she said. Jonathan didn't respond. "Or would you advise me to do what you and Claire did? Marry out of convenience and not for true love?" She immediately regretted having said that.

"Marie, I can't advise you what to do. You have to listen to your own heart. I told you I have no regrets with my marriage, but that may not work for you. Besides Richard, what have been your other experiences?"

"Pretty much none. A few dates in college, but nothing serious. Richard was my first. And now…well, legally, I'm still married, so I haven't seen anyone."

"What are you going to do about your marriage?"

She sighed. "I don't know. According to one lawyer, I don't have good grounds for divorce, so I've been just waiting it out."

"Waiting for what?"

"Well, he has grounds, but I doubt he'll file for divorce. My only other option is to wait the seven years for the marriage to be nullified, which may be better all the way around. It's bad enough I'm looked upon as different because I own my own business by myself, but who wants to be labeled a divorcee?" Not to mention a mulatto once people find that out, she thought.

"How much longer would you have to wait for that?"

"It's only been a year and a half."

"I have a few lawyer friends. Let me see what I can find out."

* * *

The Feinsteins arrived at six o'clock, all four of them. Marie, of course, had already met Gregory. With him were his wife, Gloria, their forty-one-year-old son, Ben, and Ben's twelve-year-old daughter, Rachael.

Dinner conversation included talking about Marie's interior design business, Ben's medical practice, and Rachael's school and extracurricular activities. Rachael, with shoulder-length dishwater blonde hair, sad blue eyes, and an expressionless face, answered any question asked of her but didn't offer up anything on her own. Marie was curious about her mother; there had been no mention of her before or during dinner.

After dinner, the men retreated to the main barn to enjoy the Cuban cigars Greg had brought with him. The women and young Rachael cleared the table and tidied up the kitchen. Afterward, they settled in the living room where Claire, Gloria, and Marie enjoyed a glass of port wine.

"My mom is missing," Rachael said with a flat voice and vacant look on her face. Her words stung the air at first and then hung there like a morning fog.

Gloria looked at her granddaughter with loving eyes and then focused on Marie. "Rachael's mother left the family in May. We don't know where she is."

Marie glanced at Rachael. The girl had not yet displayed even the faintest of smiles during the few hours she had been there. Marie could almost see the sad thoughts going through her head. "That must be very hard for you. I'm sure you miss her."

Rachael jumped up and sat close to her grandmother for comfort, burying her head in Gloria's bosom. Gloria clenched her mouth and rolled her eyes but didn't say anything. Then the men entered the room. "Have a good smoke?" Claire asked, trying to ease the tension in the room.

The men had big grins on their faces. "Nothing like a good Cuban cigar," Jonathan said.

"What do you think, dear?" Gloria asked, with Rachael still cradled in her arms. "Should we be getting home? Rachael has an early morning riding lesson."

The Feinsteins got up to leave. Marie, Jonathan, and Claire walked them to the door and said their goodbyes. Claire had her hand on the doorknob, about to close the door, when Rachael ran back into the house and hugged Marie. And just as quickly, she was gone.

Back in the living room, Claire explained Ben's situation. "Maybe we should have told you this before they got here, but I didn't know if it would come up, and...well, I thought it better not to say anything. Anyway, Ben didn't even know he had a daughter until a couple of years ago." She turned to her husband. "Has it been that long?"

"I think so."

"He and Judy had dated sometime back, and then she broke it off and moved to Chicago. Greg and Gloria and eventually Ben all thought it was for the best. Then one day out of the blue, Judy calls Ben and tells him he has a ten-year-old daughter. Ben did what he thought was the right thing to do, and that was move them here and marry Judy."

"That must have caused quite a disruption in his life."

"That's putting it mildly. It was a disaster. Judy spent more time away from the family than she did with them. Rachael started going to Greg and Gloria's after school because her mom was rarely there for her. Then one day, Ben came home from work only to find Judy, their checkbook, and all her clothes gone."

Marie sat in silence, mouth agape, while she listened to the story. "That poor child." She wondered how anyone could up and leave their child like that. Could there be any legitimate explanation for her actions?

"Greg and Gloria play a big role in Rachael's life these days," Jonathan added. "And Ben is trying very hard to be a good father, although I'm not sure if she's actually his daughter."

"Jonathan!"

"Well, let's be honest, Claire. What proof do they have? Judy's word? That's worth about as much as teats on a boar hog."

"Jonathan Brooks! You apologize for your language."

"Sorry, ladies. It's an old Southern expression."

"You and your old Southern expressions. No more, ya hear?"

"Yes, dear."

Claire yawned. "Well, it's been a long day, and I'm going to bed."

Marie glanced at her father whose eyes were half closed. "I think I'll turn in too. Good night," she said.

"Good night, sweetheart."

* * *

After lunch on Sunday, Jonathan disappeared in his den to prepare for his roundtable discussion. Claire invited Marie for a horse ride. Marie didn't know what to expect and was nervous about being alone with Claire, completely out of earshot from anyone.

"So you've been here a little more than a week, Marie. How does it compare to what you expected?"

Marie slowed down her horse. *Here's your chance. Whatever you do, don't blow this.* "Honestly, it's been so much more than I expected." She paused. She wanted to choose just the right words. "And I have to say it's as much because of you as it is Jonathan."

"Me?" Claire acted surprised at Marie's remark.

"Claire, I'm pretty sure this visit would never have taken place if it wasn't for you. And please don't believe for a minute that I don't appreciate that. I'll never forget this visit."

"Well, I'm glad to hear you say that, dear…and…um…I want you to know you're welcome here anytime. You're family now." She looked directly into Marie's eyes. "I mean that."

This is my chance to get closer to her. Here goes. "Thank you." She flashed Claire a smile that she hoped came across as genuine. "And I'd like to come back." She thought about her many conversations with Jonathan. "You know, I have so many questions, and…"

"I hope you're getting all the answers you were hoping for."

"Well, not all of them. Jonathan and I have had talks about how to deal with my…shall we say, my identity crisis, but I'm still pretty much in the dark about that."

This was the most at ease Claire had appeared since Marie's arrival. "What's your biggest concern?"

"Romantic relationships. I can pass for white. Heck, I've been doing that my whole life. And I don't have any problem attracting white men. But as soon as they find out about me, that's likely to be the end of it. And quite frankly, if I wanted to, I could keep it a secret and everything would be fine, at least on the surface. But I can't live with that, and I do still want children some day, so I really can't keep it a secret."

"Jonathan and I talked about this before you got here." The distant expression on her face told Marie Claire was carefully thinking through her next words. "Marie, have you ever considered going out with a colored man?"

Marie's thoughts wavered while she considered what she was about to say. "Yes, I've thought about it. But to be completely honest, it wouldn't feel right." She shook her head and stared downward. "And you know what's so bad about that?" She didn't wait for an answer. "That makes *me* prejudiced—just what I can't tolerate in other people." She peered up at Claire. "It's very confusing."

The two women rode back to the stable at a slow gait and then handed the horses over to Zach. They walked back to the house. "You're talking about a very complicated issue. There won't be any easy answers. Let's make ourselves some tea, and I'll tell you a story that may help you sort through things."

The shift in Claire's attitude lifted Marie's spirits. She followed Claire into the house.

"Do you know what is the best advice I have for you, Marie?"

"No, what's that?"

"To thine own self be true."

"Shakespeare."

"Yes. Powerful words. Very powerful words. And so many people leave this earth never having learned that lesson."

Marie thought about the quote while she helped Claire prepare beef stew for dinner. They were just six words, six simple words. But each time she thought about what they meant and all the ramifications of being true to herself, her thoughts took off in a different direction.

"To thine own self be true," she repeated to Claire after half an hour had passed. "I would think that first you have to know who you are, and I'm not sure I know that. Or am I making this more difficult than it needs to be?"

Claire put down the knife she was using and focused on Marie. "Yes, I agree you have to know who you are, and there's nothing simple about it. For you, part of the equation has already been defined. You're a woman who happens to be part Negro but looks white. That's one of your truths. Being true to yourself, I believe, means developing, believing in, and following your values based on your truths. Does that help?"

Marie nodded, and then shook her head. "I'm not sure. I'm going to have to give that some more thought." Her instincts told her to hug her, but she wasn't sure if Claire was ready for that. "Thanks."

"As for relationships, find someone who appreciates you for who you are and what you have to offer, and you'll do fine."

Marie found a handwritten note on her pillow later that evening.

The Serenity Prayer

God grant me the serenity
to accept the things I cannot change,
the courage to change the things I can,
and the wisdom to know the difference.

Marie had expected that on this visit she would derive explicit answers to the race issues that had exasperated her for so long, but she was now more perplexed than ever. But at least she was feeling more comfortable with Claire, and to some extent, that was more important.

* * *

"So how did it go, dear?" Claire asked Jonathan when he returned from Chicago.

"It didn't." He walked past his wife, poured himself a Scotch, and sank down in his favorite chair in the living room.

Claire followed him. Marie wasn't far behind. "What do you mean?"

"There wasn't any roundtable discussion. Any legitimate one anyway."

Marie and Claire both gave him confused looks.

"Join me in a drink, ladies, and I'll tell you all about it."

Claire poured the drinks while Jonathan began the story. "It was all a sham. Orchestrated by none other than the illustrious Mr. Richard Marchetti, no doubt."

Jonathan's retort caught Marie completely off guard. "What?!" she exclaimed.

"Don't get too upset about it, Marie. I'm not."

"Tell us what happened, Jon," Claire said.

"I suspected something was not on the up-and-up the night before when five of us had dinner together, and we started talking about how each of us had been contacted. Things didn't add up."

Marie strained to listen to what he was saying, but she was having a hard time getting past the Richard factor.

"It started out okay. There was someone there taking notes, so it seemed legitimate and everything. We talked about all the things I figured we would, and the discussion, while lively, was conciliatory...in the beginning. But when the moderator got to civil rights, he started firing questions directly at me—the only colored man on the panel I might add—like I was responsible for all the civil unrest in the country."

Claire's face turned red. "What did the other panel members do?"

"They were all dumbfounded, but they saw I was handling things on my own, and so they let it continue."

"That's just not..."

"Let me continue. It gets worse. Without any provocation, this short, rather stout white man in an ill-fitting suit barges through the door and looks at us like a cougar scoping out a herd of gazelles, and then points at me and says, 'Why are you listening to this nigger?'"

Both women gasped.

"He went on to say I was nothing but a two-bit horse breeder trying to fit into society and that I'd cheated more people than he could count."

"What?" Marie called out.

"Then what did the others do, Jon?"

"At first I think they were all so surprised by this man's outburst, they just sat frozen in their chairs…except for the moderator, that is. He seemed to be enjoying it all. Then that little piece of shit—I'm sorry, ladies—the little fat man went on to say I…okay, I'm not going to use the exact language he used because it's vulgar. He went on to say I caused a white woman to become pregnant, and I now have a secret illegitimate half-breed daughter."

"I don't believe this." Marie hoped the infuriation revealed on Claire's face wasn't being directed at her.

"Calm down, Claire. Don't let it get to you. It's not worth it."

"If Richard had anything to do with this, I swear I'll…"

"You, too, Marie. It's not going to help to lose control. Anyway, two of the other panel members jumped up and escorted the worthless little…out the door and then blocked it so he couldn't come back in. Then they each had their say to the rest of the group, defending me. One of them said, and I'm glad he did, that as far as having an illegitimate daughter, well, that was true, and he added that she is a welcome member of my family and an upstanding citizen in her own community."

"So where was the moderator all this time?"

"Edging his way toward the door, and as soon as Harold and Gene moved away, he fled, mumbling 'meeting adjourned' on his way out."

"Unbelievable," Marie muttered.

"After the phony meeting adjourned, everyone except for two guys I didn't know stuck around, and we talked. I knew, of course, that a few of those present were aware of my past and of Richard's threats because I told them as much last month. That, as you recall, was part of my plan— to admit to my indiscretions, shall we say, before Richard had the chance to expose me. But what I didn't know was that almost everyone else in the room knew as well. There had to be at least a dozen other men there, besides the ones I told. Seems like the word got around faster than Greg and I ever anticipated. Everyone was on my side, and quite supportive I might add."

Claire drew in a big breath. "Well, I'm relieved to hear that, but..."

"Me too," Marie added. "And I'm glad that little shenanigan backfired on him. Serves him right."

Claire's eyebrows were raised. "I wonder if he'll try something else."

"I don't know, Claire," Jonathan responded. "But we're not going to worry about it. We're stronger than that little twit. Sorry, Marie."

"No need to apologize to me. I agree with you. Only I have a much worse name for him."

Jonathan smiled. "But what Mr. Marchetti doesn't know is that because of his little escapade, I may have gotten myself a lucrative horse deal. The CEO of Granite Industries, whom I didn't know until yesterday, wants to meet next week to talk about the small ranch he and his wife just acquired in Geneva. There's a horse barn on it that will accommodate six horses." He puffed his chest out. "Ha! Take that, you big ciola."

"Jonathan! Your language."

He swallowed the last gulp of Scotch. "I'm going to bed. I've had one helluva day. Good night, ladies."

Marie waited for him to leave. "What does 'ciola' mean?"

"I have no idea." Claire threw up her hands. "But you can be sure it wasn't very nice."

CHAPTER 5

' Til Next Time

Tré's two daughters, Denise and Brenda, arrived on Tuesday to spend the day while their school was closed for parent/teacher day. Marie and Claire took the girls shopping in the morning. Marie could see that the girls loved spending time with their grandma, especially when it involved shopping. Afterward, the four of them stopped for lunch at the Hotel Baker, another special treat for the girls. Brenda scooted into the chair next to Marie before anyone else could.

When Marie noticed that most of the people seated around them were staring, she shot Claire a puzzled look.

"We're not your average patrons." Claire lowered her voice to a whisper so as not to let her grandchildren hear. "Now more so than ever." With that, Claire gave her a wink.

"So how long are you staying?" Brenda asked Marie after they ordered their meals.

"Three more days."

"Are you coming back?"

Marie glanced at Claire.

"She'll be back," Claire said.

"When?"

"I don't know, Brenda," Marie replied. "Soon I hope."

"How about Christmas?"

"Brenda!" Denise gave her younger sister a gentle poke on the arm.

"We would love for you to spend Christmas with us, Marie," Claire chimed in. "And if it works out for your friend Karen, bring her too."

Marie shook her head, somewhat in disbelief of how well the visit was now going. "Okay. And I'll check with Karen. I know she wants to meet all of you."

"Is she white?" Denise asked.

"Denise," Claire said. She gently grabbed her granddaughter's wrist. "Some things just aren't polite to ask."

Marie smiled. "Yes, she's white."

"Is she another relative?"

"Denise!"

"That's okay, Claire. No, she's just a friend—my best friend."

Claire and Marie took the girls on an easy horse ride in the afternoon. The day was sunny and unseasonably warm for November in the Midwest, and they rode the whole property, ending up at Tré's favorite place high on the ridge.

Claire let the girls ride ahead. "Marie, what happened back there in the restaurant..."

"It made me so uncomfortable. There were some people in there who stared at us the whole time, and even whispered to each other. How rude of them."

"I know. But I don't let it bother me. I don't think they mean any harm. They're just curious because the other Negroes in town don't come into places like the Hotel Baker. They're poor, most of them, and they keep more to themselves. Add you to the mix, and their jaws really start flapping."

Brenda turned around and said to Marie, "Hey, did you ever see my dad's tree house?"

"No, I haven't. Where is it?"

Brenda pointed farther into the woods, off the main trail.

"Why don't you two go exploring, and Denise and I will meet you back at the house," Claire suggested.

Marie helped Brenda tie up her horse, and they made their way into the brush and trees until Brenda stopped and pointed upward. "There it is!"

Marie looked up to see the bottom of a tree house—roughly five-by-five and at least twenty feet off the ground. "How on earth did anyone ever get up there?"

"Grandma said Dad climbed the tree."

"How? There aren't any low limbs."

"Grandma never liked Dad going up there, but Grandpa said it gave him character...whatever that means." Brenda hunched up her shoulders and did a comical impression of Claire. "Then Grandma would say, 'Give him character? All it will give him, Jon, are two broken legs.'"

Marie put her arm around the little girl's shoulder as they walked back to the horses. When she helped Brenda on to her horse, Brenda said, "I'm glad you're here, Aunt Marie. I really like you." Marie smiled but then turned her head so Brenda wouldn't see her swipe away the tear.

* * *

After their morning ride the next day, Jonathan said to Marie, "I have business in Chicago this afternoon. Would you like to join me? You could do a little shopping or something while I'm at the bank, and then we could have a late lunch. What do you say?"

"Sure." Her thoughts went immediately to Marshall Field's where she used to work. "How long do you think you'll be?"

Jonathan scrutinized her face as if he knew what was going through her mind. "As long as you need me to be, sweetheart."

They talked mostly about Marie's mother while Walter drove them into the city. "Mom was great. We lived in this little apartment on the north side, and she seemed to be able to schedule her work around my school." She smiled at him. "I have a feeling you had something to do with that."

"Let's just say I made sure the two of you had everything you needed."

Walter pulled the limo up in front of the bank where Jonathan had business. "Take Miss Costa to wherever she wants to go." He turned toward Marie. "How much time do you need?"

"Can I have two hours?"

"Sure. I'll meet you in the lobby of the bank."

Walter nodded and then looked at Marie for further direction. "Marshall Field's, please." The anticipation of going back to her old place of work made her shiver. So many memories. When Marie had found herself in a position where she had to flee from her husband, it had meant she had to flee from her job as well, something she regretted up to this day.

Marie walked with a taut chest through the cosmetic department where she and Richard had had their first encounter. It hadn't changed much in four years. The store's impressive architecture, with its twenty-foot-high ceilings and massive ornate columns, was awe-inspiring, especially the center of the floor which opened up into a nine-story domed ceiling that crested with colorful mosaic tiles.

She made her way to the seventh floor where her office used to be. That had changed. The seventh floor was now menswear. She walked toward the elevator looking for a directory.

"Oh my God! Tell me it's not you."

Marie turned around to the sound of the familiar voice. Esther looked the same. They hugged each other tight and then in unison swiped tears from their cheeks. "Is there somewhere we can talk?" Marie asked.

Esther pushed the elevator button. "My office is one floor up."

"Your office?" When Marie was there, Esther had held a junior position in the store that didn't warrant an office. "And what may I ask are you doing these days?"

Esther grinned. "Assistant buyer."

"What? Congratulations!" Marie hugged her again.

Esther closed her office door and examined Marie's face. Marie had been her former boss and friend. She shook a finger at her. "Marie Marchetti, we all thought you were dead!"

She flashed open palms. "I know. I'm sorry. C'mon, let's sit down, and I'll explain everything. I have only two hours, so all I can give you are the highlights. But I'd like to get together again when I have more time."

Marie talked nonstop for the next hour, telling Esther how she escaped from Richard and ended up in Atchison. She told her about her design business there and her coach house apartment. Then she told her about Jonathan.

Esther's mouth was agape the entire hour. "You've *got* to be kidding."

"I know. It's a lot to absorb."

"So you're telling me that sweetheart of a husband of yours turned out to be a real creep? Do you know how we all envied you? Oh my God! And your father is a *Negro*? C'mon, Marie. That's hard to believe."

"I know. For me too."

Esther's brows met in the middle. "Why didn't you contact us to let us know you were okay?"

"That was so hard, Esther. But I didn't want you to know anything about me in case Richard contacted you. If he found out you knew something and didn't tell him...well, let's just say it wouldn't have been good for you. I did call Mr. Bakersfield eventually, when I thought it was safe."

"That rat—your husband, that is. You know we called your house that night."

"The night of the retirement party when I didn't show up?"

"Yep. He told us you were running a little late."

Marie smiled. "That was putting it mildly. Did you have any other contact with him after that?"

"No, but I could swear I've seen him drive by our house a few times over the years. That car of his is unmistakable." Richard drove a 1936 Auburn Boattail Speedster.

"I know." She paused a few seconds while her mind changed gears. "Esther, how is Catherine?" Catherine was Marie's old boss, and the last time she had seen her she had been in an iron lung suffering from polio.

"She passed away, Marie, a few months after you left."

More tears. "I'm so sorry. I feel so awful I wasn't here for her."

"Don't feel bad. Looks like you had your own things to worry about. Besides, we heard that you were the one responsible for getting her an iron lung in their home, and believe me, that helped her through a very difficult time."

"Well, it was Richard actually. But in any case, I'm glad we were able to help in some way." She let out a wispy sigh. "Look, I have to go. I came in with my father, and we're meeting for lunch in a few minutes." She took out a pen and piece of paper from her purse. "Here's my address and phone number. Let me have yours too. And I'll call you when I'm in town next and we'll talk more."

The two women hugged again before Marie hurried to the elevator.

* * *

"How did it go?" Jonathan asked after they were seated at a lunch table.

She smiled a blissful smile. "It went well. My best friend at the time still works there, and we had a long talk. I had a lot of explaining to do."

"I'll bet you did. Will you keep in touch?"

"Oh, yes."

"You're not afraid of Richard?"

"Not anymore. He can try anything he wants. I will not let him affect my life any longer." Marie thought about her response. "You know, at first that scared me."

"What's that?"

"Not being afraid of him anymore. Because I think I may have been hiding behind that fear in some respects. Then when I decided I wasn't going to let him do that to me, I felt a little naked."

"And now?"

"I've moved on from that."

Jonathan put his hand over hers. "That's the spirit."

Jonathan told Marie over dinner that evening that he and Claire thought it would be nice to spend Marie's last two days in Lake Geneva, Wisconsin. The Feinsteins owned a lake house there and had said it would be free for them to use.

* * *

They got an early start for Wisconsin. Jonathan drove in his 1947 Chrysler Town and Country woody. Marie rode shotgun, and Claire sat in the backseat. Marie spent more time turned around talking with Claire than she did talking with Jonathan. The roads were clear of snow and light on traffic, so they were able to make good time. They arrived at Gregory's lake house mid-morning.

Marie was surprised to find that the lake house they had talked about so nonchalantly was quite the place. They pulled up in front of a three-car attached garage and walked the circular driveway through the front door under the twenty-foot-high pillars surrounding the portico. Inside, the foyer spanned both stories, and the large crystal chandelier in its center hung from a long heavy-gauge anchor link chain.

"Would you like a tour?" Claire asked.

"Of course," Marie responded.

"I'll meet you on the sun porch," said Jonathan.

The home had an oversized eat-in kitchen perfect for entertaining. On the first floor, in addition to the large sun porch, were a formal dining room, large living room with a stone fireplace that took up one entire wall, two bathrooms, and a mud room. Upstairs were five bedrooms and three more bathrooms. Marie chose a bedroom facing the back of the house overlooking Lake Geneva.

They met Jonathan on the sun porch that faced the lake, where he was sitting next to a table holding a pitcher of lemonade and several glasses. "Aren't you the perfect host, dear?" Claire commented with a sarcastic smile. "I didn't know you could even make lemonade."

"I can't."

The two women looked at each other and then at Jonathan.

"Ben and Rachael are here."

"Oh?" Claire said. "Was there some kind of mix-up?"

"You could say that. Apparently Ben thought he and Rachael needed to get away for a few days and without telling his parents decided to come up here." He glanced at his wife, then his daughter, waiting for a response, when Ben and Rachael walked through the French doors into the sun porch.

"Looks like I did a pretty big goof, eh?"

Claire spoke first. "Not to worry. We can find a hotel."

"I won't think of it. You stay here. We'll find a hotel."

Rachael stomped a foot and crossed her arms. "But Dad!"

Jonathan jumped in. "Look, this house has enough bedrooms. Why don't we all stay here? That is, as long as no one has a problem with it." His eyes circled the room.

"I'm okay with it," Marie said.

"Me too," said Claire.

"Okay," Ben added. He turned toward Rachael.

She extended both arms, palms up. "The more the merrier, I always say!"

"When did you ever say that?" her father asked.

"Just now. Didn't you hear me?"

Ben tousled her hair while everyone laughed.

"Can I have the room closest to Marie?"

Ben hesitated before responding. "Why don't you and Marie go upstairs and figure out the sleeping arrangements."

When Marie and Rachael returned, the five of them sat in the expansive sun porch drinking lemonade and watching the weightless snow fall. Toward noon, Ben told them he and Rachael had gone to the grocery store earlier, and there was enough lunch for everyone.

Rachael jumped up. "Can Marie and me make lunch?" she asked.

"Marie and I," Ben said.

"No, I want to..."

"C'mon, Rachael. Let's do it," Marie said before Ben could respond. "He was just correcting your grammar," she whispered.

They spent the afternoon relaxing mostly in the sun porch. Each time Rachael left the room, Ben filled in the others with his thoughts about what was going on with her.

"I'm very concerned about her," Ben said. He focused on Claire and Jonathan. "After we left your house the other night, she started to cry in the car. When I asked her what was the matter, she wouldn't tell me." He paused while he let out a sigh. "Then later that night, she crept into my room and sat on the edge of my bed until I woke up." He shook his head. "I don't know how long she'd been sitting there. Well, she let it all out, saying she missed her mom so much and wanted her to come home. This is so hard."

Ben turned around to make sure they were still alone. "Judy was an unfit mother as far as I'm concerned," he whispered. "But she was all Rachael had, and she's just too young to understand that." The sound of footsteps behind him caused him to stop.

Ben treated everyone to dinner at the nearby yacht club. When they returned to the lake house, he lit a fire. Rachael toasted marshmallows while the others talked in whispers at the other end of the room.

"It breaks my heart," Ben said. "There's only so much I can do as a father, and that my parents can do as grandparents. She needs her mom."

"Do you know where she is, Ben?" Claire asked.

"No, but I don't think it would take much to find her. I haven't done that because I thought we were both better off without her. Now I'm not so sure."

"That's a tough one, my friend," Jonathan acknowledged.

Ben shrugged his shoulders. "I thought by coming up here we could talk it through, but all I got was the silent treatment on the way here."

"And then we showed up," Marie interjected.

"Well, there may be a silver lining here. I haven't seen Rachael this enthusiastic in a long time." He turned toward Marie. "Thanks to you."

"Me? I really haven't done anything."

"She can't stop talking about you."

"So what's going to happen tomorrow afternoon when the three of us leave? Will you and Rachael stay here?" Claire asked.

Ben shrugged. "I don't know. I'll have to figure that out."

"When will she turn thirteen, Ben?" Claire asked.

"Christmas Eve. Why?"

"Just curious, that's all."

* * *

The next morning, Marie was awakened by a knock on her bedroom door a few minutes before seven. Half asleep, she shuffled over to the door and opened it. There stood Rachael, fully dressed and sporting a big smile. "Wanna build a snowman?"

Marie rubbed her eyes in an effort to conceal her smile. "Give me ten minutes."

For the next hour, Marie and Rachael rolled a big, bigger, and bigger yet ball of snow for their work of art. After they put the smallest one on top of the other two, Ben came out with an old hat, two Oreo cookies for the eyes, and a cigar for the mouth.

While Ben placed the hat on the comical snowman's head, Rachael wadded up a hard-packed snowball and hit her father square on the back of the head, which started an all-out war. Not wanting any part of it, Marie went back inside where she joined amused onlookers Jonathan and Claire.

Claire watched the two of them fiddle with the snowman's hat. "She seems like a changed girl, Marie, and Ben thinks you had a lot to do with it. What did you two talk about when you were alone with her this morning, if you don't mind my asking?"

"Oh, just girl talk. Turns out Rachael and I have a little something in common." She tilted her head. "Maybe more than a little."

"Well, Ben is very pleased to see the change, but we're all a little concerned that it may be short-lived." Claire's gaze strayed back to the window. "Look at those two."

"I know. Me too. I can't believe two weeks have passed," Marie said to Claire as they prepared lunch for everyone. "It seems like I just got here."

"You can stay longer if you want."

"Oh no. I couldn't. Claire, will you be coming with us tomorrow when Jon takes me home?"

"I thought about it, dear, but I think it's better you have that time alone with him. Time to wrap up any loose ends you two may have. Maybe next time."

After lunch, Marie and Claire tidied up the kitchen. Rachael asked her father if she could ride back with Marie and the Brookses instead of him. Ben gave her a disappointed glare. "Damn, Dad. She's leaving tomorrow. I may never see her again."

"What have I told you about that language, Rachael?"

"But it's okay when you say it."

"You're not me."

"Thank God."

"Alright, that's enough."

Rachael left the room.

Ben let out an audible sigh. "One minute she's okay, and the next minute she's impossible."

"It's okay for her to ride back with us," Claire said.

"Not after she acted like that."

"Aw, c'mon, Ben. Let her come with us. She'll be fine."

"Okay, but if she acts up, you have to promise me you'll tell me."

"We promise," Claire said.

Rachael was nowhere to be found. Finally Jonathan opened the front door and looked outside.

"She's in our car, Ben. Must have overheard us talking."

"I don't know what I'm going to do with her." Ben shook his head. "I have some things to do here to close up the house, so I'll pick Rachael up at your place on my way home."

As Jonathan would later tell Marie, he and Claire weren't sure who more enjoyed the ride home in the back seat of their car, Marie or Rachael. They talked about every subject imaginable and like two schoolgirls, they laughed at the silliest things.

When Ben showed up at the Brooks' home, Rachael's pouty face was back on.

"Did you behave yourself?"

Rachael, who had behaved herself just fine, was about to say something when Jonathan jumped in. "Ben, why don't you two join us for dinner? We were planning on going to that new Italian restaurant on Main that just opened up."

Rachael clasped her hands. "Please, Dad? Please?"

Ben rolled his eyes and smiled. "I can see when I'm being railroaded. Okay, we'll go."

"Ben, can I talk to you for a minute...in private?" Marie asked. They disappeared into Jonathan's office.

When Marie and Ben emerged several minutes later, Rachael had a scared look on her face.

Marie looked at Ben. Ben looked at Rachael. "Maybe we should tell her now," Marie said.

"Tell me what?" Rachael asked.

"Well, we weren't going to say anything until it got closer to the date," Ben said, "but we want you to know that Marie is coming back here for Christmas, and..."

"Really? What a gas!"

"What?"

"A gas, Dad." She rolled her eyes. "That's great."

"Well, excuse me, Miss Almost Teenager. Anyway, here's the deal. If you want to, you can ride to Atchison to pick her up and..."

"What? I can do what?"

"If you keep interrupting me, you'll never hear the rest of this."

Rachael rolled her eyes and pretended to zipper her lips.

"As I was saying, Marie has invited you to stay overnight with her and then ride back here the next day."

Rachael stared at Marie. "Really? But ride with who? How would I get there?"

"By limo, of course."

"Are you kidding?" She made a face. "Me, in a limo?"

"Now I may bring my girlfriend, Karen, back with me. I haven't talked to her yet." Marie paused. "You'll like her, Rachael. She's a lot of fun. Sound like a deal?"

"Are you kidding? I'm all fired up and ready to go."

"Okay, young lady. That's enough." Ben turned to Marie. "'Fired up'? I don't know where she gets this language."

* * *

The Brooks children and grandchildren came by the house for breakfast the following day to say goodbye to Marie. Walter arrived mid-morning.

Marie waited for the right moment to thank Claire when they were alone. "I don't know how to thank you," Marie said in a tight embrace. "I had such a nice time."

"I told you this before, but it bears repeating. You are always welcome here, Marie. You're family now." Based on the look on Claire's face and hitch in her voice, Marie was fairly certain she meant it.

The snow had let up from the previous day, but the roads were still hazardous, making the ride home longer than normal. "So what are you thinking, dear daughter?" Jonathan asked after they had ridden the first mile or so.

"What am I thinking?" She turned her body toward his. "I'm thinking you have made me a very happy person. You have no idea." She held his gaze. "I mean it." She reached out for his hand. "My life has changed. I mean *really* changed. But it's going to take me awhile to process it all."

"Tell me more."

"For starters, I have a family now. Mom has been gone for almost eight years. That's a long time to be without family. Well, except for Karen. She's like a sister to me. But other friends and the people you work with come and go. A family is there forever." She heaved a heavy sigh. "For me, family is everything." She paused to reflect. "I have to say, these past two weeks I have felt stronger and more confident than I ever have before. And safe." She nodded. "It's been a long time since I've felt that."

"You don't feel safe back in Atchison?"

"It's just that there's this constant kind of underlying anxiety I have, like something bad is lurking around the corner. Even though I know in my brain I'm safe, I still don't feel safe. I don't know exactly how to explain it."

"I think I may know what you mean."

"And then there's the emotional security, like I felt with Richard— during the good times, I mean. I felt that again these past two weeks, and I have to tell you, it felt good."

"But you're a successful businesswoman. That must have taken a certain amount of strength and confidence."

"Maybe so, but I never *felt* it. Everything I did was a struggle. And, then of course, there's the identity factor. For years I knew just half my identity. I had practically no family history. Now I feel a connection." She paused. "I know all about your God-given identity. But knowing who your parents are, well, that's a whole other layer."

Jonathan stared out the window. "When I think of identity, I think of what makes a person an individual, what a person does with his life, what gifts they have to offer. But I hear you saying it's much more than that." He glanced at Marie and smiled. "I understand that, which proves you *can* teach an old dog new tricks." His face turned serious. "Claire and I want to help you with this. You deserve at least that much from us. I just hope it's not too late."

"No, it's not too late." She gave him a big smile. "Just knowing you is a major milestone for me. And the more I know about you, the more I know about myself." She thought through her next words. "What do you think Claire really thinks about me?"

"Hmm."

"And be honest, please."

"Honestly...I don't think she knows yet how she really feels. She goes from feeling empathy toward you and harboring no ill feelings, which she knows is the right thing to do, to being angry about the whole affair. And unfortunately, I think the more she thinks about it, the more questions she has about our own relationship."

"I must have really messed things up by coming into your life. Everything was probably perfect before I showed up."

"No, far from it. We've had our share of family issues just like anyone else. Claire will be fine. I'm sure of that. In fact, I noticed a change in her attitude toward you during your stay. Did you sense a change?"

"Yes, I did. I was just hoping it was real and not because she felt she had to."

"Let me tell you something about Claire. She doesn't do or say very much just because she has to. Look, I don't want you to worry about her. You let me do that." He looked out the window. "It won't be long before you're home. Is there anything else you wanted to talk about?"

"As a matter of fact, there is. Two things, actually."

"Go ahead."

"When Claire and I and the girls were at the Hotel Baker, the other patrons looked at us like we were from some other planet. Claire said it was because they were curious, but I wasn't so sure. Exactly how are you treated by the whites in this town? I mean, what do you think when people stare at you like that?"

Jonathan sighed and stared out the window for a few seconds. "I think it's easier for me than it is for Claire. With me, I gained a good reputation selling horses before anyone even realized I was a Negro. So when they did find out, I was already established in the business community. But with Claire, it's a whole other matter. She can't join the afternoon tea clubs or go to lunch with 'the girls,' so to speak. There's no one for her to relate to in this town."

"She said most other Negroes here are poor and keep to themselves."

"Not most. *All* of them. But Claire is strong-willed. If she wants to have lunch at the Hotel Baker, then by God, she's going to have lunch there. And unlike in the South, she can."

"I guess I understand that." Marie paused. The next thing she was about to say was more difficult. "There's something I need to get off my chest." She took in a deep breath. "Mom always told me you loved us very much but couldn't be in our lives. I believed her, but that didn't mean

I didn't still feel abandoned by you." Her voice cracked. "And when I was pretty sure you were a Negro, which was long after she died, I felt betrayed by her as well. Maybe there was no other way, and I'm sure she thought she was doing the right thing...but I just had to tell you how that felt for me."

Jonathan squeezed her hand. "I know, Marie. Believe me, I know."

Walter dropped Marie off at her apartment and then drove Jonathan to Rita's Bed & Breakfast where he would stay the night. Marie had made the arrangements for him. She had stayed there while looking for a permanent place to live, and Rita had been her friend ever since.

The last thing Jonathan said to Marie was, "'Til next time, sweetheart."

CHAPTER 6

Library Cards

"Okay, start at the beginning. I don't want to miss even one small detail," Karen said. "But first, do you have any idea how much I've missed you? Can't tell you how many times I went to the phone to call you, and then stopped short when I remembered you weren't there." She paused to take a breath. "What did I do before you?"

"I missed you too. And I kept a journal so I wouldn't forget anything." Marie got up to get the journal and came back with it, two glasses, and a bottle of red wine. "I have a second bottle...I have lots to tell."

The two women talked well into the evening hours, Marie doing most of it. A bottle-and-a-half of wine later, Marie finished with her account.

"So I'm getting some mixed signals from you. Are you happy about the way it went?" Karen asked.

"Yes, all in all, I am. Melvin actually apologized for his behavior. I forgot to tell you that. And Claire...well, I think Jonathan knows her best, and he said to give her time."

"But she was better by the end of the visit?"

"Definitely. Maybe not all the way, and who knows, maybe she'll never be. I wouldn't blame her."

"So you learned more about Jonathan's relationship with your mother, more about his family, his roots."

"Yes, and they are the most beautiful people, Karen, and the way they all welcomed me into their family, into their lives really, just makes me feel so good."

"So do you think being with them has changed you?"

Marie thought about her question for a few seconds. "No. It hasn't changed me. But being part of their family has changed how I perceive myself."

"How so?"

"I don't know. Just the fact that I feel like I'm part of a family now. That makes a big difference."

"So do you have this whole thing figured out now?"

"No. I don't have *anything* figured out. I just feel better somehow, like I belong somewhere."

"As long as you're inside their home."

"What do you mean?"

"The same old world still exists outside of their home," Karen pointed out.

If she wasn't such a good friend, Marie would have challenged her statement. "My trip was just a beginning. I'm not going to abandon my idealistic dreams just yet." She thought about the Serenity Prayer Claire had left on her pillow and wondered if Claire and Karen were more alike than she and either one of them. "But I didn't tell you about the best part of my visit."

"What?"

Marie told Karen about her plans for Christmas and that the invitation had been extended to include her.

Karen's head jerked backward. "You're kidding! They want me to come too?"

"Yes. And so do I. I'd like you to meet them."

Karen hesitated. "I don't know, Marie. I'd feel so out of place there."

Marie looked at Karen without saying anything.

"You know what I mean. I'd be the only..."

"Nothing I've said has had any affect on you, has it?"

"C'mon, don't be mad at me. I just see things how they really are."

Marie sighed.

"Okay." Karen relented. "Count me in."

"Good. Now tell me about the things you wanted to talk about while I was gone."

"Oh, nothing really."

"They must have been important then."

"Well, maybe one thing. Remember Maurice Cooper?"

"The lawyer next door to your shop?"

Her face flushed. "Well...we sorta went out."

"What?! You waited all this time to tell me that? You louse! You went out with him? Where? And how did that come about?"

Karen pulled out a piece of chocolate from her pants pocket and popped it in her mouth.

"Okay, so one day I was locking up the back door of my store, and he was leaving his office the same time, and we kinda bumped into each other. Our cars were parked side by side, so we walked over to them together, just passing the time of day kind of thing. I was unlocking my door, and he said, 'Are you hungry?' I said, 'Yeah, kind of.' And he said, 'Want to grab some dinner with me?' And I said, 'Okay.' So we went to Mario's and had pizza."

"What's he like? When I talked to him in his office that one time, I remember thinking he was kind of stiff. I don't remember him ever smiling, even once."

"I know he gives off that first impression sometimes. But he's nice, actually."

"So are you going to see him again?"

She grinned. "Already did."

Marie threw up her arms. "Okay, tell me more."

Karen pulled another piece of chocolate from her pocket and ate it. "Well, while we were at dinner, he asked me what I was doing for Thanksgiving, and I told him I wasn't doing anything, and he said he wasn't either, so we ended up at his house cooking a turkey."

"You're kidding. What else? Wait a minute. I rarely ever see you eat candy, and now you've shoved two pieces of chocolate in your mouth in the last two minutes. What's with that?"

"Did I? Anyway…we went out again last Sunday. Saw *On the Town* and then had dinner at Madame Woo's."

"So you really like him?"

"I like him okay. But don't get carried away. He's just a nice guy."

"Wait! What about Christmas? Wouldn't you rather spend it with him?"

"No. He's going back east to spend it with his family."

Marie flashed a smile. "Well, I am so happy for you. It's been quite awhile since you've dated. How long has it been?"

"Whoa! We're not dating really. Just friends. Nothing more than that." Karen didn't meet Marie's gaze.

"Right."

"No, really."

"Did you kiss?"

"Well, yeah, but…"

"Then it's a date, my dear."

"It wasn't that kind of kiss."

"Doesn't matter. It's still a date."

She shot Marie a lopsided grin, reaching in her pocket and pulling out yet another piece of chocolate. "Forget it. You're hopeless." She wolfed down the chocolate and got up to leave. "Gotta go. See ya later."

Even though she knew she had had enough, Marie poured herself another glass of wine after Karen left, the rampant thoughts of her Thanksgiving visit still swirling in her head.

* * *

Jonathan called Marie the following week. "Marie, did you say Richard went to jail for a short time earlier this year?"

"Yes. For skimming."

"Well, my dear, if that was a felony, I think I may have some good news for you."

"What's that?"

"I spoke with an attorney client of mine who practices family law, and he told me you would have solid grounds for divorce if your husband was ever convicted of a felony subsequent to your marriage."

Marie's heart raced. It may have been good news on one front, but it frightened her to think about what Richard would do if she filed for divorce.

"I don't know, Dad. What concerns me is that I know he won't just accept the fact I want a divorce and be civil about it. He'll do something… anything he can to either try to get me back or scare me."

"What do you think he'll do?"

"I don't know. That's the scary part."

"Here's what I propose. Let's you and I meet with this attorney when you're here at Christmas and make sure we know all your options, and then you can make an informed decision as to what to do."

The next day, Marie went to the local library to renew her library card with the intention of looking further into divorce law for herself. When she arrived, the clerk behind the counter was giving an elderly woman a hard time about something. The woman was a Negro and appeared to be somewhere in her seventies. Marie had never seen colored people in the library before, or anywhere in town for that matter.

As soon as Marie reached the counter, the clerk looked at her and said, "May I help you?"

Marie looked at the elderly woman's helpless face and said to the clerk, "I think she was before me."

"No. I'm through with her," the clerk said with a disgusted tone in her voice.

The older woman turned and walked away. Marie followed her out of the library.

"Ma'am?" Marie said. The woman kept on walking. "Ma'am?" Still no response. Marie caught up to her and tapped her on the shoulder.

The woman stopped and turned to look at Marie. "What do you want?"

"What just happened back there? That clerk was so rude to you."

"And so what else is new?" She seemed to be out of breath.

Marie took her arm and tried to lead her to a bench, but the woman jerked her arm free.

"What do you think you're doing?"

"I was just trying to help you. You look like maybe you need to sit down."

The woman looked into Marie's face for several seconds and said, "You're really trying to help me."

"Of course I am. Come on, let's sit down over here."

The two women sat down on a nearby bench.

"All I wanted was a library card."

"And she wouldn't give you one?"

"No. She said, 'Your kind is not welcome in here.' I knew that, but the closest library for us is in Kansas City, and that's too far for me to go."

Marie held out her hand. "My name is Marie."

The woman shook her hand. "I'm Doretha. Doretha Scott. I'm sorry I snapped at you. I'm not used to white people trying to help me."

Marie smiled. "I'm not white. That is, I'm not all white. My father is a mulatto." She paused. "Want to have some fun?"

The woman looked at her with a curious eye.

"Was there a particular book you were interested in or just the card?"

"I was told there might be a book on Harriet Tubman." She paused. "She was my grandmother."

"Really?"

The woman nodded.

"You wait here. And don't you dare leave this bench. Just keep watching for me to wave you in."

Marie walked as fast as she could back into the library and renewed her card. Then she went outside and waved to Doretha. At first Doretha didn't understand what she was trying to say to her and just waved back.

No, come here, Marie mouthed, gesturing her to come to her.

Doretha finally came over to her and was about to say something, when Marie interrupted.

"Just follow me."

Marie walked into the library with Doretha on her arm.

"Hold it," the clerk said. "What is she doing in here?"

"She's my grandmother!"

Doretha gasped.

Marie proceeded to walk past the clerk, Doretha still on her arm and holding on tight.

The two women disappeared behind a row of shelving, looked at each other, and giggled.

"C'mon. Let's find that book and get out of here before they kick us out," Marie said.

They never did find the book. Marie offered to walk with Doretha to her home on the other side of town, but Doretha said she didn't think that was a very good idea. "You'll be just about as welcome in my neighborhood as I am here."

"Then you start walking. I'm going to pick up my car and come get you. I want to hear about your grandmother."

Doretha gave Marie a peculiar look before she shrugged her shoulders and said, "Okay."

On the way to Doretha's neighborhood, she told Marie about her grandmother, Harriet Tubman. A railroad conductor for the Underground Railroad, she had helped hundreds of slaves to freedom in the early 1850s. "They called her Moses for what she did." Doretha laughed. "My mother told me there was a forty-thousand-dollar bounty on her head for that."

"She sounds like quite the woman."

"Oh, it gets better. Later, at least from what my mother was told, she worked for the Union Army as a spy during the Civil War. And after that, before she died, she was involved in women's suffrage in New York. Do you know she was given full military honors at her funeral, with Booker T. Washington himself giving her eulogy?"

"I wish we could have found the book. That's quite a story."

As they neared Doretha's neighborhood, the scenery changed. A world apart from Marie's neighborhood, the homes here were small and in need of repair. The lawns, if you could even call them that, were mostly dirt and weeds. Doretha asked to be dropped off.

Marie wrote down her address and phone number for her. "You call me any time you want a book from the library, Doretha. I mean that."

She watched her walk down the dirt road toward a long row of unpainted houses until she disappeared in one of the driveways, the smell of poverty drifting into the car. She hoped she would hear from her, but was afraid she might not.

The next day, Marie called her friend Esther at Marshall Field's and asked her if she could ask their guest services girl to locate a book on Harriet Tubman. A week later, Esther called her back and said they found one titled *Harriet Tubman, the Moses of Her People*.

"Will you order two copies for me? I'll send you a check."

CHAPTER 7

She's Here

Marie was grateful she had unlocked the ground floor door to her apartment right before Rachael was due to arrive, because when she came, the young girl appeared to defy gravity as she raced up the steps two at a time. "Marie, I'm here!" Walter trailed close behind with her suitcase.

Marie gave her a big hug. "How was the trip?"

Rachael rolled her eyes. "Boring," she moaned. "So this is your pad? Cool." She took in everything as she walked around. "Man, I can't wait 'til I can have a place of my own someday."

"You've got quite a ways to go, don't you think?"

"I guess so."

"You must be hungry. What shall we do for dinner? Go out or stay in? Your choice."

Rachael was reading the book titles on Marie's bookshelves. "Stay in."

"Do you like Chinese food?"

"I don't know. Never had it."

Marie gawked at her in disbelief. "You've never had Chinese food?"

Rachael shook her head.

"Well, you're in for a surprise tonight then. Let's get you settled, and then we'll walk over to Madame Woo's."

On the walk back to Marie's apartment, Rachael asked her a question Marie had a feeling would come sooner or later. "How come I've never seen you at the Brookses' house before?"

"That's a long story." Marie wasn't sure how much she should tell a twelve-year-old. "What have you heard so far?"

"I asked Dad, and he said it was grown-up business. Then I asked Grandma, and she said you were part of the family. But that didn't make sense 'cause you're...uh, well, you're not..."

"They're colored and I'm not? Is that what you're trying to say?"

Rachael nodded.

"Well, the truth is I am colored...part colored, anyway. It's just that I have very light skin, so not many people would know that."

Rachael's eyes grew wide.

"I know. It's pretty weird."

"So how are you part of the family? I don't get it."

Marie hesitated before deciding the truth was the right route to take. "Rachael, Jonathan is my father."

They were halfway down Marie's driveway. Rachael stopped dead in her tracks. "Get out of here!"

Marie led her to the bench under the overhang of the coach house porch. "I know that's probably shocking to you."

"I guess! So is Claire your mother? Wait. No, that can't be, 'cause you told me your mom died when you were sixteen." She glared at Marie with a crooked smile and cocked head. "This is crazy."

"It's complicated."

Rachael's face fell. "You're not going to explain this to me, are you?"

"Like your dad said, it's pretty grown-up stuff."

"I'm not a baby."

"I know you're not. But some things are hard to explain to someone who hasn't had that much life experience yet."

"Try me. I've probably had more than you think."

Marie bit her lip and studied the face of the wide-eyed young girl sitting next to her, fearful she was telling the truth. "Okay. You see, Jonathan had a relationship with my mother years ago…many, many years ago. And then I was born."

"So let me get this straight. Jonathan and your mother were married?"

"No. They weren't married."

Rachael shook her head. "Was your mother a Negro?"

"No. She was white."

"This is so crazy."

"Let's go in before our food gets cold. We can talk more about it over dinner."

* * *

Walter was waiting for them when they got back to Marie's apartment after breakfast the next morning. Karen was in the car. The three girls talked the entire way to St. Charles. They talked about Marie's background, how Karen and Marie met, Marie's estranged husband, and Karen's current friend who happened to be a man (she refused to call him her boyfriend). Rachael followed suit and talked about herself.

"Mom and I lived on the south side of Chicago, always in some piss-poor neighborhood."

"Rachael!"

"What?"

"Your language."

"Sorry. Anyway, I didn't like where we lived much, but I never really complained. We couldn't afford anything better."

"Was it just you and your mother?"

"Not usually." Rachael rolled her eyes. "I remember when I was pretty small, maybe four or five, being curled up in the corner of my mother's bedroom—a lot. I would cover my ears with my hands so I wouldn't hear Uncle somebody-or-other beating up on her. There was always someone I was told to call Uncle in our house. Every one of 'em drank, and they all had bad tempers."

Marie cringed at Rachael's story. "I'm sorry you had to go through that, sweetheart. What did your mom do?"

"Oh, she would get through the beating and just go in the bathroom, clean herself up, and then act like nothing happened. Just like always."

"Did your mom have a job?"

"She said she did, but I don't know what it was. She said it was a waitress job, but I don't…sometimes she would leave late at night sayin' she was going to work. And she wasn't always home when I got up. And if she came home and I wasn't in school, she'd get mad. Well, sometimes. Other times she would say it was nice to come home to someone else in the house. She was pretty messed up. Still is, I guess."

Marie wanted to show support for Rachael's mother without condoning or minimizing her seemingly bad behavior. On the surface it appeared once Judy found a place to dump her child, she took off, which Marie couldn't understand any parent doing. "I'm sure she would have done better if she were able."

Rachael shrugged. "The worst part was never knowing where we were going to live or if there would be any food in the house."

"You moved around?"

"All the time. We'd go from one dirty apartment to another, until the landlord kicked us out."

"Do you have any good memories of your childhood?"

"Nope. Well, there was this one time my mom came into a pile of money. I mean a pile of it. And we moved into this nice apartment in a neighborhood where I could actually go outside and play. She bought me all new clothes. We had food in the fridge. And no grease-ball guy in the house." A slow smile formed across Rachael's face. "Mom told me things would be different from now on. And they were—for about a month. Best month we ever had."

"I'm so glad your mom had the good sense to remove you from all of that," Karen said.

"She didn't fit in at Ben's, you know. Ha! Maybe that's why she left. To go back to her old shitty ways."

"Rachael. Watch your language," Marie warned.

"Sorry."

Marie tried desperately to find the good in Rachael's mother. "If that's why she left, at least she didn't drag you with her. Maybe she thought you deserved better."

Rachael twisted up her mouth. "I doubt it."

"And school, how was school in Chicago?"

"Not like St. Charles. The classrooms were dirty, and so were most of the kids. Some days the teacher wouldn't even show up, and we had to sit there and twiddle our thumbs until they found someone to babysit us."

"Not fun, I would think," Marie acknowledged.

"Nope. Most kids flew the coop every chance they got."

"Why did you leave Chicago?"

"Mom got fired." Rachael clapped her hand across her mouth. "Oops. I wasn't supposed to tell anyone that."

"That's okay. We won't tell," Marie promised, thinking it probably didn't matter much now.

"Anyway, then we came here, Mom and Dad got married, and that was that."

"Rachael," Marie asked, "did you know who your dad was before you came to St. Charles?"

Rachael lowered her head. "No. Why?"

"Just curious. So your mom never talked about him?"

"Nope."

"Where's your mother now, Rachael?" Karen asked.

Rachael shrugged. "Who knows, and who cares?" She stared out the window. "I know I don't."

Marie gave Rachael a motherly look. "Don't be too hasty to write her off. You don't know the real story of why she left."

Rachael rolled her eyes. "Whatever it is, I'm sure it's bogus."

Karen and Marie turned toward each other. "Bogus?" Karen asked.

"Full of shit," Rachael responded.

"Rachael!" Marie blurted.

"Well, it's true."

"You need to stop with the swear words, young lady."

Rachael pursed her lips and shrugged. "No sweat."

Marie just shook her head. She completely understood Rachael's anger toward her mother, but at some point she felt Rachael needed to accept things and move on. She didn't know if that was too much to expect from a twelve-year-old. She wished she had a magic wand to wave over her to erase the bad times the girl had experienced in her short life.

CHAPTER 8

Christmas

Walter dropped Rachael off at the Feinsteins' before bringing Marie and Karen to the Brookses' house, where they were greeted by Jonathan and Claire. Claire had decorated the house to the hilt. The scent of pine filled the air inside.

"Would you like a glass of wine?" Jonathan asked. Both women nodded. When he handed Karen her glass, he gave her a wink. "So how's that place of yours in Geneva?"

A red flush crept up her neck. "I guess I should apologize for that."

"No need to. Marie told me all about your escapade on trying to find me, and quite frankly, I was impressed. So you're not married to any doctor either?"

"No, that was all part of the sham."

"No harm done. So tell me about your trip. What all did you girls talk about?"

Marie filled him in, leaving out what Rachael shared with them in confidence.

Claire joined them and filled them in on the agenda for the next three days. Marie was glad to hear all four of the Feinsteins would be joining them on Christmas Eve.

* * *

Claire, Marie, and Karen spent Christmas Eve morning preparing an elaborate brunch as various family members arrived. By eleven o'clock, all ten of them sat down to eat.

More interested in the lively conversation than the food, Marie didn't eat much. It wasn't the content of the conversations she found so enthralling, but rather the endless stream of voices interacting with each other and captivating each other's attention. Unlike Thanksgiving, when there had been so much tension, the atmosphere at this meal was light and lively.

After the meal, Evan and Arthur volunteered to clean up and wash dishes to "give the womenfolk a break," as Evan put it. None of the womenfolk objected.

Finished with the dishes, Arthur and Evan joined the group, and everyone talked until it was time to pile into two cars and go to the food pantry in Kansas City where the Brooks family had volunteered their time for the past five Christmas Eves. Three hours later, they headed back home, tired, a little sad, but feeling fulfilled.

"When do you expect the Feinsteins?" Marie asked.

"Any time actually," Claire responded. "I just called Gloria to let them know we're home."

Right on cue, the doorbell rang, and a minute later Rachael burst into the kitchen where the women were gathered.

"Hi, all! Hi, Marie." She gave Marie a big smile.

"Come here, you," Claire said to Rachael. "You look so pretty today." She patted her on the head. "And different somehow. How was your trip to Kansas?"

"Pretty nifty. Marie has the coolest apartment."

"Nifty?"

"It's a whole other language," Marie explained.

Claire put her hands on her hips. "Well, Rachael. I'm glad you had such a kick. Now tell me what else is buzzin', cousin."

"Mrs. Brooks!"

"Well, tell me what's new."

"My birthday is today."

"No kidding. That's just crazy!"

The roar of laughter brought Ben into the kitchen. "Rachael, are you behaving yourself?"

"Yes, Daddio."

Ben squinted and frowned. "Rachael..."

"Just kidding," she said back in a sing-songy voice.

"Why don't you come into the living room with Brenda and Denise?"

Marie was certain Rachael would have rather spent her time with the grownups, but she followed her father's orders anyway. "Okay," she groaned.

"Ben," Claire called to him before he left the kitchen. She lowered her voice to no more than a whisper. "She's so bubbly. I've never seen her like this."

Ben glanced at Marie, then back at Claire. "She hasn't stopped talking about her trip to Atchison since she got back. I hate to say it, but I think I'm going to have to loosen the reins on her a little. It seems to have done a lot of good, thanks to Marie." He gave Marie a heartfelt smile.

"Hey, it was my pleasure. She can be a handful, but she has such a good heart. I thoroughly enjoyed being with her." She gave Ben a wink. "I think I had just as much fun as she did. I wanted to..."

"So when can I go back there, Dad?" Rachael's voice swept into the room from somewhere around the corner.

Ben glanced at everyone and heaved a big sigh. "She's a handful, alright."

* * *

Claire made her traditional lasagna for Christmas Eve dinner. Everyone groaned afterward before they retreated to the living room for a glass of port. It appeared everyone had enjoyed Claire's cooking a little too much.

After everyone had settled down in the living room, Marie shot a glance at Claire, who then went into the kitchen. She came back with a cupcake that had a candle in it. Everyone sang "Happy Birthday," while Rachael beamed. Marie waited for her to blow out the candle before saying anything.

"Well, you're officially a teenager now, Rachael. How does it feel?"

Rachael smiled a sweet smile. "It's cool."

Marie handed her a small gift box. "Happy birthday."

Rachael tore open the box, grinning from ear to ear. Inside were two gold heart-shaped earrings. But her smile soon faded to disappointment. "They're for pierced ears," she said softly.

Marie tried hard not to smile. "I know."

Rachael stared at Marie for a confused moment, and then her face lit up. "Get out of here. Pierced ears?!"

Marie nodded. "Read the note."

She read it out loud.

I hope you like the earrings
I may just have to borrow
Both your ears, they will be pierced
The day after tomorrow!
Love, Marie

"What?!" Tears filled Rachael's eyes. She ran over to Marie to give her a big hug but then quickly pulled away from her, eyes wide, mouth open. She clutched Marie by the shoulders with a tight grip. "Wait! Does Dad know about this?"

Her question was enough to make everyone roar with laughter. "Yes, of course your dad knows." She put her hands on her hips. "I had to ask him first, you knucklehead."

"The day after Christmas?"

"Mm-hmm."

"Man, that's fantabulous!"

"Okay…is that good?" her father asked.

"Really, Dad. Yes, that's good."

"Oh, okay."

After the commotion set off by Rachael settled down, Claire and Jonathan talked about the next morning, how they would open gifts and then attend the ten o'clock church service.

* * *

Marie woke up on Christmas morning to the sweet smell of Claire's cinnamon rolls. She and Karen dressed quickly and joined the others at the fireplace for the opening of the presents. The day had dawned dreary, but that didn't hamper the cheery moods in the Brooks household.

Claire had picked Marie's name for her gift. The room went silent while she tore off the wrapping paper from the leather-bound book. In the lower right-hand corner was inscribed *Brooks Family Album*. Marie glanced up at Claire and gave her a curious smile.

"Go ahead. Open it," Claire said.

Marie's heart fluttered. She flipped open the cover. The year 1891 had been printed on the upper left-hand corner of the first page. A picture of a dark-skinned Negro woman holding a baby was the only picture on the page. She glanced up at Jonathan. "This is you?"

"Mm-hmm. Keep going."

Claire had arranged the family photos by year. The number of pictures per year increased as their children and then grandchildren were born. Marie flipped through the pages, not believing Claire had gone to all that trouble for her. When Claire said, "The blank spots are so you can insert photos of yourself," Marie couldn't hold back the tears that were pushing their way out.

The last picture was a family portrait they had taken a few weeks earlier, and below it a handwritten note:

Welcome to the family, Marie.

Below were everyone's signatures. Marie looked up to see that there wasn't a dry eye in the room.

Marie went over to Claire and gave her a strong hug and then did the same to Jonathan. While still in the hug, he whispered, "That was *her* idea." And then Marie realized that Jonathan had been so right. In her heart, Claire knew what she had to and wanted to do, but it would take her time to completely shed the hurt, resentment, and maybe some pride too.

Karen, who could be heard crying all the way from the other room, returned in time to see Jonathan begin to open his gift from Marie. Aware of what Marie had done for him, Karen turned on her heel and went right back to the other room where she could cry in private.

Marie tried to contain her smile while he opened the two-part gift, the first being an album she had put together of her life—school photos, copies of report cards, pictures of her and her mother, a copy of her college transcript, photos of her and Richard and their Lakeview brownstone, and more. The second gift was a copy of *What Really Went on in the Big House*. Jonathan, who rarely showed emotion, had to swipe a tear from his face.

Marie went into the kitchen to find Karen blotting her eyes with a handkerchief. "It's safe now. You can come back in. It's time for your gift." She put her arm around her.

"My gift?"

Not wanting her to be left out, Claire had bought Karen a red, white, and black silk scarf. More tears.

"Boy, you guys sure know how to make a girl cry," Karen groaned.

After church and following an early supper of Cornish game hens and all the trimmings, they spent the rest of the day talking, laughing, and reminiscing. Marie placed herself in her own timeline each time a story about Jonathan and Claire's sons surfaced. The twins were six years older than she, and Tré was five years her senior, so Claire was raising three small boys while Jonathan was having an affair with her mother. It hadn't hit Marie like that until now.

One by one, everyone left the Brookses' home, Rachael last of all. Since Ben had dropped Rachael off but hadn't stayed, Marie offered to drive her home in Claire's car.

Rachael held the open gift box in her lap the whole way home. Marie explained to her what she could expect the next day when she would be getting her ears pierced.

When they reached Rachael's house, before she got out of the car, Rachael said, "No one has ever done anything like this for me before." Tears flooded her eyes before she flew out of the car and into the house.

* * *

The next day, Jonathan and Marie drove into town for an early morning appointment with family law attorney, Mike Cavanaugh, to discuss Marie's marriage issues. Karen came along for the ride. A big man, middle-aged Cavanaugh had a stern face Marie thought could intimidate just about anyone in a courtroom. He pulled out a list of possible grounds for divorce from Illinois law, the same list Marie had found in her own research.

"I'm familiar with the list, Mr. Cavanaugh, and except for the felony one, I don't think I can get him on any of the charges. However, he could get me on several."

He slid the list across his desk to her. "Which ones?"

Marie studied the list. "Gross neglect of marital duty." She glanced up at Cavanaugh. "I left him in May of last year. And abandonment."

"And he hasn't filed for divorce?"

"Not that I know of. I'd know, wouldn't I?"

"Not if he doesn't know where you are."

"Oh, he knows where I am, alright."

"Do you know why he hasn't filed?"

Jonathan jumped in, his face sober. "He wants her back."

"Do you have any intentions of going back to him?"

"No."

Cavanaugh sighed. "Before we go any further, have you thoroughly thought this through? Divorcees aren't looked upon very favorably, shall we say. Do you really want to live with that?"

Marie sat up a little straighter in her chair. "Mr. Cavanaugh, one of my main goals in life is to not let other people's opinions affect the way I live. If someone looks down on me because I'm divorced, so be it. I have done nothing wrong, and I will continue to hold my head high."

"Okay, Miss Costa. I just wanted to cover all the bases." He cleared his throat, signaling he wanted to move on. "Let's get to Richard's arrest. What was the felony?"

"He was arrested, along with Joey Aiuppa, for skimming."

"While you were with him?"

"No, after I left him."

Cavanaugh stared down at his desk for several seconds. "You may or may not be successful filing under the felony grounds since you were already separated at the time." He turned toward Jonathan. "I did a little checking on him. He's not a mobster. He's an associate at best and probably not even that, but the guy has potential for being a big earner, and my guess is that's why the Outfit is interested in keeping him around. Does that surprise you, Miss Costa?"

Marie shook her head. "No, I've been aware of his association with suspicious characters for some time."

"He's tight with cops—corrupt ones, that is. Not only in Chicago, but in Milwaukee, Gary, and New York as well. Maybe other places, but that's all I could tie him to. He's good at skirting the law, and if it wasn't for Aiuppa getting arrested and snitching on others in order to get a lighter sentence, your husband probably wouldn't have even been caught."

Jonathan turned toward Marie. "What do you want to do?"

"Before you answer that, let me just get one more possibility out of the way. You and Richard were married in Illinois, right?"

"No, we were married in Crown Point, Indiana. Why?"

"Hold on a minute." He retrieved a thick law book from his bookshelf and paged through it. Cavanaugh smiled. "Well, this may be interesting. Are either of you aware of anti-miscegenation laws?"

Jonathan and Marie shook their heads.

"Anti-miscegenation laws make it illegal for whites to marry people of other races. Illinois repealed their anti-miscegenation law years ago, but Indiana's is still on the books."

"What exactly does that mean?" she asked.

"It means if you're caught, it's punishable by imprisonment. And it's the white person who goes to prison."

Marie and Jonathan stared at each other in disbelief.

"Don't get too excited about this. I'll have to look further into it. Did Richard know of your ethnicity before you married?"

"No. But then, neither did I."

Cavanaugh gave Marie a skeptical eye, and then Jonathan.

"She's being honest, Mike. It's a long story."

"Does Richard know now?"

"Yes."

"Did he find out while you two were still living together?"

"That I'm not sure."

"But he knows now."

"Yes."

"You're sure?"

"Yes."

"I'll have to look into this further. When I do, I'll get back to you, Miss Costa."

They drove home in silence. When they reached Jonathan's ranch, he pulled the car into the garage and asked Karen if he and Marie could have a minute alone. Based on the scared look on Karen's face as she entered the house, Marie had the feeling she wasn't that comfortable being alone with any of the Brookses.

Jonathan took Marie's hand. "I probably shouldn't say this, but I'm going to anyway. I'd give my right arm to see the look on Richard's face if he were to learn his marriage to you was voided because of your ethnicity and he was going to jail for it. What a coup!"

"Dad…"

"I know. I know. Something else, Marie. I was real proud of you back there standing up for what you believe in. Never give in to what other people think you should be. Claire's favorite saying, to thine own self be true, very powerful words, very powerful words indeed."

* * *

Rachael was anxiously waiting inside for Marie. Karen sat beside her on the sofa, her coat still on. "I'm ready," Rachael said. "Let's burn some rubber!"

"Hold on, Miss Antsy Pants," her father warned. "Let Marie catch her breath, okay?"

"That's okay, Ben," Marie said. "Just give me a minute to freshen up, Rachael. Then we'll be off."

The local St. Charles jewelry store didn't do ear piercings, so they had to drive to Aurora, which Rachael didn't appear to mind. Karen sat in the back seat, allowing the birthday girl to ride up front with Marie.

"You brought the earrings, right?" Marie asked Rachael.

"Are you kidding? They've been sitting by our front door ever since I got them. Dad said if I checked to make sure they were in the box one more time, he was going to take them away from me."

"Dads are like that."

"Marie?"

"Hmm?"

"There's something I've wanted to ask you, but didn't know exactly how."

"You can ask me anything, sweetie."

Rachael turned around and looked at Karen.

"It's okay to say anything in front of Karen. There's not very much we don't know about each other."

"Okay. How old are you?"

"I'm twenty-four. Why?"

"'Cause I know the Brooks twins turned thirty last year—they had this big party—so that means you were born after them."

"That's right," Marie said, afraid of where this was going.

"And Mr. Brooks is your father."

"Mm-hmm."

"So you were born when he was married to Mrs. Brooks."

"Mm-hmm."

"So how does that work?"

"What do you mean?"

"How was he your father and married to Mrs. Brooks at the same time?"

Marie took in a big breath. With no simple way out of this, she wasn't going to make any excuses for Jonathan, but she also didn't want him to lose any credibility with Rachael. Not sure if a thirteen-year-old was old enough to know the truth, she took a chance. "Rachael, Jonathan had an affair with my mother while he was married to Claire."

"And she was okay with that?"

"Well...she didn't know at the time."

"I meant was she okay with that when she found out?"

"I'm sure she wasn't, but I think Claire is a forgiving woman."

"That's crazy. I wouldn't have forgiven him."

"Don't be so sure, Rachael." Marie paused. "Look, relationships are complicated. No matter how perfectly matched the couple is, there will always be problems. And people make mistakes. They make bad decisions." Marie glanced into the wide, innocent eyes of the young girl sitting beside her. "Some people say you can tell how strong a relationship is by how the couple handles their problems. I suspect Jonathan and Claire's relationship is very strong. At least that's what I see."

"Marie?"

"Yes?"

"So is everything forgivable?"

"According to the Bible, everything is."

Rachael gave her a wanting look. "But what do *you* think?"

Worried she was getting in too deep with someone else's child, Marie took a few seconds to gather her thoughts. "I think some things are pretty hard to forgive, but I can tell you that when you do forgive someone for something, even if it's one of those hard things, you always feel better."

Rachael stared out the side window for the next few miles before she spoke again. "Your parents weren't married when you were born either... like mine. Is that something you can forgive?"

"Yes. I can forgive them for that."

"Well, I think it stinks."

"It's not ideal, hon, but so many things in life aren't. In fact, most things in life aren't. You just have to learn how to make the most of any situation you happen to be in." *Look at who's giving advice on this subject. I've struggled with this practically my whole adult life.*

"I guess I get it."

"Did you ask because you want to understand your own situation better?"

"Yeah."

"These are complicated things we're talking about. There are no easy answers."

"I know."

"Well, here's the store. Got the heebie-jeebies?" Marie teased.

"Just so you know, that's not 'in' anymore."

"Oh. So are you nervous?"

"Hell, no."

"Rachael..."

"Sorry."

The jewelry store clerk directed them to the back room. "Have a seat, honey," he said to Rachael. He pulled out a very long needle.

Rachael took a step back. "Whoa. Spread out! What are you going to do with that thing?"

"Don't be afraid, Rachael. It will only hurt for a second. Do you have your earrings?"

Rachael handed the clerk her earrings.

"Now just relax," he told her. Rachael took in a deep breath and scrunched up her face until he was done. He held up a mirror for her.

"Cool."

"How do they feel?" Marie asked once they were outside the store.

"Weird."

"Well, don't fiddle with them too much. Just give them a gentle turn two or three times a day and you'll be fine. C'mon, let's do a little shopping before we head home."

Marie took Rachael to a whimsical boutique she'd noticed across the street. Marie and Karen scanned the silk scarves while Rachael looked at earrings.

"You haven't said much all day. Are you okay?" Marie asked Karen.

"I'm just taking it all in."

Marie shot her a glance.

"How the two of you interact with each other. It's all very…"

"What do you think of these, Marie?" Rachael asked, holding up a pair of earrings.

Marie scrutinized the long, dangly red earrings Rachael held and gave her a disapproving look. Rachael rolled her eyes and put them down. "These?" Marie glanced at the next pair, more flamboyant than the first. She didn't have to say anything. Rachael put them down and kept looking while Marie paid for a scarf.

"If you're going to buy a second pair of earrings, I suggest something solid gold—and conservative. Solid gold because you don't know how your ears will react to something impure, and conservative because you don't want your father to…shall we say, go ape?"

"Okay, I get it."

CHAPTER 9

Outsiders

Marie and Karen spent the following week talking about their Christmas visit. While Marie had accepted her new role as a member of the Brooks family as normal, Karen was still at the "I can't believe this is happening to you" stage.

"How can you be so calm about it?" Karen asked her.

"Well, I wasn't all that calm at Thanksgiving, believe me, but Christmas was different. I think it happened when we were opening presents. All of a sudden, it all felt so, I don't know, legitimate maybe."

"The album?"

Marie focused on the album prominently displayed on her coffee table and nodded.

"Was that a pivotal moment for her, do you think?" Karen asked, referring to Claire.

"I think so, but maybe even more so for me."

"How so?"

"I spent the whole two weeks at Thanksgiving, and weeks afterward really, trying to read Claire. I mean, there were times I didn't like her much, and I was sure she totally resented me. But when I opened that album and realized she had been the one who put it together, I knew that was her core. Not any of the negative stuff like I'd feared."

"Marie, how do you think that Christmas image looked to an outsider?"

"What do you mean?"

"I was thinking if someone off the street peeked in the window, what would they have thought?"

Marie laughed. "We were quite the diverse group, weren't we?"

"That's one way to put it."

Marie shot her a curious glance.

"C'mon, Marie. You mean to tell me you don't feel the least bit out of place there? Don't get me wrong, I think they're great people, and I'm very happy for you and all, but..."

"But what?"

"But they're..."

"They're what?"

"Marie, they're different from you. You know what I mean."

Pretty sure the wine they were drinking was causing both of them to say things they might not otherwise say, Marie didn't let it go like she knew she should have. "No, tell me." As soon as she said it, she wished she hadn't.

"Now, don't go ape on me, like Rachael would say."

"I'm interested in what you meant."

"You *have* to admit you had to change just in order to fit in with them. C'mon. Otherwise, you would have felt as uncomfortable as I did."

"I didn't realize you were that uncomfortable. I guess it was a bad idea to invite you."

"Now c'mon. Don't go there. I went because of you. As a favor to you."

"So what exactly made you so uncomfortable?"

Karen rolled her eyes. "You know darn well what I mean."

"No, I don't."

"They're Negroes, for Pete's sake. They're not like us. You had to feel just a little uncomfortable being the only white person in the room... besides me, that is."

"No, *you* were the only white person in the room." Marie got up from her chair, walked over to the window, and peered out.

"Look, it was all sugar and spice and everything nice while you were there, but now you're back in the real world."

"Back in the real world where there's bigotry, racial prejudice, and nowhere for me to fit in. You mean *that* real world?"

"Well...yes. Marie, that's reality. Negroes aren't accepted by whites. Don't get mad at me. I didn't create it."

"I think I've heard about enough of your narrow-mindedness, Karen. You're not talking about just some other people here. They're my family, and I don't appreciate your ignorant judgments about them."

Karen got up and headed toward Marie's apartment door. She turned around to face Marie. "And don't think for a minute they weren't judging you. That was obvious!" With that, she left.

Karen was halfway down the stairs when Marie shouted at her, "Jonathan is my father, Karen. That man could have two heads, polka-dot skin, and a bushy tail, and it wouldn't change anything. He'd still be my father!"

Marie slammed the door shut, poured herself another glass of wine, and retreated to the living room. She sat still, staring out the window for a full minute before the tears came.

Karen didn't get it, and if her best friend didn't get it, who would? That is, if she was still her best friend.

* * *

Tired the next morning from a fitful night's sleep, Marie's thoughts went back to her argument with Karen. They had known each other a year and a half, and while Marie was very aware of Karen's prejudices, admitted or not, they had never fought over it, or over anything for that matter. She wavered between calling her now and waiting for things to cool down.

She thought about the way Karen became so emotional in the Brookses' home when Marie had opened the Christmas present from Claire, and then again when Jonathan opened his from Marie, and yet again when she opened her own present from Claire. If she was that detached from the Brookses, or more specifically Negroes in general, why all the emotion? Marie didn't get it.

She hoped the fight with Karen would have positive consequences. Now that Karen knew how strongly Marie felt about accepting people for who they are instead of for their skin color or cultural background, she would give it more serious consideration, or at the very least be more sensitive to Marie's beliefs. One thing was for sure, the last thing Marie wanted was to lose Karen as a friend.

The phone interrupted her thoughts.

"I called to say I'm sorry." Karen's voice was soft and contrite.

"I'm sorry too. I shouldn't have lost my temper yesterday. Maybe it was the wine."

"Look, I did a lot of thinking after I left, and I'm not sure I'll ever see things like you do. But there is one thing I *am* sure of, and that's you're my best friend, and I never want that to change." She paused. "Can we just agree that we don't see eye-to-eye on this and go back to being best friends?"

Marie swiped the tears off her cheeks. It was less than what she had hoped for, but heartfelt. She had to accept Karen's apology. "Of course. I'd like that."

"Good, because I can't go another night with no sleep. I'm a walking zombie today. Do you want to come over for dinner tonight? I'll make fried chicken."

"You're on."

Later that day, when Marie arrived at Karen's house, the two women hugged, their fight behind them.

"When does Maurice get back, by the way?" Marie asked.

Karen tried to stifle a smile. "Tomorrow."

Marie shot her a teasing look.

"Stop it."

"How's it going with you two these days? You haven't said two words about him since we've been back."

"Everything's good."

"That's all? Just good?"

"Yeah."

Marie smiled. "You're hiding something."

"Am not." Karen reached for her purse.

"What are you getting?"

Karen put her purse back down. "Nothing."

"You've got chocolate in there, don't you?"

"Maybe."

"Every time we talk about Maurice, you start eating chocolate!"

"No, I don't."

"There's more going on between you two than you're letting on, isn't there?"

"Well, I wasn't going to say anything, because I don't know if he would even appreciate my saying anything...but, well, I met his mother."

"And?"

"Well..."

"What's wrong?"

"She's...well, she's the worst hypochondriac on the face of the earth. Maurice didn't even want for us to meet, ever, but when we came back to his house one day after dinner, she was sitting on his front porch, crying."

"Why was she crying?"

"I forget exactly. Something about a pimple on her cheek that she was convinced was going to eat all the flesh off her face."

"Really."

"It gets worse. After Maurice calmed her down, which took all evening I might add, she talked nonstop about all her illnesses. He put her to bed in his spare room, and she spent the night, but not before doing his laundry."

"She does his laundry?"

"Not all the time, only when she comes over. And only when it's her time of the month."

"You're making this up."

"Do I look like I could make this up? And wait, there's more. When he was young, she had such huge fears about what she fed him, because she thought she was going to kill him, that he ended up losing all his teeth because of bad nutrition."

"What?"

"I'm not kidding. All his teeth are false. The man wears dentures, which he probably puts in a glass next to his bed each night." Karen made a face, like she had just bitten into a sour grape.

"No wonder he never smiles. So does this change things between you two?"

"I'm trying not to think about it."

* * *

Karen spent New Year's Eve with Maurice. Marie spent it alone. But not having been a big fan of New Year's Eve since being married, Marie wasn't disappointed. She needed the alone time.

On New Year's Day, Marie drove to the home of Doretha Scott, the woman she had met at the library. She parked her car and walked up the crumbling walk to her front door. Doretha was standing in the window with a somber look on her face, shaking her head. Marie knew she was advising her to leave. She held up the book she had bought for her. Doretha kept shaking her head. Marie made sure Doretha saw her put the book on the porch and then left.

As she drove away, people came out of their homes and onto their porches, giving her icy stares. Then, without warning, something hard hit her back windshield. She sped up until she reached the outskirts of the colored neighborhood and the beginning of more familiar territory, where she pulled off the road, put her car in park, and wept.

She was just trying to be a friend. And under different circumstances, but perhaps in some other world, she knew Doretha would have liked to have been a friend back.

* * *

Two weeks later, Marie received a phone call from attorney, Michael Cavanaugh.

"I'm afraid I don't have great news for you, Marie."

"Oh?"

"I consulted with my partner about the Indiana anti-miscegenation laws. He's much more familiar with them than I am. Whether or not Richard would be found guilty of violating this law would likely depend on when he found out about your ethnicity, and even if he did know of it when the two of you were still together, it wouldn't be a cut-and-dried case. There's no case law in Indiana for a situation like yours, where you yourself didn't know your ethnicity."

"So where does that leave us?"

"Your options as I see them are to either file for divorce based on his felony conviction, wait out the seven-year statute of limitation for the involuntary dissolution of your marriage, or try to get the marriage voided under the anti-miscegenation law in Indiana."

"What are you recommending?"

"The least amount of risk lies with the seven-year statute of limitation for estrangement. But, of course, that's also the option with the greatest constraints; you would be legally married for another five and a half years. Trying to get the marriage voided under the anti-miscegenation law, in my opinion, comes with the greatest amount of risk, since there is no relevant case law."

"So you're recommending filing for divorce based on his felony conviction?"

"I'll represent you under any of the three scenarios, but yes, I would say that's the way to go. Keeping in mind, of course, that the conviction came after you left him. The judge will likely take that into consideration."

Marie thought sending Richard to jail for marrying her would be unscrupulous and just plain wrong, no matter what he had done to her in the past. And while it appeared to be the easy way out, waiting five and a half more years to meet the statute of limitation requirement was too restricting. She called her father the next day to discuss it.

"I'm leaning toward divorcing him based on his felony conviction."

"Whatever you decide, I'll support you on it, Marie. But I have to tell you it would be quite satisfying to see…well, you know how I feel about him."

"Yes, Dad. I know."

She and Karen talked about it over dinner the next evening. "If you decide to go ahead with it, how do you think he'll react when he finds out?" Karen asked.

"Well, let's see. The last time I saw him was when he showed up at Lulu's. He was still wearing his wedding band. He told me he still loved me. He begged me to come back to him, and when I didn't acquiesce, he threatened to do something to Jonathan. So how do you think he'll take it?"

"So maybe you'd rather wait the five and a half years and play it safe?"

Marie took in a deep breath. "I don't know what I want to do. But I just remembered something else Richard said that day."

"What's that?"

"Somehow I got up enough nerve to tell him I wasn't attracted to him anymore, and do you know what he said to me?"

Karen shook her head.

"He said as soon as any other man finds out who I really am, he'll throw me away like a piece of moldy fruit."

"Eewww!"

"He also told me I could move to another country and he'd find me."

"Don't know, hon. I'd let sleeping dogs lie if I were you."

"Well, I don't have to make a decision right away. Maybe I'll think about it some more."

CHAPTER 10

How Nice to See You Again

For the next few weeks, Marie was unable to think about little other than what to do about her marriage to Richard, and what transpired on the trip she took to New York the following month delayed her decision even further.

The American Institute of Decorators had invited Marie to sit on their board the previous year, which meant she had to attend semi-annual three-day meetings in New York. She invited Karen to join her for the February meeting. They stayed at the Algonquin.

"Richard and I spent many nights here," she told Karen through a sigh. She let her mind wander for a few seconds to the good times.

"Nice hotel. But of all the hotels you could have picked for this trip, why did you pick this one?"

"I don't know. Maybe to show I'm not afraid of him anymore."

"Show who?"

"Mostly me, I guess."

The two women headed for Fifth Avenue after settling in. Too shocked over the prices to buy anything, Karen stuck to window shopping. Marie bought a silk scarf and bottle of French perfume not available in Atchison. "So this is the type of life you and Richard had?" Karen asked. "Trips to New York and spending lots of money?"

"He had very expensive taste. If I was here with him this trip, I would probably go home with at least one piece of jewelry from Tiffany's and perfume twice as expensive as the one I just bought. He might have gone back with a new fedora, several silk ties, and maybe a new suit. On one trip he bought us matching fur coats!"

"Must have been nice. And he made that kind of money selling medical equipment?"

"That was all I knew about. I'm sure there were other ways he made money."

"Probably better you didn't know about the other stuff."

"As I've said before, the good times were *very* good." Marie opened the door to their hotel room. The distinctive scent of roses drifted out to greet them. Marie took a step back when she saw the huge bouquet sitting on the coffee table. "What the...?"

Karen walked around her. "Gee, do they do this for all their guests?"

"No." Marie inched over to the flowers and noticed a white envelope perched in between two of the stems. "Marie" was written on it. "It's from him."

"Who him?"

"Richard."

Karen pursed her lips. "How do you know?"

Marie stared at the envelope.

"Aren't you going to read the card?"

"No."

Karen walked around to Marie's side of the table. "Want me to read it?"

"No." Marie sat down on the sofa and stared at the flowers. She picked up the envelope and crumpled it in her fist. "I hate him."

"May not even be from him."

Her mouth was rigid. "Oh, it's from him alright."

"How would he even know you're here?"

"I don't know. He has spies."

Karen shot her a twisted smile. "Marie, you're being silly."

Marie dropped the crumpled envelope on the table and went into the bathroom. When she emerged several minutes later, she slumped down in one of the upholstered chairs near the window overlooking 44th Street. She threw her head back.

"You okay?"

"Yes, I'm okay," she said through a sigh. She stared at the opened envelope on the table. "It's from him, right?"

"Yeah. He said happy anniversary. Is it your wedding anniversary?"

She thought for a moment. "What's the date today?"

"Fifteenth."

"Three-year anniversary."

"I can't get over the fact he knew you were here."

Marie glanced at her friend, stood up, and then stared out the window. "It doesn't surprise me."

"Think he's here too? Or did he just have the flowers sent to you?"

"I don't know. Let me see the note." Karen handed it to her. "It's not his handwriting, but that doesn't mean he's not here. If he is, he'll show his face somewhere."

"What makes me nervous about that note is where he says how nice it is to see you again. What do you think he meant by that?"

"I don't know. Could be nothing. Just a scare tactic."

"What if you run into him?"

"I can handle Richard." She put her hands on her hips. "In fact, I hope I do run into him. I'd like for him to know just how not afraid of him I am."

Karen glared at her friend's face for several seconds. "I hope you know what you're doing, hon."

She smiled a false smile. "So do I."

To play it safe, Marie arranged a security escort to and from the hotel for Karen. Fortunately, no further incidents occurred during the remainder of their trip.

They talked about Richard after returning home.

"So what are you going to do?"

"About my marriage, you mean?"

Karen nodded.

"I've been thinking about this a lot. And the only thing I'm sure of is that whatever I do won't have any effect on what Richard does. He's going to do what he wants to do no matter what. That's just Richard. So I may as well file for divorce. At least then I'll have the freedom to see someone else if I want to. And if the judge doesn't grant the divorce because Richard was convicted of a felony after I left him, then I'll just have to deal with it." She glanced at Karen. "What do you think?"

"Or the judge may not grant it for other reasons."

"Just because it's not done very often you mean?"

"Something like that. Did your attorney say what he thought the chances were that a judge would grant it?"

"He said it depends on the judge." Marie met Karen's gaze. "And Richard knows judges."

"Is he really that influential?"

"Mr. Cavanaugh did a little checking up on him and said he has potential for being a big earner, and that's why the Outfit is interested in keeping him around. My guess is that's why cops and politicians keep him around as well. It's all about money. Richard is all about money."

"What about your other issues? What are you going to do about them?" Marie was puzzled, but was pretty sure she knew where Karen was going with her question. "Now that you're involved with your new family, what are you going to do about...well, you know...who you are."

Marie stared past Karen, out the window and into the dark night sky. They hadn't discussed Marie's race issue since they had the fight. "Until I figure this out, I'll have to keep pretending I'm white," she said. Marie shrugged her shoulders and fought to keep back the tears. "I don't know what else to do."

The two women sat in awkward silence while they sipped wine. "It's just not fair," Marie said softly but with a tense jaw. "At least Negroes with dark skin know where they stand, know their place. It's not right, but that's how it is. And as light-skinned as Jonathan is, he's dark enough so everyone knows who he is. But I don't even have that!"

Karen smiled a weak smile. "And to think we wouldn't even be having this conversation if it hadn't been for that fat Southern...woman. You would never have had a clue you were anything but white."

Marie's mind drifted back to the incident with Southern-born and -bred Mrs. Hollingsworth, the woman who had called her a half-breed nigger girl. It had been a life-changing incident. "You're right. I wouldn't have had a clue if it hadn't been for good old Mrs. Hollingsworth. I have her to thank."

Karen met Marie's gaze and cocked her head in a once-again-I-don't-understand-you sort of way. "What would be the worst thing that would happen if you just continued to be white?"

She flinched at Karen's continued ignorance, or perhaps naiveté. Karen was pushing her again, but Marie was convinced she didn't even realize it. How could someone be so narrow-minded? "The guilt would eventually consume me."

"Guilt about...?"

Marie fiddled with her empty wine glass before responding. "Denying the fact that my father is colored. Denying my race."

"Denying your race."

"Denying my race."

"As you are well aware, I know a little something about guilt," she said, referring to her husband's suicide. "Guilt is all about something you did. You, my dear, haven't done anything."

"The guilt I have is about what I haven't done, and believe me, that can be just as bad."

Karen's eyebrows came together as one. "And exactly what is it again that you haven't done?"

She knew Karen would never understand. She drew in a big breath and let it out slowly. "By going through life pretending to be white, I'm denying the existence of my Negro heritage."

"Look, guilt is like a dam that holds you back. You have to break through it. Otherwise, you'll never reach the other side—another thing I learned in therapy after Ed died," Karen explained. "And I know we've been through this, but at the risk of us getting into another fight, which I don't want to do, I just have to say this. You're forgetting about basic human traits, and as a result, you're shortchanging yourself."

"I'm not following you."

"I think you've set some unrealistic goals for yourself, your dreams, and it's just going to end in failure. If you're more realistic about things, how the races are not compatible, for example, you can set more realistic goals for yourself."

Now Karen sounded like that little voice in Marie's head she often tried to ignore. She took a moment to collect her thoughts. "Karen, somewhere in this mixed-up brain of mine, I think I'm somehow ostracizing Negroes by not acknowledging I'm one of them, like they're inferior or something. And I don't feel that way at all. In fact, I find that very offensive."

"Okay, so let's say you join the Negro side. Then aren't you ostracizing us whites?"

She cringed at Karen's choice of words but knew she didn't mean anything disrespectful by it. "I shouldn't have to choose. I want to be included in both worlds. I want to be loyal to both sides. I *am* both sides."

"You can't change the world, Marie."

"I know. But I don't want to have regrets after it's too late to do something about it." She had given this considerable thought ever since she had confirmed Jonathan was her father. "Believe me, I wish some light would go on inside my head and guide me in the right direction. Because if I don't do the right thing, the guilt will continue to be that noose around my neck."

"Well, I think you're beating yourself up over something you have no control over."

Marie sensed Karen was trying to bring closure to the conversation, and that was probably a good thing.

"You've tormented yourself over this, and now you're in a no-win situation."

Marie digested Karen's words. "I don't have the answers, Karen. I wish I did. All I know is living like this is like living without a floor beneath you. Do you know what I mean?" She didn't give Karen time to answer. "I just wish I knew someone like me, someone who's faced the same issues as I'm facing, someone who understands what I'm going through and knows what to do." She heaved a sigh and got up from her chair. "I had hoped that would be my father, but..."

Later that evening and alone with her thoughts, Marie poured herself another glass of wine, turned on the radio, and curled up on the sofa half-listening to Frankie Laine sing "That Lucky Old Sun."

> *Show me that river,*
> *Take me across*
> *And wash all my troubles away*

Even though she thought Karen might be right about her being in a no-win situation, she wasn't going to give in. At least not yet.

Like that lucky old sun,
Give me nothin' to do
But roll around Heaven all day

She thought about her deceased mother and asked herself the same questions she had asked so many times before. *Why didn't you tell me, Mom, and why couldn't you have helped me through this when you were alive?*

The third glass of wine took effect, and Marie's thoughts remained with her mother, a mother who had devoted her life to Marie and would have done anything for her. Except tell her who her father was. Was there a special significance to the things her mother didn't tell her before she died? Or was it that she didn't know how to deal with it herself? As usual, Marie had more questions than answers.

Before falling asleep that night, she picked up a copy of *The Call*, a weekly Negro newspaper she bought whenever she was in Kansas City. She mindlessly flipped through it, her thoughts still on her mother.

The tiny announcement in the lower right-hand corner of the page caught her attention. "Doretha Scott of Atchison, granddaughter of famed abolitionist and women's suffragist Harriet Tubman, died in her home yesterday, the cause of her death unknown."

CHAPTER 11

Paul

"This isn't good," Karen said to Marie on the phone. "It's like World War II all over again." It was June, 1950, and war had broken out between North and South Korea. President Truman had sent U.S. troops to aid in the defense of South Korea. "Paper said fifteen other countries have sent troops over there. That scares me. Just when I thought things were getting back to normal, this happens. Why do we have to stick our nose in other people's business? It's not our war. Damn Koreans."

"Well, I'm sure there are many factors we don't know about." Karen rarely showed much emotion over current events; her reaction to the news surprised Marie. "Before you damn an entire culture of people, though, just remember their soldiers have wives, mothers, fathers, brothers, and sisters just like ours."

"They're terrible people. They eat dogs."

"Karen!"

"Well, they do."

What frustrated Marie more than anything was that more people likely thought like Karen than not, people who made judgments about an entire group of people based on some of its individuals. *Let someone walk in my shoes for one day. Even Karen.*

"Let's get our minds off war. Would you like to go with me to the antique show at the fairgrounds this weekend?"

"Sure. Maurice is busy with some big case he's working on. Won't see him all weekend."

At the antique show, Marie and Karen meandered arm in arm through dozens of dealer booths. Halfway through, Marie stopped to admire a collection of Roseville pottery. "May I help you with something?" asked the man who tended the booth.

Marie examined the pottery in awe. "I have a couple of pieces in this foxglove design, but nothing like this."

"Well, if you're interested in any of them, let me know. I can give you a good price." He extended his hand. "My name is Paul Foster. I own the Treasure Trove in Leavenworth," he said with a dimpled grin. He shook Marie's hand and then handed her his business card. Tall, slim, with tousled, sandy-colored hair, Marie found him to be boyishly handsome.

The two of them chatted about his collection of pottery. Karen wandered over to another booth where there were items of more interest to her.

"I have more in my shop. If you're from the area, why don't you come by someday and have a look?"

She got caught up in the quietness of his eyes for an instant, his sea-green eyes. "Thanks. I may just do that."

"Well, *he's* a cutie," Karen said when Marie caught up to her. She hooked Marie's arm. "Wasn't he?"

Marie didn't give her the satisfaction of a smile. "Mm-hmm."

"And he wasn't wearing a wedding ring, either." She gave Marie's arm a squeeze. "I saw the way he was looking at you."

"Cut it out, Karen," Marie whispered roughly, "and keep your voice down. I'm just interested in his pottery, that's all. But...he did invite me to visit his shop in Leavenworth. Want to come with me?"

"Nope. He's *all* yours."

"You just don't get it," Marie said. They walked to the next building. Marie glanced at the bag Karen carried. "What did you find?"

"Coolest set of cuffs ever. English Dowlers."

"You're sick, Karen." Karen's bizarre collection of antique handcuffs, leg irons, and chain nippers, also known as come-alongs, constantly amused Marie. Karen claimed she couldn't remember exactly how she got started collecting them, which made the whole thing even more bizarre. They finished the show and went home.

Marie decided to visit the Treasure Trove the following weekend. She thought about her father as she drove down the back roads to Leavenworth, roads rich with horse ranches similar to the one he owned. She pictured him riding one of his horses, sitting so tall in the saddle with his head held high. Her mind wandered to her Christmas visit with him six months earlier. He rode with such purpose, as if to dare anyone to challenge him. She longed for that kind of confidence.

Located on the corner of Cherokee and 6th Street, right in the heart of the quaint downtown district, the Treasure Trove resembled an old Victorian home, its storefront complete with gingerbread trim, shutters, and stained glass windows. Two rocking chairs sat on each side of an old rain barrel on the wraparound front porch.

More excited than she expected to be, she walked inside and was greeted by the familiar smell of a large collection of antiques. Paul's cheery greeting soon pulled her back to the present.

"Hi!" His eyes were wide and his smile open, letting her know he recognized her right away. "I was hoping you'd come in for a visit."

He turned around toward the pale young woman who stood on the other side of the main room. Noticeably underweight, she wore orthopedic shoes and an ill-fitting brown dress. "Beth, can you please mind the store while I show this young lady around?"

The woman nodded. She unclenched her bony hands and pointed. "There's a fresh pot of coffee and some cookies on the buffet…" Her soft voice gradually faded to nothing.

Paul was all smiles. "I'm so glad you came in…" He stopped midsentence. "I'm sorry. I don't know your name."

"Marie." She held out her hand. "Marie Costa."

His eyes didn't leave her face for several seconds before he led her to a display case on the far side of the room. "I assume you came in to see some more Roseville."

Marie peered in the case that contained an abundance of the pottery she so admired. Her eyes vacillated from one piece to the next. "These are gorgeous."

"I don't always have this many. The older pieces aren't that easy to find."

"They're beautiful. I have just one piece in the dogwood pattern. It's a small vase, and it would look lovely with these."

"Here, let's put them on the bureau over there so you can get a better look."

Marie examined the pieces more closely. The largest one was an elegantly shaped oblong basket with a twisted vine for the handle. The other two pieces were ornate candlesticks in the same pattern. She glanced up at him and smiled. "I'll take them."

After a few drawn-out seconds, he said, "Since I'm giving you such a good price on these, maybe you could do something for me."

"Sure. What is it?"

"Have dinner with me sometime?" His smile was eager. He stood behind the large brass antique cash register and added, "That is, if you're not involved with anyone."

Marie hesitated. The unexpected effect his question had on her caused her cheeks to feel like they were on fire. She must have hesitated a little too long because before she could respond, Paul said, "Look, I didn't mean to put you on the spot like that. You don't even know me." He wrapped her purchase without looking up. "If you're not interested, I'll understand."

She focused her eyes everywhere but at him while she stumbled for the right words. "It's not that." She fiddled with the strap of her purse. "It's just that I'm a little out of practice, and you took me by surprise."

He raised his downward gaze up into her eyes. "Well, think about it. Here's another one of my cards." He reached out to hand it to her, but then drew it back to write his home phone number on the back. "Call me anytime. And it doesn't have to be dinner. It could be lunch or just a cup of coffee sometime."

She held his gaze for a moment before allowing a smile to reach her lips. "Okay. I will." She gathered up the packages. "And thanks for the good deal," she said. "I really do appreciate it. Bye."

"Bye, Marie," he said. Beth reentered the front of the shop and stood next to him. "Come back soon," he called after her.

"He must think I'm such an idiot," she said out loud once behind the steering wheel, her face still flushed. Oh well. She didn't ever have to see him again.

It took her several miles before she realized she hadn't even considered her race issue when Paul asked her for a date. She was so taken by his interest in her, she'd forgotten who she was. She hated herself for that. Now having thought it through, she knew she couldn't date him even if she were divorced.

Once home Marie rearranged things so her new pottery pieces held the most prominent positions on the bookshelves. Pleased with her purchases, she poured herself a glass of wine, turned on the radio, and sat back in her easy chair to admire them. The Andrews Sisters were singing "I Can Dream, Can't I?"

> *No matter how near you'll be*
> *You'll never belong to me*

She stared past her new pottery pieces in deep thought.

> *But I can dream, can't I*

She asked herself, *Why me?*

> *For dreams are just like wine*

She silently scolded her mother for doing this to her.

> *And I am drunk on mine*

Marie heard Karen's words in her head as if she were present: "You don't have to do this to yourself, Marie."

Two glasses of wine later, she was half-listening to the news when her ears perked up.

"Earl Young, son of medical equipment mogul Benson Young, died this morning from injuries sustained after being struck by a train. The accident is thought to be Mob related and is being investigated."

Benson Young was Richard's boss, and his son, Earl, was Richard's nemesis in business. Marie cringed at the thought of Richard's potential involvement.

* * *

"So what did you buy from lover boy?" Karen asked the next day when Marie stopped in her shop to pick up a jacket she had ordered. Karen clasped her heart with her hand and sighed.

"Will you stop it?" Marie asked, haunted by how Karen referred to Paul. Her former coworkers at Marshall Field's had often referred to Richard as lover boy. "You're making something out of nothing."

Karen maintained the gleam in her eye. "Did he ask you out?"

Marie didn't answer.

"Ha! He did, didn't he?"

Marie rolled her eyes and gave Karen one of those "I hate it when you're right" looks. "Okay, so he did ask me out, but I didn't accept."

Karen put her hands on her hips and gave her a disapproving look. "You are nuts, Marie, you know that? The man was cute as all get out. He wasn't wearing a wedding ring. And he owns his own business. What more do you want?" She rang up the jacket.

Marie scanned the store for customers within earshot. "Let's not forget I'm still married, Karen."

"Only legally."

"I can't date anyone. You know that." She paused when she heard the door bell tinkle, signaling a customer had entered the store. She waited until the customer was out of sight and whispered, "And even if I could, as soon as he finds out who my father is, it'll all be over anyway."

"That would be just like you to tell him right away."

Marie stepped away from the cash register and pretended to be interested in a display of argyle sweaters while Karen rang up the other customer's merchandise.

"So anyway, you were saying…"

"I actually didn't say no to him. I just didn't say yes."

"So what does that mean?"

"He gave me his home phone number and said to call him if I was interested in getting together."

"And you're not going to call him, are you?" She didn't wait for an answer. "You are being *way* too cautious. As usual. Just remember, what we regret later in life are the chances we never took."

"Another one of your mother's sayings?"

"Yes, and if you don't call him, I'm never going to speak to you again. Just keep that in mind."

"You're all talk."

"Dating doesn't have to be a prelude to marriage. 'Course, a little action in bed wouldn't be all that bad either."

"Karen!"

"Well, it wouldn't. Promise me you'll call him," Karen ordered. "And remember, new life chases away old ghosts."

"Enough with the sayings."

"She had a million of them."

Marie headed toward the door. "I'll think about it," she called without looking back.

"See ya later. And wear that new jacket you just bought when you see him. Looks good on you."

Marie thought about their conversation on the way home. So what would be the worst thing that could happen if she went out with him? She and Richard had no marriage, no chance of ever getting back together.

Legally, it would be adultery. Hmm…more grounds for divorce for him. The more each of them dated, the less chance there was of Richard wanting her back. Maybe. She wished old emotions would stop surfacing so she could be sure she wasn't harboring any feelings for him. She wondered if she was wavering in order to avoid the pain of ending her marriage once and for all. The more she thought about it, the more confused she became.

The torment of having unfulfilled dreams didn't stop with having a meaningful relationship with someone again. The issue of having children, a dream of hers for as long as she could remember, still loomed. But now that she was aware of her true identity, that dream had sorely degenerated. Even if she was able to find someone who was accepting of her mixed race, she had to ask herself if consciously bringing a mixed-race child into such an unwelcoming world was fair. As painful as it was, Marie had to admit the answer was no.

"What about adoption?" Karen asked her one evening over a glass of wine on Marie's porch. The sky had begun its lazy fade to black, and there was a chill in the air.

Marie shivered. "What color?" she asked. Karen didn't respond. Marie paused for a moment before saying slowly and deliberately, "It's just color. It's your outward appearance. It has nothing to do with the person inside. Why don't people get that?"

"Hey."

"Hey what?"

"Best friends?"

Marie figured that was Karen's way of saying they should change the subject before getting into another fight. Marie flashed a faint smile.

We may be best friends, she thought, *but our values, at least when it comes to race issues, are staunch adversaries.*

CHAPTER 12

That Kind of Child

"Hello, Paul?"

"This is he."

"This is Marie Costa. The reason I'm..."

"You've changed your mind and you're going to have dinner with me."

"Well, something like that."

"I was hoping you would call. After you left my shop, I thought maybe I may have come across a little strong. I'm usually not that forward."

"Well, I...anyway, I'm calling to say I would love to have lunch or dinner with you sometime."

"Wonderful." His tone was sincere. "I have an idea. There's an arts and crafts show in Leavenworth this weekend. How about if we have lunch and then take in the show?"

"Sure, sounds like fun."

"Does Saturday work for you?"

"Saturday would be fine."

They made plans to meet at his shop. As she hung up the phone, Marie tried to ignore the prickly feeling inside her. She had given it a lot of thought before calling him and had pretty much decided not to. And that was something she didn't understand about herself—the way she could think through something long and hard, decide in her head not to do it, and then do it anyway.

Marie picked up the phone and called Karen to tell her about her date.

"Don't put too much thought into it, Marie. Just have a funky time. Hey, speaking of Rachael, what do you hear from her these days?"

"That girl writes the best letters. I got one just yesterday telling me all about what she's doing in school and with her friends. And of course, the ongoing issues she has with Ben. I haven't answered it yet and don't know how I'm going to respond, with regard to Ben, that is. It's just normal child-parent stuff, but to her he doesn't know what he's doing."

"I felt the same way about my parents. She'll look back one day and thank him, like most kids do."

"I hope so."

* * *

When Marie pulled into the driveway of the Treasure Trove, Paul came out the front door and signaled her to park next to his car in the back. His smile was wide, and his eyes sparkled in the radiant sunlight even from afar. He followed her to the back and opened the car door for her.

"You look lovely today, madam," he said. She wore a skirt splashed with colorful flowers that flared out from her narrow waist to right below her knees. The yellow jacket she had bought in Karen's store partially covered a lace-trimmed white cotton tee that softly caressed her breasts, just low enough to show the promise of cleavage.

"Why thank you, sir."

He held out his arm. "We can walk from here." He wore gray trousers with heavy pleats, a pale green long-sleeved dress shirt rolled up to his elbows, and a gray and green pin-striped tie. It was much more subdued and casual than what Richard would have worn, but Marie thought the look suited him.

They walked at a leisurely pace equal to the gentle breeze coasting in and out, the early June air warm on their faces. He led the way to Binyon's, a restaurant located on the widest part of Threemile Creek. He requested a table overlooking the water.

Marie gazed out the window after being seated. The luminous reflection of the sun danced on the slow-moving water, like thousands of tiny ballerinas in their twinkling costumes, mesmerizing anyone who stared at them for too long. "It's pretty here." She turned to him. "Good choice."

They entered into the usual first-date conversation, the voices of the other patrons around them rising and falling in the background. Paul told her about himself, and she did the same—limiting the information she conveyed to only the safe stuff for now. They had a few common interests and talked about them while they ate.

He told her about his home in Leavenworth, about how he and his sister, Beth, had inherited the business and family home, which he now occupied, when their parents died.

She found his demeanor somewhat dull compared to Richard's quick wit, high level of confidence, and ability to cultivate a stimulating conversation. And while Paul was more educated than Richard, he didn't have half of Richard's vocabulary. *Stop comparing him to Richard*, the little voice in her head told her.

After lunch, they walked the short distance to the arts and crafts show. They strolled through the aisles of exhibits, gravitating toward the same booths, discovering they liked the same type of artwork.

At the end of the afternoon, they headed in the direction of his shop. "Did you enjoy yourself?" he asked. "Maybe it was my imagination, but I kinda got the impression you were a little on edge about something back there."

"I had a *very* nice time, Paul. The art show was a great idea. I'm so glad you suggested it." She had to admit to herself, it felt good being with a man again. Marie gave him a relaxed smile as they walked back to her car. She turned to him and said, "I really did enjoy the day, Paul. If I appeared to be nervous, it's only because I haven't been on a date in a long time."

"Hmm. Well, can I call you?" His words were tentative and slow.

Marie nodded, regretting she didn't know how to politely decline his offer on the spot. "Okay. I'll give you my number." She rummaged through her purse for a pen and paper.

She relived their encounter on the drive home. She didn't know what surprised her the most—the fact that she had agreed to go out with him in the first place, the fact that she hadn't thought about her ethnicity even once during their date, or the fact that she actually looked forward to seeing him again.

Marie called Karen when she got home.

"So how'd it go?"

"It went okay."

"You don't sound very enthusiastic. Going to see him again?"

"I don't know."

"Why not? Didn't you have a good time?"

"No, I had a good enough time."

"And did he?"

"I suppose."

"So…are you going to see him again?"

"I don't know," she said through a sigh. "He asked me if he could call me, and I said yes, but now I don't know whether I really want to see him again or not. I keep going back and forth about it."

"See him again. You deserve to have some fun."

* * *

Paul called Marie the very next day. She wished he hadn't called so soon. She needed more time to think things through. *My marriage. My race. What I would give to not have to agonize over these things just to go out on a date.*

"Would you like to have dinner with me on Saturday?" he asked.

She hoped her hesitation was short enough for him not to notice. "Sure." She made a face, not sure why she said yes.

"I'll pick you up at six." He cleared his throat. "That is, I *would* pick you up at six if I knew where you lived."

Marie gave him directions to her home, and after chatting a few more minutes, they hung up. She caught herself smiling, a smile that soon faded the more she thought about what she was doing.

Paul arrived a few minutes before six on Saturday. He took everything in as Marie showed him around her apartment. "Nice place," he said. He glanced out the spare bedroom window overlooking the expansive backyard. "It sure is private back here. Who lives in the big house?"

"I'll tell you about them on our way to dinner."

They went to his car, a dark blue 1947 Pontiac coupe—not on the order of anything Richard would drive, but a definite step up from Marie's slightly dented 1946 Ford sedan.

"Where are we going, by the way?"

"I made reservations at Anthony's. I hope you don't mind the drive. They have a steak Delmonico that's to die for. Have you ever been there?"

She forced a guarded smile. "Anthony's...uh, the one in Kansas City?"

"That's the one," he said proudly.

Marie had never been to Anthony's, but she recognized the name from a conversation she had had with a Kansas City lawyer she once met. He represented mobster types from time to time, and in the course of their conversation, he had mentioned two Kansas City restaurants to stay away from. Anthony's was one of them.

Marie tried not to let Paul see the panicked look on her face. He opened the door for her and then walked around the car to the driver's side.

"Uh...don't start the car yet, Paul. There's something I have to tell you." She paused a few seconds to gather her thoughts. "I'd prefer we didn't go to Anthony's. There's a chance that people who know my ex-husband will be there, and they're not people I want to run into." She watched his face. "It's a long story. Can we go somewhere else? Do you mind?"

He gave her a puzzled look. "Sure. Don't even worry about it. What about Fulton's? They have great seafood." He paused. "So...you were married? You didn't mention that before."

She shifted her weight in the seat. "Paul, can we not go to Fulton's either?" She wondered what he must be thinking of her. "And it wasn't that I was married before. I'm still legally married." She looked him straight in the eye. "Look, if you want to call this whole thing off, we can." She fumbled for the door handle.

"Hey, not so fast." He took a gentle hold of her arm. "Look, you don't have to explain anything to me right now, although your having a husband or ex-husband, whatever he is, well, uh..." He forced a chuckle. "You're not still with him, are you?"

She shook her head. "No. We've been apart for two years."

"Okay." Paul paused an endless few seconds. "So...would you like to tell me where we *can* go for dinner?"

Marie managed an awkward smile through tight lips. "There's a nice place called Wick's Inn that's about twenty minutes north of here. I can show you where it is."

"Perfect."

Wick's Inn was an old Victorian house that had been converted into a restaurant shortly after World War II. They had kept most of the rooms intact, allowing for several small, more intimate dining rooms instead of one large one. They were seated with three other couples in what used to be the front parlor.

Marie fidgeted with the napkin on her lap. "Tell me, Paul," she said after they had ordered their food, "do you go to Anthony's and Fulton's often?"

"No. In fact, I've only been to Anthony's once. I sold an old roll-top desk to someone who came into my shop one day. The guy lived in Chicago but wanted the desk delivered to an address in Kansas City. He didn't have any way to get it there, so I offered to deliver it, and he thanked me by taking me to Anthony's for lunch." He smiled. "Here I thought I was going to impress you with a downtown restaurant. Well, I guess *that* backfired."

"What was the man's name?"

"What man?"

"The man who bought the desk." She had a mental picture of the roll-top desk in Richard's home office.

"I don't remember. Why?"

"Do you remember what he looked like?"

"I really don't remember. It's been a few years. One thing I do remember though is he smoked a terrible-smelling cigar. I practically had to fumigate the place after he left. Why?"

Reference to the cigar was enough to put Marie on edge. She was sure Richard had had one of his short, fat, cigar-smoking cohorts follow her from time to time. "No reason. I asked about Anthony's because it's known for being a hangout for mobster types." She watched the expression on Paul's face change.

"You're kidding." His brows scrunched up until they met each other in the middle. "Are you sure? Do you mean I sold that desk to a mobster?"

"Well, I don't know about that, but if he knew people in Anthony's, there's a good chance he was mixed up with them in some way."

He shook his head. "The restaurant looked normal to me."

"There are probably rooms in the back."

"Come to think of it, the guy did know a lot of people there." He paused. "Well, I won't go back there. That's all there is to it. And I apologize for wanting to take you there. I feel like a real schmuck."

"Don't feel bad. You didn't know." She recalled some of the similar restaurants Richard had taken her. "To an outsider, it looks like any other restaurant."

"So your husband is mixed up with these people?"

Marie explained some of the aspects of her life with Richard on the way home. She watched his eyes grew big when she talked about what had gone on in their marriage.

"So where did you grow up, Marie?"

The knot in the pit of her stomach expanded the more family-related details she revealed to him. "I grew up in Chicago with my mother. While my father supported us financially, he didn't live with us." She inhaled a few breaths in a slow deliberate manner, and after filling her lungs with an ample amount of air, exhaled through slightly parted lips, preparing for what she was about to reveal next. "He's a pretty amazing man—probably the most prominent Negro horse rancher in the country."

The car swerved sharply to the left before Paul hit the breaks and pulled off onto the shoulder. He brought the car to a slow stop. Expressionless, he gazed deep into her eyes. "Marie, you're either testing me or trying to shock the heck out of me. Which is it?"

Her eyes met his. "It's neither. I'm just telling you the truth."

After staring at her for a lasting few seconds, he pulled back on to the road, stared straight ahead, and said nothing the rest of the way home, his hands gripping the steering wheel like vices. When he pulled the car into her driveway and put it into park, he asked, "Can we talk?"

Once in her apartment, thinking she had little to lose at this point, Marie spilled out more information about her father, not leaving much out. She did the same about Richard.

Paul's arms were crossed. "Well, I guess it shouldn't matter who your father is." He smiled a weak smile. "Everyone has something in their past they're not comfortable with. Hey, I do too." He shot her an edgy grin and whispered, "We all have at least one dirty little secret."

Dirty little secret?

"Of course, as far as Richard goes, I would feel a lot better if you were legally unmarried to him."

Dirty little secret?

"Look, Paul, maybe this isn't going to...see, you're the first date I've had since I left Richard two years ago, and the first date since I've known about my father. So maybe now you realize..."

"Oh, I realize a *lot* of things now." He fingered his earlobe. "And if I'm going to be honest..."

"I understand completely." She got up from her chair and headed toward the door. "Goodbye, Paul."

"Let's not call it off just yet, okay?" He stood up but didn't head toward the door. "Can we talk more?"

Marie sat down on one end of the sofa, and Paul sat down on the other. Marie's cat, Sheana, immediately jumped up between them and stared at Paul as he spoke.

"Can I just tell you something more about myself? Maybe get to know each other better?"

She wasn't sure she wanted to get to know him any better.

"I was married once myself. Georgia and I were very young. She was eighteen. I was twenty. We thought she was pregnant, and that's why we got married. Turned out she wasn't, but we stayed together anyway. Not exactly the perfect marriage, but we liked each other enough, and it was convenient." His eyes drifted from one side of the living room to the other as he spoke.

"Then my sister and I inherited the antique shop from our parents, and the three of us ran it together for awhile. Georgia was much better at knowing what to buy for the shop than we were, so she always went on these road trips while Beth and I managed the store. Anyway, after a few years, Georgia and I split. It just wasn't meant to be. She wanted out, and I didn't fight it. But we stayed friends. We're still close."

Marie wasn't sure why he wanted to talk about himself when there was a much more important factor looming.

"Okay, so you said who my father is doesn't bother you, but does who *I* am bother you?"

"Uh...of course we'd have to be discreet about being out in public together...that is, because of your husband and everything."

She gave him a weak smile. Part of her wanted to ignore the fact he was dodging her question. The other part wanted to ask him to leave. "So just for clarification, you'd like to keep seeing each other, but only if we're not seen out in public together?"

He leaned in toward her and then quickly backed off when Sheana issued a short hiss.

He stared at the cat. "I wish I could say I'd be your big protector, from your ex and all, but the truth is I'm pretty much a wimp when it comes to tough guys." He leaned even farther back from the cat. "I was beat up as a kid. Quite a bit." He had a crooked smile on his face. "So maybe we can just keep a low profile?"

She examined his face, still not sure what to make of him and his avoidance of her direct questions. She suspected Richard didn't bother him as much as her father did. "Look, I'm trying to understand what you're saying..."

"All I'm saying is I would like to get to know you better."

She took her time responding. "Okay. And then what?"

"Then what?"

"Yes. Where could we go with it?"

"With what?"

"The relationship?"

Paul gave her a blank stare. "Well...let's not get too far ahead of ourselves."

She bit the inside of her cheek. She had already opened the door, and now she was going to barge through it. "Let me be a bit more direct, Paul. Could you ever see getting serious with someone like me?"

Paul's eyebrows arched up. "Serious?"

"Yes. Serious. Like in marriage."

Even Sheana's ears perked up.

He looked down at his feet with an unfocused gaze and then leaned over to swipe a smudge from the toe of his shoe. "Well, unless I misunderstood you before, I thought technically you were still married."

"I plan to get a divorce."

Paul stared at her for a long moment before responding. "Okay."

"What if I was divorced, what then?"

"What do you mean, what then?"

"Would you feel differently about me, about our situation?"

He gazed out the window with a fuzzy expression on his face.

"Are you going to answer me?"

"I don't know what to say. What situation?"

She knew she was pushing him too hard and too soon, but all of a sudden she felt as though she was talking to all of mankind and had to get things off her chest.

"What about children? Do you want children someday?"

He eyed her like she had just sprouted horns. He rubbed his forehead with one hand and then took in a jerky breath. "I have to admit that not having children has always been something I've regretted. Georgia wasn't able to have kids, and that, quite frankly, may have been the downfall of our marriage." His Adam's apple appeared to have a mind of its own. "But I'm not here to talk about marriage...and certainly not children, Marie. I'm..."

"Well, let's just say that having children is important to me. What would you say to that?"

"I'd say you're talking to the wrong guy."

"Why?"

"Marie, we just met."

"That's not the real reason."

Paul got up. "I think I should go."

Marie dug in her heels. She wasn't about to let him off the hook that easily. "And *I* want to finish this conversation. Would it be out of the question to have children with me?"

His words were slow and deliberate. "Okay. No. I couldn't do that with you."

She stared at him for an uncomfortable few seconds. "Why?"

"Because...you know...they could be...colored. I would think you wouldn't want children because of that as well."

A surge of blood crept up her neck, causing her to lose focus. Even though she saw it coming, hearing him say the words was shattering. Her open hand drifted up to her mouth and slid down her neck. "I can't believe you just said that," she said, feeling as though someone had punched her in the stomach—hard.

He headed toward the door. "This conversation is going all wrong. All I'm trying to..."

She didn't wait for him to finish. "All you're trying to do is..."

"Look, up until now, I kinda liked you, but all this talk about marriage and children...well, to be blunt, I couldn't bring myself to father that kind of child." He stumbled over the words. "C'mon, who could?"

If he had set off a bomb in the room, it would have had less of an impact. She faced him. "*That* kind of child?" Her glare flew to his face. "You just don't get it, do you?" She tried hard not to be controlled by her emotions, but by this time they had all swirled to the surface. "For your information, I *am* 'that kind of child.' How in the hell do you think that makes me feel hearing you say that?"

Before he could answer, Marie continued her barrage, the words cracking from her mouth like a boxer throwing punches. "You are nothing but a bigot! And you're too damn *stupid* to even realize it. Get out! Just get out!"

She slammed the side of her fist into the wall, unable to hold back the tears. "Go home! Go to hell for all I care! I never want to see you again!"

When he reached the door, he muttered something Marie didn't comprehend. She waited until she heard the sound of his car engine and then drifted to the sun porch and into the welcoming gloom of the moonless night sky. She watched him pull out of the driveway, the emptiness sweeping over her like a slow fog.

The light drizzle of rain that had been coming down all evening suddenly turned into a downpour. Marie poured herself a glass of wine and curled up on the living room sofa. Sheana jumped up, sat on her lap, and looked at her sympathetically.

She tried to sort through the details of the evening. *That kind of child.* The words gnawed at her. Marie spent the rest of the evening reflecting...on everything. "I'm not going to let him or anyone else bring me down. I've made it through worse situations than this," she said aloud, not succeeding in holding back the tears. "Well, you won't be seeing him around here anymore, Sheana." She stroked the purring cat's back. "But it looks like you didn't like him much anyway, did you, sweetie?"

The wind picked up, pelting the rain against the windows, almost drowning out Billy Eckstine.

The night is like a lovely tune
Beware my foolish heart

She watched the rain fall, trying to make sense of things, swiping away the tears with the soggy handkerchief she clenched in her hand.

Take care my foolish heart

She went to bed, and in time, she fell asleep, in spite of the roar of the pounding rain.

CHAPTER 13

A Very Special Lady

Marie awoke before dawn the next morning after a fitful night's sleep. Needing to get out of the house to clear her head, she drove down to the river.

A man and small boy fished off the bridge. Two young boys rowed downstream in a bright red canoe. Gulls called to each other in the distance. Useful distractions. She stared at the mirror-smooth, slow-moving water.

Marie got out of her car and sat on a bench near the water's edge, allowing the healing warmth of the sun to penetrate her skin. Dragonflies skimmed the surface of the water, catching sunlight on their iridescent wings. She tossed a pebble into the water, breaking its peaceful surface.

She stared at the water in a trancelike state until a frog on the riverbank diverted her attention, its fat belly dragging on the ground as it stumbled along, probably looking for its next meal. She breathed in the cool fresh air until her emotions, still ripe from the day before, subsided.

When home, she called Karen and told her about the fight with Paul.

"Well, lady, what did you expect when you backed him into a corner like that?"

"I know. I know. But I could see what was running through his mind, and I had to hear him say it."

"Well, you asked for it, then."

"I suppose." Marie paused, not sure if she wanted to admit everything. "I think I was unconsciously just using him."

"How so?"

"Maybe all I was doing was testing the waters as to what might happen if I started dating again."

"Keep talking."

"I didn't know what to expect when I told someone I was still married, and even more so that my father is a Negro."

"And you thought Paul might be a good patsy?"

She didn't like Karen's choice of words but accepted it. "Mm-hmm. If I'm really honest with myself, I'm afraid so. And now I feel terrible about it."

"Because of the way you treated him?"

"I feel bad that I used him. I feel bad that he reacted the way he did. I should have just ended it without any confrontation, or not gone out with him in the first place."

"I'm not surprised at all at his reaction. Look, you've got to understand that no one likes to see whites and coloreds mix. You may not like that or think it's right, but that's the way it is. Paul's no different."

"He probably thinks I'm some kind of freak show. I wonder why he wanted to get to know me better anyway."

"What did you really want from him?" When Marie didn't respond, she added, "Be honest."

"I wanted him to accept me for who I was."

"Maybe that's what he was trying to do."

Leave that go, Marie. "I don't know. I've made a mess of things, haven't I?"

"Have another glass of wine, hon. You'll feel better. Meanwhile, I gotta go. Talk to you later."

* * *

Marie called her father that evening and told him about Paul.

"I can't say I'm surprised. It sounds like you pushed him into it."

"I know I did. And it was wrong, but..."

"No, I see why you did it. Just learn from it, sweetheart. By the way, have you filed for divorce yet?"

"No. I keep going back and forth about what to do, and in the meantime, I do nothing."

"Can I give you some advice?"

"Of course."

"Do something. And even if that's waiting until the statute is up, make up your mind what you intend to do, and do it. To think too long about doing something often becomes its undoing. I'm not sure who said that, but it's worth following."

"I'll work on that. And thanks...Dad."

* * *

Later that week, as Marie turned the corner onto her street after a shopping trip in Leavenworth, she saw his car parked in front of the main house—a dark blue 1936 Auburn. It had to be Richard's. With nowhere else to go, she cruised by the house. The car was empty. She drove around the block, and when she returned, the car was gone.

She called Karen.

"How long has it been since you've heard from him?" Karen asked.

"It's been almost a year, but less if you count when I've felt his presence."

"You've got to get over him. He's going to drive you crazy."

Karen should have known better. She of all people knew that things that happened years ago could still reach out and grab you by the throat. "I know. I just wish I knew how to do that."

It took several glasses of wine that evening for Marie to drift off to sleep, her last thoughts being maybe she needed to confront Richard once and for all. As fate would have it, she got that opportunity the following day.

Karen had invited Marie out for dinner and a movie for her twenty-fifth birthday. Marie stopped in Karen's dress shop after work to pick her up. Karen was in the back room closing things up when Richard entered the front door.

He walked in with a casual gait, looked around the store, and then smiled at Marie.

"What are you doing here?" she asked.

Richard exuded his usual level of confidence. "Just in the neighborhood and thought I'd do a little shopping. What a nice surprise to see you here."

A wave of confidence swept over her. "You know damn well whose shop this is. Why are you doing this?"

"Doing what?"

"Don't be coy with me. You didn't drive five hundred miles to shop in a woman's clothing store. Why are you really here?"

"I'm here to do some shopping, but I must say it's always nice to see you again. Happy birthday, by the way. You're looking as beautiful as ever, sweetheart."

"Quit patronizing me, and stop stalking me. I've had enough!"

"You're still my wife, don't forget. But that's neither here nor there, is it?"

"Please get out, and don't come back here. Stay in Chicago where you belong."

Richard shifted his weight. "In case you don't already know this—and I'm sure you do, 'cause you're a very smart girl—I can pretty much go anywhere I please. The last time I looked, this was still a free country. At least it is for me." She cringed at the obvious implication. "Right, Karen?" He looked toward the back of the store.

Karen came out from the back room and stopped abruptly when she saw Richard.

"May I help you?"

"This is Richard, Karen. He was just leaving."

Karen had a look of horror on her face. She appeared unable to move.

"Karen, can you give us a few minutes alone?"

Karen looked at Marie, who nodded. *Are you sure?* Karen mouthed. Marie nodded again, and Karen disappeared into the back room.

Richard walked toward Marie.

"Stop right there, or I'll…"

"You'll what? And don't be stupid. I've never hurt you."

The tightness in her chest hurt. "You're the stupid one, Richard. And you *have* hurt me…in countless ways, and you're still doing it." She couldn't believe she had just called him stupid.

Richard didn't respond right away. Instead he stood up a little straighter and pressed his shoulders back. "The only thing that makes me stupid is still being in love with you." He tilted his chin up and looked down his nose at her. "Come back to me, Marie. We can make it together. We need each other."

"I don't need you. Not anymore." She had difficulty controlling her breathing given her heart was beating so fast.

"You're nothing without me."

"Get out."

He tipped his hat. "You need someone who'll be there to protect you, darlin'." He headed toward the door. "Someone like me." He opened the door and exited, but not before dropping a piece of paper on the floor.

Marie walked toward the door and locked it before picking up the piece of paper. It had been torn out of a newspaper. The headline read, "White Man Lynched for Dating a Negro."

Karen came out from the back of the store. "I heard everything. That man scares me."

Marie concealed the scrap of paper in her clenched fist. "Me too."

* * *

On her way to work the next day, Marie swung by the trash can to throw out a bag of garbage. When she popped off the lid, she stood there in a trance-like state for several disheartening seconds. On the top of the garbage was a Roseville vase, the foxglove design, shattered into little pieces. The note on top read, "For a very special lady. Happy birthday."

CHAPTER 14

Catching the Monkey

Marie's interior design firm, Genesis Design Group, continued to flourish. With World War II embedded five years into history, the economy was stronger than ever, and people were no longer afraid to invest in new and improved furnishings, in both residential and commercial settings. She added two more designers to her staff in order to keep up with the demands from all the referrals she was getting.

It had been almost three months since she had confronted Richard, and she had a constant nagging feeling that he was still occasionally around, but she never actually saw evidence of him until one evening when she and Karen were in Marie's apartment watching *The Ed Sullivan Show*. Marie left the room during a commercial and went into her bedroom. Ten minutes later, Karen came in to check on her.

"Come here, Karen, quick! See that?" She pointed to the house next door. "That's Richard's car, the blue Auburn."

"Are you sure?"

"It's him. You know who lives next door, don't you?"

"The policeman?"

"Yep. Somehow Richard must know him. That lousy son of a..."

"Are you sure it's him?"

Marie cracked open the window, hoping to hear something. They watched the neighbor's driveway for another ten minutes from their second story vantage point, but no one came out of the house.

Marie wiped her sweaty palms off on her trousers and peered out the window. "He's trying to scare me again, and I must admit he's doing a good job at it."

Karen took hold of her arm. "Let's go in the living room. You're getting all worked up over what's probably nothing."

She ran her fingers through her hair. "Nothing." Her mind drifted. "Maybe you're right," she said, but inside she thought that "nothing" could be a whole lot of "something."

They retreated to the living room just as the television show ended. Karen turned it off.

"Let's say that *was* him. What's it going to take for him to leave you alone?"

"I don't know. He's pretty relentless."

"Well, you know what they say. If you want to catch the monkey, you have to climb the tree."

Marie gave her an uncertain look. "Another one of…"

"My mother's sayings. I know some of them are kind of corny, but they're true. In other words, he wants you, the monkey, and he's willing to climb any tree to get you. Unlike Paul. I think he may have wanted you, but he wasn't willing to climb the tree."

"Let's get serious. Paul wasn't even willing to stumble over a low-lying bush for me."

"Hey, good one, kiddo."

Marie tried to suppress a smile.

"Wonder if that's the difference between being in love and just loving someone," Karen suggested. "Whether you're willing to climb the tree."

"I never thought about it that way. What is love anyway? I'm not sure I know anymore."

"One thing I figured out when I was married to Ed is to be in love with someone, you need passion. Once that passion is gone, there's no more being in love."

"What about you and Maurice?"

A flush of red crept up Karen's neck up into her face. "Are you kidding? We can't keep our hands off of each other."

"And Ed? I mean, how does that compare to Ed?"

"When I think back to my marriage with him, which seems like a hundred years ago, I thought we had passion in the beginning. I remember times when we couldn't rip off each other's clothes fast enough before we made love. Hell, there were times we would come home and we couldn't wait to make it into the house, so we did it in the back seat of our car."

"You said you had passion in the beginning. What changed?"

Marie knew Karen still had a hard time talking about her late husband's sexuality. It had been years after his suicide that she'd realized he was a homosexual, and she still didn't completely understand or accept it, especially since during their marriage he seemed to have been a normal loving husband. This was the most she had said about him in a long time.

"I don't know. Somewhere along the way we lost it. Maybe that's when he discovered...did I ever tell you there was a time I thought maybe he was having an affair? I even confronted him about it."

"Really? What did he say?"

"He denied it, of course. Told me he loved me and that I was the only woman for him. Now I know what that meant, but I didn't have a clue back then. He'd get emotional whenever we talked about it, and my Ed did not like to show his emotions, so eventually we just stopped talking about it."

"Do you still think about him?"

"Yeah, unfortunately, especially when I'm with Maurice. I keep making comparisons. Stupid, isn't it?"

"No. I've done that with Richard too."

"Yeah, but Richard wasn't a goddamn queer."

"Karen! You never swear!"

"I know, but it still upsets me. What he did was...well, it was wrong, that's all. And disgusting."

Marie wasn't sure she would have characterized it that way, but then she wasn't in Karen's shoes. "I wonder what makes people do that. I'm sure he didn't do it because he was out to hurt or humiliate you."

"I don't know. It's illegal, isn't it? Why does anyone do something that's illegal? He must have gotten something out of it." Karen made a face that said it all. "And to think I was lying in bed with him at the same time he was up to all that."

"But you had no suspicions, right?"

"None. Zero. Nothing."

"That says something about men who do that...but I'm not sure what."

"It says they're sick. That's what it says."

"So how are things with you and Maurice?" She handed Karen a bowl of chocolates she had kept on hand for such an occasion.

"Very funny," Karen said, taking two pieces. "Good. Things are really good." She shook her head. "You know, after Ed died, I never thought I'd ever be interested in anyone else." She threw her shoulders back and shrugged. "I didn't think I really needed a man."

"So tell me more about Maurice. Any more encounters with his mother?"

"She's such a basket case. Her birthday was last Saturday, and Maurice invited her over for dinner. Big mistake."

"Why?"

"She spent the whole time talking about her doctors. She must have twenty of them. I lost count after she complained that her hepatologist didn't use sterile instruments, and she needed to find another one, but the closest one she could find was in Illinois."

"What's a hepatologist?"

"Have no idea and didn't dare ask."

"You know, we never did finish our conversation about what being in love is."

"How's this? It's a combination of trust, intimacy, passion, and commitment." Karen waved her hand in the air as she spoke.

"Hey, that's almost profound, my friend! And then let's add that it's when you put your partner's interests above your own."

"Oh, and let's not forget empathy and equality."

"Yes, and what about loyalty?"

"Marie?"

"Yes?"

"We need to get ourselves a couple of puppies, because there aren't any men out there like that."

After Karen left, Marie glanced out her bedroom window at the house next door. The Auburn was gone.

* * *

Marie had finished one of her early Saturday morning horse rides when Ted Braxton, owner of the ranch where she boarded J.B., followed her into J.B.'s stall where she was rubbing down the horse. Ted's rugged good looks had caused Marie to wonder more than once if he was married. Or whether by any chance he knew or knew of her father, being they were in the same line of work.

"Have a good ride?" he asked.

"Sure did."

"Marie, do I remember you telling me you know a gun dealer in Kansas City?"

Marie had met Barry Stone the year before when she made the decision to buy a gun when Richard took his bullying a step too far. He had sold her a Smith & Wesson .38 special revolver and then taught her how to use it. Barry had asked her out at the time, an invitation Marie had declined. She told Ted about him.

"Well, I just inherited a slew of guns from my uncle, and I know I'm supposed to be a cowboy, but I know nothing about guns, and I'm interested in what they are and what they're worth. Do you think he'd be able to help me?"

"I don't know, but he seemed to know an awful lot about guns. Do you want me to ask him if he'd take a look at them for you?"

"Would you?"

The following weekend, Marie accompanied Ted to Stone Guns and Ammo. On the way, she mentioned her father's business. Ted said he didn't know him.

Barry greeted Marie with a smile and a quick run of his fingers through his hair. But the gleam in his eyes quickly faded when he saw Ted. He examined the display of guns in its entirety. "Hmm. Nice collection."

"Whatever you can tell me about them would be helpful," Ted said.

Barry picked up the first one. "This one is a Philadelphia-style derringer. Not the real McCoy, but still a good piece. Probably 44-caliber. My guess it's from around 1850 or '60."

"Do you know what it's worth?" Ted asked.

He shrugged. "Oh, I don't know exactly what you could get for a piece like this, but I would think at least a hundred bucks, maybe more. This one here is also a copy of a Colt. Pretty sure it's 32-cal. Nice engraving on the nickel. Worth less than the first one. Maybe half a yard."

"Half a yard?" Marie asked.

"Fifty bucks." When he picked up the next one, Barry's eyes grew large. "Now this one is interesting. Colt 44. Dates back to probably 1860s or '70s.

Original ivory grip. Looks Mexican to me. If you could find the right buyer, you may be able to get a couple hundred for this one."

"No kidding. Did you hear that, Marie?"

Marie heard Ted say her name but was preoccupied with the familiar-looking car that had pulled into the parking lot and was now parked in the shadow of a large shade tree. Thinking it could be Richard, she didn't understand how he could possibly have known where she was. She hadn't told anyone where she and Ted were going this afternoon, not even Karen. Had he followed them? She turned back toward Ted and Barry and half-listened to the rest of their conversation.

"This one is an Army Colt that was probably turned in after the war and refurbished. You can find a lot of these. I have two of 'em myself. And this is another one of the same. See this engraving? The eagle and snake? That's how I know it's Mexican."

The last gun was a Smith & Wesson "lemon-squeezer," the gold gilt finish worn but with little pitting. "Why do they call it a lemon-squeezer?" Marie asked.

"See this safety? You have to squeeze the grip in order to release the safety and fire the gun. Like so."

"You've been a great help, Barry. I appreciate it."

"Tell you what. I'll give you a hundred clams for the ivory-grip Colt."

Ted's face lit up. "Hundred twenty-five and it's yours."

"Deal."

Barry paid Ted, and as soon as Ted turned to leave, Barry shot Marie an eyebrow flash, smoothed the ends of his mustache, and said, "See ya 'round."

Marie tried to get a better look at the man in the parked Auburn in the far corner of the parking lot, but his face was hidden by his fedora, similar to ones Richard owned. She watched the road behind them in the passenger side mirror of Ted's car, but there was no sign of the Auburn.

CHAPTER 15

Fears

Marie's second Thanksgiving at the Brookses' felt a lot like she was just another family member. She flew in a day ahead and helped Claire in the kitchen all afternoon, in an environment that was so much more comfortable than the year before.

This morning, she joined Jonathan for an early morning ride before the big meal. Gregory, Gloria, Rachael, and Ben were expected late afternoon.

"So tell me, Marie, why haven't you filed for divorce from that illustrious husband of yours?" her father asked.

They reached an open section of the trail where the sun shone brightly on their faces. She squinted, partially from the sunlight, partially because she didn't have a good answer for her father. She told him about her confrontation with Richard in Karen's shop.

"But you and Cavanaugh decided filing for divorce was best, right?"

She turned to meet his gaze. "We did."

"And?"

"He wasn't sure a judge would grant me the divorce based on his felony conviction because I had already left Richard when he was arrested, and that was my only chance of getting a divorce. He said it would depend on the judge, and Richard knows judges."

"Family court judges?"

"I don't know. Crooked judges."

He stopped his horse. Marie followed suit. "What are you afraid of, sweetheart?"

A cold breeze swept in from the north, causing her to shiver. She took her time answering. "I don't know, Dad. I want to be divorced from him. I really do. It would make things so much easier."

"Let me ask you something. How many times have you relived that time, that horrific moment in time, when he pushed you down the stairs?"

Marie took in a gulp. "Just about every day. I have nightmares about it, and sometimes I even have flashbacks during the daytime." She hadn't shared that with anyone else, even Karen. She thought she should have been over that trauma by now and didn't want anyone to think she was weak, or worse yet, losing her mind. After all, the incident had occurred two and a half years earlier.

"Well, I'm no shrink, but it may be that you're re-experiencing that episode, maybe unconsciously, every time you think about divorcing Richard, and that scares you into doing nothing. Do you think that could be happening?"

"Could be. When I wake up from the nightmare, I usually feel the same things, physically I mean, that I did when it happened. My heart is pounding. I feel sick to my stomach. I'm sweating."

"I'll always be there for you, Marie. I think you know that. But you do realize this is something you have to face yourself, don't you?"

"Yes, I do."

"Well, I told you before, my advice is to go through with the divorce, but you have to feel comfortable with it too. And I know you've said you don't care what people think, but..."

"What's making you feel so strongly about this?"

"As we both know, I'm not in any position to give moral advice, but I will anyway. Wouldn't you feel much better if you weren't married and Richard was completely out of your life before you start seeing other men?"

"Yes, of course I would." She thought about her father's rationale. "But here's the thing. First of all, as I've said before, the judge may not grant the divorce. But secondly, I'm not sure a divorce would get Richard out of my life anyway."

"And you're not willing to take the chance?"

"I guess not." She looked at him. "So what does that say about me?"

Jonathan let his gaze linger on Marie's face before he responded. "I think you're being overly cautious. But I must admit, I'm also being somewhat of a protective father. I would like to see him completely out of your life so you can go on, and doing nothing just insures he's still in your life. And maybe that's what he's banking on."

Marie shook her head but didn't say anything.

When they reached the far corner of his property, Jonathan stopped his horse and turned to face his daughter. "I'm not an educated man, but I do know a little something about fear. When I was eight, maybe nine years old, my mother asked me to walk to the next door neighbor's house to borrow a cup of sugar she needed for whatever she was baking. Now where I lived, the next door neighbor's house was at least a mile down the road." He paused as though thinking about a related memory, perhaps a fond one.

"Anyway, so I walked down this dirt road, kicking a stone, like kids do, when out of the bushes jumped Eddie Sheets, the neighborhood bully." He chuckled. "We used to call him Dirty Sheets behind his back. Well, he had a piece of two-by-four in his hand, and he was a few years older than me, and much bigger. And did I mention he was white?"

Marie shook her head and smiled at the boyish smirk her father wore.

"He said to me, 'Hey, nigger. How'd you like the shit beat out of you?' I was thinking that was a pretty stupid question, but I wasn't about to tell him that, so I just stood there for a few seconds and then kept on walking. Well, it was late in the day, the sun was low in the sky, and I could see his shadow on the ground coming up on me.

"I don't know where I got the courage, but I turned around, faced him head on, and shouted at the top of my lungs, 'Get the hell out of here, Dirty Sheets, you good-for-nothing fucking ass-wipe cracker,' excuse my language, 'before I stick this knife in you and twist it until your guts come spilling out of your white honky body!' And I reached into my pocket and took a step toward him."

"Good heavens, Dad!"

"Like I said, I don't know what came over me, and at such a young age too. Well, it scared him but good. That little white boy disappeared into the bushes from whence he came in about two seconds flat, and he never bothered any of us again."

"That's quite a story. Sounds to me like you took quite a chance standing up to him."

"Looking back, I did, and it was quite foolish. People were lynched for less. But I told you that story to make a point. If your fear is keeping you from doing what you want to do, or in my case what I needed to do, you must confront it. Otherwise, the Dirty Sheets of the world will control what you do instead of you controlling your own actions. I used to think I was powerless over that boy, and so did every other little nigger boy in our neighborhood. But after that episode, I discovered I wasn't. I only thought I was.

"You can't back away from your fears. If you do, you sabotage your own future. You have to be stronger than your fears. Remember that. I'll bet you half my ranch that Richard lives and breathes that philosophy."

"Oh yes. He does that. By the way, what's a cracker?"

Jonathan let out a nervous laugh. "You never heard that expression?" Marie shook her head. "The word cracker comes from plantation owners cracking a whip on the backs of slaves."

Marie closed her eyes while she rode toward the main barn, trying to get that image out of her head.

They weren't in the house more than five minutes when Rachael bounded into the living room. "We're here!"

"We can see that, Rachael. Come here. Sit down by me," Claire said.

When Marie came out of the kitchen, Rachael shot her a wide smile. "Don't go anywhere," she squealed. She brushed her hair to the side to expose her new earrings. "Are these crazy or what?"

"They're crazy, alright."

Marie excused herself to change her clothes and then joined Claire and Rachael in the kitchen, where they were preparing turkey sandwiches for the evening meal. Rachael was unusually excited.

"So spill the beans, missy," Claire said to Rachael. "Tell us girls what you're so excited about."

"Oh, nothing."

Marie gave Rachael a "you can't fool us young lady" look.

"Okay. So there's this boy in school." Rachael's eyes lit up brighter than Marie had ever seen before. "He's so crazy. A little bit of a freak, but not bad."

"A freak?" Marie asked.

"He's different. That's all. Anyway, he asked me out…well, not really out, just to go ice skating."

"When?"

"Tomorrow. There's no school, and his dad is going to drop us off at Depot Pond to skate."

"And what does your dad think about this?" Rachael was one month shy of fourteen, and Marie was pretty sure Ben wouldn't allow her to date.

"He's hip about it. As long as it's not really a date date."

"What's his name, hon?" Claire asked.

"Craig Dungan."

Claire's expression made Marie wonder if she knew the boy. St. Charles was a small town, and the Brookses were pretty well connected.

"Well, I'm very happy for you, Rachael. I'll be here through Sunday. Will you call me to let me know how it went?" Marie asked.

Rachael giggled. "Sure. It'll be such a kick."

"Rachael, would you mind setting the table for me?" Claire asked. "Everything you need is on the buffet."

Marie turned toward Claire as soon as Rachael left the room. "You looked concerned when she mentioned the boy's name."

"I am. There's only one Dungan in town. There are three boys, and the older two are always in trouble. In fact, the oldest one, I think his name is Jake, broke into one of our barns last year and stole two very expensive saddles."

"You're kidding. So they caught him?"

"The sheriff found the saddles in the back of his pickup truck, but in the end we couldn't prove he stole them. The middle boy has been in trouble with the law too. Caught vandalizing school property. Both boys are school drop-outs. If Jonathan finds out Rachael is seeing their younger brother, he'll have a fit."

"Who'll have a fit?" Ben asked from the doorway to the kitchen.

"Um...Jonathan."

He walked closer to Claire and lowered his voice. "I overheard your conversation. Sorry, I wasn't eavesdropping or anything...well, maybe I was. When I heard Rachael's name, I couldn't turn away."

"I'm sorry."

"Don't be sorry, Claire. Is there anything else I should know about this family?"

"Well, there's one more thing. Pat Dungan, the boys' mother, used to go to our church until one Sunday her husband, I don't remember his name, came in during the service, yanked her out of her seat, and practically dragged her out of the church. We haven't seen her since."

"Good grief," Marie exclaimed. "What kind of man would do that?"

"The type of man I won't allow my daughter to be associated with, that's who." With that, Ben headed toward the dining room. "C'mon, Rachael, we're leaving."

"What? Why?"

"Just get your coat. We're going home."

"Dad, what are you doing?"

Ben took his daughter's arm and guided her toward the front door. Rachael pulled away from his grip and stomped out of the house. "This is so bogus."

Jonathan entered the kitchen to check out the commotion. Claire filled him in.

"Sounds like Ben didn't handle that too well," Jonathan said.

"No, he didn't," Claire agreed.

Greg and Gloria entered the kitchen. "What on earth happened?" Gregory asked.

Claire explained what had transpired.

"What do you think we should do, Greg?" his wife asked.

"Nothing. When Ben doesn't know how to handle something with that child, he runs. Drives us crazy, but Ben's an adult. She's his daughter. We don't need to interfere."

"Well, let's eat some dinner," Claire said, apparently trying to ease the tension that had built up in the room.

* * *

Ben called Claire the next day and asked to speak with Marie. "Rachael's run off, and I have a feeling she's headed toward Jonathan and Claire's, toward you." Ben's house was in the same town, a mile and a half from the Brookses' ranch.

"Are you sure she's not headed toward this boy's house or Depot Pond?" Marie asked.

"I'm pretty sure. The last thing she said to me was, and I quote, 'You don't know shit about anything. I'm going to talk to Marie.' I went after her, but the little squirt is too fast for me. I thought about going after her in my car, but decided that would only make matters worse."

"How long ago did she leave?"

"About ten minutes."

"Maybe I should start driving toward your house and see if I can find her."

"Would you?"

"Of course. I'll call you when we're safe and sound here."

Ben's sigh was audible even over the phone lines. "Thank you."

Marie borrowed Claire's car and drove the most likely route to Ben's home. Halfway between the two homes, she saw Rachael walking on the side of the road with her head hung down. Despite the forty-something-degree weather, Rachael's coat was wide open, and she wore no hat or gloves.

Marie pulled up beside her, leaned across the front seat, and cranked down the window. "C'mon, Rachael. Get in."

She stood there for several seconds looking as forlorn as a child could possibly look. She stared at Marie as she walked toward the car, but stopped short of getting in.

"Rachael, get in here before you freeze to death."

She opened the door and slid into the front seat. "He doesn't understand anything, Marie."

"I know it looks like that to you now, but why don't we get to someplace warm and talk it through."

"I don't believe this. You're going to take his side, aren't you?"

"I'm not going to take anyone's side, Rachael. I'm just going to talk this thing through with you. Is that what you want?"

Rachael nodded. "I guess."

Marie drove back to the Brookses', where Claire was waiting in the living room. "I made some hot chocolate for you two. Why don't you take it into your room, Marie, where you can talk privately?"

"Can you call Ben and let him know Rachael's here, Claire?" she asked before leading Rachael toward the bedroom. She didn't miss the disparaging look that Rachael shot at Claire.

Once in the room, they both sat down on the bed and sipped their hot chocolate for a few seconds before Marie broke the silence. "There's something you need to do before we talk."

"What's that?"

"You need to march yourself into the living room and apologize to Mrs. Brooks for that dirty look you just gave her. What happened yesterday wasn't her fault."

"Yes, it was! If it hadn't been for her, I'd be with Craig right now."

"Listen to me. Claire told me about Craig's family because she was concerned about you. She didn't tell your father anything. He overheard our conversation. You're getting bent out of shape over someone caring about your well being. You need to apologize to her."

Rachael crossed her arms and glared down at the bed.

"Now."

Her footsteps echoed throughout the house. When she returned, she said, "There, are you happy now?"

"Look, Rachael, if you don't drop that attitude of yours, this conversation is going to go nowhere, and you'll be back in your house with your dad in the same situation as when you stormed out of there. Is that what you want?"

"No," she said without looking up.

"Now, do you want to tell me what happened after you and your dad left here yesterday?"

"You know what happened. He said I couldn't see Craig. Ever."

"Did he say why?"

"'Cause he comes from a bad family." She rolled her eyes.

"And what do you think?"

"I told him I came from a bad family too. So what?"

"I'm sure that went over big."

"It's the truth. You should have seen the chumps my mom used to go with."

"Do you think that kind of talk with your dad helped you in the end or hurt you?"

Rachael met Marie's gaze. "Hurt."

They talked for close to an hour. Marie had no experience talking to a teenager, any teenager, let alone one full of so much spirit and resentment. When Marie sensed the conversation was heading for a stalemate, she changed its course. "What exactly are you afraid of, Rachael?"

Rachael shook her head. "I'm not afraid of *anything*."

While hard to do, Marie refrained from shouting, "You have so many fears, my dear, they're about to consume you!" Instead she said, "Want to know what I think?"

Rachael glared at her as if to say, *Do I have a choice?*

"I think you need to figure out a few things for yourself, because if you don't, the situation you have at home will only get worse."

"Like?"

"Like what's making you so angry."

Rachael didn't respond.

"I have an idea what part of it is."

"Yeah? What's that?"

"I think you're angry at your mother."

"I don't give a shit about her. I don't need her, and..."

"Stop with the language, or I'm going to drive you home and let you figure this out by yourself."

"Sorry."

"Look Rachael. I can't blame you for being angry at your mother. I know you don't know the whole story, and..."

"I don't *have* to know the whole story," Rachael protested in a loud voice. "She's never been a good mother, always looking out for herself first, not caring shit for me."

"I know, hon. That's not right, and you so deserve better than that. But I have to go back to something I said awhile back, and that is if she was capable of doing better, I'm sure she would have."

"Oh she was capable alright, capable of doing better for herself. She doesn't care about other people, Marie. Don't you get that?"

"You have every right to be angry...but not at me."

"I'm sorry."

"Let's talk about here and now. I know people who care a lot about you."

Rachael gave her a half-smile. "So what should I do now?"

"The first thing I'd do is go home and make amends with your father."

Rachael sighed.

"Nothing else you or I do will work until you do that."

Rachael's face lit up. "What are you going to do?"

"I have an idea that may help."

"What's that?"

"I can't tell you yet. Actually I could, but I'm not going to until I talk to your dad."

"He's such a geezer. And when he can't deal with me anymore, he runs away."

"Like you just did to him?"

"See how *he* likes it."

"He cares about you." She waited for Rachael to meet her gaze. "Even geezers deserve a break. Right?"

That was enough to bring a smile to Rachael's face.

"Okay. I'll apologize. Will you go with me?"

"Sure."

On her way out the front door, Rachael said to Claire, "Bye, Mrs. Brooks. Thank you."

* * *

Ben was reading the afternoon paper when Marie and Rachael arrived. "Can I come in?" Rachael asked before she got all the way in through the front door.

"Of course you can, Rachael."

"Marie's here with me. Is that okay?"

"Yes, of course."

Rachael apologized for her behavior, albeit clumsily, and then went to her room.

"She's a smart girl, Ben," Marie said.

"Too smart if you ask me."

"I know. What I see is a young girl who has massive pent-up anger and lots of fears she doesn't even know she has. And she needs her mother."

Ben shot her a pathetic look.

"Rachael told me things about her mother, the various places they lived in Chicago, the company she kept, so I know how bad it was. But that doesn't make her miss her any less. That's all she knew for so long."

"I know. I know. I just thought the environment here was so much better, she'd do anything to stay. Boy, was I wrong."

"Don't you see, Ben? When you're taken out of your environment, no matter if it's good or bad, the new environment scares you. It's different. It's intimidating. Especially to a young girl. Look, I have an idea. I'll be back here for Christmas. What if you were to let Rachael spend her Christmas break with me, in Atchison. We'd have time for all the girl talk she needs. I think it would be a good break for her."

"Why would you want to take this on?"

"Because I care about her. And maybe I see a little of myself in her too. Believe it or not, we have a number of things in common. I think maybe I can help her."

Ben stared out the window past Marie for several seconds. "I suppose it couldn't be any worse than the mess we've created here. Okay, she can go."

CHAPTER 16

Girls Like Me

Marie spent Christmas with her family and then brought Rachael back with her to Atchison for four days. Marie could tell Rachael was excited about coming home with her—she must have called the Brookses household a half dozen times during Marie's visit.

Rachael had never been on a plane before. Marie watched her as she peered out the window at the vast blue sky above the clouds, sitting up so straight, looking so proud in her window seat of the plane. "Having fun?"

"This is so cool. None of my friends have ever flown."

"None *has* flown."

"No, they haven't, that's what I said."

"I meant 'has' is the correct verb. It's singular, like none."

Rachael gave her a "give me a break—I'm on vacation from school" look.

"Okay, I'll stop."

"Thanks. It's hard to be this fired up and talk good grammar too."

I give up.

Marie arranged for a limo to pick them up at the airport. Once home, she showed Rachael to the guest bedroom, which she had spiced up with new curtains and a bedspread that were more contemporary than what she'd had before. On the pillow she had put a stuffed bear that Karen told her was popular with teens.

"Hey, this is cool."

"So I'm officially hip?"

"Of course you are. Now my Dad, that's another story."

"Now, now. Don't be too hard on him. Just remember, he came into his dad role late in the game. That makes it a lot harder, you know."

"I know, I know." Rachael rolled her eyes. "Grandma tells me that all the time, but I came in late too. No one seems to notice that."

"What do you mean?"

"Nothing." She tossed her suitcase on the bed, her back toward Marie. Then she turned around and said, "There's no lock on this door."

"No, of course not. Is that a problem?"

"No. I'm just used to locks, that's all."

"Okay…well, let's get you settled in." Marie showed her where to hang her clothes. "We're going to have dinner at the local pizza parlor in about an hour. Karen's going to join us. Then I thought we could take in a movie. How's *Harvey*?"

"The one about the imaginary rabbit?"

"That's the one."

"That's for…okay, I can dig it."

They met Karen at Mario's and ordered the largest pizza on the menu, loaded, the way Rachael liked it. When Marie and Karen ordered a glass of wine, a look of horror swept across Rachael's face.

"You're gonna drink?" Rachael asked.

Marie glanced at Karen and then Rachael. "Yes. Is that okay?"

Rachael stared past Marie with an emotionally flat expression.

"Rachael?" No response. "Are you okay?" Marie asked.

Rachael smiled. "Sure," she said, snapping out of the momentary fugue that had engulfed her. Marie and Karen exchanged glances, but before either one could say anything, Rachael had changed the subject.

Marie asked about Rachael's school and her studies. She asked about her teachers and how her horseback riding lessons were coming along. Karen must have had other ideas about suitable subject matter. "So, do you have a boyfriend?" she asked.

Marie shot Karen a foreboding look. Karen shrugged. "No. Well, kinda," Rachael said. "And he's from a *good* family. Anyway, there's this boy in my homeroom that's cute. Nathan. And he likes me, I know."

"How do you know that?" Karen asked.

"Because Susan Jeffrey told me."

"How does she know?" Marie asked.

"Because Nathan told Johnny, and Johnny told Susan."

Marie and Karen exchanged glances.

"Boys are so immature," Rachael explained.

"I have news for you, Rachael," Karen advised. "That doesn't change much as they get older." All three laughed, and then Marie and Karen laughed some more.

"We're going to see *Harvey* after this," Marie told Karen. "Do you want to join us?"

"No, once was enough for me. Maurice and I saw it last weekend."

"Okay. Do you want to join us for breakfast tomorrow?"

"No, I'll grab something at home. Maurice is going to call me in the morning from New York." Karen smiled through a blush.

"Maurice is Karen's beau," Marie explained to Rachael.

"He's not my beau," Karen corrected.

"Is so."

"Is not."

"Every time she talks about him, she eats chocolate."

"Do not."

"Do so."

"And they talk about us," Rachael mocked.

Marie and Rachael returned to Marie's apartment just past eleven-thirty. "We should go to bed. It will be a long day tomorrow. Do you need anything, Rachael?"

"Are you kidding?"

Marie stared at her for several seconds. "Do you need anything, like…"

"Sorry. No, I don't. But do we really have to go to bed now? It's not that late."

"It's almost midnight. How does that compare to your normal bedtime?"

"Okay. Okay." More eye-rolling. "Good night, Marie."

"Good night, Rachael."

"Marie?"

"Yes?"

"Thanks for everything."

"You're welcome, sweetheart. Pleasant dreams…about H-A-R-V-E-Y."

"Oh, Marie."

* * *

Rachael was up, bathed, and dressed by seven the next morning. "So what's cookin' for today?"

"I thought after breakfast I would give you a tour of my little town. How does that sound?"

"Like crazy. Let's go."

After breakfast they walked to Marie's studio, where Rachael was introduced to Marie's staff. Rachael sat in Marie's high-back desk chair and twirled around several times. "You've got to be kidding. This is crazy. I can't wait 'til I'm on my own."

"And just what will you do then?"

"I don't know. Not have an office like this, that's for sure."

"Why not?"

"Girls like me don't end up in places like this."

"Says who? You work hard in school, and then in college…"

Rachael shot her a look. "No way am I goin' to college."

"Why not? A lot of girls go to college nowadays."

"Right. Where I come from, you're lucky to make it through high school."

"You're with your father now. Things will be different. My guess is he expects you to go to college. Everyone in his family has gone, including the women."

"Yeah, right. 'Til my mom comes back. Then we'll see what happens." She twirled around in the chair one more time. "*If* she comes back."

Rachael jumped out of Marie's desk chair and headed toward the door. "So what's next?" she asked.

Marie wanted to take Rachael by the shoulders and shake her, but her nurturing instincts prevailed. She took Rachael's arm. "Let's walk down to Karen's shop."

"Hey, you two. What's cookin'?" Karen said when they entered.

Good grief. Rachael's slang had gone epidemic.

"I'm just trying to be hip."

"Marie has tried that, too, Karen," Rachael said. "No offense, but you two are just a little too…"

"Hey! Careful. I can have you on the next plane back to Chicago, you know."

"What I was going to say is that you two are just a little too hip already."

"Nice save, sweetheart."

Karen walked Rachael to the jewelry counter. "Pick out any pair of earrings you want, Rachael. My Christmas present to you."

"Get out of here."

Rachael spent the next twenty minutes trying on almost every pair of earrings in the case while Karen told Marie about her Christmas with Maurice. "He laid a little bit of a bombshell on me Christmas Eve."

Judging by the look on Karen's face, what she was about to say wasn't going to be good. Marie braced herself for the worst. "What was that?"

"Turns out he's Jewish." She pulled out a chocolate candy bar from behind the cash register and began eating it.

"Jewish? And this is the first he's mentioned it?"

"Yeah. A year later, and now he tells me."

"So what does that do for the two of you? Are you okay with it?"

Karen searched the area where Rachael was standing and lowered her voice. "Here's the thing. I don't think it matters to me. His mother is Jewish, but he wasn't raised in that religion. He wasn't raised in any religion. But the fact that he didn't tell me up front bothers me."

Marie thought back to the numerous times she had been faced with whether or not to tell someone something important about her background, up front or otherwise.

"His mother the hypochondriac?"

"That's the one. He said they didn't go to temple because she thought there were too many germs there."

"Good grief."

"My dad's Jewish, but I'm not. No big deal," Rachael said.

"How did you hear what we were talking about all the way over there?" Marie asked.

"I have good ears."

"Rachael, you and your good ears may pick out any outfit in the store. My Christmas present to you," Marie said.

Karen finished complaining about Maurice while Rachael tried on clothes.

"So now what?" Marie asked.

"I'm giving it time to sink in. I'm hoping it won't matter as much in a few days."

After Marie paid Karen for Rachael's outfit, they left her shop and continued with the tour of Atchison.

The next day, Marie and Rachael started to get ready for the theater where they were going to see a local performance of *Oklahoma!*. "Can I wear my new outfit?" Rachael asked.

"Sure. Hurry up. We're going to leave in twenty minutes."

Five minutes later, Rachael came out wearing her new clothes. She had a wide smile on her face. "Thank you for the outfit." She rushed to Marie, gave her a hug, and mumbled something into Marie's chest that sounded a lot like "I love you."

The following day, they had lunch at Whitey's, a coffee shop frequented mostly by local business owners. Afterward, they walked back to Marie's apartment to pick up her car so she could show her the rest of the town.

"You sure know a lotta people here," Rachael said, referring to all the people in the restaurant who singled her out to say hello.

"It's a small community, not that different from St. Charles. Both our fathers know just about everyone there too."

"Yeah, but that's different."

"How so?"

"They're men."

"So?"

"Men are different."

Marie smiled. "I'll give you that, but what's that got to do with knowing people?"

"When men know a lot of people it means they're successful. My mom knew a lot of people, too, but..." She paused. "Can we change the subject?"

"Sure."

"Cool."

Marie drove by Amelia Earhart's birth home. "First female to fly solo across the Atlantic."

"Cool."

"You could learn a lot from her."

Rachael rolled her eyes. "Yeah, right."

Marie ignored her response. "She was determined to be a pilot, even though it was a man's world, and she didn't give up, even when she was faced with huge obstacles."

"Where is she today?"

"She and another pilot were attempting to fly around the world when their plane disappeared somewhere over the Pacific. She was just thirty-nine."

"That's crummy."

"You know what I think you should do when you go home?"

"No, what?"

"Go to the library and look her up. You may find her to be an interesting role model. One of her quotes I remember from college is, 'The woman who can create her own job is the woman who will win fame and fortune.' Isn't that a great quote?"

"Mm-hmm. From someone who probably grew up in some fancy house with rich parents who gave her everything she needed to be someone."

"Think again, Miss Know-It-All. She didn't have it so easy. Her father was an alcoholic, and she didn't always live with her parents because of it. She tried to attend college on two different occasions, but dropped out both times due to illness. When she decided she wanted to take flying lessons, she didn't have enough money for them, and neither did her parents, so she worked every job she could get her hands on, even driving a truck."

"That's cool. I get it."

"She was gutsy." Marie gave her a warm smile. "Like you." She put her arm around Rachael's shoulders. "C'mon. Let's go home."

The Edwards family was outside when they arrived home. Marie introduced Rachael to each of them: six-year-old Wayne, Jr.; three-year-old Fran; one-year-old Ellen; Julia; and Wayne, Sr. Julia invited Marie and Rachael to join them for dinner. Before Marie could say anything, Rachael blurted out, "Cool, what are you having?"

"Rachael..." Someone was going to have to teach that child manners.

Julia laughed. "That's okay, Marie. We're having pot roast, and there's plenty to go around." She looked directly at Rachael. "And peach cobbler for dessert."

Rachael's face lit up. "Can we, Marie?"

Marie smiled. "Of course. What time would you like us, Julia?"

"How's six?"

"Can we come early and help with anything?"

"If Rachael would like to come a little early and spend some time with the kids, that would be great."

Marie panicked. *Without me?* "Sure."

Once in her apartment, Marie and Rachael sat down in the living room. Marie gave her a solemn look, and Rachael burst out laughing.

"What's so funny?"

"The look on your face when Julia asked me to come down early to be with the kids. That was crazy."

"First of all, you should have waited for me to respond to her invitation to dinner. It wasn't your place to accept it. Secondly, it's Mrs. Edwards to you, not Julia. Third, it was rude to ask what they were having. And fourth..."

Rachael put her hands on her hips. "And if you're going to tell me you don't trust me with her kids..."

"I wasn't going to say that at all."

"I'm fourteen years old, and..."

Marie sighed. "I wasn't..."

"I'm sorry for the other things I did."

Marie peered deep into Rachael's eyes and into the wounded soul she suspected was in her all along but was too scared to emerge. "Why don't you wash up? It will be time for you to go down to Julia's before you know it."

"Marie?"

"Yes."

"I'm glad you invited me here."

"Me, too, hon."

* * *

The car ride to the airport the next day was a solemn one. Marie kept trying to lift Rachael's spirits, but Rachael kept sinking back into an unpleasant mood. While Marie thought she needed to snap out of it, she also had to keep reminding herself of Rachael's troubled past and the fact she had just turned fourteen.

Once seated in the gate waiting area, Marie presented Rachael with a small white box tied with a blue ribbon, Rachael's favorite color.

"What's this?"

"Open it."

She removed a gold bracelet from the box. A heart-shaped charm with her initials engraved on it dangled from the bracelet. She glanced up at Marie.

"Read the back."

Rachael turned the charm around.

Happy 14th birthday
Love, Marie

Tears welled up in Rachael's eyes and then rolled down her cheeks. She made no attempt to swipe them away. She leaned in for a hug. Marie held her until her shoulders stopped jerking.

"No one has ever done this much for me. Not in my whole life." She pulled herself away from Marie's hold and gave her a sad look. "So what's in this for you?"

Marie stared at her for several seconds. "What's in it for me? I'll tell you what's in it for me. It gives me great pleasure doing something nice for someone I care about."

Rachael stared back. "You know you just ended that sentence with a preposition."

The stewardess announced they were ready to board the plane. Rachael wiped her eyes and got up from her seat. She turned to Marie and saluted. "Later, gator."

* * *

On the hour-and-a-half-long drive home from the airport, Marie reflected on the past four days with Rachael. Her initial objective of merely wanting to be there for her, during a time period in her life when she so desperately needed a female adult to talk to, had been accomplished, but she hadn't been prepared for the delicate psyche she discovered when she peeled back a few of Rachael's layers. Most disturbing had been Rachael's comments about how success wasn't in the cards for someone like her.

She thought about Rachael's moodiness and unexpected reaction to things, like when she and Karen had ordered a glass of wine with dinner, and when she'd asked if there was a lock on her bedroom door. She rehashed their conversation outside of Amelia Earhart's home about how men knowing a lot of people was different from women knowing a lot of people, and the so-called uncles who had periodically stayed with them, men who got drunk and routinely beat up on her mother. Marie wondered what else these uncles had done.

Rachael's mother. How could she abandon her own daughter like that? It had been eighteen months since anyone had heard from her. Even if Marie gave Judy every benefit of the doubt, unless she was dead, there could be no legitimate excuse for not getting in touch with

Rachael or Ben, if for no other reason than to make sure Rachael was alright.

Marie thought about her own abandonment issue with her father, and while he at least provided for her financially while she was growing up, she still felt the consequences of his not being in her life in other ways. She could only imagine how Rachael felt.

CHAPTER 17

Segregation

The next day, worn out from craving more now than ever to someday have a family of her own and understanding the consequences of her racial identity, Marie phoned her father.

"Can I ask you a huge favor, Dad?"

"Sure. Anything."

"I want to see the South."

"The South?"

"Yes. I want to see where colored people live and how it differs from white people. I want to see where you and your parents and grandparents lived. I want to…"

"Hold on, daughter. Let's talk about this. What are you really looking to gain from going there?"

"I want to be closer to you and Claire. And everybody. I want to understand your background—which is my background too."

"Sweetheart, you don't want to see the South firsthand, believe me."

"Yes, I do."

"I'll tell you as much as you want to know about it. That will be just as good."

"No, it won't. I need to understand things for myself. I was going to ask you if you would go with me, but if you won't, I'm going alone."

"You're not going there alone."

"Why not? Maybe Karen will go with me."

"No. You don't know the lay of the land. You'll end up in the wrong places, and they'll eat you alive."

"Then you'll go with me?"

"It's not pretty, Marie. And it's not safe."

"But you know the lay of the land and where to go and not go."

"You're determined to do this."

"Yes."

She heard his sigh over the phone line. He waited several seconds before speaking. "Okay. I'll go with you, but only because I'm afraid you'll go alone and get into who knows what kind of trouble."

"Thank you, Dad."

"You know I love you, Marie."

He had never said those words before. He might have shown it, but he had never come out and said it.

"I love you too. When can we go?"

* * *

Two weeks later, Jonathan drove to Atchison, stayed overnight at Al & Rita's Bed & Breakfast, and picked Marie up at her apartment bright and early the next day, exactly three years to the day Marie had left Richard. The mid-May weather was perfect for a road trip.

"What have you done to your hair, child?" he asked Marie when she answered the door. Three years earlier, Marie had cut it short and dyed her almost-black hair to light brown when she felt she needed a change, a new beginning in her life. Now chin-length and back to it's natural color, the style was similar to the way her mother had worn her hair.

She spun around. "Do you like it?"

"Maybe I just need time to get used to it."

"You don't like it."

"No, it looks fine. Makes a big difference. I hardly recognize you." He paused. "I never realized until now just how much you look like your mother." He gave her a serious look. "You're sure you want to go through with this?"

Marie gave him a wide smile. "Oh, yes. More than anything else in the world." Marie had given this significant thought before, during, and after asking her father to take her there. She understood the dangers, or at least she thought she did. She recognized what she was about to witness could change her way of thinking altogether, but she was ready for that. She had to know her roots in order to understand who she was...and perhaps more importantly, who she was supposed to be.

They drove three hundred miles to St. Louis before stopping for lunch. The Missouri landscape wasn't much different from Kansas— wheat fields, expansive pastures scattered with cattle and small fenced-in pens for pigs. Not as many horse farms.

At lunch, Jonathan described the plantation where he had lived until he moved to St. Charles, thirty-six years earlier. "It was called Wisteria Belle, and when you see it—if it's stayed the same, that is—you'll know why. The main house had a huge front porch with massive two-story-high columns across the front of it and purple wisteria cascading down from the top of the columns all the way to the ground."

"It sounds gorgeous."

"It was. Of course, we never got to sit on that porch, or even go in the front yard, for that matter. It was strictly for the plantation owners and their white friends and family." He turned toward his daughter. "I hope you're ready for one hell of a story, my dear."

"Please don't leave anything out."

"The main house was huge, four stories and a basement. I'm going to guess there were at least twenty rooms in that house, including a ballroom, and all decorated to the hilt. I do know there were seven bathrooms because my father used to tell the story that his mother had to clean them all, every day."

"Were you ever in there?"

"The main house? Not very often. I wasn't allowed in the house unless the family was gone for the day, and that was when I was pretty young. I don't remember much."

"Didn't all that change when slaves were freed?"

"The way my father told it, after the slaves were freed, his family, like most of the slaves, continued to work at Wisteria Belle. They really had no other place to go. And then, like I told you before, my father was given fifty acres of land and several horses by his father. Louis Boone was his name, the plantation owner...my grandfather."

They finished lunch and returned to the car. "What was your father's name?"

"Samuel Brooks."

"So where did the name Brooks come from?"

"That was my grandmother's last name. Mariah Brooks."

"Did you ever meet your grandparents?"

"Both died before I was born. My grandmother, the house slave, died when my father was a teenager. By then he was a full-fledged slave. My grandfather died just a couple of years after he gave my father the land and horses. My father always said Louis probably knew he was dying and that's why he gave away most of his land."

They crossed over the Mississippi into the southern tip of Illinois and on to Kentucky.

"So after your father was given the land... Was it on the same plantation?"

"Yes."

"So then he managed his own land, with the horses, by himself?"

"He took on some fellow former slaves who had no place to go, and they ran it together. One of those men had a half sister whom my father married when he was forty-six. She was younger, much younger."

"How young?"

"In her twenties."

"Quite the age difference. What was her name?"

"Minervy Gulliglove."

Marie shot a glance at her father. He took his eyes off the road long enough to give her a smile.

"No one is quite sure of my mother's background. She was a Negro, but she obviously had some other race in her background. We're not sure. Actually she wasn't even sure where the name Gulliglove came from."

"Sounds like identity crises may run in our family."

Jonathan chuckled. "Well, let's hope we've put a stop to that once and for all. Now, going on with the story, my parents were married in 1889, and I was born the following year. I think I may have told you, I suspect she was pregnant before they got married. No one ever talked about that."

"What is your earliest memory?"

"We lived on the far corner of Wisteria Belle, far away from the main house, but our little ramshackle of a house was on a rise, so you could see the main house from it. That was my earliest memory, looking down at that mansion. I must have been four or five when I asked my father who lived there. He told me it didn't matter because we weren't welcome in that house."

"So this was probably thirty some years after the Emancipation Proclamation, right?"

"About that."

"But your father had relatives in that house—half brothers, you said?"

"The Emancipation Proclamation may have made it illegal to have slaves on paper, but it didn't change things all that much. Thirty years later, Negroes were still treated like shit. Sorry. Excuse my language. But it's the truth. My father would have no more tried to talk to or visit anyone in that house than they would have come knocking on his door. It just wasn't done."

"So how old was your mother when she died?"

"She was thirty-seven. I was ten. Dad was in his fifties." Jonathan pulled off the main road at the sign which read, *Welcome to Frankfort, Kentucky's State Capital*. "We'll stay here. I know a nice hotel where we can get in." Marie raised her eyebrows. "We're at the top of the Deep South. Still completely segregated."

"So what does that mean for me?"

Jonathan didn't answer immediately. "Segregation works both ways. Negroes aren't allowed in some places and vice versa. I'm counting on you being accepted in a Negro hotel, especially after I introduce you as my daughter. It's not that unusual to see very light-skinned Negroes in this part of the country."

Marie's heart raced. Up until now, ever since learning of her true ethnicity, her anxiety had stemmed from knowing she was part colored but passed for white. Looking white and trying to pass for colored was completely foreign.

"Are you okay?"

"Yes. Well, no, to be honest. I'm starting to feel uncomfortable. Am I overreacting?"

"I don't know if you're overreacting or not. But I can tell you if I get any sense that it's not a safe place for you, we'll leave." He heaved a big sigh. "Marie, you're going to see a lot on this trip. And maybe it will bring you closer to my side of the family and maybe it won't, but what I want to say is, never lose sight of the fact that your outward appearance shouldn't define who you are. I know it does to other people, but it shouldn't to you. Do you understand that?"

"Mm-hmm. I do. But here's the thing. When I'm with whites, I feel uncomfortable on the inside, because I know I'm not one of them, not totally anyway, but they think I am. But when I'm around Negroes, I feel uncomfortable on the outside, because they think I'm not one of them. Does that make any sense?"

"Oh, I understand what you're saying. It's not easy. I know that. And I wish I had all the answers for you, but I don't. You know who you are, and you're confused about who you should be. And when I or anyone else tells you to just be yourself, you say, 'But that doesn't work very well.' Well, you have to figure out how to make it work. No one can do that for you."

They approached the hotel. "I was thinking of separate rooms," Jonathan said. "Are you okay with that?"

She didn't know which scenario was more daunting—being alone or with him in the same room.

"Marie, the farther south we go, the worse it gets. I tried to prepare you for this, but…"

"I know. I insisted. I'm sure it will be fine." She paused. "Let's keep separate rooms and see how that goes, okay?"

"Welcome to the South, my dear."

At the hotel, Jonathan asked for a room for himself and one for his daughter. The clerk gave him a curious glance but handed him two room keys without asking any questions. Jonathan handed Marie her key with slight smile.

"You okay?"

"I'm fine."

That night as she lay in bed, Marie mulled over all the family history Jonathan had shared with her. She thought she had appreciated Jonathan, his family, and his life fairly well up until this point, and she harbored nothing but good feelings over it, all of it. Now she wasn't so sure. All of a sudden she felt overwhelmed by the family history.

One of Jonathan's comments kept surfacing in her mind. "Segregation works both ways," he had said. Segregation was a word Marie was learning to hate. If she lived in the South, she'd be only one shade of skin color away from not being able to use the same public restrooms as white people, get the same education, work in the same jobs, and ride in the front of the bus. Segregation. She had looked the word up in the dictionary shortly after meeting Doretha Scott. "To separate or set apart from others or from the main body or group; isolate."

Isolate. Like they had some contagious disease. The main body or group. They were hurtful words, ones Marie thought she would never understand. But what troubled her even more was she hadn't thought much about segregation when she was going through life thinking she was white.

She had heard the term "Jim Crow laws" but didn't know what they meant, so she had gone to the library to research it. Statutes enacted in the South as far back as 1880, they were designed to legalize segregation between Negroes and whites. The name was derived from a character in a popular minstrel song of all things.

> *Old Jim Crow*
> *Where you been baby?*
> *Down Mississippi and back again*
> *Old Jim Crow, don't you know,*
> *It's all over now*

She had read the full lyrics a few times, but didn't fully get the connection. She read further and found the term Jim Crow originated when a white minstrel show performer blackened his face with burnt cork and danced a silly jig while singing the song. He had created the character after seeing a crippled old black slave dancing and singing a song ending with these chorus words:

> *Wheel about and turn about and do jis so,*
> *Eb'ry time I wheel about I jump Jim Crow.*

So what does all this mean for me? she asked herself for the millionth time. *How do you segregate someone like me?*

CHAPTER 18

Wisteria Belle

At breakfast the next morning, Marie asked how much farther it was to Wisteria Belle.

"I thought we'd have lunch in Greenville, South Carolina. We should reach Chesterfield by dinner. That's where Wisteria is. The only problem is that I've been away so long, I don't know where we can have dinner or even stay, so that could be an adventure."

Marie had a feeling he was downplaying a potentially disquieting situation so she wouldn't fret over it. But she did anyway.

They reached Greenville by two o'clock and searched for a place to eat lunch. When Jonathan reached a fork in the road, he veered to the right. "We're not going to eat in this part of town, but I want you to see it anyway."

Marie observed the nicely maintained homes on either side of the road. After they drove for a mile or so, the residential section turned commercial—hardware store, real estate office, clothes stores, and restaurants.

"This looks like a nice place to stop. What's wrong with having lunch here?"

He slowed down. "Look closely at the signs in the windows."

She gasped at the first crudely made sign. Prominently displayed in the window of a restaurant, it read

NO
Nigger or Negro
ALLOWED
Inside Building

The next one read

Colored Served
In Rear

Three signs hung over the doors of a public bathroom.

White Women   White Men   Coloreds

She shook her head in disbelief. "I had no idea it would be like this."

"I know you didn't. I tried to tell you."

"I know."

Jonathan turned the car around and drove back to the fork in the road. This time he took a left turn.

Marie wondered how anyone could live in the tiny run-down houses, some with no front doors, and others with gaping holes in the roofs. Skinny little shoeless colored children played in the grassless yards, their clothes dirty and torn. The unmistakable aroma of cotton, mingled with the earthy smell of the dirt the children were kicking up as they ran through the yards, permeated the air and drifted up her nose. "It's like being in a different world."

A dilapidated building with a car repair shop on one side and a coffee shop on the other stood at the end of the street. Jonathan slowed down the car but continued driving. "I'm not going to stop here either."

He drove back to the white section of town to the back of the restaurant with the sign directing Negroes to the rear of the building. He picked up two sandwiches to go and drove a half mile to a park they had seen on their way in.

The sun still shone brightly, and the scent of blooming dogwoods wafted through the air. Jonathan parked the car, and they headed toward a park bench. Marie sat down, but Jonathan stayed standing, his gaze directed beyond her.

"What's the matter?" she asked.

He continued to stare past her, the look on his face soulful. She got up and followed his gaze. The sign read:

Negroes and Dogs
Not Allowed

They walked back to the car in silence. Jonathan turned on the ignition but didn't put the car in gear. Marie couldn't look at him. She tried to conceal her reaction but didn't have what it took to hold back her emotions. She buried her face in her hands and sobbed. Jonathan leaned over and held her until her shoulders stopped shaking. He held her face and forced her to look at him.

"I tried to tell you."

"I know."

After eating their sandwiches in the car by the side of the road, they drove another hundred and fifty miles to Chesterfield. When they reached the middle of town, a smile crept over his face.

"What are you thinking?" she asked him.

"I was just thinking of when me and my friends would go to the swimming hole that was on one of the neighboring plantations. We were eight or nine I guess. One of us would stand as lookout because if we were caught, it would mean a terrible whuppin' by the landowners."

"So did you ever get whipped?"

"Caught, yes. Whipped, no. I was a spindly kid, but a very fast runner."

The sign for Wisteria Belle Plantation appeared to have been recently painted and held a prominent position twenty-five feet from the long driveway leading to the house. Jonathan pulled off the side of the road and parked the car by a narrow clearing where the main house was in clear view.

Marie drew in a long breath. "It's beautiful." The wisteria were in full bloom—hundreds, maybe thousands of clusters of large purple flowers pouring down like a waterfall all the way to the ground from the second story balcony. Only the front door and slivers of the two-story windows peeked through the dramatic flowering drape.

The house sat back at least two hundred yards from the road. Two rows of thirty-foot-tall live oak trees, their branches forming a perfect canopy, lined a wide path to the house. Stalactites of jade-green moss dangled from their branches halfway to the ground, causing an eerie, almost unwelcoming greeting for a visitor approaching the house.

"I've never seen anything like it."

"It was something else," Jonathan said, his voice fraught with sadness.

"What's the matter?"

"It's been more than thirty years since I've been here, and all I can think about is the life my grandmother must have had here—a slave, raped by the reprehensible owner of this place at the age of eighteen and dead by twenty-five."

"It's hard to believe...hard to understand."

"And it happened all the time...I mean all the time. That's why the woman who made that remark to you in Marshall Field's that day said what she did. She was from the South. She'd seen people who looked just like you many times. It was very common practice."

"Did that at least end when the slaves were freed?"

"Not entirely. You have to understand, freedom was a misnomer really. And even after they were so-called free, most Negroes didn't think freedom was possible in reality anyway. My own people stayed here and worked after they were freed. I was the first to leave."

"Do you think we can see where you lived?"

"Maybe." Jonathan put the car in gear and proceeded down the road they had come in on, turning onto the first road on the right past the main house. The dirt road was wide enough for only one car. He drove for ten minutes before slowing down.

"See over there, on the rise?"

Marie looked in the direction of his gaze to a row of small unpainted houses.

"There was only one house when I lived there. I'm not sure now which one it was. They all look the same to me."

"They look pretty small."

"Just one room with a fireplace for cooking and cold nights. There was a small loft upstairs where I slept. And you can't see it, but there was a rather large front porch where we sat most evenings after dinner. Looks like the outhouse is gone." His facial expression was placid. "I see the houses still aren't painted."

"Why is that?"

"When I was living there, we didn't want the owners of the big house to think we didn't feel inferior to them, and an unpainted house helped to do that."

"Tell me the good memories."

"There was a swimming hole on the main property, far enough from the big house so no one could see us there. Felt pretty good on those hot, sticky summer days."

"Did you have friends to play with?"

"A few, but most of the colored kids were working the fields during the day."

"How young?"

"Four, five years old. If they weren't picking cotton, they were pumping water and bringing it to their daddies or chopping wood or running errands. There were a few kids like me whose parents wouldn't allow them to work the fields, but never enough for a good game of kickball or anything. Sometimes we could get white kids to join us, but if we were caught playing with them, we would get in big trouble."

Jonathan turned the car around and headed toward the main road. "Let's see if we can find a place to eat dinner and a hotel for the night."

They had to drive to Bennettsville before finding a decent restaurant that allowed Negroes to come inside to eat. The patrons were mostly white. Before they left, Jonathan asked the colored waitress if she knew of a hotel where they would be welcomed.

The waitress glanced at Marie and then gave him a puzzled look before she said, "If she goes in alone, you can go just about anywhere."

Marie and Jonathan faced each other and nodded. On the way out, a man's voice blurted out, "So long, nigger lover." The laughter was daunting.

Marie slowed her step, wanting to turn around and say something back, but Jonathan took her arm and guided her out the door instead. "It's not worth it, believe me."

They drove three miles to the edge of town where Jonathan had previously noticed an inn. He parked his car out of view of the inn's entrance and let Marie go in and make the reservation. When she came back to the car twenty minutes later, she told Jonathan about the back door where she could let him in. So he drove around to the back, parked the car, and waited for her to emerge from the building.

"There's more than one way to skin a cat," he said as they climbed up the back stairs to their room.

The Victorian-style Briden Inn had once been someone's home, they learned after reading about the history of it in their room. Converted to an inn in 1925, the owners maintained the home's original lush gardens and dogwood-lined walkways around the property.

The next day they drove ninety miles to Charlotte, where Jonathan had made arrangements for his driver, Walter, to pick up his car and drive it back to St. Charles. Jonathan and Marie would fly back to Chicago.

The drive to Charlotte was ninety miles. Jonathan took Marie through Cheraw in South Carolina and Wadesboro, Monroe, and Matthews in North Carolina—all small towns with plenty of dirt-poor Negroes living in crowded, rundown shanties with no running water or electricity. He relayed stories to Marie that had been handed down by his mother and father.

"Growing up in the South as a colored person was downright humiliating. By the time I was born, it was better, but still not good. My father said when he was growing up, the white folks made them feel even more helpless, ignorant, and dependent. And the rules were much stricter then."

"The rules?"

"The rules about how to act around whites. Social etiquette, they called it. I have a better name for it."

"What were some of these rules?"

"Like when you were walking down the sidewalk and a white person was coming toward you, you had to step to the side and hang your head down. And if you were wearing a hat, you'd best have taken it off. And if you were a man, and the white person was a woman, you'd better not look her in the eye."

"Really?"

"Really. And you were never allowed to eat in the same room as a white person. It didn't matter if you were the one who prepared their food, you were never allowed to eat within their viewing distance."

"So what happened if you broke the rules?"

"Anything from a tongue lashing to a whipping to a lynching."

"You'd get lynched for looking at a woman?"

"You bet. And then it would be a public lynching and people would come from all over to watch it. They'd even bring their children."

"That's hard to believe. They don't still do that, do they?"

"There are still lynchings to this day."

"How did they get that way?"

"Who?"

"The whites."

"Greed, I think. The more subordinate they could keep the Negroes, the less it cost them to keep them working for them."

"Didn't anyone stand up for you? There were no Negro politicians or lawyers back then?"

"My father used to talk about Booker T. Washington all the time. He was born into slavery himself. In fact, his mother was a slave, and his father was white."

Marie recalled the story Doretha Scott had told her about her grandmother. She relayed it to her father. "I remembered learning about him in school when Doretha told me he gave her grandmother's eulogy. He helped build better schools for Negroes, didn't he?"

"That and much more. He was our spokesman in Washington and gained respect from some very influential white people. You should read his book, *Up from Slavery*. You'd appreciate his writings."

When they were a few miles outside of Charlotte, the landscape changed. The homes were bigger and in much better condition. Redbud trees with intense pink flowers lined the streets. Taller buildings lined the horizon.

They stopped for lunch at the Dunhill Hotel and then waited for Walter in the lobby afterward. Jonathan talked more about influential Negroes who had made a difference during his lifetime, including Thurgood Marshall and his work for the NAACP, and Harvard graduate W. E. B. DuBois.

Walter dropped them off at the airport before heading back to St. Charles. On the plane, they talked about their trip.

"Are you glad you went?" Jonathan asked.

"Yes. I am. But it wasn't anything like I expected. I knew I would see poor people who lived in rundown homes, but I didn't expect it to be that bad. And I really didn't expect to be treated that way…the signs and all. I wasn't ready for that."

"Initially, you said you wanted to feel closer to my family—your family, your roots—by seeing where we came from. Do you feel that?"

Marie thought about his question. "Yes, but not because I went there."

"How so?"

"I feel closer to you and your ancestors because of the stories you told. Thank you for…"

"You're going to get an 'I told you so.' You know that."

Marie laughed. "Okay, so you did tell me that. But I'm glad I went anyway. And I'm so glad I saw Wisteria Belle. You know what's so amazing to me?"

"No. What?"

"You look at that house and you think it's so beautiful. You picture big gorgeous furniture inside, a huge dining room and lavish bedrooms, with elegant people dressed to the nines. But if you're not familiar with this way of life, you would have no idea it looks like it does because of hundreds of poorly treated Negroes who have done all the cotton-picking that brought in revenue, and who cleaned the house, raised the white children, and cooked all the meals. It's just not right."

"There are a lot of things that aren't right in this world, my dear. A lot of things."

* * *

Marie took off from work the day following her return from South Carolina to reflect on everything she had observed and everything her father had said.

Surprisingly, she had been thinking a lot about Paul lately. She thought there was a bigger lesson to be learned from her brief relationship with him. It had to be more than merely not letting the lure of a relationship obfuscate what the man was all about and whether his values and beliefs were compatible with hers. She just wasn't sure what that lesson was yet.

Lamenting the fact that her primary objective of feeling more connected to the Negro side of her ethnicity had not been entirely accomplished on the trip, she tried to understand why. After all, those were her people. She kept going back to the Shakespeare line Claire had quoted to her when they had first met: "To thine own self be true." She looked up the quote in its entirety.

"This above all: To thine own self be true, and it must follow—as the night and the day—thou cans't not be false to any man."

She thought about what it meant to be true to herself and concluded she must first know who she was, and to know who she was meant knowing her goals, values, wants, and needs—not what others expected of her, but what she truly felt in the core of her inner self.

And then it hit her. Until she was true to herself, she could never succeed in a relationship, no matter who the man was or the values he held. Because if she didn't know her own goals, values, wants, and needs, she could never determine compatibility with anyone. Why hadn't she thought of that before? Had that also been true about Richard? Before she knew her real ethnicity, she'd thought she had had a good handle on what she wanted out of her marriage, and it worked. But when she discovered who she really was, all that changed. And right around that same time, she realized Richard wasn't who she thought he was. No wonder it all fell apart.

That made her think about her inner versus her outer self. Her inner self was not reflected in her outer self, nor could it ever be, but was that important? Though she was certain she couldn't keep pretending to be something she wasn't and be alright with herself, she also wasn't sure that meant ignoring her outer self, how others perceived her. She invited Karen over the following evening.

"Your hair!"

"I know. What do you think?"

"I had forgotten all about your natural hair color. I was so used to it being light brown. I like it."

"Me too." She shared with Karen her thoughts about how she needed to determine exactly who she was in order to be true to herself.

"So what *are* your goals?" Karen asked.

"Aside from the obvious, like being financially secure, healthy, and happy, I want to stop pretending to be something I'm not. I'm not willing to settle for half of my reality. Now that I know the whole of my reality, I want to live it."

"Have you figured out how to do that?"

"No, that's the problem, I guess."

"So what more do you need to get out of life in order to live your 'whole reality,' as you put it?"

Marie stared out the window at the last remnant of the red-orange sunset disappearing behind the tree line across the street, hoping this discussion was not going to lead to an argument. She shook her head. "I don't know."

"What's keeping you from being who you really are?"

"I don't know that either."

"You've said before that you don't like living a lie. But isn't it only a lie if you allow others to influence how you think about yourself? I mean, *you* know who you are. What difference does it make what others think of you?"

Marie continued to stare out the window and sipped her wine while she mulled over Karen's words. "In other words, if I live what I believe to be a truthful life, then I'm being true to myself, and that's all that matters." She paused to reflect. "Why was I having so much trouble figuring that out?"

"Sometimes it's the obvious that's so hard to see."

"Another one of your mother's sayings?"

"No, I came up with that all by myself!"

CHAPTER 19

Camelot—Then and Now

The next day Marie called her lawyer, Michael Cavanaugh, and advised him to move ahead with divorce proceedings based on Richard's felony conviction. Then she called her father to tell him of her decision. Jonathan congratulated her and acknowledged the degree of fortitude it must have taken to proceed with it.

"Someone I know who knows a lot about guns told me, 'Your finger has to stay off the trigger until you're ready to shoot.' I think now I'm finally ready to shoot," Marie said.

When she got off the phone with him, she called Karen, who suggested they do something special to celebrate.

"You know where I've always wanted to go?" Karen asked. "Alaska."

"Alaska? Like near the North Pole Alaska?"

"That would be the one."

"Why on earth would you want to go there?"

"Because it's different."

"It's different, alright."

"Ed and I talked about going there someday, and so that's one place I never wanted to go...after he died, that is. Now I see you making this hard decision to confront Richard with a divorce, and well, if you can do that, I can go to Alaska. Want to go?"

"I don't know, Karen. Alaska?"

"We'll make it a celebration trip. C'mon! We'll celebrate our braveries. Is that a word?"

"Alaska..."

"Want to know what my mom used to say?"

"Lay it on me."

"She said, 'Losing something can lead you to positive paths.'"

"Where on earth did she get all these sayings?"

"I don't know 'cause she didn't read much." Karen laughed. "In fact, whenever she picked up a book, the alcohol would kick in before she finished the first page, and she'd be out like a light. I swear, a copy of *Life with Father* sat on the end table in our living room for four years without her ever getting past page one. I still have that book, vodka stains and all." Her mother had died of an alcoholic seizure two weeks before Karen's wedding.

Marie shook her head. "But Alaska? Why not Hawaii or someplace in Europe?"

"Because you've already been there. You need someplace you've never been before, and I need to get past my Ed roadblocks."

"I've never been to Europe, Karen. Let's think Paris."

"If I ever have the opportunity to go to Paris, no offense, honey, but it won't be with you."

When Karen had an idea stuck in her craw, it would take dynamite to get it out. "Okay. Alaska it is."

"Really? You'll go?"

"I'll go."

* * *

They planned to be in Alaska in the middle of June. Before they left for the trip, Karen asked Marie about Barry's gun shop.

"I was cleaning out the basement the other day and ran across the gun Ed used to...well, to kill himself. I had forgotten it was even down there. I don't know what to do with it. Can't just throw it away. Wonder if Barry would buy it from me."

"If not, I'll bet he may know someone who would."

"Would you go with me?"

"Sure."

They drove Karen's 1949 Ford convertible with the top down, the brightly colored kerchiefs on their heads flapping in the breeze. When the "Stone Guns and Ammo" sign came into view, Marie said, "There it is. On the right."

When they entered the shop, Marie couldn't help but notice Barry stand up a little straighter, tuck in his stomach, and quickly pitch a *Playboy* magazine under the counter. "Hi! How's the best shot this side of the Missouri River?" he teased through a dimpled grin.

She felt a warm flush creep up her neck. "I'm fine. And you?"

"Couldn't be better." He gave Karen an abrupt glance and then focused on Marie. "I don't get many girls in here. It sure is a nice change of scenery." Marie hadn't noticed before how luminous his blue eyes were.

"Barry, this is my friend, Karen. She has a rifle she wants to sell, and I thought maybe you could help her." Barry followed the two women to Karen's car, guiding Marie out the door with his hand in the small of her back. Karen opened the trunk and showed him the gun.

He picked it up, made sure it wasn't loaded, and then pulled it up to his cheek to peer through the sight. As she watched Barry handle it, Karen's expression appeared to reflect the morbid memories associated with the gun.

"Not bad. I don't buy used guns myself, but I could keep it here if you want, and if I hear of someone who's interested in buying it, I could put you in touch with them." Barry's gaze fell upon the pair of antique German handcuffs that lay between the spare tire and first aid box. He picked it up gingerly between his thumb and index finger, the way a new father might pick up a dirty diaper. "Come alongs?" He gave Karen a teasing smile. "So...do ya use these much?"

The blood quickly rose up to Karen's face. Marie stood to the side laughing.

"Well, I sort of collect them."

"You have more?"

"Oh, she has tons more, and leg irons too," Marie said through laughter. "And a ball and chain."

Karen lowered her head and drew a circle in the dirt with the toe of her shoe. "Okay, you can stop now."

Barry gave Karen a suspicious once-over before setting the object back down in the trunk. Then he picked up the rifle, and the three of them headed inside where he said he'd write up a consignment receipt.

Turning to Marie, he asked, "Have you done any target shooting since you were here last?"

"No, but I wish there was someplace close to me where I could. I must admit, I really enjoyed it."

"You're welcome to come to my place anytime." He ran his fingers through his hair and smiled just enough to make the corners of his mouth turn up. "You've got my number, right?"

"Yes, I think I do."

"Here's my card in case you don't." He put his thumbs in the belt loops of his jeans in a cowboy stance. "Call me anytime, and I'll take you to the next level."

Marie wasn't sure what he meant by that.

"Of shooting."

"Oh. Okay."

"Well, see ya 'round."

"What a nice guy," Karen said once they were back in the car.

"Mm-hmm."

"You're going to call him, right?"

"I wish there was someplace in Atchison to target shoot. Do you know of any place?"

"Marie. He was so flirting with you. And he couldn't have been any cuter if he had been holding a cocker spaniel puppy. Why not call him?"

"Karen, after Paul, I may never be interested in any man ever again."

"C'mon. That's just nonsense."

"Who's to say Barry doesn't hold the same views as Paul...and just about everyone else out there? No, I may be done. And let's not forget, I'm still married." She wasn't ready to admit it, but she did miss being with someone. "And besides, he has my number. If he was that interested, he would call me."

"You don't know men very well, do you? Most of the time they need to be led to where they want to be. Look, your marriage has long been over. Anyone can see that. You're going to divorce him. And Barry is obviously smitten with you."

"Smitten? You are so funny. Although he did ask me out."

"Really? When?"

"After a few shooting lessons."

"And you said no?"

"Yes, I said no. I told him then I was married."

Karen shook her head. "Here's what I would do."

"Whatever you're about to say, I'm not going there. If I'm going to try another relationship, which I'm not even sure I'll ever do, I'm going to be divorced first."

"Well, have it your way, but..."

"I know. I know. You'd do it differently."

Karen rolled her eyes. "You bet I would."

"So why don't *you* make a play for him?"

"It's you he's interested in, Marie. He didn't look twice at me."

"And if he knew who my father was, he wouldn't look twice at me either."

"If you say so."

* * *

They left for Alaska the following month, right after Michael Cavanaugh told Marie the divorce papers had been filed and Richard had been given ninety days to appeal.

They flew into Fairbanks and checked into the Wedgewood Resort the first night. Karen had been right. The new scenery was a welcomed change.

The next day they rode a train through Denali National Park, where they stayed two days. In Anchorage, they took a sightseeing tour and a floatplane ride over the glaciers. Twenty-three continuous hours of daylight took some getting used to.

Next, they went on a three-day cruise on the *M.S. Noordstrom*, where they met photographer Adam White. It was close to ten o'clock in the evening when Adam walked into the bar, scanned the crowded room, and asked Marie and Karen if he could join them at their table. He was tall, with dark curly hair and a welcoming smile. Marie thought he looked harmless enough and welcomed him to join them.

They sat there for hours as Adam told them fascinating stories about his adventures all over the world, photographing wildlife and nature. Contracted by *National Geographic* to photograph Alaskan wildlife, he shot during the day while the ship was in port, and in the evenings he mostly sat in the ship's bar and drank beer. The three of them drank and talked into the wee hours of the morning.

Adam's flirtatious demeanor made it obvious he was attracted to Marie. But his attention was the last thing she wanted or needed, so she tried to brush it off. Later in their room, Karen pushed it.

"Go for it! He's a nice guy. He lives in Indianapolis. You'll never have to see him again. So why not?"

"I have no interest, Karen. *You* go for him."

"He's not interested in *me.*"

"Well, I'm not interested in him."

On the second day, Karen became seasick and had to stay in the cabin for the rest of the day. Marie stood on the deck waiting for the ship to port in Sitka, where she had planned to do some souvenir shopping, when Adam walked up behind her. "Where's your friend?" he asked. He had more camera equipment hanging around his neck and off his shoulders than she thought one person could carry.

"Seasick," she responded.

Adam's face lit up. "Would you like to accompany me on a shoot?"

Not able to think of a polite way to decline fast enough, she said, "Okay." They walked down the gangplank together. "What are you shooting?"

"Eagles."

"You're kidding." She pictured them soaring high in the sky and wondered how he would ever get a good shot at them.

They were walking down the boardwalk in the harbor when Adam dropped his equipment in a patch of grass and readied his tripod and camera for a picture. Marie looked up into the sky, but she didn't see anything. She turned back toward him and looked in disbelief at where he had focused his camera.

There, perched on a low branch of a tree not more than twenty feet from them, sat a bald eagle. She had no idea eagles were that big…or that majestic. It sat motionless on the branch, looking right at Adam, its blackish brown feathers gently moving in sync with the breeze coming in off the water.

Adam clicked off several shots and then took a step back to admire the bird without hindrance from the camera. "What do you think?" he asked without taking his eyes off the eagle.

"I think he's amazing."

"It's a she."

"How can you tell?"

"I'm not always right, but this one has an unusually deep beak, and she's large. Females are generally larger than males."

Marie studied its massive hooked yellow beak. "I'll bet that beak could do some serious harm."

"Just ask the salmon."

"That's what they eat?"

"Yeah, they'll snatch a salmon out of the water, but they'll also feed on carrion."

Without warning, the eagle let out a high-pitched twitter and sprung from its perch, its piercing eyes focusing on something in the distance.

Marie's glance moved toward the harbor where a half dozen other eagles were perched on pilings. "Just amazing." Adam joined her gaze and pointed his camera on another large female just about to take off, clicking the shutter twenty times while the bird glided up into higher altitude.

"What a wingspan!"

"Well over six feet, I'd say."

Adam took over two hundred photographs in all. Picture-worthy subjects were easy to find. At one point he let Marie look through the lens, putting his arm around her while he explained what she was seeing, what he wanted her to capture. She felt uncomfortable with his arm around her but found the birds so captivating, she allowed it.

Marie found herself smiling as they walked back to the ship, and when he asked her if she wanted to join him for dinner, she agreed, knowing Karen would still be holed up in their cabin. They talked about his work during dinner and how he planned to spend the rest of his time in Alaska. He put his arm around her waist while they walked to the Eagle's Nest for a nightcap. He ordered a bottle of wine.

Fascinated with his work, she leaned in with her elbows on the table and continued asking him questions. Sitting with his legs outstretched, ankles crossed, and his left hand supporting the side of his face, he responded to her questions, but only with short, abrupt answers. When his eyes kept wandering around the room, she changed the subject and asked him about his family.

He sat up straight, put his arms on the table, and leaned in toward her. "Look, honey. This has all the makings of a fuckin' one-night stand, not a remake of *Camelot*, for God's sake. Can we skip the small talk?"

Marie got up from the table. "No, but we *can* skip the one-night stand."

She told Karen about the incident as soon as she returned to their cabin. "So this is why half the time I say I'm done with men. Who needs that?"

"Hey, everyone needs a little romp in the hay now and again."

"Karen!"

Their trip ended in Vancouver. All in all it was a trip they would remember for a long time, and Adam White was a name Marie would throw up in Karen's face for a long time too.

* * *

During the weeks following her Alaska trip, Marie allowed her work to save her from dwelling too much on whether Richard would appeal the divorce proceedings.

With few exceptions, Atchison local businesses were owned and managed by men, and more than a few eyebrows had been raised when she had opened her interior design business doors two years earlier. But not about to have her goals and aspirations diminished by that fact, and not afraid to go against the grain, Marie forged ahead as if she were one of them. And it worked.

Earlier that year, Marie had been elected president of a floundering group of local business owners she had joined when she had first opened her business. She eagerly accepted the challenge and grew the group from fifteen members to close to forty. Karen was voted secretary, and they renamed the group TABOO (The Atchison Business Owners Organization). When word about the group spread to neighboring towns, similar groups, all modeled after theirs, were formed.

Marie was honored when the American Institute of Decorators asked her to create a committee and forum that would award national prizes for best interior designs. After a few months of brainstorming, she and her committee members determined prizes for best-designed furniture, fabric, and wallpaper. The AID board liked their proposal, but when Marie suggested that the award-winning pieces be displayed in New York's Metropolitan Museum of Art, the AID president, who was originally from Chicago, suggested the Chicago Art Institute instead.

Since Marie was the committee member who lived closest to Chicago, she was asked to work with the Art Institute when the winning designs were to go on display, requiring her to make two trips to Chicago. The initial trip went well. The second trip was scheduled for the middle of September.

It was a pleasant walk from Chicago's Union Station to the Blackstone Hotel on Michigan Avenue where Marie was staying. The morning clouds were gradually shooed away by a gentle breeze, warming her face as she strolled down the avenue. She thought it odd not to see streetcars. When Marie had lived in Chicago, the Green Hornets, as they were called, ran on almost every downtown street. Now cars and buses had replaced them.

As she got closer to her hotel, Marie saw that a crowd of people had formed outside of it and was told Governor Adlai Stevenson was inside the hotel meeting with some Chicago bureaucrats and businessmen. Stevenson was someone many Chicagoans wanted to see run for president in 1952. Marie pushed her way through the crowd into the hotel lobby and to the front desk.

After getting settled in her room, she headed out for her meeting at the Art Institute. Afterward, near the end of her five-block walk back to her hotel, she saw him standing outside the main entrance. It was too late to turn back.

He wore a feral grin of triumph. "Hello, Marie. How was your meeting?"

"What are you doing here, Richard?"

"I live here. Remember?"

She tried to get past him, but he took a step sideways to block her. "Can we stop inside for a drink?" he asked.

She looked him in the eye and held her head high. "I see no purpose in that."

His face was calm, including his eyes. "You don't think you at least owe me that?" he asked in a soft voice.

Marie took in a deep breath and let it out slowly. "Okay." Richard led her across the lobby to a sitting area farthest from the groups of people still wanting to get a glimpse of the governor.

"How are you?" he asked.

"I'm fine, and you?"

"Not so fine. As you know, I was served with divorce papers."

She didn't say anything.

"I want you to withdraw it." His gaze didn't leave her face.

"Why, Richard? We'll never have a life together again. You know that."

"You know something? I *do* know that. I know that now. But that's not why I'm asking you to withdraw it."

"Why then?"

"I'm doing it for you. My felony conviction was expunged from my record, and so your grounds for divorce won't hold any water in court."

Her heart sank.

"So why let it go through the court process when it will obviously be denied?"

"How did you get that expunged?"

Richard raised an eyebrow.

"Sorry. Stupid question." She peered deep into his eyes. "So now what?"

"My lawyer tells me I have all sorts of grounds to divorce you."

Marie gulped and hoped he didn't notice. She held her breath waiting for him to continue.

"And while this still isn't what I want, I'm willing to file...to make things easy for you."

"Why would you do that if it isn't what you want?"

He gave her a weak smile. "When you took that little road trip to South Carolina with your father, I knew I had lost you for good. I know you too well, sweetheart, and while I can't say I understand it, I can't compete with that. So...I may as well let you off the hook, let you go." He leaned in closer. "And believe me when I tell you, this is the hardest thing I've ever done in my life. Because, despite whatever you think of me, whatever you think you know about me, I have never loved anyone like I loved you, and I don't think I ever will."

Richard stood up and turned away from her. He took one step and then hesitated. After a brief moment, he continued his stride through the lobby and out the front door of the hotel.

Marie remained in her chair, staring straight ahead, trying to remain calm, and trying not to cry. It almost didn't matter that he knew about the trip with her father, that he knew she was staying at the Blackstone right now, and that she was in town for a meeting. What she couldn't get over was what Richard had said about not being able to compete with Jonathan.

It didn't sink in at first. Here was a man who had been telling her for three years in one way or another that he still loved her and wanted her to come home. And now, because she took a trip with her father to his hometown, the town where he grew up, the town where he became the man he was today, Richard gives up.

He said he knew her too well. Maybe he knew her better than she knew herself.

CHAPTER 20

Compassion

Nearing the end of an early morning ride on J.B. one balmy fall day, Marie spotted Ted and several of the ranch hands gathered near one of the stables. Ted walked in front of Marie's horse, forcing her to stop. "Don't go in there just yet."

"How come?"

"One of our mares just had a stillborn birth in the stall next to J.B.'s." He took the reins from Marie and led her to the next barn. "We can put him in here until things settle down. Mama's pretty upset and won't let anyone near her dead colt."

She dismounted and walked next to Ted as he led J.B. to the last stall. Marie reached for the brush hanging on the nail outside the stall, but before she could start rubbing the horse down, Ted took the brush from her hand. "I'll ask one of the hands to do that. Would you like to come in for a cup of coffee?"

Over coffee, Marie found out Ted had been married—twice. His first wife had run off with their next door neighbor, and his second wife had died in a riding accident. That had been two years ago.

"I'm so sorry to hear that. How awful that must have been for you."

"It was. I was the one who found her. I don't know what caused that horse to be so aggressive. And he wasn't any crow-bait horse. He'd never shown any sign of bad behavior before, nor since. Just goes to show you how unpredictable animals are. Say, would you like to have dinner with me sometime?"

She liked his smile. "Only if you allow me to tell you about myself. And then, if you want to back out, I'll understand." She told him about her father and Richard.

"Your father sounds like someone I'd like to get to know, but that husband of yours, well, that's a different story."

"So who my father is doesn't bother you? I'll understand if you want to back out. Really."

"I ain't backing out." He laughed. "My great-grandfather was a Cherokee Indian. Does that bother you?"

"No. Not in the least."

* * *

The next evening, while they sipped wine on Marie's porch, Marie told Karen about her talk with Ted.

Karen's face lit up. "He's so handsome, in a rugged sort of way. Is he single?"

"Of course he's single. I wouldn't go out with him if he wasn't."

Karen gave her a peculiar look and then smiled. "Well, *you're* not."

"Right. Well, you got me there."

"Any word on the divorce?"

"Not yet. I guess Richard hasn't filed yet."

Karen smiled. "I can just see the two of you riding off into the sunset together..."

"It's just dinner, Karen. And I'm not even sure if he's my type."

"Oh really? And what exactly is your type?"

Marie's mouth went into an instant smile. Both women knew she didn't have an answer to that question. "For one thing, when I told him I was separated but still married, he referred to me as a California widow."

"What does that mean?"

"I have no idea. I was afraid to ask. And when I described Richard to him, he called him a regular flannel mouth."

"Huh?"

"It must be a whole other language."

"A real cowboy then?"

"I guess."

"Well, it doesn't take away from that handsome face of his, and those tight jeans. Whew!"

"Cool down, Karen."

"Well, I just can't stand to see you alone. You have so much to offer someone. And that someone is out there. I just know it. Someone who will accept you for all that you are, including who your father is. Maybe that's Ted."

"Tell me, why do you think Paul was interested in me even after I told him about my father?"

"Honestly? I think he had never met anyone like you before—college-educated, gorgeous, and secretly colored—and that was exciting for him."

"Really?" Marie pondered Karen's rationale. "What do you think the odds are of meeting the true love of your life? And just how many frogs do you think you have to kiss before you find him?"

"Who knows? Maybe hundreds. Or maybe he's right under your nose, and you don't even know it. My mother used to say, 'What's meant to be will always find its way.' I think she was right."

"Maybe. How are things going with you and Maurice these days?"

A vivid red blush crept up Karen's neck. She smiled.

"Okay, tell me. What's going on?"

"He told me he loved me."

"And you said?"

"I told him back."

"I knew there was something different about you today! I'm so happy for you. What about his wacky mother?"

"I'm trying to ignore that. Makes things a lot easier. And he told me if it ever came down to it, he would choose me over his mother."

"You two make a great couple, you know that? So how much chocolate have you eaten this past month?"

"Shut up, Marie."

* * *

Ted picked Marie up the following Friday in his pickup truck. He was wearing jeans, boots, and a cowboy shirt. She came to the door in a silk dress and three-inch heels. As soon as they saw each other, they both laughed.

"I'll go change," she said. Ted waited in his truck.

They went to a restaurant/bar on the outskirts of Hiawatha where everyone seemed to know Ted. He led Marie to a table in the middle of the room, near the bar, where he promptly sat down. Used to a man pulling out the chair for her, she tried to overlook it. Maybe it wasn't a cowboy thing to do.

"They do a bang-up job here with their chuck wagon stew. And their biscuit pie is fine as cream gravy. Do you want a beer?"

This wasn't going to work.

"I'll have whatever you're having," she told him.

When the waitress brought two beers and chuck wagon stew, Ted held up his bottle and said, "Here's how!"

It was going to be a long evening.

Between Ted's cowboy lingo and the boisterous bar activity, Marie understood only about half of what he said during dinner. Toward the end of their meal, when he told her they should probably get a wiggle on, she admitted to herself she liked this man's personality and character, but definitely not as a love interest.

Ted pulled his truck up in front of Marie's apartment. She reached for the door handle, but he gently grasped her other arm and said, "Can we talk a spell?"

Marie turned to face him. "Sure."

"I like you." He had the calmest deep brown eyes.

"I like you too, Ted."

"But not as your home-skillet."

She wasn't familiar with the expression, but based on the connotation, she figured it meant something like boyfriend/girlfriend. "I agree."

"Whew! What a relief." His smile was wide. "The whole time we were talkin' through dinner, I was thinkin', 'I wonder if she's thinkin' the same thing I'm thinkin'.'" He grinned. "When it comes to understanding women, I'm afraid I'm usually pretty much lost at sea."

Taken in by his innocent charm, Marie couldn't help but smile. "Then we're on the same page?"

"I think so. How about if we go riding sometime?"

"I'd like that."

He leaned over and kissed her on the cheek. "Good night."

"Good night, Ted."

"Hey, and just remember, I'm someone you can always ride the river with, so if you ever need anything, anything at all, you call on me. Ya hear?"

Marie smiled. "You can count on that, Ted. Good night."

* * *

"So how did your date go?" Karen asked the next day.

"Oh, we had a real hog-killin' good time."

"That bad, huh?"

"No, it wasn't bad at all. In fact, I rather enjoyed it. And he did too. But we both decided when he dropped me off afterward—in his freshly washed pickup truck, I might add—that we're probably better off as just friends."

"It's nice to have a good male friend."

"I think so too. Hey, do you want to come over Monday night? There's a new television show everyone is talking about called *I Love Lucy*."

"I'll bring the wine."

* * *

The divorce papers were served to Marie at her studio. After immediately informing her attorney, she phoned Jonathan.

"You're going to sign them, right?" Jonathan asked her.

"Yes. I am definitely going to sign them."

"What did he charge you with?"

"Abandonment."

"I would take it and run."

"I'm going to."

"Claire wants to talk with you. I'll talk to you later. Congratulations, Marie. I'm proud of you, sweetheart."

Claire got on the phone. "Marie, will you be spending Thanksgiving with us this year?"

"Yes, I will." It would be her third Thanksgiving spent with them.

"And what about Christmas?"

"I'll be there."

"Well, we would be thrilled if you could spend the month with us— the month between Thanksgiving and Christmas."

Her heart raced. "Oh my. Uh…let me give that some thought, Claire. What a wonderful invitation. The only reason I'm hesitating is because

I have a business to run and customers who wait until the last minute to get their homes ready for the holidays. This is a very busy time of the year for me."

"I understand." The disappointment in her voice was obvious.

Marie had managed to build a successful business despite predictable odds for the times, and putting it in possible jeopardy by taking a month off wasn't something she wanted to do. But spending a month with her family had the potential of enriching her life as nothing else could. Somehow she would make this work.

"Claire, my staff will just have to handle things while I'm gone. Yes. I would *love* to stay the month."

"Wonderful. You and Jonathan can work out the details. And Marie..."

"Yes?"

"There's someone besides your family who will be thrilled with your visit."

"Is she fourteen and talks in teenager?"

"You guessed it. Ben brings her around every once in awhile, and you're all she asks about."

"That's interesting because she plays it pretty cool in her letters and our occasional phone calls. Any word from her mother?"

"No. Not a word."

"Well, please tell Rachael I'm looking forward to seeing her, and maybe we can do a few things together while I'm there."

"I can hear the squeal now. I don't think I'll tell her just yet. If I do, she'll be calling me every other day to see if I know anything more about when you'll be here."

"Good idea."

* * *

Marie didn't have to wait long to find out the court date, which was set for November 16, three days before she was to leave for St. Charles to be with her family for the holidays. She asked Karen if she would go with her for moral support, and Karen readily agreed.

They flew into Chicago the morning of the trial. Marie met with her attorney at the courthouse a half hour before they were scheduled to go in the courtroom. Karen sat on a bench down the hall.

Cavanaugh explained how the proceedings would go. He told her the whole case shouldn't take any more than a half hour.

"What if he changes his mind?"

He gave her a puzzled look. "He was the one who filed." He flipped the document in his hands to the last page. "And he signed it."

"I'm just trying to think of all possibilities."

"I understand. But I've been in touch with his attorney. In fact, I know him."

"Really? What's he like?"

"Let's just say he's not someone I would ever play a round of golf with. Anyway, everything seems to be in order." A clerk came out of the courtroom and told them to come in. "Ready?"

"As ready as I'll ever be."

Richard wore a navy blue pinstriped suit, bright white shirt, and perfectly knotted striped tie. He looked at Marie with a somber expression. Standing beside him was his attorney, who reminded Marie of one of the many characters Richard had brought into their home from time to time—dark slicked-back hair, shiny suit, and a large diamond pinky ring. He presented Richard's case, and when he went on and on about Marie's abandonment, Richard cleared his throat loudly as if to say, "Enough."

Marie swiped the palms of her hands on her dress before taking her seat on the witness stand. While she had no intention of denying she had left Richard, her attorney had advised her she would likely be asked why she left him. She needed to reveal enough to justify her leaving, but not so much as to incriminate him. And she had to be truthful.

"Tell me why you left Mr. Marchetti," the judge said.

"I left, your honor, because of my husband's business."

The judge peered down at the papers on his desk and then at her. "He sells medical equipment. You had a problem with that?"

"You see, in his business he has to meet with all kinds of people, attend all kinds of functions, and I just didn't feel comfortable around them. I didn't understand what he was doing half the time."

The judge glanced at Richard and then his attorney. Marie was certain Richard's attorney gave the judge some kind of signal with his facial expression. "You may leave the stand, Mrs. Marchetti. Divorce granted."

The proceeding lasted just twenty minutes. Marie joined her attorney and walked toward the door, but before they reached it, Richard approached them.

"May I have a private word with your client, Mr. Cavanaugh?"

Cavanaugh turned to Marie with a questioning look.

"It's okay," Marie said. "I would like a moment with Richard if that's okay."

"I'll wait for you in the hallway."

Richard led the way to the back row of spectator seats and waited for Marie to sit down. He sat down next to her. He didn't say anything at first; he merely focused on her with the same endearing eyes she remembered from when she was with him during the good times.

"I still love you. I want you to know that." His voice was soft, and his words came slowly.

"I know."

"This doesn't have to be it, you know."

"Yes, it does."

He stared deep into her eyes and then past her. After a few seconds, he looked back at her and said, "I want to be there for you."

She looked at him, puzzled.

"You're going through a difficult time right now. I can be there for you. I want to be there for you."

"I'm not following you."

"Marie, it can't be easy dealing with who your father is. I've met him, and he seems like a decent enough man, but it doesn't matter how decent he is, he's still a Negro, and so are you." Jonathan had told her how Richard had finagled his way into a dinner party at his home two years earlier by posing as someone interested in horses. "I can help you with that. You need help with that."

Richard had always taken exceptionally good care of her physical and material needs, but had never shown such consideration toward her emotional needs. She shook her head. "I'm handling things just fine."

He stared into her eyes for several seconds, then got up and left. Marie took in a deep breath of air and sat alone for a minute before joining Karen and her attorney.

"Everything okay?" Cavanaugh asked.

"Yes. Everything is okay."

He reached out for her hand. "Congratulations, Marie."

"Thank you."

* * *

Marie didn't say anything on the way back to their hotel room, and Karen didn't ask any questions. Once in their room, Marie called for room service and ordered a snack for the two of them, including a bottle of wine. She then went into the bathroom and had herself a good cry. When she came out ten minutes later, Karen was waiting for her.

"You okay?"

Marie nodded. "I just needed to get that out of my system." She sat down in the chair across from Karen. "I don't know why I cried like that. This is what I wanted."

"What did he say to you? If you don't mind saying, that is."

Marie told her about their conversation.

"Wow."

"Yeah. Wow." Marie heaved a healthy amount of air out of her lungs. "He was like a totally different person."

"Why do you think that is?"

"I don't know. It almost seems like when he finally realized there wasn't any way I would be coming back to him—and that took three and a half years, I might add—he saw that he didn't control me, and I don't know… it was like there was this other person inside who took over."

"Like a broken soul?"

"No, more like he conceded, and once he did that, he could take off his game face." She stared past Karen, out the window.

"What are you thinking?"

"I'm curious about who that other person is."

"Marie, you aren't…"

"No, I'm not thinking of finding out." *I'm not, am I?* "I'm just curious, that's all. I lived with the man for over two years, and I never saw that side of him." She looked at Karen. "I know you're probably not going to understand this, but deep down, he's not a bad person."

Karen gave Marie a disparaging look.

"And you know what I hope for him?" Marie went on.

"What?"

"I hope he figures out someday how to live his life without that game face."

"To thine own self be true?"

Marie nodded. "Something like that."

After Marie returned home, she thought about why she cried so hard back in the hotel room. It unnerved her to think it was because of the finality of their relationship. She didn't want that to be the reason after all she had gone through to get to that point. But her mind kept going back to Richard's words after the trial, his demeanor, his compassion.

It wasn't as if he hadn't been compassionate when they were together, she thought. But this compassion was different somehow. She thought back to when they were together, before he'd gotten in so deep with the unsavory cast of characters he referred to as his business associates. She went back to the good times. He had compassion back then, lots of it. Or had he? *No, that wasn't compassion. It was passion. He lacked compassion.* She wondered why she had never realized that about him before.

She was pretty sure her crying jag had nothing to do with Richard, but it had everything to do with now being totally free to pursue other love interests...and confront her ethnicity head-on.

To thine own self be true? Marie knew she would have to figure that out completely before she could ever have a meaningful relationship with anyone.

CHAPTER 21

Champions

Karen came over to help Marie pack for her six-week visit at Jonathan's.

"How are you going to pack six week's worth of clothes into one suitcase?"

"I'm not. I've got two."

"Isn't that kind of hard, managing two suitcases on the plane?"

Marie turned to Karen and smiled. "I didn't tell you. Rachael talked her dad and Jonathan into having Jonathan's driver pick me up, and..."

"And she's coming with."

"You guessed it."

"She's a little hustler."

"She is so excited about my being there for six whole weeks, she can't stand it. I talked to her yesterday, and she must have said the word 'crazy' a hundred times."

Marie put the last of her things in the second suitcase and poured them each another glass of wine before relaxing in the living room.

"I'm going to miss you," Karen said.

"Aw...you've got Maurice."

Karen looked at Marie with a deadpan face.

"What?"

"I haven't talked to him all week."

"Why? What happened?"

"Found out his daughter Hannah isn't his only child."

"What?"

"Apparently he had an affair with another woman when Hannah was just two, and she had a baby."

"*What?* Did *he* just find this out?"

"No." Karen teared up. "He's been sending her money for years."

"Karen, I am so sorry." Marie put her arms around her as she sobbed.

"But I loved him," she wailed into Marie's shoulder.

"I know you did, hon." Marie left the embrace and looked into Karen's eyes. "And you still do, right?"

Karen sighed. "I don't know." She swiped the tears from her face. "It was one thing to not tell me he was Jewish, and then of course there's his insane mother he could have told me about sooner, but this…this is something else. He should have told me about her long before this."

"Karen, you still love him."

"He may as well as have lied to me."

"How did you end it with him?"

"Told him I never wanted to see him again…ever."

"Karen, his office is two doors down from your shop. How are you going to help but see him occasionally?"

"I'll move. I hate him."

"No you don't. Has he tried to contact you?"

"Yeah. He calls me every day, both at home and at my shop. He's come to my house several times, but I don't answer the door. I keep my door locked at the shop and let customers in only when I see who they are. He knocked on the door once. I ignored him."

"You can't go on like that. He's a good man, Karen, and he still loves you, and I know you still love him. Have you given any thought to forgiving him?"

"Do you have any chocolate?"

"Promise me something. Promise me you'll give serious consideration to forgiving him. And if you can't, that's fine, but just remember..."

"Remember what?"

"I was trying to think of one of your mother's sayings that fit, but..."

"It's okay to make mistakes, but you don't want to make one that follows you the rest of your life."

"Yes, like that one."

* * *

When Rachael arrived, Marie took her to a new Italian restaurant that had recently opened. Karen joined them. Rachael talked nonstop about...well, everything. Marie had to interrupt her several times to ask her to slow down so she could appreciate everything she had to say.

"He's okay, I guess." Rachael's face took on a frown whenever she talked about her father. "He's still a geezer though."

"He let you miss two days of school to come here."

She rolled her eyes. "He doesn't dig my friends, or anything I do, for that matter. He's always hounding me about something."

"Tell me about your friends."

"Okay, so they're not from rich families that go on vacations and have summer homes and shit like that."

"I don't want to hear you use that kind of language, young lady."

"Sorry." Another eye roll.

"So he's met your friends?"

"One or two. But when they come over, he drills them about their families. He's so hung up on good families. I don't come from a good family. I wish he'd get that."

"First of all, you are part of his family now. Maybe he wishes you'd get that."

"I knew you were going to say that."

"Well, I think he cares about you very much, and he just wants what's best for you."

"I guess. And he has no respect for my privacy. Can you believe this? I came home from school one day, and he was in my dresser drawer, actually in it."

"Why do you think he was in it?"

"He *said* he was putting away clean clothes, but I *know* the cleaning lady does that."

"How did you react to that?"

Rachael looked away. "Bad."

"Badly."

"He treats me like a stupid child. One day he gave me the royal shaft for not coming home from school right afterward. I'm fifteen!"

"Not quite."

"Close enough." A smile slowly crept across her mouth.

"C'mon. Let's go home."

Marie hoped she wasn't getting in too deep with Rachael. She wanted to help her get through this difficult period in her life, but she was also aware if Rachael got too attached to her, Marie may not be able to fulfill all that Rachael needed. And she wasn't sure exactly what that was. Being only eleven years older than her, Marie was too young to be her mother, but too old to be a close sister.

The one thing Marie clearly understood was that according to Ben and Claire, Rachael looked up to Marie like no one else, and she couldn't wait to be around her.

* * *

Walter picked up Marie and Rachael the following morning. They arrived at the Brookses in time for dinner. Ben greeted them at the door. "I hope she behaved herself," he told Marie. With that Rachael stomped her way to the kitchen. "Did she act that way the whole time she was with you? Because if she did..."

"No, Ben. She behaved beautifully." She searched Ben's face for a clue as to how much she could say to him without interfering. "I think she just took the way you greeted us the wrong way."

"That child takes pretty much everything I say the wrong way," he said as he headed toward the living room to join Jonathan and Rachael's grandfather, Greg.

* * *

After Ben and Rachael left, Marie spent the rest of the evening helping Claire prepare for the next day's holiday meal. Marie filled Claire in on her observations of Rachael and Rachael's tumultuous relationship with her father.

"It's hard to know what to do in your case, I know," Claire said. "You want to be there for her, but you don't want to interfere. I understand that. And Ben has told us it has gotten so bad at times with her, he wonders if he should try to find her mother."

"Rachael has a lot of resentment toward her mother, and I can't say I blame her. The way she feels is that it doesn't matter what her mother's reason was, she still deserted her."

"She has a point...unfortunately."

They joined Jonathan in the living room. "So how did it really go with Rachael?" he asked.

"It went fine. It was a pleasure having her with me."

"To hear Ben talk, she's impossible to live with."

"I think that feeling is pretty much mutual," Marie responded.

"Are you still going to go ahead with your plans with her for spring break?"

Marie had talked to Ben about letting Rachael spend spring break in Atchison with her. "As it stands now, yes. But given her rocky relationship with Ben, anything could happen between now and her birthday, when I plan to tell her about it."

"What plans do you have spending time with her while you're here?"

"Well, if I go along with Rachael's thoughts, we'll be doing something every weekend."

Claire smiled. "I was afraid of that. She told her grandmother we could have you during the week when she's in school."

"She's a shrewd one, she is," Jonathan said. "You need to be on your toes with her."

* * *

The Brooks family members arrived throughout the morning, greeting Marie as though she had always been one of them. At the end of the day, as Marie and Jonathan were heading toward their respective bedrooms, Marie teared up.

"What's wrong?" Jonathan asked.

"Nothing. I'm just glad to be here, that's all."

"So am I, sweetheart. So am I." He put his arm around her. "And you want to know something else? Claire feels the same way."

She wiped the tears from her face. "Are you sure?"

"I'm sure."

"Thanks, Dad."

* * *

Marie spent the next week mostly with Jonathan—accompanying him on business calls, going on long morning rides with him, and sitting with him in his den, just talking. On one of those morning rides, he shared more memories of her mother.

"I had a book of love poems in my Chicago apartment, and we would read them to each other.

"She walks in beauty, like the night
Of cloudless climes and starry skies;
And all that's best of dark and bright
Meet in her aspect and her eyes:
Thus mellowed to that tender light
Which heaven to gaudy day denies."

"Lord Byron," Marie said.

"You've read his poetry?"

"Yes, in college."

"For someone so confused when it came to his own romantic interests, he sure could write about it."

"My college professor thought he was misunderstood."

"I suppose that's one way to put it. Are you still feeling misunderstood, sweetheart?"

"What do you mean?"

"We haven't talked about your…shall I call it your identity issue, for some time. Now that you're divorced, do you have any plans for bringing someone new into your life?"

"Oh, I've thought about it, alright. But to answer the question I think you're really asking, I still don't know how to handle it." She laughed. "I'm laughing at it like it wasn't something very important, but you and I both know it is. I'm still at a loss, I guess. I keep going back to the fact that I don't think I could bring a child into this world knowing he or she would have to face the same impossible issues I'm facing."

"So you have it figured out then."

"Not really. It's just not fair. It shouldn't be that way."

"Some things you have no control over."

"Now you're sounding like Karen."

"Hmmm."

"Karen thinks you need to live your life based on what others think in order to survive. But I'm more of an idealist than that."

"Maybe the answer is a compromise."

They finished their ride and were headed toward the main barn when it happened. At first Marie thought Jonathan was merely having trouble dismounting his horse, but when he slumped down over the horse's neck and head, she realized he was in trouble.

"Zach! Come here. Come quick!"

Marie jumped off her horse and ran to her father's side with Zach several steps behind her.

"Call for an ambulance, I'll get him off the horse," he instructed.

Marie ran to the house and called for Claire. "Dad needs an ambulance!"

Claire ran to the phone. Marie waited while she made the call. "Is he breathing?" Claire asked while still on the phone.

"I don't know! Tell them to hurry!" she cried.

Claire hung up the phone and followed Marie to the barn. Zach had Jonathan off the horse and lying on the ground. "Is he breathing?" she asked Zach.

"He's unconscious but breathing. It's shallow." Despite the thirty-five-degree temperature, Jonathan's face glistened with sweat.

"It may take awhile—all we have out here are volunteer doctors who have to be picked up by the ambulance," Claire said. She stared at Marie. "What happened?"

Marie's stomach churned. Her voice was weak. "We were close to the barn door when it looked like he was going to dismount. Then he slumped down, and that's when I knew he was in trouble." She swiped the tears off her cheeks. "Is he going to be alright?"

Claire shook her head. "I hope so. God, I hope so."

* * *

It had been six hours since the ambulance transported Jonathan to Delnor Hospital. He was still unconscious but in stable condition. The doctors thought it was a heart attack, but wouldn't be sure until more tests were run.

Claire and Marie sat in a small waiting area near to his room, mostly in silence.

"Has he had anything like this before, Claire?"

Claire shook her head. Her face was sallow, and Marie saw the worry in her expression.

Thoughts flew through Marie's mind. She worried about Claire. On the way to the hospital she had told Marie she didn't know what she would do without Jonathan. He had always been the strong one in the family, the one who always kept a level head no matter what the circumstances. She had called him her champion.

Jonathan had turned out to be Marie's champion as well, and the thought of losing him now, after not having had him in her life for her first twenty-four years, devastated her. The last two years of knowing him had been the most fulfilling ones of her life.

The doctor approached them with a serious expression.

"Is he alright, doctor?" Claire asked.

The doctor nodded. "He's just gained consciousness."

"Will he be okay?" Marie asked.

"We think so. The ECG is confirming a mild heart attack. He was pretty lucky."

"Can we see him?" Claire asked.

"For just a minute. He needs to rest."

Jonathan opened his eyes when they entered the room, his face ashy. Claire went over and kissed him on the forehead. "How are you feeling, Jon?"

He tilted his head and smiled. "I've had better days."

"Well, you had us scared, that's for sure." Claire stepped aside to allow Marie to get near to him.

"I'll second that," Marie said, taking his hand. "I feel like I can actually breathe now."

"Have they told you how long you'll be here, dear?"

"I asked the doctor, and he said it was too early to talk about that." He made a face. "If they think this is going to slow me down, they've got another think coming."

"Jonathan, you are going to listen to doctor's orders if I have anything to say about…"

"It was mild. The doctor said so himself. I'll be fine."

Both Claire and Marie gave him stern looks.

"Okay, we'll see."

A nurse entered the room and advised Marie and Claire they would have to leave so Jonathan could rest.

"I'll be out in no time," he said to them as they were leaving.

"We'll see about that," the nurse echoed back.

* * *

Claire spent the next several days driving to the hospital in the mornings. Marie took the afternoon shift. In between, Jonathan had a regular flow of other visitors, including all the family members. After ten days, he came home. Claire made sure she had a written list of instructions from the doctor before he was released.

"Things are going to change around here," she told Jonathan when they were home and Jonathan was settled in. He rolled his eyes. "For one thing, I'm going to start cooking differently. The doctor said you could stand to lose a few pounds."

"Yes, dear."

"And I've already talked to Zach. He's going to take over running things for…"

"Hold on a minute. I'm not an invalid, Claire."

"You didn't let me finish. I know you're not an invalid, but the doctor said you need to rest for a good month. So what I was about to say before you interrupted me was that Zach can take over things for the next month."

"And just what am I supposed to do?"

Claire took out a piece of paper from her purse. "Take your medication. I'll handle that. Light exercise twice a day. We'll go on walks together. Diet low in fat and high in fiber. No sweets. That's my department too. And weekly doctor visits until he says you're okay to return to your normal lifestyle." She glared at him. "C'mon. Get that look off your face. We'll get through this."

"Maybe...but it won't be easy with you as my drill sergeant." He managed a smile.

"She's only doing this because she loves you," Marie added.

"I know. I know."

* * *

Marie had been in St. Charles two weeks and hadn't spent any time to speak of with Rachael, and while Rachael hadn't said anything to anyone, Marie knew she was probably disappointed. Now that Jonathan was home and out of danger, she felt secure in making plans with her.

Rachael had been taking horseback riding lessons since living in St. Charles but hadn't seen any type of equestrian competition, so Marie arranged for them to go to the Kane County Fairgrounds where the American Quarter Horse Association was sponsoring a two-day meet.

"This is so crazy," she said to Marie in the car on their way to the fairgrounds.

They arrived early to insure good seats. The stadium-style benches in the large indoor arena accommodated close to five hundred people. They found an opening in row three near the center.

The Western Pleasure competition was up first. Marie and Rachael watched each rider show off their horse's soft smooth gait, flawless conformation, and even temperament. The last rider was a female.

"You've got to be kidding," Rachael remarked. "Girls compete?"

"It looks that way." She glanced at Rachael. "Is that something you'd like to do someday?"

She shot Marie a look. "I could never do that."

"Why not?"

"It's for people with…"

"With what?"

"I don't know. Can we get something to eat?"

Marie tried to continue the conversation while they ate barbeque sandwiches in the makeshift lunchroom in the building next to the arena, but Rachael kept changing the subject. "So what's going on after this?" she asked.

"Reining competition. Do you know what that is?"

"Riding through circles and doing spins and how well you can get the horse to stop?"

"Mm-hmm."

The judges were looking for how responsive the horses were to their riders' commands and how effortless the rider made it look. At the end of the competition, after the awards were given out, the master of ceremonies asked the crowd if there were any experienced riders who wanted to give it a try.

"Raise your hand, Rachael."

"No. Are you kidding?"

"Go ahead. You're an experienced rider, and it may be fun."

"I said no!"

"Okay. Sorry. I didn't mean to push you."

Rachael got up and headed for the door. Marie followed.

Rachael was quiet on the way home. Marie wondered if her silence was just more normal teenager behavior or spurred on by Marie's suggestion she try her hand at reining. Either way, it was disturbing.

"Should we go out for pizza tonight?" she asked her, knowing it was her favorite food.

"Cool."

* * *

Jonathan followed doctor's orders and felt better with each day, and while he grumbled at Claire's strict oversight every chance he got, he was an obedient patient. Ten days out of the hospital, he and Marie went on a short ride.

"It's been almost three weeks since I've been on a horse. I don't think I've ever gone that long, ever. It's good to be back."

"It's good to have you back." Her emotions got the better of her. She stopped her horse.

"What's the matter, sweetheart?"

Marie looked at her father through tearful eyes. "When I thought we were going to lose you..."

"I'm not going anywhere, and..."

"And what?"

"I'm fine, my dear daughter, here with you."

"I know, but while you were in the..."

"I'm fine. And thanks to my wonderful wife, I think I'm in better health than before." He laughed nervously. "She calls me her champion, but really she's mine."

"And mine."

* * *

Marie picked Rachael up from school on her last day before Christmas break. "Hey, what are you doin' here?" she asked when she got into the car.

"I'm taking you home so you can pack."

"Pack? Where are we going?"

"I thought we'd go on a little weekend shopping spree for your birthday."

"What? Where?"

"Downtown Chicago. Where else?"

"Get out of here. What did Dad say?"

"He said yes, of course."

"So he didn't tell you the trouble I got into at school?"

"Yes, he told me." Rachael had been caught with three other students who had stuffed birdseed in all the nooks and crevices of the principal's car. The principal found his car that day covered in bird droppings.

"And he's still letting me go?"

"Well, he didn't say yes right off. But I assured him…and I really went out on a limb for you. I assured him you would benefit from the trip and give serious thought to what it meant to be a mature, respectful soon-to-be fifteen-year-old."

"Really? He was so mad at me. Said I was grounded for a month."

Once in Rachael's room, as she helped her pack, Marie realized how few clothes she had. Ben could easily have afforded to buy nice clothes for her, but Marie suspected that was something he wouldn't have come up with on his own. While Rachael finished packing, Marie talked to Ben in the living room.

"I was going to let Rachael spend the Christmas money I intended to give her on anything she wanted, within reason, of course, but now that I see her closet, I think I'm going to steer her toward clothes." Ben gave her that "have I loused up again?" look. Marie confirmed his thoughts with her weak smile.

"So how do I resolve this?"

Marie shrugged.

"How about if I give you what I would have spent on her for Christmas and her birthday, and you two can have a…dare I say, a ball shopping?"

"Cool."

They talked mostly about school and boys on the way to Chicago.

After settling into their hotel room, they went to dinner and then saw *Angels in the Outfield*. They talked about it on their walk back to the hotel.

"So what do you think the lesson was in that movie," Marie asked her.

"Lesson? What lesson?"

"There was an important lesson in that movie. Think about it."

Rachael sighed. "Marie, school's out, remember?"

"And I told your dad you would come back a more mature fourteen-year-old, remember?"

"Okay. Uh, okay, the manager was a different person at the end of the movie."

"Why?"

"I don't know."

"What did you notice about him that was different?"

Rachael thought about it for awhile. "He had a better attitude."

"Bingo."

"Why do I get the feeling this has something to do with me?"

"Because, my dear, you're a very smart girl. What should it mean for you?"

"Okay, so my attitude isn't always that great. So what?"

"What did a change in attitude mean for the baseball manager?"

"His players played better."

"You are smarter than you think. That's exactly right. A positive attitude can affect the whole team, and your team is you and your dad."

"Hmmm."

"That's all I get is a hmmm?"

"Let me think about it."

"Okay. That's fair."

The next morning, they headed out to Marshall Field's. Before they started their shopping spree, Marie tracked down Esther, who cried when she saw Marie.

"God, I think about you all the time. How are you, and who's this?"

Marie introduced her to Rachael and asked if she was able to meet them for lunch so they could catch up.

"Are you kidding? Of course, I can."

Esther walked with them to the young adults section of the store. "You girls have fun, and I'll meet you downstairs at one."

Marie steered Rachael toward the dresses, but Rachael kept looking over at the racks of trousers instead.

"Okay, I have something to tell you." When she got Rachael's attention, she told her about the money Ben had given her. Rachael shrieked.

"Keep your voice down, will you?"

"I can't believe he did that. How much do I have to spend?"

"Enough to buy several outfits, maybe a couple pairs of shoes, and some accessories."

"So why is he being so nice all of a sudden?"

"I don't know. Could it possibly be that I presented your case to him with a very positive attitude?"

Rachael smiled and rolled her eyes. "Okay, I get it. I get it."

They managed to spend half of Ben's money before meeting Esther for lunch. Esther brought Marie up to date on everything and everyone at Marshall Field's, and Marie reciprocated by filling her in on her business and family.

"What about lover boy?" Esther asked.

Rachael's ears perked up. "Yeah, what about lover boy?"

"Never mind, young lady." She turned to Esther. "We're divorced... finally."

"No kidding."

They said their goodbyes to Esther and finished shopping. Burdened with almost too many packages to manage, Marie and Rachael collapsed on the bed of their hotel room. "I can't believe we bought all this stuff," Rachael said. "It's crazy."

"Are you saying 'crazy' because it's current slang, or are you really in disbelief?"

"Both, maybe. I'm in shock I have all these nice clothes."

"Do other girls in your class have nice clothes like these?"

"They all do."

"But you didn't."

"Right."

"Why do you think you didn't?"

"'Cause I'm not as good as them."

"By whose standards?"

"Dad's. Otherwise he would have bought me nice clothes long before this."

Marie fought to keep back the tears. "Rachael, sweetheart, that is *not* the reason."

"Why then? When I was with Mom I didn't have nice clothes because she couldn't afford them. But Dad can."

"You've got to understand that your dad came into your life late. We've talked about that. What has it been, a little over three years? So he had no experience raising you when you were little. It wasn't gradual like with most parents. And even while your mother was living with the two of you, I'll bet she didn't parent with him, did she?"

Rachael shook her head. "She wasn't there most of the time."

"So you see, you can't expect him to know very much about being a parent. You've got to cut him some slack, Rachael."

Rachael pursed her lips. "But I'm just a kid."

"Are you a kid, or a teenager who's not that far away from graduating high school and deciding what you're going to do with the rest of your life?"

"Okay. I get it." Rachael paused. "I'm hungry."

"When aren't you hungry?"

* * *

Rachael, Ben, Gregory, and Gloria were expected for Christmas Eve dinner along with the whole Brooks clan. This year, Claire made a healthy pasta dish instead of her famous lasagna. Jonathan made a face but didn't say anything.

After dinner, everyone sat around the table and sang "Happy Birthday" to Rachael. After she blew out the candles, she looked at her father and smiled. "I know I already got my birthday gift. Thanks, Dad."

"You didn't get mine though." Marie handed her an envelope. "Read it out loud, Rachael."

Happy birthday, dear Rachael
As you turn fifteen
I have no present to wrap
But I'm not being mean.
Think ahead to April
When you're on spring break
A trip to Atchison
Will be a kick, for corn's sake.
So I hope you're excited
And you think this is boss
Because if you don't
I'm just at a loss!
Love,
Marie

"You better not be kidding." The tears welled up in her eyes. She got up, ran over to Marie, and then whispered, "I love you."

* * *

The sweet aroma of Claire's cinnamon rolls wafted through the house on Christmas morning.

"Claire, dear, please don't tell me you made those for everyone but me," Jonathan whined.

Claire flashed a big smile. "I suppose one cinnamon roll won't hurt you." By the look on his face, Marie would have thought he had just won it big at the race track.

Tré's ten-year-old daughter, Denise, had drawn Marie's name for the Christmas present exchange. Marie opened the crudely wrapped present—a handmade embroidered sampler. All around the perimeter were red hearts, and in between each one a yellow flower. In the middle she had embroidered in cross stitch, "The love of a family is life's greatest blessing."

Marie glanced up at Denise and through tears said, "This is so sweet. Thank you."

* * *

The Christmas church service was particularly relevant for the Brookses. Their pastor focused on the relationship among body, soul, and spirit and the importance of each. Marie sat on one side of Jonathan and Claire sat on the other. Claire grasped her husband's hand a little tighter whenever the pastor talked about body.

The Brooks clan sat in the living room after dinner—there would be no traditional cigar-smoking in the barn this holiday. Jonathan's son, Arthur, brought up the new Amos 'n' Andy television show.

"So what do you think, Dad?"

"About what?"

"Do you think the show is amusing or insulting?"

A direct descendent of the radio program that had originated in the twenties, the television version showcased several Negro characters who mimicked so-called Negro dialect and were stereotypically characterized as ignorant, scheming, untrustworthy, lazy, and loud-mouthed.

Jonathan hesitated before responding. "I don't know. I guess I have mixed feelings. I would certainly prefer that the only show on television showcasing Negroes would present us in a more positive light, but let's face it, there are characters out there like them, and it's entertaining. Hell, I knew someone just like Kingfish back in South Carolina. In fact, he makes Kingfish look like an amateur."

The look on Arthur's face indicated he didn't like his father's answer. "Well, the NAACP doesn't like it, and I'm with them." Arthur had strong ties to the NAACP through his law practice.

"So what are they saying?" Jonathan asked.

"They're up in arms over it because they think millions of white Americans will think our entire race is like this. We know differently, but..."

Jonathan turned toward Marie. "What do you think?"

All eyes were on Marie. She was aware why Jonathan put her on the spot—better to have to face a question like this for the first time among family.

She took in a deep breath. "Well, I saw just one episode, so I'm not sure if I can give a very well-informed opinion."

"One episode is all you need, believe me," Arthur said through a scowl.

"I honestly don't think most white people who watch that show think that's how all Negroes are. The sad thing is they probably don't think anything at all about us as a people beyond the program. I think they're amused by it, and that's where it ends."

Arthur's twin brother, Evan, chimed in. "So is that a sad thing or a good thing?"

"I can tell you from firsthand experience, that's a sad thing," Marie said.

* * *

Marie had a particularly hard time saying goodbye to Jonathan this trip. While he looked like his old self, he wasn't completely back to normal, and Marie feared he would get back to his busy routine too soon and risk another heart attack. Claire was doing everything she could to keep that from happening, but Jonathan was stubborn when it came to being the patriarch of the family and in charge of his business.

"You're going to take care of yourself, right?" she asked him.

"Yes, Mother," he responded sarcastically.

"You know it's only because I'm concerned about you."

"Yes, dear."

CHAPTER 22

Spring Break

Spring break snuck up on Marie. After a day of making sure the spare bedroom and the contents of the refrigerator suited Rachael's needs, Marie met her train in Kansas City. It was eight p.m., and Rachael had been on the train almost ten hours. She looked a little weary but was smiling. "So how was it?" Marie asked as they exited the train station.

"It was cool. There was a girl my age on the train most of the way, and her parents let us sit together, so it wasn't boring or anything."

"Did you eat?"

"I ate lunch."

"Well, you must be starved then. Let's check into our hotel, and we'll order room service."

"Crazy. I've never had room service."

"Well, there's a first time for everything, my dear."

"Right on."

Whenever Marie had to spend overnight in Kansas City on business, she stayed at the Hotel Phillips in the historic district of the city, and so that's where she made the reservation. Rachael scanned the lobby as soon as they entered the hotel. "This is so crazy," she exclaimed in awe of the art deco furnishings. "This place must really be old."

"Built in the thirties, I think. Look at that." Marie pointed to the eleven-foot likeness of the Goddess of Dawn. They continued walking through the hotel. "Do you know who Harry Truman is?"

Rachael rolled her eyes. "Of course I do. He was the thirty-something president."

"Thirty-third. He used to run the haberdashery in this hotel before he got into politics."

"The what?"

"Haberdashery. Men's clothing."

"Like Brooks Brothers?"

"Like Brooks Brothers." *She knows about Brooks Brothers?*

The next day, they spent a leisurely morning in their room while Rachael filled Marie in on school, boys, and how she was getting along with her dad.

"We've both changed a little, I guess. I'm trying to drop the attitude, and he doesn't have a cow every time I say or do something. He's trying his best to not be such a pooper."

"A pooper?"

"Yeah, as in no fun."

"You have new words since the last time I saw you."

"You ain't heard nothing yet."

"That's what I'm afraid of."

After leaving the hotel, they window-shopped down Main Street before stopping in a quaint café for lunch.

"How about a movie before we drive home?"

Rachael gave Marie a big smile. *"Too Young to Kiss?"*

"I was thinking more along the lines of *An American in Paris*."

Rachael quickly suppressed a pout. "Okay."

"Well?" Marie asked her after the movie.

"It was cool. I liked it."

"It's good for you to enjoy a wide spectrum of things, like going to more educational movies. Broadens your horizons."

"Yes, Marie. I get it. I'm not just some boondocker, you know."

"Where *do* you get all these sayings?"

Rachael thought for a moment. "Why, it must be from the *wide* spectrum of things I expose myself to." She flung her right arm in the air like a symphony conductor.

"Okay, young lady. Don't get smart with me."

They talked about the movie on the way home. "Must be cool to be an artist," Rachael said. "Draw whatever you want when you feel like it. Don't have to go to a boring job."

"Artists have to eat and pay rent just like anyone else, don't forget."

"Yeah, I dig it."

Rachael's mood changed, and Marie recognized the signs that something was on her mind. Ten minutes later, Rachael felled the silence.

"How do you know Mr. Brooks is really your father?"

"That's a long story."

"How long until we get to your place?"

"A little over an hour."

"Well?"

Marie told Rachael the short version of how various clues had led her to Jonathan. Rachael didn't interrupt.

"But what I mean is how do you *really* know?"

Marie didn't know how much a typical fifteen-year-old knew about the birds and bees, but then Rachael wasn't your typical fifteen-year-old. "What do you mean?"

"Marie, can we talk woman to woman?"

She didn't know how to answer that question. "We can try. But you are just fifteen after all."

"I probably know more than you think. Like just because someone tells you he's your father, he may not be."

"And what are you basing this on?"

"Mostly a friend of mine from Chicago. My best friend back then. We talked about everything...I mean everything. Anyway, her mother had a baby, and nobody thought too much about it. But by the time the kid turned three, everyone could tell he looked more like the Mexican next door than her husband. My friend said her father left her mother when she admitted the neighbor was the *real* baby's father."

"Well, I know Jonathan is my father because all the puzzle pieces fit, but more importantly, because the first time I saw him, I felt the connection. I can't explain it, Rachael, but it was definitely there. Do I have scientific proof? No. No one gets that. You have to go on what you know, whom you trust, and your gut instincts."

Rachael was silent for several seconds. "Boy, am I in trouble."

"Why?"

"'Cause I have very few puzzle pieces, I don't trust anyone, and my gut tells me Ben isn't my father."

Marie concentrated on her driving while she mustered the right words. "Rachael...I'm not sure how much I can help you with this. My initial thought is if you're having doubts about it, start with Ben. Just keep one thing in mind: he's accepted you into his life as his daughter. That has to count for something whether he is or isn't. Now I'm not saying you shouldn't pursue it, but just be sensitive to his position. I've had enough conversations with him to know he loves you, and he would do anything for you."

"I can't say I love him," Rachael said with a sad tone. "I guess that makes me a pretty bad person."

"No. Not at all. Some people need more time than others to develop those types of emotions. You were how old when you and your Mom moved in with him?"

"Twelve and a half."

"Three years isn't..."

"But you said he loves *me*."

"That's different. A parent's love for a child is different."

"How so?"

"A parent's love is hard to explain. It's almost a level beyond love, unconditional for one thing. You'll find out some day."

"What does unconditional mean?"

"It means you love someone no matter what else the other person says or does."

"Hmmm." She shook her head. "I don't think I could do that."

"Wait 'til you have children. You'll understand then."

"So do you think I should come right out and ask him?"

"Maybe you could start by asking him about his original relationship with your mom, before you were born. How they met, how long they were together, why they split. Stuff like that. And then just let the conversation evolve from there. Just remember, it's never good to go into a discussion with both guns drawn if you know what I mean. If you do, it will probably turn into a battle." Marie glanced over at Rachael. "Make sense?"

"I guess so."

"Here we are, kiddo. Let's go in and take a load off."

"Marie?"

"Yes?"

"You're getting better with the lingo."

"Gee, thanks."

"And Marie?"

"Yes?"

"Thanks."

* * *

Rachael and Marie spent the next morning preparing for Sunday dinner in honor of Karen's birthday. It had taken Karen and Maurice a week of talking things through, but in the end, Karen forgave him for not telling her about his secret offspring.

Rachael's experience in the kitchen was pretty much limited to opening cans, something she had done often in order to survive when living with her mother, so Marie took time to teach her some cooking basics. They talked about a myriad of subjects while cutting up vegetables for the salad; peeling carrots, onions, and potatoes for the pork roast; trimming string beans; and cooking the orzo. While the meal simmered on top of the stove, they made an apple pie together.

Karen and Maurice arrived at noon with two bottles of wine. Marie asked Rachael if she would bring some wine glasses to the living room for them. Her temporary sullen mood reminded Marie that Rachael had a difficult time with grown-ups' drinking.

Maurice turned toward Marie with a sympathetic look. "I have a teenage daughter, so..."

A timer went off in the kitchen. Rachael jumped up. "I'll get it."

Marie looked at Karen and shrugged her shoulders. "It's going to be an interesting week," she whispered.

Rachael ate up being the center of attention while they ate. "I *love* your earrings, Rachael," Karen offered. "I wish I could wear pierced earrings, but my ears get infected every time I try. Hey, I may have some earrings you may like."

"Really?"

"Yeah, really. Marie, can you two stop by while she's here? I've got some really cute ones that would look good on her."

"Cool. Thanks."

"How did you like the Phillips Hotel, Rachael?" Karen asked.

"It was crazy. The bed was so squishy, I could hardly get out of it. And they gave you this big fluffy bathrobe for when you got out of the tub. And then room service was such a kick."

"Where did you grow up?" Maurice asked.

"Chicago."

"What side?"

"South."

"White Sox fan, then?"

"All the way."

"Ever see a live game?"

"Oh yeah. My mom dated this one guy for a while, Mike something or other. He brought us to games all the time."

"So what do you think of Richards?"

"He's alright, I guess."

"And your favorite player?"

"Number 19. How'd you like that slider he started throwing? Was that cool or what?"

Marie looked on in awe as the two of them discussed baseball.

"When's the last time you went to a game?" Maurice asked.

"Years. I tried to get Dad to take me, but he's not really into baseball."

"I love the sport. I grew up on the south side of Chicago myself, so I'll always be a White Sox fan."

"So who do you root for now? There aren't any teams in Kansas."

"White Sox, of course. They're the closest team to here. Well, and the Cubs."

Rachael made a face. "Boo, Cubs."

"So you learned all this about baseball from your Mom's boyfriend?" Marie asked.

"Yeah. That's about all he was good for."

"Rachael."

"Well, it's true."

"So what grade are you in, Rachael?" Maurice asked.

"Eighth." When he didn't say anything more, Rachael added, "I was put back a year. Missed too much school."

"Dessert, anyone?" Marie asked.

* * *

Rachael and Marie started with a tour of the state capitol building in Topeka on Monday, including the forty-five-minute walk up 296 stairs to the top of the dome. They visited Reinisch Rose Garden and Old Prairie Town where the original home of Mary Jane Ward, the so-called mother of Topeka, had recently been opened up to tourists.

"This area was occupied totally by Indians at one time," Marie explained to Rachael. "Do you remember reading about the Oregon Trail in school?"

"Not really."

"It crossed over the Kansas River right here in Topeka."

Having sensed Rachael had had enough history for one day, Marie planned a lighter agenda for Tuesday. They had breakfast at Lulu's with Karen and then walked to Karen's shop, where Marie let Rachael pick out a new outfit. Then they went to Marie's studio, where Rachael chatted with Marie's staff while Marie took care of some business in her office. They ate lunch at a restaurant on the river and strolled down the bank afterward toward a craft show Marie had read about. Marie bought Rachael a silver bangle bracelet she had admired at one of the booths.

"This is so weird."

"What's that?"

"My mom used to say all the time, 'That's how the other half lives.' I guess this is how the other half lives." She touched her new bracelet. "We walk through a craft show. All I did was look at this bracelet, and you buy it for me. That's crazy."

"You deserve to have nice things."

"And I didn't when I was with my mom?"

The statement stopped Marie for a moment. "No, you deserved it then too."

"It's not fair."

"I know, Rachael. I know."

They headed toward Karen's. She had invited them over for some of her famous fried chicken, which was a hit with Rachael. "Best I've ever had," she told her. After dinner, Karen showed Rachael her collection of earrings as promised, and Rachael picked out three pairs she liked. Without any coaching, she steered away from the three-inch hoops and the ones shaped like bananas, pleasing Marie.

Rachael wandered over to Karen's handcuff collection. "Hey, cast an eyeball on these."

"Go ahead. Make fun of them," Karen invited.

"Make fun of them? I don't even know what they are." She picked up a pair of nineteenth-century leg irons. "Like these."

"They were used on slaves, Rachael," Marie explained. "Leg irons to transport them from one place to another."

"You're kidding."

"I wouldn't kid about a thing like that, my dear."

"I'm sorry. I didn't mean it that way." She set them back down and picked up a key. "What does this fit?"

"Let me see it." Karen examined the key. "That fits an Adams cuff."

"And this one?"

"Cummings."

"What's the story on these?"

Karen shrugged and gave Rachael a befuddled smile.

Rachael raised her brows and smirked. "Okay. It's all cool."

* * *

Marie and Rachael sat on Marie's sun porch that evening. Marie shared with Rachael some of the profound and not so profound talks she had had with Karen on the porch.

"Marie, don't you think Karen's handcuff collection is a little weird?"

"Mm-hmm."

"Me too." She looked like a younger version of Karen the way she curled her legs up under her in the chair. She stared out the window. "Do you think you'll stay here forever?"

"I really like it here. so I don't see myself leaving any time soon. But…you never know." Rachael's face registered disappointment. "Why do you ask?"

Rachael shrugged. "No reason. Just curious."

* * *

Rachael was excited when Marie told her they would spend Wednesday afternoon on horseback. Marie rode J.B. They gave Rachael a gentle, deep brown mare named Brownie. Marie led the way toward her favorite riding path. When they reached the top of the rise, halfway up the trail, Marie stopped so they could take in the landscape.

"It's beautiful, isn't it?"

"Sure." Rachael appeared to be in some other world.

"You okay?" Marie asked.

Rachael shot Marie a disconcerted look. "Yep."

"You looked a million miles away."

"I was just thinking."

"About what?"

"Having to go home and then back to school."

"I thought you liked school."

"Oh, I do. But this break has been such a kick. I don't want it to end."

"All good things must come to an end. I'm not sure who said that, but it's true."

"What a drag."

"I left tomorrow open. What would you like to do? Your choice."

"I want to call Dad."

"Aw, you miss him, huh?"

"No. I want to tell him I want to come live here with you." Rachael gave her horse a tap with her heels to get him moving faster, ahead of Marie and her horse.

Marie kept a safe distance behind Rachael and Brownie, grateful for the time she had to process what Rachael had said at the top of the rise. Thoughts rushed in and out of her head like a yo-yo. *Come live with me? What is she thinking? Maybe she was just being funny. But it wasn't funny. Good heavens, what have I done?*

Rachael had reached Marie's car by the time Marie and J.B. arrived at the stable. From behind, she watched Rachael swipe the back of her hand across her face. Was she crying? Before she approached her car, Marie spent a couple of minutes talking to the ranch hand who was preparing to rub down the horses.

"You okay, Rachael?"

Without turning around, Rachael responded in a soft voice, "Yeah."

Marie sat behind the steering wheel of her car and stared straight ahead without starting the engine. She glanced over at Rachael. "Pizza tonight okay?" Rachael nodded without turning her head. "We can talk after dinner."

Marie kept dinner conversation to idle chatter. When they got home, they sat on Marie's porch to begin what was likely going to be a challenging conversation. Marie sipped a glass of wine while a gentle southern breeze wafted through the open windows, bringing in the sweet smell of early lilacs. Rachael sipped on ginger ale.

"Okay. Let's start with what prompted you to say that back on the rise."

Rachael heaved a sigh, lowered her head, and shrugged her shoulders.

"You miss your mom, don't you?"

More shoulder shrugging.

"And you're not sure if your dad is your dad? And we've had so much fun this week."

Rachael tried to hold back the blissful smile, but couldn't.

"Rachael…" She gazed into Rachael's eyes, into the eyes of a confused, scared child who deserved better. "It's just not that easy." She scrambled to put her thoughts together. "Look at all the factors involved, not the least of which is your father. Whether he's your father or not, you can't just up and leave him."

She made a face. "Why not? My mother ditched *me* enough."

"And how did that make you feel?"

"Lousy."

"Okay. So what's the golden rule?"

The words dragged out of her mouth. "Do unto others as you would have them do unto you."

"Those aren't bad words to live by, by the way."

"I know."

"And speaking of your mother, you can't leave her out of the equation."

Rachael crossed her arms. "Why not?"

"Because she's your mother."

"So? She's not acting like one."

"I know. But you can't choose who your parents are, honey. She's still your mother, and she will be forever."

"Well, that stinks. What if she never comes back?"

"She'll still be your mother."

"I hate her."

"Rachael, what she did to you was unconscionable. You just don't abandon your children. But I suspect there's a whole lot going on inside her we don't know, and I'll bet any amount of money, she wishes she was in a better position to take care of you."

Rachael dug in her heels. "I doubt it. So what am I supposed to do, wait for her until I'm eighteen and I'm legally on my own? Fat chance."

"I know you're struggling with this, and that's okay. We all struggle with things from time to time."

"I know." She turned her head away from Marie and stared out the window. "But what if it's all the time?"

Marie let out a sigh. "And what about school?"

"They have schools here, don't they?"

"Yes, of course they do." Rachael wasn't making this very easy. She sat next to her on the wicker love seat. "Look at the moon." They both stared into the murky night sky for several seconds. "I've never seen it quite so full and bright."

"You're changing the subject."

"I know."

"So?"

"Rachael, have you given any thought to how it would affect *my* life if you were to come live with me?"

"Knew *that* was coming."

"Well?"

She looked at Marie with wide-eyed innocence. "I wouldn't be much trouble."

Marie gave her a dubious look.

"I said not much." Rachael smiled.

"That's not what concerns me."

"What concerns you, then?"

Marie couldn't think of any convincing reasons it wouldn't work out. "For starters, my apartment is fairly small, and I use the spare bedroom for other things."

"Looks like just a spare bedroom to me."

"My sewing machine is in there."

"When was the last time you used it?"

"And what about my social life? I've been used to coming and going whenever I please and not worrying about another person in the house."

"You wouldn't have to worry about me."

"Maybe worry wasn't the right word. I would be concerned about you."

"Will you think about it?"

How could I not think about it? "I'll tell you what. You have that talk with your father, the one about him being your biological dad, and then we'll talk again after that. Fair enough?"

"I guess so. But I wish you could be there with me when I talk to him. I'm sure he'll flip his wig."

"Look, Rachael, you've decided to take on some grown-up issues on your own, so you're going to have to face them as a grown-up."

"No sweat."

"So what do you want to do tomorrow?"

"Can we go see *Singin' in the Rain?*"

"Good choice."

"And then afterward, can we visit with the people in the big house?"

"I suppose so. Why?"

"Just to make sure we get along for when I live here."

Marie shook her head and couldn't hold back a smile. "You little..."

* * *

They hummed songs from *Singin' in the Rain* all the way home. "You Are My Lucky Star" was Marie's favorite. Rachael liked "Make 'Em Laugh."

"They were all so happy."

Marie gave her a heartfelt look. "Like you want to be?"

"I just want to fit in somewhere. The happy can come later."

Pretty profound for a fifteen-year-old. Marie couldn't get Rachael's words out of her head as she lay in bed that evening. "I just want to fit in somewhere." She saw a lot of herself in Rachael. Not only her wanting to fit in, but other things too. Like her need for family, her determination, and her self-control. And perhaps most importantly, her need to establish a true identity for herself.

A true identity was something Marie still hadn't determined for herself, at least not to the point of where she saw herself in a few years. When she was married to Richard, before he'd gotten in so deep with the Chicago underworld and before she knew Jonathan was her father, she had a well-thought-out plan in her head of where she wanted to be three years out, five years out. But things had changed.

Lying in bed that night, she thought about the prospect of having Rachael come live with her. She could picture them sharing the same space, chores, laughs, insights, and love. She had plenty of love in her heart for that child, and while she didn't have any experience, she thought she had a lot to offer to her in the way of guidance. Rachael needed a strong female role model, and Marie thought she could be the right person for the job.

While Marie didn't have strong religious convictions, she was certain some higher being was responsible for bringing her and Rachael together, and for that she was grateful. But she had to keep reminding herself that Rachael already had a mother and father, regardless of their insubstantial relationships among themselves.

* * *

They met Karen for breakfast on the last day of Rachael's visit. Karen presented her with a stylish young person's purse as a parting gift—a shoulder bag with a thin rope strap made of brightly colored fabric in an abstract design. "I just got these in last week, and they're selling like hotcakes."

"Cool. Thanks, Karen. And thanks again for the earrings too. I can't wait to wear them."

Marie and Rachael proceeded to the train station. Both had tears in their eyes as they said goodbye. Rachael promised to call her after she talked with her father. Marie promised to think about their talk. Rachael took a seat next to the window on the side of the train, where she waved goodbye to Marie and mouthed, *I love you.*

As the train left the station, Marie sat in her car, staring straight ahead but not seeing anything, listening to it roll away on noisy rails, until the noise faded into the distance, the lump in her throat refusing to go away.

* * *

"What would you do?" she asked Karen after she explained her last twenty-four hours with Rachael.

"Don't know. You could call her father, give him a heads-up, but then you told her to handle it like an adult, so he should hear it from her first. Then again, maybe she'll think it over on her train ride back home and chicken out."

"Oh, I doubt that." Marie shook her head. "I guess I should just let Rachael handle it in her own way. I gave her some examples of how to start the conversation. From what I know of Ben, he may not handle it well."

"Marie, would you let her live with you?"

Marie sighed. "I've thought about it, believe me. On one hand I think it may be the right thing to do, but then I think, what do I know about raising a teenager? And what about Ben? He's the controlling factor here."

"*If* he's really her father."

"I don't think that matters. He's assumed that role. And we can't forget about her mother either, even if she *is* missing."

"Wonder what a lawyer would say."

"God, I hope it never gets to that."

* * *

Ben called Marie the following Sunday. "You know the reason for this call," he began.

"Yes, I believe I do."

"Rachael is at her grandparents' house, so I can talk freely. Marie, I don't know quite what to say to you." She shut her eyes and waited for what was to come next. "At first, I was so grateful that Rachael took a liking to you. She went from being a mopey little girl to a happy, smiling young lady, and I credited you with that. But now this? I don't know what to think. Quite frankly, I regret having allowed her to come stay with you."

Marie didn't know what to think either. Was he referring to Rachael questioning her parentage, or wanting to come live with her? She blew out a gush of air through her lips which she hoped he didn't hear.

"To be honest," he continued, "I myself have questioned whether or not I'm Rachael's father as well. But what could I do? They needed a place to live, and I wasn't about to turn Judy and a ten-year-old away. I know I did the right thing." He paused. "Marie, I've treated Rachael as my own, so when she raised the question to me, what could I say? It was more than just an awkward moment."

Marie swiped one sweaty palm on her trousers, then the other. "I know. It was awkward for me too."

"What do you mean, for you too?"

"When she told me she didn't know whether or not to believe you were her real father."

"So you didn't put that notion in her head?"

"Of course not. Did she tell you that?"

"Well, no, I just assumed…"

"Ben, I would never do such a thing. No, she asked me in the car one day how I knew Jonathan was my father. I figured she was raising the question because of our different skin colors. But the more she asked, the more I knew she was really talking about her own situation."

"Did you tell her to talk to me about it?"

"Yes, I did do that. It was so heavy on her mind, I thought that was best. I hope you're not upset with me."

His tone softened. "Well, I was, but now that you've…now that I know how this all got started…I just wasn't prepared for her questions."

"Believe me, I thought about calling you as soon as she got on the train, but…"

"No, I understand. You didn't want to betray her. You did the right thing. And the more I think about it, even if she hadn't ever met you, she probably would have asked the question eventually."

Marie sighed. "When did she ask you this?"

"This morning." He laughed. "She's a very bright girl. She spent all day yesterday giving me a blow-by-blow description of how the two of you spent the week. I've never seen her so upbeat. She even got excited about the trip to Topeka and all the history you bestowed upon her." He let out a sigh. "So that little stinker made sure I knew what a great time she had, and then the next day she dropped the bomb on me. Maybe that's why I thought you put the idea in her head, by the way she wanted to build you up so I wouldn't be mad at you."

"If I'm not being too nosy, Ben, how *did* you respond to her?"

"I told her we'll probably never know for sure, but as far as I was concerned, she is and will always be my daughter. How'd I do?"

"I think that was a perfect response."

"Now about the other thing."

Marie's chest pounded. "Other thing?"

"Yes, the earrings. The ones Karen gave to her."

"You don't approve?"

"Don't you think they're a little too grown up for her?" Ben asked.

"Well, maybe just a little, but remember she is a teenager, so she's constantly going to test the waters. You know what I would do?"

"No, what?"

"I would tell her she could only wear the fancier ones on special occasions. That may be a reasonable compromise."

"You know what?"

"What?" Marie asked.

"I like the way you think."

She let out a silent sigh. "Rachael is a very special girl. You're lucky to have her."

"Can I call you from time to time when she's driving me completely crazy?"

Marie laughed. "Any time, Ben. Any time."

* * *

"So she didn't tell Ben she wanted to come live with you?" Karen asked the following evening.

"Apparently not."

"Wonder why."

"I don't know. I'm hoping she thought it over and decided maybe living with Dad isn't so bad after all. I kind of wish she would call me, though, to let me know what she's thinking."

Marie didn't have to wait long to find that out. A letter from Rachael came the following week.

> *Dear Marie,*
>
> *First of all, I want to thank you so much for the crazy time I had with you. It was such a kick! Thank you for all the places we went, that cool outfit you bought me, and especially our talks. No one has ever done anything like that for me before — ever.*
>
> *I thought about what we talked about on my way home. I thought about it a lot. I was glad there wasn't anybody in my car to talk to, cuz I really wanted to be alone. At first, I rehearsed how I was going to tell Dad I wanted to*

come live with you. But then I decided maybe one thing at a
time would be better. So I'm going to wait.

You were right about so many things. Like the way
Dad acted when I asked him how he knew he was really my
father. He didn't blow a fuse like I thought he would. He was
pretty cool about it. He told me no matter what, I'll always be
his daughter. I have to admit that felt pretty good.

One more thing. Mom called Dad while I was with
you, and boy was she mad!!! Dad didn't tell me everything
she said, just that she didn't like some other woman taking care
of me. Ha! But I don't really care what she thinks. She's such
bad news.

Well, I gotta go. I have a mess of homework. Please
say hi to Karen and Maurice for me. I think they're cool.

Love,
Rachael ♥

P.S. Dad's making me save the earrings Karen gave me
for special occasions. I guess I'll have to get creative on just what
a special occasion is. Ha Ha

"Writes a nice letter for a teenager. What do you think of it?" Karen asked after Marie read the letter to her.

"I think she handled herself very maturely. And I also think she has every intention of moving down here with me. She's just strategizing."

"What do you think about her mother calling Ben?"

"I'm not sure what to think. But I know she must have been referring to me when she said she didn't want some other woman taking care of Rachael."

CHAPTER 23

Judy

It was Good Friday. Marie was sitting on her sun porch sipping tea, too deep in thought to realize it had started to rain. Rachael had been gone two weeks, and Marie had to admit not a day had gone by that she didn't think about her. She thought about her own teen years and how much harder a time Rachael was having in hers. "I just want to fit in somewhere," she had said—a sad, unsettling statement. The phone interrupted her thoughts.

"What?!" Marie couldn't believe she had heard Claire correctly. "When did this happen?" She sat down, afraid her knees would buckle from underneath her. "Have they checked with all her friends?"

Marie hung up the phone and let everything Claire had said sink in. Then she called Karen.

"I have some terrible news. Ben's been shot and is lying in some hospital room, and Rachael is missing."

"What?!"

"Claire just called me. I don't know what to think or what I should do."

"Are you thinking of going there?"

Thoughts raced through her mind. "I would, but what if Rachael tries to call me? I'd want to be here," she said with a tremorous voice. "On the other hand, if something's happened to her, I want to be there for her. I'm not sure what to do."

"Well, if you want me to stay in your apartment while you go there, I can do that."

Marie mulled that over for a moment. "You wouldn't mind? What about your shop?"

"Don't worry about the shop. I'll have someone look after it."

Marie was on the next flight to Chicago. Jonathan agreed to send a car to pick her up. By the time she arrived at Jonathan's house, Ben had taken a turn for the worse. "Is he going to make it?" she asked her father.

"It doesn't look good, Marie."

"Any news on Rachael?"

"I'm afraid not."

Marie sank into the living room sofa and stared into space. Claire brought her a glass of wine. After taking a sip, she turned to Jonathan. "I just don't understand who would do such a thing. What are the police saying? How much does anyone know?"

"Greg said Ben's next door neighbor heard a loud bang shortly after midnight and went outside to investigate. He found Ben half-hanging out of Rachael's bedroom window, like he was trying to climb out of it. The neighbor called for an ambulance and then got his wife, who's a nurse, out of bed, and I guess she at least got the bleeding to stop. As soon as the neighbors realized Rachael was missing, they called the police."

"That poor child," Marie said. "Like she hasn't gone through enough in her life. Is Ben conscious? Has he been able to tell the police anything?"

"No, at least not as of a couple of hours ago."

"How are Gregory and Gloria holding up?"

Jonathan shook his head. "Gloria is still at Ben's in case Rachael shows up there. Greg is at the hospital hoping for a change in Ben's condition."

"Nothing like this has ever happened in St. Charles before," Claire said.

Jonathan told them the police had asked the Feinsteins a lot of questions about Rachael's mother.

"So they think she had something to do with it?" Marie asked.

"We don't know. We're not even sure if they don't think Rachael had something to do with it."

"That's preposterous! Dad, Rachael told me in a letter that Judy called Ben while she was with me in Atchison and wasn't at all happy about Rachael being with me."

"Really? You should tell the police that," Jonathan advised. "Come in here. You can use my office phone."

Marie made the call and told the police all she knew about Judy. She grimaced as she came out of Jonathan's office.

"Are you okay?" Claire asked.

"Not really. It just occurred to me if Judy had anything to do with this, she may have Rachael…and a gun."

Claire gasped.

"Okay, let's not jump to conclusions," Jonathan warned. The phone interrupted his thoughts.

He emerged from his office a few minutes later, his face pallid. "Ben didn't make it."

* * *

Ben's remains were buried the next day according to Jewish tradition. Two days passed without any word from Rachael. Claire had to force Marie to eat, reminding her if she didn't take care of herself, she wouldn't be of any help to Rachael once they found her. Sleep was next to impossible;

whenever Marie lay down, she couldn't even get her eyes to close, much less doze off.

On day three, Jonathan forced Marie to go on a ride with him before the family started arriving for Easter dinner. She nervously bit the inside of her lip while the horses were being saddled. "It's been too long," she said to her father. "Three days is too long. Isn't there something more we can do?"

Jonathan helped her onto the horse and then got up on his own. "I've been assured the police are doing everything they can."

"Well, maybe that's not enough."

Jonathan gave her a sympathetic look. "If I knew what else we could do, I would. You know that."

"I know. I'm sorry, Dad. It's just that I'm having all these crazy thoughts about what might have happened to her or what she is going through right now, and…"

"Don't go there, sweetheart. Let's keep the faith that she's alright. And if Judy has her, we have no reason to believe she would harm her."

They rode for thirty minutes at a slow pace, and when they reached Tré's favorite place on the rise, they stopped to admire the view.

"What about posters? We could put posters all over town. Maybe someone's seen her."

"Greg's neighbors took care of that."

"What about a reward? Maybe that…"

"There's a $5,000 reward, and it's on the poster."

"Who put up the reward?"

"Greg put up half. I put up the other."

When they returned from their ride, Claire told them the police had called the Feinsteins and told them they'd caught up with Judy in Wisconsin.

"Was Rachael with her?" Marie asked.

Claire shook her head. "When they asked about her, Judy said she didn't know where she was."

Marie heaved a heavy sigh, not knowing if that was a good or bad sign.

Claire's expression revealed she had more information. "When they searched her car, they found a Colt 38, the same kind of gun used to shoot Ben."

"What!?"

"They took her into custody and questioned her about the shooting, but she wouldn't say anything without an attorney."

Jonathan called Gregory. Claire and Marie listened with bated breath to the one side of the conversation.

"How many? Which ones? What can we do to help?"

Jonathan hung up the phone, his face as dour as Marie had ever seen it.

"What did he say?" Claire asked.

Jonathan took in a deep breath. "Greg asked the police how many shots had been fired from the gun they found."

"And?"

"Two."

Both women gasped.

"How many shots did Ben take?" Marie asked.

"One."

Marie couldn't hold back the tears. Claire moved over closer to her and put her arms around her. "You've got to stay strong, Marie. Stay strong for Rachael," she whispered.

Marie swiped the tears from her face. "What else did he say?"

"He said three radio stations committed to interrupting their programs periodically to announce Rachael's disappearance. I wrote down the station numbers. They're on my desk if you want to listen to them."

"What did he say when you asked him what we could do to help, dear?" Claire asked.

Jonathan's voice cracked. "He asked us to pray."

Day five. Still no word from Rachael. While no one said it, Marie knew everyone feared the worst. Jonathan knew the police chief well and was told they were doing everything possible to find her. Every available cop was on the case, bloodhounds were searching for her throughout Kane County, and the FBI had been called in when they found Judy across the state line.

In spite of Claire's force-feeding, Marie had lost five pounds since her arrival, and the dark circles under her eyes made her look even more gaunt. Jonathan had his work to keep his mind off of Rachael's whereabouts. Claire had her house chores. But all Marie had was time to think about what had happened and what could currently be happening to that child.

Strong emotions welled up inside of Marie with seemingly nowhere to go—fear, anguish, frustration, and anger, all bottled up inside of her, ready to blow. She felt more helpless, tired, and discouraged with each passing hour. Was Rachael being held against her will? Was she physically alright? Was she wondering why no one was coming to rescue her?

CHAPTER 24

That Peaceful Place

Day seven. Marie had another fitful night's sleep. She felt guilty sleeping in a clean, comfortable, safe place knowing that Rachael was likely having to deal with something much more exposed. Alone. Or maybe not alone.

As the morning dragged on, Marie's intense emotions were interjected with feelings of numbness. While she tried to keep her thoughts positive, her mind kept going back to the worst scenarios. She wished everything inside of her would shut down, at least until the uncertainty ended. The not knowing was the worst.

Claire answered the ringing phone and a minute later came running out of the kitchen. "They found her!" she shouted. "And she's alright!" She gave the phone to Marie, who was sitting at the kitchen table.

Marie was shocked to hear Karen's voice on the other end of the phone. She listened with tears rolling down her face while Karen talked.

"Rachael is here, and she's okay. She's had a rough week, but she's here now and she's okay."

"What happened?"

"I'm going to tell you all I know. It isn't much. Judy broke into Ben's house and tried to kidnap Rachael. When Ben came into Rachael's room, he tried to stop her. That's when she shot him."

"Who? Judy?"

"Yes, Judy. Judy shot Ben, and she and Rachael ended up in Kenosha, Wisconsin. Rachael said she hitchhiked here. I don't know any more details. She was so worn out that after I checked her over, I let her go to bed."

"I'll be home just as fast as I can. Can I talk to her? Do you think she's awake?"

"No, she's sleeping. Do you want me to wake her?"

"No. Let her sleep. Sounds like she needs it." She let a jittery laugh escape. "Just tell her I love her, and I'll be home as soon as I can."

"So what happened?" Jonathan asked after she hung up the phone.

"Wait. Don't start until I get back. I need to call the Feinsteins."

"Claire, you call Walter. He can drive us to the airport while Marie tells us what happened. And I'll call the chief too."

In the car, Marie filled them in on as much as she knew. "Oh, good heavens!" Claire gasped.

"I don't know anything more. Karen said it was all she could do to get Rachael to tell her the bare facts of what happened before she collapsed in the guest bedroom."

"Oh my God in heaven. That poor girl," Claire sighed.

"Karen made sure she was okay, physically anyway, before letting her fall asleep."

Jonathan and Claire shook their heads. "She probably doesn't know her father is dead," Claire said.

Marie nodded. "No. I guess I'll have to be the one to tell her."

"It won't be easy."

"I know."

"What are you going to do, Marie?"

Marie understood what he meant. "First I'm going to go home and make sure that child is alright. Then I'll call Greg and Gloria, and we'll figure it out. Rachael can certainly stay with me, temporarily at least—if it's okay with the Feinsteins, that is. But it's complicated, given her mother is still around."

"Oh, she'll go to jail for sure," Jonathan assured them. "Rachael was a witness, for God's sake. I think you can count on her being out of the picture for a long while." Walter pulled the limo up to the airport curb. Jonathan turned toward his daughter. "We're here for you if you need anything, sweetheart. Have a safe trip, and call us when you know more."

Claire gave Marie a sympathetic look. "We'll make sure the Feinsteins are kept in the loop. I think their week of Shiva ends today."

* * *

Marie entered her apartment feeling like she was walking into someone else's home. Karen greeted her with a hug. "How are you, hon?"

"I'm okay. The question is, how are *you?*" Marie asked.

"I'm okay. C'mon, let's go out here," Karen whispered, guiding Marie to the porch.

"No, wait." Marie went to the spare bedroom and peeked in on Rachael, who was curled up in a fetal position, her back facing the door. She tiptoed toward her, just far enough to see the peaceful expression on her deceptively callow face, then left the room.

She joined Karen on the porch. Two glasses of wine sat on the wicker end table, but Marie, wanting to have all her wits about her when Rachael woke up, didn't drink hers.

They kept their voices to a whisper. "She's still sleeping?" Karen asked.

"Mm-hmm. You're sure she's okay?"

"I think so. Like I said on the phone, I checked her out pretty well. She's exhausted, that's for sure, and very relieved it's over."

Marie took in a deep breath. "Tell me more about what happened to her."

"Don't know much more than what I already told you. She rang the doorbell because, of course, I had locked the outside door. I went down to see who it was, and when I looked out the window, I didn't see anyone at first. Then I heard scratching at the bottom of the door, and so I looked down, expecting to see a cat or something, and saw her, kind of crumpled up, leaning against the door."

Marie sighed. "Good grief."

"I know. So I opened the door and looked down at her. She looked up with the most pitiful face you ever saw and started to cry. I helped her up the stairs, sat her down on the sofa, and asked her if she was alright. She just shook her head, not saying anything."

"Do you think she was in shock?"

"I don't think so now. But then, I didn't know what to think. She asked for a glass of water. So I got that for her, and after she took a sip, she asked me where you were. I told her, and she asked me to call you. And I said, 'Not until you tell me what happened.' That's when she told me her mother broke into their house, shot Ben, and kidnapped her. She said they stayed in this dirty room in Kenosha, Wisconsin, and she escaped in the middle of the night and hitchhiked here."

Marie shook her head. "I can't believe this. She was missing a week! Were you able to tell her I was on my way?"

"Yeah. And when she heard that, she started to cry again." Karen's look was serious. "She really needs you, Marie."

Marie nodded and waited for the tears to stop welling up in her eyes. "I can't wait to put my arms around her and tell her everything's going to be alright."

"I know, hon. I know."

"You said she had bruises. Are they bad?"

"Not really. I gave her one of your nightgowns and stayed with her while she undressed. There are black and blue marks on her legs and one on her back, but that's about it." Karen paused. "I hope I did the right thing by not bringing her to the hospital or the doctor or something. It looked to me like the thing she needed most was sleep."

Marie reached over and patted Karen's hand. "You did the right thing. And I can never thank you enough for staying here…and being here for…"

"I could use a hug," Rachael said in a soft, broken voice. When their eyes met, Rachael started to cry.

Marie jumped up and put her arms around her, burying Rachael's face in her chest. "You're safe now, sweetheart. You're safe here with me."

The held each other until Rachael's sobs waned into soft tears. Karen mouthed, "I'm going to go. Okay?"

Still holding onto Rachael, Marie peered over her shoulder at Karen and nodded. They stayed in the hug several more seconds. Then, with a gentle touch, Marie pushed her away and examined Rachael's red swollen face. "C'mon, let's sit."

They stared at each other for a long moment before Rachael spoke, her hands clasped in her lap. "Are you mad at me?" she asked in a shaky voice.

Marie reached out for her hands. "Of course not, hon." She gave her hands a gentle squeeze. "I was worried sick about you, and I'm just so glad you're here and alright. Are you alright? Maybe we should have a doctor look you over."

Rachael shook her head. "I'm okay."

"Do you want to talk about what happened now, or do you want to wait until morning?"

"I can talk some now," she said, her voice barely audible.

"Your mother broke into your house. Is that when it all started?"

Rachael gulped before talking. "Mm-hmm. She came in through my bedroom window. I was sound asleep, and the next thing I knew someone had their hand over my mouth."

"You didn't know it was her?"

"Not at first. I tried to scream, but her hand was so tight, I couldn't. And then she grabbed my arm and started dragging me toward the window. I started kicking and knocked my Dr. Pepper sign clear across the room." She paused to take a couple of breaths.

"Your Dr. Pepper sign?"

"Yeah. Something one of Mom's boyfriends probably stole. Mom wanted it, but he gave it to me."

She rubbed the back of Rachael's hands. "Go on."

"She had this wild look on her face. It was crazy." She paused while she took in a couple of deep breaths. "Anyway, Dad must have heard the noise and he came in. They said some things back and forth, like Mom said she wasn't going to let Dad have me any longer, that I was going with her, and Dad tried to get me away from her, and that's when she pulled out the gun."

Marie shook her head and let her talk.

"Then she shot him." She barely got the words out. Tears welled up in her eyes. "Right in front of me." She squeezed her eyelids tight and took in another deep breath. "Is he alright?" she asked with a distraught face.

Marie put her arm around her shoulder. "No. I'm sorry, honey. He didn't make it."

She held Rachael until she stopped sobbing. "Do you want to stop?"

"No."

"What happened next, hon?"

"She dragged me out the window and to her car and threw me in the back seat and then floored it. I couldn't get out on her side 'cause there were just two doors, but I looked over at the other door and thought maybe I could get out that way, but she had tied that door with rope."

"Sounds like she had this planned out pretty well in advance."

"Yeah. We drove a long time. I thought about hitting her or something from the back seat, knock her out or something, but I was afraid maybe that would cause a crash, so I didn't."

"Did she say anything while she was driving?"

"No. She was too peed off to say anything. After awhile I asked her if she would just let me go on the side of the road or something, and I told her I wouldn't say anything to anyone. But she just kept telling me to shut up."

"Karen said you ended up in Kenosha, Wisconsin."

"Yeah. But I didn't know where I was then. We stopped at this sleazy motel or something. She dragged me outta the car and pounded on the door, and this creepy-looking big daddy opened the door and let us in."

"Could you describe him to the police, do you think?"

She nodded. "Anyway, they locked me in the bathroom and started talking, but I couldn't hear what they were saying, even with my ear on the door. Then I heard footsteps, and he said, 'I gotta take a piss.' Next thing I knew the door flew open and I flew out. Mom was standing by the front door with the gun dangling from her hand and told me, 'Don't even think about leaving.' I asked her why she was doing this, and she just told me to shut the ...well, to shut up again."

Marie tried not to let the horror she felt inside leak out onto her face. "You must have been scared to death. I am *so* sorry you had to go through that, Rachael. Do you want to go on or finish in the morning?"

Some color came back to her face. "I want to go on, but I'm a little hungry."

"When's the last time you ate?"

"Yesterday."

"Come on. I'll make you a sandwich."

Rachael continued to talk while she wolfed down the sandwich. "By this time it was almost daylight, but Mom was tired and said she was going to get some sleep. So she went into the bedroom and closed the door. But first she threw out a shirt and a pair of pants of hers for me to put on, 'cause I was still in my PJs, and then she left me with what's-his-name."

"Do you know his name?"

Rachael shook her head. "She called him 'dog.' But I could think of a few other names for him. Anyway, I had to sit in the living room with cootie guy while Mom slept. He had the TV on but nothing much was on at that time. He kept getting up to change the channel, and when all he could get were test patterns, he got mad and kicked it."

"You said your mother had the gun before. Where was the gun now?"

"Sitting on the coffee table. Anyway, he got a beer from the fridge and before he could finish it, he fell asleep on the couch." She gulped down a breath of air. "So I bolted out the front door and ran as fast as I could. Through the parking lot and across the street."

"He didn't try to stop you?"

"He was passed out. There were a lot of beer bottles lying around. Too boozed up to even know I was gone, probably."

Marie rested her arms on the dining room table. "Go on."

"I really didn't know where I was running to, I was just running." She took the last bite of sandwich. "I was running through this truck stop when I ran right into, I mean right into, this big fat dude. He put his hands on my shoulders and gave me a creepy look and then asked me where I was going in such a hurry. I told him away from here, and I tried to get away from him, but he held me pretty tight."

Marie got up to fill Rachael's glass with more milk, her stomach doing flip-flops.

"He started talking to me like he wanted to help me, but he was so big, he kinda scared me, and I just wanted to get away. Then this other guy came up to us. He was much smaller and looked nicer. He asked the big dude—his name was Prick—what he was doing with such a young girl, and I go…well, I lied and said, 'I'm not so young. I'm sixteen.' Then the short guy asked me where I was headed, and I said Kansas."

"What did you say his name was?"

"Which one?"

"The first guy."

"The short guy called him Prick."

"That's what I thought you said. Okay, go on."

"Probably just a nickname. Anyway, after I said Kansas, they both started laughing, and the short guy asked me if my name was Dorothy." She rolled her eyes. "Very funny. Then Prick said, 'I'm going as far as Chicago. You can ride with me.' I looked at the short guy, and he said Prick was okay, that I could go with him. Then he asked me if I was hungry, and I said yes, so he went into the truck stop and brought me back a burger."

"So you got into the truck with this guy?"

Rachael nodded.

"Oh my." All sorts of thoughts raced through Marie's head. "Did he hurt you at all, Rachael? Be honest with me. You can tell me anything."

Her eyes went wide with innocence. She shook her head. "No. We just rode without saying much. He told me he was headed for Akron, Ohio, I think it was, where he had a wife and three kids. A daughter my age."

Marie let out a big sigh. Rachael kept her gaze on Marie's face a long moment. "Don't worry. I've spent most of my life depending on people I don't trust or even know, not Ben or anything, but before. Maybe it wasn't the smartest thing for me to do, but..."

"I know, hon. Go on."

"Anyway, then when we got to Chicago, he talked to another truck driver on the radio, and he told me he was going to drop me off at the bus station where this other guy would take me the rest of the way."

"He dropped you off at a bus station?"

"Yeah. But no other trucker ever came by."

"So what did you do?"

She shrugged. "I just sat in the bus station all day, and when it got dark, I found a spot in the corner and dozed off and on all night."

Marie listened with intensity as Rachael's story unfolded, feeling a sinkhole of fear in her own gut she hadn't felt for years. "Weren't you scared?"

"Yeah, I was scared. But I just kept telling myself to look forward, and I did something my mom taught me."

"What's that?"

"First you sit with your ankles crossed. Then you put your hands in your lap and close your eyes. Then you take in a deep breath and let it out slowly, and you have to think about what you're doing, how you're breathing. In and out, or it won't work. You do this ten times. Now this is the best part. Then you let your head go to your peaceful place."

"Where's your peaceful place?"

"Well, everybody's is different. You just make it up. Mine is in the middle of a rainforest. And while I'm there, I listen real carefully so I can hear the waterfall in the background and the birds singing." She closed her eyes. "If I really concentrate on it, I can even feel the air on my face and little sprinkles of water from the waterfall." She opened her eyes. "And you can go there anytime you want to."

"That's beautiful, Rachael. I think I'll have to remember that the next time I'm scared."

"You? You get scared?"

"Everyone gets scared. You will never know how scared I was for you when you were missing."

Rachael flashed a guarded smile. "Anyway, so the next day someone in the bus stop said there was a soup kitchen down the street where you could get a meal, but you had to listen to a church sermon first, which I didn't mind. I'd done it before with Mom. So I walked over there and ate."

"What was that like?"

"Pretty crummy, but I was really hungry, so it was no big deal." She paused with a distant look on her face. "As far as soup kitchens go, I guess it wasn't that bad. I've been in worse. Anyway, I asked someone in there if they knew of any shelters who took kids, and this woman told me of one. It took me awhile to find it, but I did. I wanted to go there because sometimes if your timing is right, you can make a connection. Sometimes you have to stay a few days and be part of the scene before connecting, but after crashing there for three days, I didn't. That's the longest a kid can stay, because then they call Juvey."

"Juvey?"

"Juvenile Hall."

Marie couldn't believe that was their actual policy, but she didn't question it. "What kind of connection?"

"On whatever it is you need. Place to live. A ride somewhere. Booze. Drugs. That kind of stuff."

Marie tried to absorb it all but had a hard time visualizing a young teenage girl making it alone in a shelter. "So where did you go from there?"

Rachael sighed. "I went back to the bus station thinking if I asked enough people, maybe I could collect enough money for a bus ride here. Then this woman came up to me and asked me if I was okay. We started talking, and she was nice enough, so I told her where I was headed, and she said she would drive me there if I would go with her to Social Services and pretend to be her daughter. So I did that and she drove me here."

"Wait a minute. Pretend to be her daughter?"

"Mm-hmm."

"Why?"

She shrugged. "I dunno. Probably to get free money."

"Good grief," Marie mumbled. "So she drove you here, to my apartment?"

Rachael shook her head. "Not exactly. She dropped me off on Main Street. It took me awhile to find your apartment."

Marie sat back and stared at Rachael in awe, trying to connect all the dots of what the child had gone through. "You are so lucky you didn't get hurt. Tell me, though, why didn't you just try to find someone who could call the police or your grandparents for you?"

Rachael's lip quivered as though she was about to cry again. "All I could think of was my Dad might be dead, my mom is really messed up, and I wanted to be with you."

"Did you try to call here first?"

Tears welled up in her eyes. "I didn't want to talk to you just to have you tell me not to come here."

Marie took Rachael to her bosom and held her tight. "Well, I'm glad you're here now and by some miracle not hurt." She pulled out of the hug. "But you took some mighty big chances, young lady."

Rachael bit her lip. "I know. How much does Grandma and Grandpa know?"

"Just that you're here and safe. We'll call them tomorrow. I think the best thing now is for us to get some rest. I'm tired, and I know you must be too." Marie paused and made direct eye contact with her. "Rachael... what your mom did—abandoning you, shooting Ben, and whatever else—I can assure you didn't have anything to do with you."

"How do you mean?"

"It was all about her—her issues, her insecurities, her demons. They have nothing to do with you. You were just an unfortunate victim. Do you understand that?"

"I guess so."

"C'mon, let's get some sleep. Sound like a plan?"

Rachael rubbed her eyes. "Okay." Marie followed her toward the spare bedroom. Rachael turned around to face Marie. "Later, gator?"

Marie shook her head and gave her a heartfelt smile. She responded with, "Later, gator yourself," and then promptly called the St. Charles police, who informed her they would be sending someone to Atchison first thing in the morning to get Rachael's statement.

She then called Jonathan and Claire and relayed to them Rachael's harrowing account of what had happened to her. Their phone conversation ended close to midnight. The call to Gloria and Greg would have to wait until the next day.

CHAPTER 25

Change

The St. Charles policewoman arrived promptly at nine o'clock to take Rachael's statement. Marie could see that Rachael was nervous, but she handled herself extremely well for someone who had gone through that experience, especially a fifteen-year-old.

The Feinsteins were appreciative of Marie's offer to keep Rachael for a few days, understanding that if that was where she had fled, it was where she wanted to be, and it would be best, at least for now. They agreed to come to Atchison on Sunday, at which time the four of them would come up with a plan for Rachael's immediate future. Marie relayed this to Rachael while they sat at the dining room table.

"What's to discuss? I'm here now. Can't I just stay?"

"Rachael, it's not that simple. Gregory and Gloria are your grandparents, and my guess is that legally they have the final word on what happens to you."

"What about my mom?"

"Well, she's been arrested, and Jonathan thinks she'll probably go to jail. If that happens, she may not have any say in the matter."

"But they're not really my grandparents."

"You don't know that for sure."

"Yes, I do."

"How?"

"'Cause when Mom broke into the house, she told Dad he wasn't really my father."

"She did?"

"Yep. Threw it up right in his face."

"Well, you know we're back to that discussion we had the last time you were here. How do you really know? How do we know your mother is now telling the truth?"

"All I know is that it would be just like her to say Ben was my father when she was down and out and needed something from him. That's how she is. She uses people."

Marie peered long and hard into Rachael's discontented eyes. "Is that what you really want...to come live with me?"

She leaned forward. Her face was serious. "More than anything else in the world."

"I wouldn't be a pushover, you know."

Rachael sat back in her chair. "I know."

"And I wouldn't let you do whatever you want to do. There would be rules."

"I'm cool with that."

"You'd have to go back to school. And get good grades."

Rachael nodded. "No sweat."

"And no boys."

"What, for the rest of my life?"

"No. For the rest of mine."

A slow smile came across her face. "No boys. Can we at least get a dog?"

Marie half-smiled. Nothing she had done in her life had prepared her for raising a half-grown child.

* * *

The Feinsteins arrived at noon on Sunday as planned. Rachael took care of preparing lunch for the four of them. Gloria started the discussion. Her voice was warm but unyielding.

"Rachael, we know what you're going through, and we want you to know that whatever you need, you can count on us for it." She gave her a comforting smile. "Greg and I miss you very much. What we really came down here for is to take you home with us. We have that big house, so there's plenty of room. We need to get you back in school, into your riding lessons, back with your friends." She struggled to keep the tears in check. "And we think Ben would want that too."

Gregory nodded throughout Gloria's opening statement and then picked up from there. "I agree completely. We really do want you to come live with us and try to pick up the pieces. We think what's best for you is to be with family in a time like this."

"Before Rachael responds," Marie said, "I want to tell you that Rachael and I have talked pretty much since she got here about what may lie ahead for her. And believe me, I want what's best for her too. I've gotten to know her very well these past few months, especially these past few days, and there isn't anything I wouldn't do for this child." She looked at Rachael with tear-filled eyes. "I mean this young woman. And if what's best for her is to live with you, then I'm one hundred percent for it. But I have to tell you that she and I have also talked about her staying here…permanently."

Gloria and Greg exchanged glances. Greg let out a sigh and responded, "I can't say we're surprised. We're both aware of how much Rachael cares about you, and there's the fact that she sought you out when she was in trouble. That speaks volumes." He turned his attention to Rachael. "You're fifteen, Rachael, and you should have a say in the matter. Is that what you want to do, live here with Marie?"

Rachael nodded. "I love you guys. I really do." She swiped the tears off her cheeks. "But I'd like to stay here."

The Feinsteins turned their focus on Marie, who nodded. "Can my wife and I have a few minutes alone, Marie?" Greg asked.

"Of course." She led them to the spare bedroom and closed the door.

Rachael and Marie were silent while they waited for Greg and Gloria to emerge. When they did, Marie saw Rachael cross her fingers and put them behind her back.

"Here's the deal, young lady." Gregory's tone was serious, but everyone saw the glint in his eyes. "You'll come visit us often, and when you can't visit, you'll call us. And we may pop in here for a visit as well. If you don't do well in school, you'll have to answer to us." He gave Rachael an affectionate look. "Because I can assure you, we are *not* going to forget about you."

Gloria added, "And if you ever need anything, anything at all, even if it's just someone to talk to, you know how to get a hold of us."

Gregory turned to Marie. Marie glanced at Rachael. They both put their hands on their hips and said in unison, "We're cool with all that."

* * *

Marie and Rachael spent the next month getting Rachael settled in. There was school to consider, redecorating Marie's spare bedroom to match Rachael's personality, and establishing a routine that worked for both of them. School was the big issue. Rachael should have been starting her sophomore year in high school, but because of the amount of school she had missed, the Atchison High School wouldn't accept her. Academically, they thought she belonged in eighth grade.

Rachael went berserk. "They can't do that to me. I can't go to school *two* grades behind. Forget that shit!"

"Rachael! Your language."

"Sorry."

"Let me see what I can do."

It took a lot of convincing, but Marie was able to get the high school administrator to allow Marie to work with Rachael over the summer and then take an achievement test to see if she qualified to be a freshman in the fall.

During the next weeks, in between Marie and Rachael's long study sessions together, more of Rachael's story emerged of how she escaped from her mother, especially stories of the three days she spent in the shelter—stories about the squalid conditions and dealing with social misfits, the mentally ill, and garden-variety weirdos. She talked about how she'd had to sleep, or pretend to sleep, next to pie-eyed old men and then try to find something to do outside the shelter between ten in the morning and two in the afternoon when everyone had to leave.

Marie cringed when she heard her tell these stories like it was just another day in paradise. Fortunately or unfortunately, depending on how you looked at it, Rachael had been there before.

The Feinsteins boxed up Rachael's belongings and sent them to her. They included a card to wish her well in her new home and a check for fifty dollars for her to buy something special to make her new start a memorable one. With part of the money, Rachael bought a picture frame. She put a photo of herself and Marie in it and then sent it to the Feinsteins.

The Feinsteins had included a second check made out to Marie, a check for a thousand dollars. The note read, "Please use this toward Rachael's education. Ben would like that."

"I'm so proud of her," Marie told Karen one day when they met for lunch. "But just when I think I have her figured out, she does something else to surprise me."

"Like what?"

"Like the fact that she didn't tell the Feinsteins that her mom said Ben wasn't her father after they told her they wanted her to live with them. That was very mature of her. And what teenager would take the

fifty dollars they gave her and turn around and spend some of it on them?"
She told Karen about the picture frame.

"What else did she buy with it?"

"She bought a glass bud vase at the five-and-dime for her room, and
whenever I have flowers in the house, which is just about all the time,
she takes one for her vase. Or sometimes Julia will give her a stem or
two."

"Doesn't seem like something your average teenage girl would be
interested in. Maybe she's just looking for brownie points."

"Maybe, but I also think that's her way of expressing herself. She wants
that bond with me but doesn't know how to put it into words, so she finds or
maybe even creates a commonality between us, like the flowers, to show me
instead. Another thing is whenever I work late, I'll come home and find she's
done something without being asked, like taking out the garbage or dusting
and sweeping the sun porch, stuff like that."

Karen laughed. "Have to give her credit. She's very...let's say shrewd
for her age. How's she doing with the studying?"

"Really well. She's a bright girl and determined not to have to go
through eighth grade again. I give her an assignment in the morning
before I go to work, and she has to have it done by three when I get home.
Then we go over it together, and I quiz her on it."

"That's great."

"I told her she could take off weekends, but she suggested we keep
going." Marie sighed. "I'll be glad when this is over. It's running me
ragged."

"But you love every minute of it, don't you?"

Marie smiled and nodded. "Hey, how's Maurice? I've been so wrapped
up in my own life, I haven't asked you about yours lately."

"We're good. What are you two doing on Memorial Day?"

"Jonathan and Claire invited us up for the weekend, so that's where
we're going. I'm sure we'll see the Feinsteins as well, which will be good
for Rachael. How about you and Maurice?"

"He wants me to meet his daughter, but we haven't quite figured out how to do that yet. His ex-wife is a real pill. Goes out of her way to make things difficult for him."

"That's too bad. How old is the daughter now?"

"Just turned seventeen. Maurice is trying to get her interested in the University of Missouri, but her mother is against it."

"Well, she'll be eighteen before you know it, and then she can decide things for herself."

"That's what he's banking on. He's going to Kansas City next week on business. Do you and Rachael want to take in a movie? *Heidi* may be fun."

"Are you kidding? That would be *way* too immature for her," Marie said sarcastically.

"How about *Don't Bother to Knock* with Marilyn Monroe?"

"Um...come back down a notch...or two."

"*The Greatest Show on Earth?*

"Perfect."

* * *

It didn't take long for Rachael to befriend thirteen-year-old next door neighbor, Phyllis Armstrong, and as a result, Rachael's home territory expanded. Marie just hoped Phyllis was the one she was interested in being with and not Phyllis's seventeen-year-old brother. Rachael and Phyllis would spend time in each other's bedroom or in the yard behind the coach house. Marie and Phyllis's mother, Linda, talked about it one day.

"I'm glad the two of them are friends," Linda remarked. "There are no girls Phyllis's age in the neighborhood."

"Me too. It keeps Rachael close to home but gives her a little freedom as well. If she's ever around too much, be sure to let me know."

"You know, Phyllis is going away to camp for two weeks next month. I wonder if Rachael would want to go."

"Where is it?"

"Up in Hiawatha. Lots of horseback riding, swimming, and hiking. I think the age group is eleven to fifteen."

"I'll ask her. May be good for her."

Rachael was excited to go. Mr. Armstrong drove the girls to camp in his prize '31 Ford roadster complete with rumble seat.

Marie invited Karen over for dinner one night while Rachael was at camp. "So what have you been doing while she's gone?"

"Well, for one thing, I am totally digging the silence. I almost forgot what that sounded like."

"I'll bet."

"And the TV is getting a break. She has a habit of turning it on and then going off to do something else. Like listen to the radio in her room. Do you know how many times a day I have to tell her to turn it down?"

"Plenty, I'm sure. Who does she listen to?"

"Have you ever heard of Johnnie Ray?"

"No."

"Neither have I, but he's on the radio, and she likes him. I don't much."

"What else have you noticed with her gone this week?"

"I noticed an overdue library book in her room…on Amelia Earhart. And here I thought she hadn't heard a word I'd said about her."

"What about her?"

"I took her to her museum and told her Amelia was a stubborn and determined individual, just like Rachael. Now she's reading a biography about her."

"Got to give her credit, even if the book is overdue."

Marie laughed. "Well, I guess I can't have everything. She's a handful."

They continued talking while preparing dinner. "Your life sure has changed with her here," Karen remarked.

"I'll say, but with Rachael at camp, I can tell you I don't miss picking up after her or straightening the bathroom towels six times a day."

Karen shook her head. "I don't know how you put up with her."

"Did I tell you I discovered she was using my razor? So now I have to have a talk with her on feminine hygiene when she gets back. Good grief."

"Just wait 'til you have to have the birds and bees talk."

"Ugh. I hadn't even thought about that. When am I supposed to do that?"

"Well, she *is* a teenager."

Marie shook her head while she thought about their conversation. "And all that eye-rolling. Drives me crazy."

"Anything else?"

Marie smiled. "God, I miss her."

Karen chuckled. "Who said, 'Love knows not its own depth until the hour of separation?'"

"I don't know, but they sure knew what they were talking about. She wrote me a letter from camp, you know." Marie got up to retrieve the letter and let Karen read it to herself.

Karen glanced up at Marie after reading it. "Well, she writes a good letter."

"I think so too." Marie tried to stifle a smile. "And guess what else? I got a letter yesterday from Greg and Gloria. Turns out Ben had an insurance policy, and they wanted Rachael to be the beneficiary, so they enclosed a check for $10,000."

"You're kidding. So Rachael doesn't know yet?"

Marie shook her head. "I haven't decided how to handle it yet—the money, that is. What I may do is give her a small amount now to do with as she pleases, then another amount for us to invest together so she learns about how that's done, and the largest portion set aside for her college. What do you think?"

"Sounds good to me." Karen smiled and gave her a peculiar look. "What?"

"You know, you're like a different person these days."

"Why do you say that?"

Karen shook her head. "I don't know. Just the look you get on your face when you're talking about Rachael. You just seem happier to me. Not that you looked unhappy before…"

"I know what you mean. I was just thinking about that last night too. It's almost like I'm a different person living in a different world lately."

"You have other things to think about now."

"Ain't that the truth." Marie fingered the stem of her wine glass before taking a sip. "I know I did the right thing by taking Rachael in. I wouldn't change any of that. I'd do anything for that child."

"But?"

"I've been feeling a little guilty lately."

"About what?"

"I don't know. It's just that prior to Rachael, all my spare time was spent thinking about Jonathan and my background and how I needed to deal with all that. And now…"

"If it's change you're concerned about, you've gone above and beyond on that."

"What do you mean?"

"You changed a young girl's life, don't forget."

Marie smiled a soft, slow smile. "I know. And you have no idea how good that makes me feel."

"So what's with the race issue?"

"What about it?"

"No longer an issue?"

Marie gave that some thought. "Yes, of course it is."

"When's the last time you thought about it?"

Marie bit her lip and stared past Karen for a moment. "It's been awhile." She looked back at Karen. "I feel like such a hypocrite."

"You shouldn't."

"Yeah. Easy to say."

"You were searching a long time for what you thought would change your life, make it better. You just didn't expect it would be...well, Rachael."

Marie stared right through Karen. "You're right."

"Maybe race wasn't really your most crucial issue after all."

She met Karen's gaze. "You know, we've never been on the same page on this subject."

"Not even close."

"Well, we're still not." Marie focused her eyes on Rachael's letter. "But now I think we may be at least reading from the same book."

CHAPTER 26

Trust

Rachael returned from camp, and in no time the coach house apartment was back to its normal teen-induced craziness, with Marie back to her quasi-mom role.

Rachael passed the eighth grade achievement test and was allowed to enter high school as a freshman. Much to Marie's surprise and gratification, Rachael appeared to be fitting nicely into her new world. In a relatively short period of time, she had a diverse group of friends Marie thought helped to keep her balanced. For the most part, she was a well-behaved and -mannered teenager. But every so often, she regressed into her old ways—like the time she ditched school.

Johnnie Ray was scheduled to visit Leavenworth Prison, and Rachael had asked Marie if she could skip school to see him. One of her friends had talked her mother into driving them there in hopes they would catch a glimpse of him. Marie said no. Rachael went anyway. Marie found out a week later when a photograph of a long black stretch limo fell out of one of her textbooks.

"What's this?"

Rachael shrugged.

"Rachael, what *is* this?"

"Looks like a photograph to me."

"Don't get smart with me. Tell me why you had this photo in your math book."

"'Cause I like limos?"

Marie put her hands on her hips and narrowed her eyes. "You went to Leavenworth last week, didn't you?"

Rachael looked down.

"I'll find out anyway when I call the school, so you may as well 'fess up now."

"Please don't call the school!"

"Why?"

She met Marie's eyes. "Because they think you excused me that day."

"And why would they think that?"

"Because of the note you wrote."

"What?"

Rachael bit the inside of her bottom lip. "I sorta forged a note from you so I could go."

Marie glared at her...hard. In a surprisingly calm tone, she said, "You did what?"

Rachael drew her right arm across her body and clasped her elbow. "I know it was wrong, but I *really* wanted to go."

Marie held up the picture. "So you could get this? A picture of his limo?"

"Well, you can't tell from the picture, but we could see him inside it. He waved at us."

"Well that wave is going to cost you dearly."

"What are you going to do?"

"Go to your room for now. I need time to think. You know what's the worst part of all this? That I can't trust you anymore."

Rachael wasn't in her room more than five minutes when she reemerged, her eyes red and puffy. "Can we talk?"

"Okay."

She couldn't hold back the tears. "I'm sorry. I'm so sorry. I don't care what the punishment is; I'll take anything you give me. But *please* don't say you can't trust me, Marie. I can't take that."

"Come here." Marie put her arms around her. "Do you understand *why* I feel that way?" She felt Rachael nod into her chest. She gave her a squeeze and then gently pushed her away, keeping her hands on Rachael's shoulders. "No more lying or sneaking around?" Rachael shook her head. "And when I say no, I mean no."

Rachael pulled out from Marie's hold to wipe her eyes. Her voice quivered. "I promise. But please say you trust me."

"You've got to regain that trust, Rachael."

"I will. I promise." Rachael took in a big breath of air and let it out through a smile. "He was so cute."

"A real flutter bum?"

"Yeah.

Rachael stared a long moment into Marie's eyes. "If I ask you something, will you promise to tell me the truth?"

"That depends."

"On what?"

"If I think you're mature enough to handle the truth."

"Have you ever done anything that would cause someone not to trust you?"

Marie thought back to her days with Richard after she discovered who she really was but felt too disconcerted by it to tell him. Then, when she was convinced he was in over his head with sinister activities, she'd plotted for months to leave him. That was followed by her breaking into someone's home after fleeing from Richard and scaring an old lady half to death.

"Yes, I have. I suppose we all have if we're honest about it."

"So what did you do to earn back that trust?"

I can't get into this with her. "That part is complicated."

"So I'm not mature enough to handle it? Is that what you're saying?"

"Something like that."

Rachael turned from her and went into her bedroom, the sound of her door closing causing Marie to feel even more remorseful for not having come up with a better answer.

Marie stopped in Karen's shop the next day and told her about the ditching school incident. "So what was her punishment?" Karen asked.

"She has to come straight home after school for the next two weeks and do her homework. No friends. When she's done with her homework, she has to help me cook dinner. But the hardest thing was I made her tell her girlfriend's mother and the principal that she forged the note."

"Oh, I'm sure that went over big."

"Well, she didn't fight it, and I know she did it because I got calls from both of them afterward." She let out a sigh.

"All things said and done, though, she's turned out to be a pretty good kid, hasn't she?"

"Mm-hmm. Especially when you think of what all she's gone through."

"I think you two were meant for each other."

Marie smiled and nodded. "And you know what's really cool?"

"What's that?"

"That I catch myself all the time thinking of us as one. I think that's telling."

"Sounds like the start of a family to me."

Karen's comment took Marie aback. She hadn't thought about it in those exact terms. *The start of a family. I'm mixed race but look white. We don't know who Rachael's father is.* "It's the start of something, that's for sure."

"Whatever happened to her mother, by the way?"

"I didn't tell you? She pled guilty and got twenty-five years in prison." Marie was grateful Rachael didn't have to testify in court against her mother.

"What did Rachael say to that?"

"She didn't say much. I asked her if she wanted to have any contact with her, and she said no. But she could change her mind later on. I'll let her make that choice for herself."

"Does she ever talk about her father, who he might be?"

"No. Not since she's been with me."

"Do you think about it?"

Marie frequently struggled with how much to get involved with Rachael's parentage. She thought the right thing to do would be to provide guidance for Rachael when it came to her biological father, but she also knew from firsthand experience that some matters were best handled on one's own—in one's own time and on one's own terms.

"All the time. Look what happened to me when I found out who my father was. Changed my whole life."

"For the better."

"Right."

"Doesn't mean it would necessarily be for the better for Rachael, though."

"I know." Marie drifted off to another place for a few seconds. "Well, I didn't find out until I was twenty-four. She's got time."

"So…going to let her have a dog?"

"Did she tell you that?"

"She told me she's been working on you."

"That child. No, we're not home enough for a dog, and besides, it's in my lease, no dogs. Don't tell her, but I've been thinking of taking her to the pet orphanage to pick out a kitten before school starts. It turns out Sheana is a one-person cat and isn't taking to Rachael very well."

"Promise you won't tell her I told you this?" Karen asked. "She said she really wanted a cat, but she thought you'd say no, and that would be the end of it. But if she started with a dog, she thought she could work you down to a cat."

"She is too smart for…"

"Her own good."

"Have I said that before?"

"Just about a million times."

* * *

Marie arranged for Rachael to continue riding lessons on Saturday mornings, and when she was sure her interest in equestrianism was sincere, she bought her a horse of her own. Rachael named him Fiducia, the Italian word for trust.

Both horses were boarded together, at Ted's ranch in Hiawatha. Thanks to Ted's easy-going nature, for which Marie was extremely grateful, there hadn't been any awkwardness between the two of them given their first and last date. He gave Rachael a warm welcome and invited her to come visit any time.

There was an assortment of trails on Ted's ranch, each with varying degrees of difficulty. Following Ted's advice, Marie and Rachael tried a different one each time they went out, Ted sometimes joining them.

When Marie felt Rachael had eased into her new life comfortably, she took her to the animal shelter in Kansas City and let her pick out a kitten. She chose a black-and-white one and named her Miska. The kitten immediately attached herself to Rachael and took up residency in Rachael's bedroom on the first day, pretty much ignoring Marie and Sheana.

Shortly after the beginning of her school year, Rachael asked Marie, "Can you take me to Olathe to see an exhibit of Grace Bilger's artwork? I have a class project where I have to study an artist and write a report on what inspired them."

They went to the Bilger exhibit the following Saturday. Karen accompanied them. They learned that Bilger was a prolific local artist who taught art at the Kansas State School for the Deaf. They all thought her watercolors were particularly impressive—landscapes, portraits, and still-lifes.

"Some day I want to paint like her," Rachael said.

"I didn't know you had any interest in art, Rachael."

"Well, you don't know everything about me, you know." She smiled.

"Should I be worried?"

"No, you pretty much know all the bad stuff."

They were driving through Leavenworth when Rachael announced she had to go to the bathroom…badly. "Isn't Barry's place near here?" Karen asked.

"It's right up the road. We can stop there."

When Marie pulled into the parking lot, Rachael quipped, "Guns and ammo? What kind of place are you taking me to?"

"Just what it says. They sell guns and ammunition."

"How would you know a gun dealer?"

Marie laughed. "I guess you don't know everything there is to know about me either, young lady."

Rachael raced through the door and headed toward the back of the store before Marie could say anything to Barry.

He flashed her his slow, sweet smile. "What was that?" he asked.

"That was Rachael. I hope you don't mind. She had to go *really* bad, and we were in the neighborhood. How are you, Barry?"

"No complaints here. How have you been?"

"Busy. But good. You remember my friend Karen?"

"Of course. Nice to see you again. No takers yet on your rifle, by the way." His gaze quickly went back to Marie. "So have you done any target shooting lately?"

"I'm afraid not. I've been busy with…" She glanced toward the back of the store. "Who's she talking to back there?"

"Olivia is in the back room. But she doesn't speak any English."

"Olivia?"

He gave her an uneasy look. "Long story. Don't ask."

A small, wide-eyed little girl peeked out from the doorway, her long black unkempt hair covering much of her heart-shaped face, her dress dirty and worn. Marie cocked her head and looked back at Barry.

"Every once in awhile I watch her for a couple of hours while her... well, I'm not sure who she is, runs errands or something." He glanced at his watch. "She should have been back by now."

The girl stayed in the doorway of the back room while Rachael approached the front of the store.

"That's Olivia," Rachael said.

"Yes, we know," Marie responded. "Were you talking with her?"

"Yeah. But she's pretty shy. I couldn't get her to say much."

"Well, she doesn't speak any English."

Rachael rolled her eyes. "I know a Mexican when I see one. I spoke Spanish with her."

"You can speak Spanish?"

"Sure." Rachael answered with a shrug, as if to ask, "Doesn't everybody?"

Marie let out a sigh. "Okay, one more thing I didn't know. Are we ready?" She turned to Barry. "Thanks for the use of your facilities."

"Anytime." He shifted his weight and smiled. "And don't be such a stranger," he said as they left his store.

"Hey, look at this," Rachael said. She stood halfway behind a bush next to the building and pointed to an open beat-up duffle bag. A stuffed teddy bear stuck out of the top. She reached down to pick up the bear.

"No, don't touch it!" Marie blurted. "Let me get Barry."

Barry came out and stared at the bag. He bent down, picked up the bear, and handled it as if it were a live hand grenade.

"Osito!" Olivia ran up to Barry and grabbed the bear from his hands.

He glanced at Marie, then Karen, then Rachael, his eyes wide. "Can you ask her if that's her toy?" he asked Rachael.

"*¿Es tu juguete?*" she asked Olivia.

Olivia hugged the bear and nodded. Barry peered over the duffle bag and then bent down and gingerly picked out a piece of clothing. "Ask her if this is her dress."

"*¿Es tu vestido?*"

The girl nodded. Barry's jaw dropped. He picked up the bag and stared at Marie. "Can you come in for a minute?"

Marie followed him into the store and then turned around to face Karen. "Will you be okay out here for a few minutes?"

"Sure," Karen said. "We'll be fine."

"What's going on, Barry?" Marie asked.

"This woman usually comes back to get her in two hours or less." He glanced at his watch. "It's been over three."

"Do you think she's not going to come back this time?"

He took out the contents of the duffle bag and laid them on the counter: two pairs of pants, two tops, pajamas, a pair of shoes and socks, several pairs of underpants, and the dress. "What do *you* think?"

"What are you going to do?"

"I don't know." He looked up at Marie with total panic on his face. "What am I supposed to do with her?"

"Do you know how to reach this woman?"

He shook his head. "I don't even know her name. She'd talk to me, but I never understood a word she said."

"Do you know any relatives?"

"No."

"Do you know her last name?"

"The woman's, no. But Olivia's father's name was Flores."

"Was?"

"Yes. He's dead."

"Well, you'll have to call the police. I would…"

"*¡Ningún policía!*"

Everyone's attention shifted toward Olivia, who was running toward Barry. She grabbed his leg and held on tight. The look on his face begged for help.

"She said no police," Rachael interjected.

Barry let out an audible sigh. "She's had her share of police in her short life." He allowed Olivia to keep hold of his leg. He patted her head and said, "You'll be safe with us, Olivia."

Marie got more curious by the minute as to what had brought this little girl and Barry together, but refrained from asking any questions for the time being.

"Rachael, can you take Olivia to the back room and keep her occupied while we figure this out?" Barry asked. Rachael did as she was told.

"Barry, I know you said it was a long story, but maybe we could help you through this better if we knew how you've come to know Olivia."

He took in a deep breath. "About two months ago, I was sleeping in the back room. Sometimes if I'm here late, and I don't feel like driving home, I go out to eat and come back here for the night. Anyway, I was asleep when I heard a noise, like someone was trying to break in. I grabbed a gun and hid behind the door to the back room, and it was light enough—there may have been a full moon that night, I don't know. Anyway, there was enough light for me to see this guy break in the door and head for the gun cases. So I yelled, 'Stop or I'll shoot,' and this guy pulled a gun on me." He gulped. "I shot it out of his hand before he could pull the trigger."

Karen gasped.

"Oh my God. How awful," Marie exclaimed.

"Tell me about it. The guy yelped and hightailed it out of my store. I called the police and then ran out to see if I could see where he went, but he was gone. Left his car behind."

"That seems odd, don't you think?"

"Well, there was blood splattered all over my front window, so I suspected then his hand got shattered pretty good and so maybe he couldn't drive. And I found out later his hand *did* get mangled because they found his body down by the railroad tracks."

"His body?"

"Turns out he was in this country illegally, with a criminal record, and the police suspected he tried to hop a train before they caught up with him."

"And what? He was run over by the train?"

"They think he missed the train and...well, it wasn't pretty."

"How awful."

"Anyway, back to the night of the break-in. The police took my statement and left, and I was going to pour me a healthy glass of bourbon—and I haven't had a drink in over ten years, so you know the state of mind I was in—when one of the policemen came back in my shop and told me when they searched this guy's car, they found a little girl. Olivia."

"What?"

"They suspected this guy I shot was her father, and she was in the back seat waiting for him."

"Good grief!" Karen said. "So what happened to her?"

"They took her with them...crying all the way to their car. It was horrible, but what could I do?"

Marie could tell by the compassionate way Barry told the story that he had been deeply disturbed by the whole ordeal.

"To make a long story even longer, two weeks later, this woman comes in my store with Olivia, says something to me in broken English that I didn't understand, and then leaves. So here I am with this...how old would you say Olivia is? Four, five maybe?" Marie and Karen shrugged. "This little girl who doesn't speak a word of English, and I don't know if this woman's coming back or not."

"Barry...that poor child. So what did you do?"

"I had shot the girl's father. The least I could do was wait to see if the woman was coming back for her. So I showed Olivia the back room, 'cause I had customers coming in and out, and she stayed back there the whole time."

"So the woman came back?"

"Yep. Two hours later. She said *gracias* and left."

"Unbelievable."

"And she did that a few more times...until today."

Karen had tears in her eyes. "I'm going to check on them. I'll be right back."

"Well, you have to call the authorities, Barry. What else can you do?" Marie paused. "Why are you looking at me like that?"

"By any chance, do you remember when I gave you all those free shooting lessons, you said if there was any way you could repay me...?"

"Okay, what are you thinking?"

"Can you just stay here until we get this resolved? I'm in way over my head here."

She gave him a friendly smile. "Of course."

They called the police and requested a meeting away from the gun shop. Marie accompanied Barry to a nearby coffee house where they met up with Sergeant Farber. He brought along Spanish-speaking social worker, Pilar Hierra. Barry explained the situation.

Miss Hierra spoke first. "The only Spanish-speaking orphanage I know of is in Topeka. I'm willing to take her for the night, and then I can drive her there tomorrow."

"An orphanage?"

"That's about all I can do for now. I need time to see if I can locate the woman who dropped her off or some family member or something."

"And what if you can't find anyone? Will someone adopt her? Some other family? A good family?" Marie asked.

"Maybe. But I can tell you, it's hard to adopt out Mexican children."

We can't let this happen, Marie thought. Barry, Miss Hierra, and the policeman got up to leave. "Wait," she said. All eyes were on Marie. "We can't send this little girl to an orphanage. She'll be scared to death. Look what's happened to her so far."

"I don't see any other way," the social worker said. "We don't know where she belongs."

"She can stay with us." The words came out faster than her mind could reconcile what she was saying. "Until you can find her family."

No one sat back down. Marie stayed put. "We have the room, and I have a daughter who speaks Spanish." *Daughter?* "Would there be anything wrong with that?"

Miss Hierra raised an eyebrow. "It would be highly unusual."

"I have found, Miss Hierra, that sometimes you have to take unusual measures to do what needs to be done."

Miss Hierra turned toward Barry. "What do you have to say about this?"

"Me?"

She gave him a puzzled look. "You're the husband, aren't you?"

He shook his head. "No, I'm not the husband. But I am a very close family friend, and I'll be here to help out any way I can." He put his hand over Marie's and gave it a squeeze.

"My daughter is also very responsible," Marie said. "She's fifteen and good with children."

"So where's your husband?"

"I'm divorced, Miss Hierra."

Barry shot her a surprised look.

"A divorcee?" The look on Miss Hierra's face was nothing short of dubious.

"A divorcee with a college degree who owns her own business in Atchison and is a pillar in her community, I might add," Barry blurted.

The social worker shot him a disparaging look. "I assumed you were married," she said to Marie.

"No, I am not."

Hierra peered over her glasses and down her broad nose at Marie. "So who all lives with you?"

"It's just Rachael and me."

"And Rachael is your daughter?"

"She's my surrogate daughter."

"And what exactly does that mean?"

"Her father was killed in April, and I took her in."

Marie didn't know how to interpret Hierra's frown. "Okay, for one night, and I'll come visit you tomorrow to inspect your house to make sure it's suitable. We can take it from there. Maybe I can get a temporary custody order or something until we find her family."

Marie got up and shook her hand. "Thank you. We'll take very good care of her. I promise you that."

Barry took her elbow as they walked toward his truck. "Are you okay?"

"I don't know." She glanced up at him. "What have I just done?"

"The right thing, darlin'. You did the right thing. And Marie?"

"Yes?"

"I meant what I said in there. I'm responsible for all this, and trust me, I will do whatever I need to do to help." Marie knew by his expression he was being sincere.

Rachael kept Olivia occupied in the back seat on their drive home. Rachael's Spanish seemed to be fluent enough to keep a good conversation going. After they got Olivia settled in Rachael's bed for the night, Marie asked Rachael how she learned Spanish.

"We lived in a Mexican neighborhood once for awhile. It wasn't hard to pick up from the other kids. I had to if I wanted to play with them."

CHAPTER 27

Daughters

The social worker arrived at ten the next morning, giving Marie barely enough time to discuss her situation with Julia. Fortunately, with three children of her own, Julia was completely understanding. She and Marie carried a rollaway bed Julia had in her basement up to Rachael's room and threw a blanket and pillow on it, Olivia's teddy bear perched high on the pillow being the final touch.

At the end of the inspection, the social worker took a photograph of Olivia and said she would try to locate any relatives. In the meantime, she was okay with Olivia staying with Marie.

The sudden addition of Olivia to Marie's household caused her mind to spin in different directions. While she knew it was unwise to start thinking about the three of them as a family, it was hard not to, especially when she saw how Rachael and Olivia interacted with each other. She knew the minute Olivia's relatives were found, she would be taken away from her, but even that didn't stop her from thinking how this unlikely ménage had started to spell out family.

The last thing Marie wanted to do was disregard her ethnicity in favor of fulfilling her desire to have a family. *But I would be giving two children a good home, two children who needed and deserved a good home.* She thought about Olivia's ethnicity, being a Mexican in a white world. She laughed to herself at the thought of Rachael being the only one without a race issue. God knew she had enough other issues to make up for that.

Suddenly the concept of having her own biological family someday didn't seem so important. Had the most troubling aspect of her mixed ethnicity been suddenly abolished? Marie didn't know how she felt about that. Was she compromising her most intrinsic belief that race shouldn't matter? Or was she making the most of an impossible situation given whites' current attitude toward Negroes?

Marie's thoughts occupied every spare minute of her day and kept her up most nights. In the meantime, she didn't hear anything from the social worker except for when she periodically checked in on them, and life went on.

She was more than just a little pleased to see it didn't take long for Olivia to fit in her household. And it didn't take Rachael long to start teaching Olivia English—on her own, without being asked, making Marie a proud...a proud what? She wasn't sure what to call herself.

Ten days into Olivia's stay, Marie and Rachael were sitting on the sun porch at the end of the day. The cool mid-October evening breeze was enough to make them don sweaters. Marie drank merlot. Rachael drank Coca-Cola. Olivia was sound asleep in her room.

"Can we talk?" Rachael asked.

"Of course, sweetheart. What's on your mind?"

"So how have I been doing?"

Marie was puzzled. "What do you mean?"

"I mean, you're pretty hip when it comes to telling me when I've done a good job in school, or horseback riding, and now with Olivia, but how am I doing as your...well, I heard you say to that social worker... you called me your daughter."

Marie peered deep into Rachael's anxious eyes. She knew the time Rachael was talking about. She had wanted Miss Hierra to see a stable home life for Olivia until they found a permanent place for her, but she hadn't realized Rachael had overheard her.

The truth was Marie had struggled with the possibility of trying to legally adopt Rachael. The huge step of adopting a child as a single parent was difficult enough without factoring in race. In her heart, she had no issue with being a Negro and adopting a white child, her passing for white notwithstanding. But she knew it would raise more than just a few eyebrows from other people. And while she tried not to let other people's opinions affect her own actions, it was hard not to think about the potential problems they would likely face down the road.

Marie stared past Rachael, out the window into the starlit night sky. When she looked back at her, she saw Rachael holding back tears. "You were uncomfortable with that."

"Sort of."

"Why, hon?"

"'Cause I'm not really your daughter."

"I know. And maybe I shouldn't have referred to you as that, but I was trying…"

"I know what you were trying to do. I'm not stupid." Rachael looked down into her lap.

Marie wasn't sure what to say. The situation was nothing short of complicated. "What about your real mother?"

Rachael shot her a disgusted look. "I couldn't care less about her."

"You say that now, but…"

"Please don't tell me how I feel about her. I hate her. I hate the way she raised me, and I hate what she did to Ben. I want nothing to do with her."

"Well, whether you like it or not, legally, your mother is still your mother." She looked deep into Rachael's eyes. "What if I was able to legally adopt you? Would that make you feel better about things?"

"Are you kidding?"

"Think about it. Remember, I'm half Negro. What would your friends think?"

"Who cares what they think?"

"You may, the first time they call me a name."

"Call you names and I'll give 'em a knuckle sandwich."

Marie peered at Rachael and smiled. Rachael smiled back.

"Aside from *wanting* to give them a knuckle sandwich, what would you do?"

"Look, if you can handle being part Negro and looking white your whole life, I think I can handle a snide comment from a kid or two."

Marie wasn't sure if she admired the child's way of thinking or was frightened by it. "Look, I'll check with an attorney, but I can't promise you anything. Your mother is a big factor."

"That's shitty."

"Rachael..."

"Sorry. Isn't that a shame?"

Marie couldn't imagine what was going through young Rachael's mind. The pain on her face told her the torment ran deep.

"I'll check with an attorney tomorrow, and I can promise you I'll do whatever I can to make our relationship bona fide." She took her hand. "But I want you to understand, even if I can't do something legal to make you my daughter, I'll always be there for you. Piece of paper or not. Is that clear?"

"Can't ask for better than that. But you know what would really put me on cloud nine?"

"What's that?"

"If Olivia was part of the deal."

Marie couldn't speak. Rachael seemed to have this all figured out. But she was just a kid. She didn't understand all the potential ramifications.

Three very different daughters living together, growing together, thriving together in a way they in all probability couldn't do apart.

Words her father had shared with her during one of their first visits suddenly came to mind: "God created us different to understand the need for each other." If he was right, nothing could be truer in Marie's life right now.

"You know what?" she said through tears. "Sometimes I don't think I give you enough credit."

Rachael rolled her eyes. "Well, it's about time you figured that out."

* * *

Miss Hierra put Marie in touch with a Spanish-speaking attorney who specialized in family law. He found out Olivia's mother had run off when she was an infant, and up until he died, her father and a variety of neighborhood Mexican women who felt sorry for them had been raising her. He told Marie that given the number of unwanted Mexican children in the state, she would likely have no problem adopting Olivia, and the fact Marie was mixed race herself would be a plus. Marie was fairly certain that would be the only time in her life she would ever hear that sentiment.

Adopting Rachael was another story. The same attorney told her that Rachael's mother, prison or no prison, would have to relinquish her parental rights before Marie could legally adopt her. And in fact, the attorney informed her, Marie was taking chances by keeping Rachael in her custody without going through the court system.

Marie called Greg and Gloria to get their input. "I bet Judy would give up her rights if there was something in it for her," Greg said.

"Like what?"

"I don't know, but it's clear she doesn't care anything about Rachael. If she did, she would have tried to contact us. She's a user, Marie. And that may work to your advantage."

"She's in prison for twenty-five years. What could she use in there?"

"I don't know. Maybe an attorney could help you with that."

Marie's attorney wasn't very optimistic. "You don't want to do anything that will look like bribery or coercion to get legal custody of the girl. If her mother really cared about her, she would give up her parental rights in order to know her daughter would be well cared for while she was in prison, but you'd be taking a risk stirring things up."

"I'm not sure I want to give her any ideas. So far we haven't had any trouble from her."

Later Marie explained it all to Rachael. "I can have my lawyer proceed, but you have to understand that your mother could potentially have you removed from my care. She has the legal right to do that."

Rachael bit her lip, appearing defeated.

"You'll be eighteen before you know it. And then she can't do anything."

Rachael stomped her foot. "It's not fair."

"Life isn't always fair, Rachael. I've told you that before. We just need to make the best out of every situation."

"I know."

"So are you okay with just keeping things the way they are?"

"I guess."

Marie smiled and gave her a hug. "I love you, sweetie."

"Aw...don't get mushy on me."

Adjustment for Olivia didn't come without its ups and downs. Once Marie found her cowering in the closet in the bedroom she shared with Rachael. When Marie approached her, Olivia threw up her arms in a defensive posture, as though she expected Marie to hit her. Olivia's English wasn't that good yet, but luckily Rachael was home and able to learn from her that she had messed her pants. Through Rachael, Marie told Olivia she never had to worry about coming to Marie if it happened again. Accidents happened, and there would no punishment.

One thing Olivia had a hard time learning was sharing and respecting what belonged to others. Judging by the way Olivia hoarded things—food and toys mostly—Marie suspected she'd had to fend for herself in the past. Marie and Rachael tried to set good examples for Olivia, but they could tell she was apprehensive. It would take time.

Meeting Olivia's basic needs—nutritious food, safety, and security— was relatively easy, but meeting her emotional needs was more challenging. Connecting to Olivia emotionally was difficult given the language barrier, but Marie could see that connection between Rachael and Olivia and knew this would take time as well.

With Rachael in school and Marie at work, Olivia needed a place to stay during the day, so Marie rearranged her office to accommodate a small desk for Olivia, her own child-size sofa, and a play kitchen complete with a tea set. Marie's staff enjoyed being served make-believe tea at least twice a day.

One day, out of the blue, Olivia asked Marie where her daddy was. "Come here, honey," Marie said. She took Olivia's hands as she spoke. "Your daddy is in heaven, sweetheart. And he's probably looking down on you right now to make sure you're okay. Do you understand that?"

Olivia shook her head.

"Do you know what heaven is?"

Olivia nodded. "Where nice people go to die."

Oh dear. Where are we going with this? "That's right."

"Where do bad people go?"

"Oh, I think there's a place in heaven for everyone."

"Okay."

Okay, what?

"Are you okay with that?"

"Yep," Olivia said as she skipped over to her pretend oven to whip up a batch of cookies or something.

* * *

The Costa family—Marie, Rachael, and Olivia—went to St. Charles for the long Thanksgiving weekend. Everyone was there, including the

Feinsteins. It had been almost a year since Jonathan's heart attack, and he was back to feeling normal. The women handled the food while the men talked about sports, business, and politics.

The Feinsteins talked about Ben and how much they missed him. He had been gone a little more than six months, and at first, Marie had learned, they couldn't even mention his name without breaking down. But once Judy confessed to his murder, Claire told Marie, they accepted the fact he was gone and were now able to talk about him without losing their composure.

Of course, there was the occasional cigar fest in the main barn. Much to Jonathan's dismay, Claire had thrown away all his cigars after his heart attack, but only after cutting them in half, something he vowed he would never let Claire forget.

"To quote the great Abraham Lincoln," Jonathan said to anyone who would listen, "'it has been my experience that folks who have no vices have very few virtues.'"

"That was ignorant the first time I heard you say it, Jonathan, and it still is, Lincoln or no Lincoln," Claire quipped in front of everyone.

"Do you realize how much they cost, those cigars you so cruelly cut up?" he asked.

"Do you realize how many additional years of life you'll enjoy without smoking them? What's the cost of that?"

"You win…dear."

After the cigar talk simmered down, Gloria pulled Marie aside to talk about Rachael. "I can't tell you how happy we are for Rachael, Marie. I've never seen her spirits so high."

"I think my friends would say the same about me. Both our lives have changed completely—for the better. Has she been writing you, by the way?"

Gloria's face lit up. "Oh yes. We get a letter every few weeks or so. And they're long letters. She's told us all about school, horseback riding, her friends, Miska, and of course Olivia. We so look forward to her letters."

"I'm so glad she's doing that. I wasn't sure, and when I ask her, she rolls those big blue eyes of hers and says, 'Yes, Sergeant.' You know, with that tone of hers."

Gloria smiled. "Well, we don't get that tone in her letters."

Marie laughed. "That's good."

"She talks about you a lot. Says you're real cool. At first we thought she meant you were indifferent toward her, and we started to get concerned. But when I mentioned it to Claire one day, she set us straight." Gloria laughed. "I guess she's a bit more hip than we are."

"I still don't understand all the lingo, believe me."

Rachael stuck her head in the door. "Everything okay in here?"

Gloria turned her back toward Rachael and mouthed *thank you* to Marie.

Olivia made a big hit with the Brooks family members. She had been with Marie for almost two months, and her bubbly personality was gradually emerging. The once sad-looking, shy little girl who hid behind her hair had blossomed into an energetic darling who loved wearing her hair in a ponytail and could light up a room with her smile and antics.

Jonathan summed it up in his Thanksgiving dinner prayer. "Dear Father in heaven, we gather together to ask the Lord's blessing as we partake of this food. We pray for health and strength to live our lives as you would have us do. We give thanks for this food prepared by loving hands. We give thanks for life itself and the ancestors who brought us to where we are now so we can enjoy it.

"As we partake of this food, we pray for health and strength to carry on our daily lives, care for those who mean so much to us, and extend what we have to offer to strangers who are less fortunate.

"We pray that you will bless all those who gather here, and help us to remember that we are all brothers and sisters, called to serve one another and walk together, despite our differences. We are particularly blessed to have Rachael and Olivia with us this Thanksgiving Day. Please watch over them as they make it through life with our daughter, Marie, and give her the guidance she needs to provide them with what they need.

"We ask all this in the name of Christ, oh heavenly Father. In Jesus' name, amen."

"A-men!" Olivia cried out through a big smile.

And that was all that was needed to set the mood for the rest of the day.

CHAPTER 28

Mi Marie

The preliminary hearing for Olivia's adoption had been set for December 12, sixty days after she'd moved in with Marie, long enough for Miss Hierra to determine there were no relatives or even close family friends to take Olivia in. Marie's attorney, Olivia's caseworker, and Miss Hierra accompanied Marie to court. Rachael was so excited about it, she asked if she could take the day off from school to attend, to which Marie agreed.

The judge examined the paperwork while Marie and the others anxiously sat in front of her. The judge called on Olivia's caseworker first. "I have read your reports, and from them I am interpreting you find the living conditions at the Costa residence suitable for Olivia. Is that correct?"

"That is correct."

"You have visited the Costa household a total of eight times. Is that correct?"

"Yes."

"Were any of these visits surprise visits?"

"Except for the first one, they were all surprise visits."

Florence Osmund

"Did anyone try to coerce you into writing favorable reports?"

"No, they did not."

"I can read here what you say about Olivia, but I would like to hear it directly from you. How would you characterize this child?"

"I would characterize her as a happy, healthy little girl with a very sweet disposition."

"How is her English?"

"Considering she just started learning it two months ago, I'd say it's pretty good."

"Is it good enough for me to ask her a few questions? If not, I can get an interpreter in here."

"I think so."

The judge looked at Marie. "Do you have any objection to my asking Olivia a few questions?"

Marie's stomach churned. "No, your honor. I do not."

"Olivia, can you come up here, please?"

Olivia looked at Marie, who nodded. Rachael leaned forward, her gaze fixated on Olivia.

Olivia walked up to the bench and peered up at the judge. *She looks so small.* She turned around and smiled at Marie. *And she looks so brave.*

"Maybe you should come up here by me." The judge came out from behind her bench, took Olivia by the hand, and led her to her chair. "This way your back isn't to the people who care so much about you. What's your name, sweetheart?"

Five Olivias could have fit in the judge's oversized chair. "Olivia," she said in soft voice.

"And how are you today?"

"Fine."

"And who do you live with, Olivia?"

She pointed to Marie and smiled.

"Let the record show Miss Olivia pointed to Marie Costa. And do you like living with Miss Costa?"

Olivia gave Marie a puzzled look. Marie stood up. "Your honor, she knows me as *mi* Marie."

The judge smiled and looked at Olivia. "Do you like living with *tu* Marie?"

Olivia nodded.

"Let the record show Miss Olivia nodded in the affirmative. Why do you like living with *tu* Marie, Olivia?"

"She takes care of me and Rachael and Sheana and Miska."

The judge looked at Marie. "Just how many people live in your house?"

"Sheana and Miska are my cats, your honor."

"I see. Olivia, tell me about Rachael."

"I like Rachael."

"What do you like about her?"

"She teached me English."

Oh dear.

"And she's my best friend."

"I see. Is there another place you would like to live instead of with *tu* Marie and Rachael?"

Marie thought Olivia was going to cry and got ready to get up to rush to her side. "No, please," Olivia said in a shaky voice.

"Okay, my dear. You may go and sit back with *tu* Marie."

As soon as the judge sat back down, Rachael stood up. *Oh my God. What is she doing?*

"Your honor?"

The judge gave her a disconcerted look. "Approach the bench if you have something to say."

Rachael walked tall to the place in front of the judge.

"State your name for the record."

"Rachael Feinstein."

"Go ahead."

"I'm sorry Olivia said 'teached' instead of 'taught.' We haven't gotten that far yet. But what I really want to say is that I've been living with

Marie since April, and when I got there, I was a mess. You have no idea. I was two grades behind in school. I didn't trust anyone. I was angry all the time, and I was a total freak."

"I beg your pardon?"

"I'm sorry. I mean I didn't fit in anywhere. Anyway, Marie took me in and turned everything around for me, and she is doing the same for Olivia. She cares about us—both of us." She paused. "Well, I guess that's all I have to say, your honor."

"Thank you, Rachael. That was very well said."

As soon as Rachael sat down, Marie put her arm around her shoulders and whispered, "That was crazy."

"Please wait while I make my decision." The judge got up and exited through a door behind her bench.

Rachael broke the uncomfortable silence. "Somebody say something. How do we think it went?"

Before anyone could answer, the judge returned. "There seems to be one important thing missing from the documentation submitted," the judge said. Marie's attorney stood up. "What is Olivia's birth date?"

"We don't know that, your honor. Her father didn't leave behind a birth certificate."

The judge gave Marie's attorney a skeptical look. "So you don't even know how old she is?"

"We think she's around five."

Olivia's caseworker stood up. "Your honor, this is a very troubling case. I personally talked to every adult in her community, and no one knows how old she is or if she has any living relatives. I even conducted a birth certificate search in every jurisdiction of Mexico.

"Your honor, I have handled hundreds of these cases, and I feel very strongly she belongs with Miss Costa. There is very little likelihood this child will fair well in an orphanage and less likelihood she will ever be adopted. What you have in this courtroom is someone who cares deeply for this child and has demonstrated she can provide a good home for her."

"My job is to do what's in the best interest of the child," the judge said. She looked at the caseworker. "You and I go back many years, Miss Hierra, and I trust your judgment." She paused to glance at Rachael. "But I have to admit, I may have been more influenced by Miss Rachael's testimony."

The judge looked toward Marie. "Based on everything I've heard, I'm prepared to extend temporary custody. I'm going to order monthly visits by Olivia's caseworker for the next six months, and if all goes well, your chances will be very good for permanent adoption. I am also going to arrange for a birth certificate for this child. All I need is a birth date."

Rachael whispered into Marie's ear, "December 24."

"Would you please stand, Miss Costa? Do you have a date in mind when you would like to celebrate this child's birthday?"

Her emotions were hard to contain. "Yes, your honor. December 24."

When they reached Marie's car, she took Rachael by the shoulders and then gave her a long hug. "I am so proud of you."

"Aw. No sweat."

* * *

Marie called Jonathan the next day. "Congratulations, my dear. The news couldn't be any better. I'm so happy for all of you. Wait, Claire wants to talk to you."

After Claire gushed over the news, Marie asked her if they would be too disappointed if they didn't visit with them over Christmas. With two birthdays on December 24 and their first Christmas together, Marie wanted it to be a special time they spent by themselves.

"Of course we understand. How about Easter, then?"

"Perfect."

Marie invited Karen, Maurice, and Barry to dinner the following Sunday to celebrate. Karen and Maurice brought Olivia a Betsy McCall doll, complete with red plaid dress and black patent leather shoes. Barry opened a savings account in her name and put five hundred dollars in it for her.

Everyone's attention was on little Olivia, and Marie realized that had it not been for Rachael's mother, they would likely have been celebrating Rachael's adoption as well. She pulled her aside after dinner.

"I know what you're going to say, and it's okay," Rachael said.

"Okay, Miss Know-It-All. What was I going to say?"

"That this is all about Olivia, and you don't want me to feel left out."

"Do you feel left out?"

"No."

Marie gazed deep into her eyes.

"But just keep in mind I'll be sixteen in ten days and old enough for a driver's license."

"You little..."

Rachael took Marie's arm and smiled. "Shall we? We really shouldn't keep our guests waiting."

When they returned to the living room, Karen and Maurice got up. "I know this is supposed to be a celebration for little Olivia, but...we have an announcement to make," Karen said. She took Maurice's hand and looked at Marie. "We got married."

"What?!" Marie shrieked. She got up and hugged Karen, then Maurice. "You guys! When did this happen?"

"Last weekend," Karen said.

"And you're just telling me now?"

"I know. I'm sorry, but you had so much going on with...well, everything, and we did it kind of on the spur of the moment...and, well, I'm..."

"That's okay. I'm just so excited." Marie gave Karen another hug and whispered, "I'm so happy for you."

"I'll explain later," she whispered back.

They spent the rest of the evening talking about Karen and Maurice's announcement. Certain there was much more to the story than what they were telling, Marie was anxious to talk further with Karen.

Barry was the last to leave. Marie walked him down to his car.

"I have a confession to make," he said.

"A confession?"

"I called Karen the other day and asked her if you were involved with anyone."

"You did?"

He nodded. "Do you remember when we first met and I asked you out? You told me you were married."

"Yes, I remember that."

"Was that true?"

"It was then."

"How long have you been divorced?"

"A little over a year."

He gazed into her eyes and smiled a curl of a smile. "Would you like to talk about it over dinner sometime?"

"Not without confessing something first myself."

He leaned up against his car beside her and folded his arms across his chest. "Okay. Shoot."

"And after I tell you this, if you want to change your mind about dinner, I'll understand."

"I'm listening."

"My father is a Negro. Therefore I am a Negro. My ex-husband is mixed up with the Chicago mob and has wanted to get back with me ever since I left him in May of '48. And the reason I haven't adopted Rachael is because her mother is in prison for killing the man Rachael thought was her father, but really wasn't." She looked him straight in the eye to get his reaction, but Barry didn't flinch.

"I have a twin brother who still lives at home and thinks he's Henry VIII—on a good day. I have just three toes on my right foot due to frostbite after I got cockeyed drunk on cheap Puerto Rican rum when I was nineteen and then passed out in the snow. I was madly in love with my fifth grade teacher, Miss Crandon, but other than that, I have never been in a relationship longer than three months. *And* I played a role in Olivia's father's death." He paused. "How's Saturday?"

"Pick me up at seven?"

"See you then."

                              * * *

"Okay, my dear friend, tell me everything," Marie said to Karen the next day.

"Can you come over?" Karen asked.

"Where? Your house or Maurice's?"

"Maurice's. I'm all moved out of mine. I just put it on the market this morning."

"I'll bring the wine."

Karen and Maurice sat on their living room sofa. Marie sat across from them. "We're expecting," Karen said.

"What?! I don't believe it! When?"

"The middle of April."

Marie got up from her chair. "Come here, you." They hugged, and when they separated, Marie patted Karen's stomach. "So you're...let's see, five months?"

Karen nodded. "Seems hard to believe, doesn't it?"

"How long have you known?"

"The week before we got married. Actually, just a few days before."

Marie studied Karen's face, then Maurice's. "You two look so happy."

"We are," they said in unison.

"Does your daughter know yet?" Marie asked Maurice.

"I told her last night. She has mixed feelings about it right now. I hope she'll come around."

"How about your ex?"

"Oh, I can pretty much guess what she's saying about it. One kid in college, one I support but don't see, and another one on the way." He shook his head. "But she can say or think anything she wants. I'm happy." He turned toward Karen and kissed her on the cheek.

"Oh my God, Karen. You're going to have a baby!"

"I know."

"So do you think it will be a boy or a girl?"

"Who knows?"

"Do you have any names picked out?"

"Clyde Edward if it's a boy, and if it's a girl..." Karen's eyes welled up. "Anna Marie."

"That is so sweet. Can I tell Rachael and Olivia?"

"Sure. It's not a secret anymore."

* * *

"Why isn't he here yet?" Rachael asked.

"Because it's only 6:55."

"He's sure cutting it close."

Marie observed herself in the hall mirror for the umpteenth time. "It isn't a matter of life or death if he's a few minutes late."

"I thought you told me it's important to always be on time."

"It is, but..."

"Maybe he's going to stand you up," Rachael suggested.

"What makes you think that?"

"Are you nervous about going out with him?"

"Well, I wasn't until this conversation."

Rachael ran to the window. "He's here! Olivia, come out here."

"Why? What are you going to do?"

"Don't worry. Just leave everything to me."

What is she up to? Marie went down to let Barry in. She had put on a navy blue striped knit top with coordinating skirt and heels. She hoped he wouldn't show up in jeans, which was what he typically wore in his gun shop. When he arrived, she smiled, relieved to see dark dress slacks beneath his wool trench coat.

"Hi. Please come in."

Rachael and Olivia were sitting next to each other on the sofa, hands clasped in their laps and smiles of their faces.

"Good evening, Mr. Stone. And how are you this lovely day?" Rachael asked in her rendition of a sophisticated tone and manner.

"Why, I'm fine, Miss Rachael, just fine. And you?"

"Oh, we're fine too. Aren't we, Olivia?"

Olivia looked up at Rachael and shrugged. Rachael nudged her with her elbow.

"Uh...nice water we're having."

Marie looked at Barry and shook her head and then went to the closet for her coat, which he took and held out for her to put on.

"Okay, my little wisenheimers, we won't be late." She turned to Rachael. "She's to be in bed by eight."

Rachael saluted. "Yes, Sergeant. But I'll be up when you get back, so..."

"That will be enough, young lady."

Rachael smiled. "Later, gator."

Barry opened the car door for her. "What was that all about?" he asked.

Marie waited until he got behind the wheel of his car before responding. "Apparently Rachael thought it was necessary to give you a good impression on our first date."

Barry smiled. "Too late. I already had that three years ago."

She blushed, grateful for the dimly lit driveway as Barry turned the car around and headed toward the street.

He took her to DaVinci's, a new Italian restaurant that had recently opened in Leavenworth. Marie's pulse quickened when he parked the car—three doors down from Paul's antique shop. Determined not to let anything or anyone ruin this date, she walked toward the restaurant, her arm linked in his, her head held high.

Like many of the businesses in this section of town, DaVinci's had once been a Victorian home. Barry asked for a table in one of the smaller dining rooms. She smiled to herself when he pulled the chair out for her—memories of Richard's good side. *I'm not going to do that this time—compare him to Richard.*

It was different talking to Barry like this, sitting directly across from him for an extended period of time. Up until then, her encounters with him had been under very different circumstances. They'd first met when she had decided to buy a gun for protection. She had been very nervous that day and couldn't even look him in the eye for very long. Then, when he taught her how to shoot, he had been by her side, standing slightly behind her. And the unnerving time when Olivia had been abandoned at his shop, she hadn't paid much attention to his personal side. This was nice. She asked about his family.

"Well, I told you a little about my twin."

"What's his name?"

"Henry."

Marie laughed. "I mean what's his *real* name?"

"Henry *is* his real name. We're not sure where everything went wrong with him. My parents have had him evaluated by more than one doctor. They call it a delusional disorder. He's very smart, much smarter than I, but he can't hold a job because at any given time he could start acting like Henry VIII, or sometimes someone even worse."

Marie couldn't even imagine what he was describing. "What does he do? When he thinks he's Henry VIII, that is."

"He can fly into a rage at the drop of a hat, and he'll complain about his wives, all six of them, and threaten to kill them. When he's feeling particularly sorry for himself, he'll walk with a limp, like the real king did."

"Oh my."

"But my parents handle it very well. They just go along with it, knowing he's completely harmless and eventually will snap out of that character and be Hank again."

"How did you end up in the gun shop business?"

"I've had a fascination with guns my whole life. My father and uncle own a saddle shop down the road, and when I turned eighteen, Dad bought the gun shop from a cohort of his who was moving out of state, and we ran it together until he trusted me enough to run it myself."

"Your face lit up when you talked about your father."

He smiled. "They don't come any better."

Barry asked Marie about her background, which she freely revealed.

"Hmm. College-educated," Barry said. "I was lucky to make it through high school. Didn't like being in school much. Now Hank, he's another story. He has a degree in mathematics. He's a genius in that area."

"School isn't the only place to get an education. It looks to me like you've done pretty well for yourself."

"I suppose so. I don't owe anything on the shop. My dad and I own it together, and I had to pull my half just like him."

"I'm impressed, Mr. Stone."

They shared a fruit and custard tart for dessert, Barry's favorite. After they left, instead of driving straight back to Marie's apartment, Barry turned down a winding road that led to the river. He parked the car a few feet from the water. The moon was full, casting enough light for them to clearly see each other. The early winter air was brisk, so he left the car running and the heater on while they talked.

"Please don't take this the wrong way, but I thought maybe we could have a few minutes alone at the end of our date before I take you home."

Marie laughed. "No, I know what you mean. There's very little privacy in my house these days."

His stare was soft. "You're a very attractive woman."

"Thank you."

"I'd like to see you again."

She turned toward him. His blue eyes were shining even in the dim light. "I'd like that."

"Can I kiss you?"

She hesitated a few seconds, then smiled and leaned in for the kiss. His lips were soft and sensual, and the kiss lingered on Marie's lips for several seconds.

He turned forward and put his hand on the gear shift, staring out at the water for a moment.

"What are you thinking?" she asked.

"Nothing." Then he put the car in gear and drove to Marie's apartment.

He kissed her again before saying good night and then left with a slow smile on his lips.

CHAPTER 29

Barry

"Well, it's about time," Rachael said when Marie arrived home from her date with Barry.

"It's ten-fifteen. What are you talking about?"

"How long does it take to…"

Marie's glare stopped Rachael from finishing the sentence. "So how was it? Where did you go? What did you talk about?"

Marie wasn't sure who was asking the questions—a daughter who was curious about what dating was all about, a friend who was just eleven years her junior, or her newfound protector. "It was fine. We went to DaVinci's and talked."

"About what?"

"Well, this was our first date, so we talked mostly about each other's backgrounds."

"So what's his story?"

"He's lived his whole life in Leavenworth. He has a twin brother and two parents there."

"A twin? Cool."

If she only knew.

"So are you going to see him again?"

She smiled. "Yes, I am. Is that okay with you?"

"Cool. I like the guy."

"Well, good. I'll sleep easy tonight."

"Marie?"

"Hmm?"

"I'm glad you're seeing someone."

"Good night, Rachael."

Ten minutes later, Barry called. "Hi. I was thinking about things, and well, uh…Christmas is this week, and I really don't want to wait until next year to see you again. What are you doing Christmas Eve?"

"That's Rachael's and Olivia's birthday."

"I know. That's why I asked. Do you have anything special planned for them?"

"I was just thinking of cooking their favorite meal and celebrating here at home."

He told her about a hayride and barbeque hosted by the community center each year on Christmas Eve, a fundraiser for the less fortunate, and asked Marie if they would like to be his guests. Marie thought about it for a few seconds. "It sounds like fun. But since it *is* their birthday, how about if I run it past them first?"

"Fair enough. Let me know."

"Tomorrow is one of our Scrabble talks, so I'll ask Rachael then."

"Scrabble talks?"

"Rachael and I started playing Scrabble a few months ago, and I think it was the third or fourth time we played when she formed the word 'teacher.' Then she looked at me in a way I knew she had something on her mind, and I asked her if she wanted to talk about it, and she proceeded to tell me about an incident she had had with one of her teachers. After that, it happened just about every time we played that one of us would form a word that sparked a conversation, so we started calling them our Scrabble talks."

"Scrabble talks. I like that."

* * *

When Marie told Rachael about the hayride the next day, she received a big smile.

"Are you kidding?" Rachael turned toward Olivia who was sitting at the table coloring. "Olivia! Do you want to go on a hayride?"

Olivia looked at Rachael with a blank stare. "A hayride, Olivia." Rachael looked at Marie. "I don't know the word for hayride." She turned her attention back to Olivia. "Uh. *¿Quieres ir de paseo en un vagón grande?*"

Olivia's face lit up. "*Sí!*"

"Then it's yes?" Marie asked.

"Like crazy."

"I thought we could come back here afterward for cake and ice cream."

"Cake and ice cream!" Olivia shrieked.

"Barry too?"

"Sure. Barry too"

"Barry too!" Olivia had been with them for barely two months, and already she was Rachael's shadow. Marie wondered how she would feel when she realized Barry was the one who had shot at her father.

Whoa—slow down, Marie, she thought. *You are getting way ahead of yourself.*

* * *

Barry picked them up for the hayride at ten in the morning. Everyone was bundled up with multiple layers of clothing, scarves, hats, and mittens in order to deal with temperatures in the teens. Poor Olivia could hardly walk, and when she did, her shiny polyester leggings rustled.

Hundreds of people, mostly families, were there when they arrived. Five wagons, each holding twenty or so passengers, were loading up. Marie's group huddled together in the corner of one of the wagons.

"Nice horsie," Olivia kept saying as she watched the horse in the wagon behind them. "Rachael's horsie."

Barry and Marie sat on top of two hay bales stacked one on top of each other. Rachael and Olivia sat in front of them on another bale. Barry put his arm around Marie and gave her a gentle squeeze, the wind sharp against their faces.

"What do you think?" he asked her.

"It's fun. Cold, but fun."

He gestured toward Rachael and Olivia. Marie smiled. "Looks like they're having fun."

Rachael turned around. "You two can smooch back there if you want. We won't look."

Olivia giggled. Marie shook her head and gave Rachael a nudge in her back. "No comments from the peanut gallery."

Rachael turned around. "Huh?"

"I have expressions, too, you know."

The girls loved the hayride, but Marie was glad it lasted only a half hour.

"Did you have fun?" she asked Olivia. Olivia smiled wide and took Marie's hand. Then she looked up at Barry and took his hand as well. Marie and Barry exchanged glances but didn't say anything.

Barry brought them their hot drinks and then disappeared toward the back of the room where they were collecting the donations. When he reappeared, he said, "I like the way they do it. Whatever they collect today will buy things throughout next year for those who are in need. Food, clothing, and school supplies for the kids. It's a good organization."

Marie thought about how Rachael and Olivia could have been on the receiving end of this type of fundraiser under different circumstances.

"Do you have plans for the girls for this afternoon, or can I surprise them with something?" Barry asked.

She looked at him, puzzled. "Well...we like surprises."

He took Marie's arm. "C'mon girls, let's go to my place."

Marie had been to Barry's home several times three years earlier when he'd showed her how to shoot but had never been inside his house. She gave him a soft smile when she saw his dining room table that had been set for four, picnic style. "What if I had said we had other plans?" she asked.

"Then I'd be eating fried chicken and potato salad the rest of the week."

"So you cook?"

"Ha! Hardly," he said. Marie helped him take things out of the refrigerator and put them on the table. "We have this great delicatessen, Rosie's. Best fried chicken in town."

Along with the fried chicken were potato salad, buttermilk biscuits, pickles, and olives. "I thought it would be fun to have a summer picnic in the middle of winter. Goes with the hayride."

"Cool," said Rachael.

"Yeah, cool," Olivia piped up.

Marie shook her head and rolled her eyes. "You're rubbing off on her," she said to Rachael.

"I know. Isn't that a tickle?"

Barry's house, a long narrow ranch, was decorated the way Marie had pictured it—a little rugged but cozy. What she didn't expect to see were several pieces of original artwork, one of which she recognized as a Durand.

"Are you two girls ready for your birthday present?" Barry asked after they finished eating.

Olivia perked up. "Present?"

"I'm ready," Rachael said.

"Get dressed then. We're going outside."

Marie shot him a glance and scrunched up her face. What did he have in mind?

Barry led them outside to a large barn where four horses were saddled and ready to go. "You're all set," a smallish middle-aged man said to Barry. A younger woman, equally as short, came out from one of the stalls and stood beside the man.

Barry faced Marie. "This is B.B. Starr and his daughter, Josie. They live in the guest house and take care of the horses and the property." He introduced Marie and her family to the Starrs.

"Olivia has never been on a horse before," Marie said.

"I'll walk beside her while she rides on Annie here," Josie said, and put her arm around the smallest horse's neck. "She's very gentle, I assure you."

Marie stooped down to Olivia's level. "Do you want to ride the horsie, Olivia?"

She smiled wide and nodded. Rachael went to the middle-sized horse and mounted it by herself. Barry gestured to a long-necked chestnut mare for Marie, and he took the remaining horse, a large black mare.

"Ready?"

Rachael didn't have to be told twice. She clicked at her horse and guided him out of the barn. The others followed.

They took a slow ride, giving Olivia time to get used to it. She did surprisingly well. When they had been gone for about thirty minutes, Barry rode ahead, turned his horse around, and stopped high on the rise. He pointed to the north. "See that?"

Marie looked toward where he was pointing at a small herd of animals. "Buffalo?" she asked. "I didn't know there were buffalo in this part of the country."

"Several small herds, mostly in honor of Buffalo Bill." He glanced at Rachael. "Do you know his story? He got his nickname because he was the one who killed buffalos in order to feed Kansas Pacific Railroad workers so they could continue building the railroad. But before that, he was a decorated soldier in the Civil War. You did learn about that in history class, right?"

She rolled her eyes. "Yes, of course I did. Fort Sumter, Battle of Bull Run, Stonewall Jackson—all that stuff."

"What Buffalo Bill was most known for, though, were his wild west shows."

They headed back toward the barn. Rachael rode on ahead of them. "She's a good rider," Barry observed.

"I know. Better than I am."

"Let's see just how good you are!" Barry kicked his horse with his heals and thrust into a gallop. Marie followed. They rode fast, side by side, the icy wind on their faces. When Rachael realized they were close behind her, she coaxed her horse into a gallop as well.

When the ride was over, Barry helped Marie off her horse. As her feet touched the ground, with his face just inches from hers, a fluttering sensation rose up in her chest. He winked at her, making her blush.

By the time Olivia and Josie reached the barn, the other horses had been de-saddled and were being rubbed down. Marie went over to Olivia, lifted her off the horse, and placed her on the ground. "How did you like it?"

Olivia took a few steps with her feet wide apart. She looked up at Marie with a scared face.

"Those are just your horsie legs. Take a few steps and you'll get your land legs back."

"We call it saddle butt where I come from," Barry said.

"Barry!" said Marie.

Rachael let out a guffaw. "Way to go."

"And I cleaned it up for you," Barry said with a smile. He put his arm around Marie's shoulders. "More hot chocolate?"

The two girls walked ahead of them toward the house. "This was nice. Thank you for helping to make their birthdays special."

"You're welcome."

"Would you like to join us later for cake and ice cream?"

"Say, yes!" Rachael shouted without turning around.

Marie shook her head. He squeezed her arm. "I thought you'd never ask."

* * *

Rachael was up at the crack of dawn Christmas morning. She tiptoed into Marie's bedroom and cleared her throat several times before Marie opened her eyes. "Olivia is pretty excited and wants to come out and open presents."

Marie had stayed up late the night before getting the presents she had hidden in the attic under the tree. She sat up in bed, stretched, and yawned. "So where is she?"

"I'll get her!"

Sleepy-eyed Olivia, who Marie was certain had just been awakened by Rachael seconds before, eyed the presents and squealed. "*¿Para quién son éstos?*"

"*Para ti.*"

"For me?" she said.

"Just some of them are for you," Rachael explained. She handed one to Olivia that she had helped pick out. Olivia ripped off the paper and hugged the stuffed monkey she had talked about for the past month after seeing it in the *Sears Wish Book*. The monkey had a serious, almost scary face, and Marie wondered why she'd wanted it, but she bought it anyway. Rachael helped her unwrap a larger gift. When Olivia saw the dollhouse, she ran into her room to get her Betsy McCall doll, which was about a hundred times too large for the house.

"Olivia, look inside. There are little dolls in there," Rachael told her. Olivia tossed Betsy to the side for the time being while she placed and replaced the two small dolls in each room of the house, looking at Rachael and Marie for approval with each move.

Rachael had asked for jewelry, and when she opened the small box with a watch and gold earrings, Marie thought she was going to cry. She got up from the floor and hugged Marie hard.

Two presents from Marie were addressed to both Olivia and Rachael. One contained a set of flash cards to help Olivia with her English, and the other one a Candy Land game. Rachael glanced up at Marie and said, "These are cool." Then she got up and went way under the tree and pulled out an envelope. She handed it to Marie.

Marie opened it up and pulled out a piece of construction paper. On it was written,

For the best mom two girls could ever ask for
Love,
Rachael and Olivia

Inside the envelope was a gold chain with a heart-shaped locket. Inside the locket was a picture of Rachael on one side and Olivia on the other.

"Karen helped us with it. Do you like it?" Rachael asked.

Olivia pointed to her name on the card. "O-l-i-v-i-a. Olivia!"

Marie scooped up both girls in her arms and thanked them through tears. "You couldn't have given me any better present."

She cooked the girls' favorite meal for Christmas—pot roast, browned potatoes, and corn. Halfway through dinner, Rachael asked Marie where Barry was.

"He's having dinner with his family, but he's coming over later for dessert."

"His horses too?" Olivia asked.

"Well, no he's not bringing his horses, silly."

She looked disappointed. Marie threw up her hands. "They won't fit in our house!" she said with a funny face, making Olivia laugh.

"When will he be here?"

Marie glanced at her watch. "In about an hour."

"So what are you giving him for Christmas?"

Marie had given a lot of thought to it. They had been on only two dates, and one of those was with the girls. She wanted to give him something, but nothing too personal and nothing that suggested she was further along in this relationship than he was. He had mentioned his love for camping and fishing on their first date, so she bought him a subscription to *Outdoor Life*. As a joke, she included a copy of an article she had found at the library titled "Understanding Henry VIII." On top she placed a picture of a little girl and a cat Olivia had colored for him.

"He's here!" Olivia shouted while Rachael and Marie finished doing the dishes.

Rachael grinned. "She's a good lookout."

"You put her up to that?" Marie asked.

"Well, sure. We need a little notice to get ready for him." She pointed to Marie's hair. "I'll let him in while you fix that."

When did she become my coach?

Barry came in with an armload of gifts. The girls cheered. Marie shook her head. He handed Rachael and Olivia each a present but kept the third one in his lap while he watched them open the gifts.

Rachael pulled out a wide western concho belt. "Cool!" She got up and headed toward her bedroom.

"Where are you going?" Marie asked.

"To see if it fits in my jeans for the next time I go riding."

Olivia tore the paper off her present—a child's book on horses. "Horsies!"

Marie looked at Barry and mouthed *thank you* before she opened her present. Inside was a pair of deerskin riding gloves.

"Looks like you're appealing to our love for horses," she said.

"It would appear that way." His smile was soft and sincere. She handed him his present.

His face lit up at Olivia's picture. "Why thank you, Olivia. I'll have to hang this in a very special place." He laughed at the Henry VIII article and glanced up at Marie. "This may come in handy." He picked up the issue *of Outdoor Life*. "Hey, this is great. I pick one up every once in awhile, but I don't have a subscription. Thanks, everyone."

Rachael walked over to him and handed him a sheet of paper. What was she giving him? Barry turned it over and stared at the paper before sporting a wide grin. "Did you draw this?"

Rachael nodded. Barry glanced at Marie. "This is really good. You never told me she was an artist."

"May I see it?"

He handed it Marie. She stared in disbelief at the pencil sketch of Barry, Marie, and Olivia on horseback, Rachael's perspective for the drawing being that she was the last one in line on the trail.

"Rachael, this is amazing. Where did you learn to draw like this?"

She shrugged. "Nowhere, I guess."

"Talk about hanging this in a special place. I'm going to have it framed!"

"Well, I'm glad you like it, Barry, but I didn't think you were going to go ape over it."

"I don't know about the ape part, but it's darn good."

Rachael looked back and forth among Marie, Olivia, and Barry. Her gaze paused on Marie. "Just think," she said, "if I didn't have to piss so bad that day coming home from Olathe, these two wouldn't even be a part of our lives right now."

"Rachael!"

"What?"

"Your language."

"Sorry. Piss so badly."

Good grief.

CHAPTER 30

Like a Real Family

"You know, if you and Barry want to go out on New Year's Eve, I'll babysit Olivia," Rachael offered.

Marie glanced up from her newspaper. "Thank you, sweetie, but Barry hasn't said anything about New Year's." They had talked on the phone a few times since Christmas, but he hadn't asked her out again. She went back to reading the paper when an article about the hayride fundraiser they had attended caught her eye.

"The annual fundraiser had its biggest success ever, thanks to the generosity of Barry Stone, son of Jeremy Stone, former state representative of Kansas," she read. *Former state representative? Looks like our Mr. Barry hasn't told me everything. I wonder just how much he contributed.*

The phone interrupted her thoughts. It was Barry. "I know this is last minute, but would you like to get together New Year's Eve? That is, if you don't already have plans."

"No, I don't have plans."

"This may sound lame, but I'm not big on going out on New Year's Eve. Too much hoopla for me. What would you say we cooked something at my house?"

"Okay, sure."

"I was thinking, maybe the girls could come too."

She hadn't expected that. "That would be great."

"There's one more thing."

"What's that?"

"Can you cook?"

"Yes, I can cook."

"I mean, will you do the actual cooking?"

Marie laughed. "Sure. I'll cook. But you have to help."

"That I can do...well, maybe."

Barry's awkward invitation made Marie smile the rest of the day.

* * *

They arrived at Barry's at five o'clock. The plan was to put the pork roast in the oven and then go on a ride. But shortly after arriving, Olivia announced she had a *dolor de estómago*, a tummy ache. Barry showed them to a spare bedroom where Olivia could lie down. After Marie talked to Olivia about what was bothering her, she joined Barry and Rachael in the kitchen.

Barry had poured a glass of ginger ale. "This may help her stomach," he said.

"That won't be necessary. Rachael, may I see you in the other room?"

Rachael followed her into the living room.

"Okay. 'Fess up."

"What?"

"Olivia told me everything, and now she's upset."

"Oh."

"Rachael, look, I know your intentions were good, but there is no need to play games. And to involve your sister is just not acceptable."

Did I just say your sister?

Rachael hung her head. "I'm sorry."

"You go in there and tell her you made a big mistake by asking her to fake being sick so Barry and I could be alone. And when you're done, both of you come out and join us in the kitchen."

"Yes, ma'am."

"And Rachael?"

"Yes."

"Just so you know, our plan was to bring you two back to our place after dinner, and then we were going to spend the rest of the evening here—alone."

Rachael smiled. "Cool."

"Go."

Rachael saluted.

Marie explained to Barry the plan Rachael had hatched. "You can't be too mad at her, right?" he asked. "She was just thinking of you."

"Barry, that's not the point," she whispered. "I'll explain it to you later."

"I guess I've got a lot to learn about kids."

Marie smiled. "Me too. Believe me."

Rachael and Olivia entered the kitchen. "We're sorry," Rachael said.

Olivia burst into tears, ran over to Marie, and hugged her. Marie scowled at Rachael. *See what you've caused?* she mouthed.

Rachael scrunched up her mouth and bit the inside of her cheek. "I'm really sorry."

Marie sat down on one of the kitchen chairs and pulled Olivia up on her lap. "Don't cry, honey. You didn't do anything wrong."

"Rachael said I did."

"Rachael gave you bad advice. You, my dear, didn't do anything wrong. And you know what? Barry is going to take you on a horsie ride while Rachael and I have a little talk here in the kitchen." She wiped Olivia's tears from her cheeks. "Would you like that?"

Olivia nodded. Barry fetched Olivia's coat, hat, and mittens. For the next half hour, Marie and Rachael talked about the consequences of being deceitful, regardless of intent, while they prepared dinner.

"Marie? I wanted this day to be so perfect, and now I've screwed it all up. I'm sorry."

"Why was that so important to you?"

"'Cause it felt so much like being part of a real family."

Her words resounded with a truth that Marie had not yet admitted to herself.

Barry and Olivia came back red-faced from the cold. He took off her outerwear and led her into the living room where he built a fire in the fireplace, letting her help by handing him the smaller kindling. Marie sent Rachael in to let Barry know he was wanted in the kitchen.

"You're not going to get off without helping with this meal, mister," Marie said to him.

"Just tell me what to do. I'll be your slave." After he said it, his face dropped. "Was that an insensitive thing to say? I'm sorry. Sometimes I don't think before I speak."

Marie smiled. "No, you're okay. But if it were the other way around, I might have had an issue with it."

"Really?"

"No, not really."

"You're confusing me, Marie."

"Shut up and get to work." She walked over to him and gave him a quick kiss. "Do you know how to peel a carrot?"

"No, but I'm trainable."

"This is going to be a long evening."

"Promise?"

CHAPTER 31

One More Time

The early summer evening was cool—cool enough for Marie and everyone else sitting on her sun porch to be wearing a sweater or light jacket. The sun began its slow descent, giving way to a full moon that hovered right above the tree line, the promise of a peaceful night ahead.

Anna Marie cooed in Karen's arms while she rocked her in Marie's newly acquired antique Thonet rocking chair. Less than two months old, the baby already took after her mother—blue eyes, sandy brown hair, and a button nose. Maurice sat in a chair close to them, the smile on his lips showing no sign of fading.

Olivia, now legally adopted, hosted a tea party around the coffee table. Guests included her favorite doll, Betsy; Dangle, her stuffed monkey; Rachael; and Marie. Rachael was preoccupied with sketching Karen and her family. Olivia, who was busy pouring water into everyone's teacups, appeared to be in a world of her own.

Barry walked in with a birthday cake he and the girls had baked that afternoon while Marie was at the hairdresser's.

"Well, this may not look as good as what my beautiful wife would have done," he said, smiling at Marie, "but I can tell you, we sure had fun making it." He took a seat beside Marie on the wicker love seat and gave her a peck on the cheek. "Thanks for cleaning up the mess, dear, and happy birthday."

"How much longer are you going to be here, Marie?" Maurice asked.

"Oh, we're pretty much all moved in at Barry's now. I just wanted for us to get together one more time here before I turn in the keys to Julia." She sighed. "I'm really going to miss this place."

"We had a good many talks on this porch," Karen reminisced.

"I'll say. Over a good many glasses of wine."

"You know what we need around here?" Rachael asked.

"I'm almost afraid to ask. What?" Marie asked.

"Music, of course." She headed toward the radio. "And I get dibs on the station."

"Not so fast, sweetheart. Your taste in music is…well, shall we say, a little too salty for us oldsters."

"Marie, you just said my taste in music was a little too angry."

"I can't keep all your sayings straight. You know what I meant."

She tuned in the radio to KSDB, which was playing Frankie Lane's latest song, "Your Cheatin' Heart."

Marie gave Rachael a motherly look. "How about some Frank Sinatra, dear?"

"How about the Four Lads instead?"

"Doris Day?"

Major eye roll by the teenager. Rachael looked at Barry with begging eyes. "Hank Williams?"

Barry couldn't help but smile. "I think Marie would prefer Bing."

"He's so…boring."

"Rachael…"

"I think you may be rattling Marie's cage, sweetheart."

Another eye roll.

Barry gave Rachael a disconcerting look. "What, I'm not hep enough for you?"

"It's 'hip,' Barry."

"Shot down again."

Rachael left the porch shaking her head and muttering, "This is crazy."

"What are you serving, Olivia?" Marie asked.

"Ice cream."

"That's nice. What flavor?"

"Pokeydoke."

"What flavor, sweetie?"

"She said pistachio, Mom...I mean Marie," Rachael shouted from the other room.

Olivia looked at Marie with wide eyes. "I knowed that."

"Hey, Marie. Where's the chocolate sauce?"

Olivia's face lit up. She stopped what she was doing and headed toward the kitchen and Rachael.

"For what?" Marie asked.

"To put on the cake. I didn't tell Barry, but I forgot to put the eggs in the mix, and it's awfully dry."

The four grownups watched a giggling Olivia, whose face was sticky with chocolate sauce, run from Rachael, who chased her with a wet paper towel.

Maurice looked at Karen. Karen looked at Marie. "Is this what we have to look forward to?" she asked her.

Marie smiled at Barry and then Maurice and Karen. "I sure hope so."

THE END

Don't miss Florence Osmund's first novel, *The Coach House*, prequel to *Daughters*.

It's 1945 Chicago. Anything can happen, and for Richard Marchetti, it usually does.

Marie Marchetti, however, doesn't know that about her husband. To her, they have the perfect life together. That is, until little things start to pop up that put her on alert: late night phone calls, cryptic receipts hidden in the basement, and a gun in his desk drawer. When she learns he's secretly attended a mobster's funeral, her feelings are confirmed. And when she inadvertently interrupts a meeting between Richard and his so-called business associates, he causes her to fall down the basement steps, compelling Marie to run for her life.

Ending up in Atchison, Kansas, Marie quickly sets up a new life for herself. She meets Karen Franklin, a woman who will become her lifelong best friend, and rents a coach house apartment behind a three-story Victorian home. But her attempts at a new life are fraught with the fear that Richard will show up at any time—and who knows what he or his associates will do then? Ironically, it is the discovery of the identity of her real father and his ethnicity that unexpectedly changes her life forever.

What they're saying about The Coach House...

"The settings in *The Coach House* are described beautifully by Florence Osmund—Chicago and its music venues, New York City, and San Francisco—we get to travel and enjoy these cities with Marie.

"The character development is Osmund's strength in *The Coach House*. Each character becomes alive in chapter after chapter. It's hard to put down the book because we get so absorbed with each character—whether it's Marie, Richard, and Karen, or Richard's cohort doing his dirty work.

"*The Coach House* is a superbly written book, in my opinion. It will leave the reader thinking about relationships, adversity, independence and growth, and prejudices. It's always nice to finish a good book with something to think about."

—Author and book reviewer, Mary Crocco

ABOUT THE AUTHOR

Florence Osmund grew up in a Victorian home in Libertyville, Illinois, complete with a coach house, the same house she used as inspiration for her first novel, *The Coach House*, and its sequel, *Daughters*. She earned her master's from the Lake Forest Graduate School of Management and has more than three decades of experience in corporate America. Osmund currently resides in Chicago, where she continues to write novels.

Visit her website at http://www.florenceosmund.com, and follow her blog at http://www.florenceosmundbooks.wordpress.com.

CPSIA information can be obtained at www.ICGtesting.com
Printed in the USA
LVOW12s2216040314

376088LV00001B/228/P